BLUE DOOR, RED BOWL

A NOVEL

JOSEPH C. FOREHAN

authorHOUSE®

AuthorHouse™
1663 Liberty Drive
Bloomington, IN 47403
www.authorhouse.com
Phone: 833-262-8899

Published by AuthorHouse   11/24/2021

ISBN: 978-1-6655-4082-7 (sc)
ISBN: 978-1-6655-4081-0 (e)

Library of Congress Control Number: 2021920809

This book is dedicated to Charlene, Shane, Liam, Papa, Ga, Mandy and Nana. You are my life and I love you.

Special thanks to Tara Filowitz for her editing skills, friendship and focus. None of this would have happened if you hadn't checked your junk mail.

Contents

1

All of This Shit Actually Happened

THE HEIGHT OF the sun suggests that it is, in the best case scenario, not yet noon. Long ago, I raced past an acceptable time to fall asleep. I can rationalize still being awake as long as it's still morning. The transfer from AM to PM destroys everything for me. The moment the clock strikes noon is when my current behavior stops making sense. Sadly for me, the clock on my desk switches over and my time runs out. When the clock strikes twelve, I know that I am truly fucked.

8:30 AM is a distant memory. This is the first time I miss the opportunity to be normal. I am operating on no sleep. I am still not ready to go to bed. It's ridiculous to still be awake. It makes no sense to be staring at my computer at this hour. It is futile to try to pull something brilliant out of my coked out mind. I've been typing for hours and I need to stop, but I don't know how. I can't sit still. I can't watch television. I can't go to sleep. All I do is stare at the fucking keyboard. All I do is stare.

9:00 AM attacks. And just like that, it is gone. No clue where 9:00 AM goes. This can't be good for my health. This is the moment of truth. If I miss this window there may not be another. Sleep *needs* to happen. If I don't go to sleep now I will surely be awake in five hours. There is no reason why I shouldn't be able to close my eyes and fall asleep. I had no excuse for doing so many lines last night. Somehow I lost control and lost focus. Now I am awake. I am the only one *still* awake. Kids are getting ready for school, trash trucks are picking up things, street sweeping begins, the sun arrives, I am on the couch, out of cigarettes, kicking myself and wondering why the fuck I am *still* awake.

10:30 AM comes and goes quicker than it should. I must now accept the consequences of my actions. Last night blended seamlessly into the next day. This complicates everything. I fully intend to keep it together. My objective was a simple one. I planned to go to sleep at a normal hour. I fail miserably. Part of me wishes that my dealer was on vacation. A spur of the moment road trip. A sick grandmother in Fresno. *Anything* to get him out of town. There is no doubt in my mind I wouldn't still be awake at this god awful hour if he was in Palm Springs. But he's not. And here I am, awake.

11:30 AM is here. This is fucking stupid. This is unhealthy. This is kind of pathetic. I should be focused on catching up on badly needed sleep. Instead, I'm dealing with a bloody nose, still going strong. I'm wearing sunglasses inside my apartment. I question the benefits of this lifestyle. I accept that sleeping is no longer an option. I finish whatever drugs I can find and continue banging away on my computer– writing everything, saying nothing. I try to understand why the hell I am still smoking cigarettes and drinking cheap canned beer on a random Tuesday morning.

1:30 PM taunts me. I'm still sitting on the couch in my dirty apartment. I'm sliding dangerously towards the far end of an alternate lifestyle that is not accepted by the masses. My alter egos are no longer safely hidden under the bed. I am a tired cliché of what happens when things fall apart and you have no clue how to respond. Instead of embracing the merits of participating in a productive lifestyle, I do nothing. I spit on the idea of working. I pity those who spend their time jogging. I avoid grocery shopping at all costs. I reinvent myself. I say an emphatic "no thanks" to a quiet and rational existence. Instead, I do whatever it takes.

I have no idea how to find an employer looking for a college graduate with a passion for spending his free time typing nonsense into an old 1950's red typewriter, cutting these shards of wit out and then gluing these random phrases onto the bottoms of Polaroid photos taken of his drunken friends. If this job exists I am not able to find it. Instead, I prostitute myself to the food service industry in order to pay my bills. I am overeducated, under-skilled and content with the flexible hours, lack of responsibility and the surplus of cash. My free time is spent in a vague attempt to harness creativity without the time consuming interference of actually creating something. A productive day includes substitute teaching, ignoring the impulse of digital cable, an afternoon nap, and filling the time in my shack cutting, pasting, cleaning or painting.

This lifestyle would no doubt confuse the adults in my life. Any assumptions my parents have concerning my activities won't be met. If they actually see what I am up to they would have no clue how to react. I have created a masterful façade that they are content to accept because the truth would stain them. They are out of their element. The frustrating aspect of my daily adventures is that I'm living a life with an unhealthy amount of dead, free, unsubstantiated time. I lack substance. I don't have the balls to live the life of a struggling writer. A struggling artist. A struggling anything. Instead, I find myself on the couch, watching *ESPN Sports Center* for the third time every afternoon without the hope of a plan.

I live on fragments of sunrises. I am delirious and I am the only one who understands. I am a rambling mess. I am the *only* one who gets it. I am wise, brilliant and sad. I convince myself that I am ready to take on the world. I am fully awake. I am going to *stay* awake and I am going to remain productive while everyone else I know snuggles under the covers of their down comforters. Their safety is based on their bullshit lives and I judge them while I smoke another cigarette. I tell myself I am more worthy. I am strong. Instead of having faith in them, I have faith in me.

4:00 PM My journey into the depths of pandemonium and dysfunction continues. I convince myself that this chaotic indifference will lead me to immortal fame. The certainty of representing without delay protects me from remorse. I am free. I choose chaos and decay. I facilitate a steep decline. It's time to hit rock bottom. It's time to see how far I fall before I figure it out and bounce back. Sooner or later sanity will prevail and normalcy will creep back into my life.

Every action I take disappoints me. The safety of my childhood home in Rossmoor no longer exists. I lost the battle against my artificial self. Mitch is gone, he is my best friend in the world and he's not coming back. My college life in San Diego underwhelms me. College is lame. College is disappointing, to say the least. It sure wasn't as much fun as I had anticipated. Vodka convinces me to seek out those I would otherwise consider mediocre. I am constantly annoyed with my situation. Moving home is hard. Having a sick sister is harder. My life is missing pieces and I can't fill them regardless of what I try. I'm stuck waiting tables because I don't know what I want to do with my life.

7:00 PM, It is early evening on a random Tuesday. I am trying my hardest to remain calm while this catastrophe of noise and motion swallows me. My attempt to sit quietly loses all meaning. Spending all day waiting for something brilliant to happen leads me to this moment. Nothing good happens. I am destroyed. I am alone. All I can do is quietly contemplate the path I am on. My only option is to accept that this moment has passed and another one is on its way.

2

Running is Stupid and Should
be Avoided at All Costs

I CAN'T THINK OF a bad memory from my childhood. I have
no memory of pain or loss. Nobody close to me or my family has
the misfortune of falling down a well. I am never bombarded with
shocking news associated with an aunt or second cousin tragically
stepping in front of a city bus. All injustices on display during the five
o'clock news are relayed as random events that lack any connection or
significance to my sheltered existence. I am encouraged to avoid all
contact with the messy world around me.

Unaware of conflicts and dangers, my childhood insulates me from
the threat of serious worries. I am just out of reach from the evil empire.
I am safely located within the "Bubble" known as Rossmoor. My youth
is comfortable. I spend Saturdays playing AYSO soccer. I always have a
buddy from school on my team. Running around for forty five minutes
is never a bad idea. My dad coached the team when I was young. I am
a decent player, never the biggest or fastest, but I survive on grit and
determination.

I walk away from each game proud of my scraped knees and grass
stains from slide tackles. My mediocre kick is made up for with stellar
defense. I am good, but I am also modest. I patiently wait for the
growth spurt that will allow me to take over the field and become a
soccer god.

This doesn't happen. I am never the best on the team. I am a step
below. I play the right way. I play hard and I get dirty. The sidelines are
full of enthusiastic parents who make sure that the kids stay hydrated.
The bourgeoisie middle class in action. Middle aged white people

dressed to kill in cashmere sweaters and penny loafers readjust their laser focus on the thirst of the local children. Oranges and cold water are offered during half time. A sugar based beverage and a tasty treat is provided, win or lose, after the game.

Here is found stock footage of speech given before every single AYSO soccer game played in the history of AYSO soccer:

"Listen fellas... I want to see the game played right. I'm more concerned with playing hard and playing fair, than winning or losing... and hey. Have some fun. It's a game."

The score matters, of course. But overzealous coaching is the exception, not the norm. Soccer is fun. Nobody is that much bigger or better than the rest. The kids blessed with talent and ability show up and enhance the game, not change it.

This all changes in middle school. Puberty, for the fortunate, is in full swing. Sadly, for yours truly, it's still lurking around some mythical corner. Some kids are already growing and developing muscles. Parity is a thing of the past. Soccer has become serious. It is now no longer insignificant if you win or lose. How you play the game is important only in theory. Sportsmanship and fair play are sadly pushed aside. AYSO is a thing of the past. Club soccer is my new reality. My new coach doesn't care about anything other than results and victories. The fat kid is out. The awkward kid has no chance to make the team. The joy is sucked dry. First life takes away toys, because you can't play with toys anymore and now life is taking away sports. Getting old blows. Keep in mind, I am twelve.

Coach: *Don't give me excuses. I want results.*

Just have fun? This is the silly nonsense only told to children. Now we learn the truth. The notions of gamesmanship and honor are over. The expectation of victory is the new reality. Instead of water we are given inspiration in the form of "move faster, you pansy mother fuckers. What do you think this is? Some type of AYSO pussy soccer?" This is a club team, we will be having *tryouts*. If you're lucky you will spend the next four months of your life driving to obscure soccer fields playing against complete strangers. No more afternoons spent lightly scrimmaging. Now we "train" three times a week and play games at night. I make the local team and continue my career as a soccer player. More accurately, I joined a soccer club and spent a year running. Running fucking sucks. Running is hard.

Mohammad is our coach. He is a strange man from Iraq. We make fun of him constantly behind his back. He has a slight build, curly hair, and is hard as a rock. Allegedly, he played for the Iraqi National Team or was a professional Middle Eastern soccer player in his youth. He is rigid and strict. He also knows the game and we are told to listen to him. We are expected to follow directions without question. He is the coach in charge of torturing us from three to five every Monday, Wednesday and Friday. His son Ernie is on the team, a nerdy kid doomed by a poorly chosen name and weighed down by his father's high expectations. He is a tad overweight and without much natural ability. The majority of his childhood is spent desperately trying not to disappoint his dad.

We hate our coach from the start. We resent putting the balls aside and running continuously every practice. We hate Mohammad for making us run. So inevitably we start to hate Ernie for his association with his dad. Sucks to be you, from here on out you will be known as Ernie the Iraqi.

During the first month of practice we are not allowed to bring our soccer balls. I come home from sixth grade, have a snack and then ride my bike to the practice field. No soccer is played these days. Instead, we run. We run so fucking much I want to die. I spend the days that have after school practice in a trance. Alarm wakes me up and I take a shower. Sleep falls away as I get warm. Life returns as I open my eyes, only to realize what day it is. Even before I'm out of the shower and my hair is dry, the dread sets in. Hope evaporates and is replaced with fear. The reminder of what is to come invades my brain and sickens me, and just like that, my day is ruined.

The practice hovers over me like a dark cloud for the rest of the day. I am consumed with apprehension for what awaits me after school ends. Most kids dread school and live for the bell to ring symbolizing the end of the day. For me, the school day sadly flies by and before I know it the bus has dropped me off and I am walking home. The next two hours are filled with significant leg pain, labored breathing, and no hope. Three days a week I am unable to enjoy life, my life is unbearable. All day fucking long the practice sticks in my mind. A lighthearted moment may find me. I may witness a humorous exchange at lunch or during math, but it's lost on me.

"Sorry, I can't laugh right now. Why, you ask? Well... because... it doesn't fucking matter, don't you get it? Nothing fucking matters. And no... Actually... I can't enjoy this moment with the group. I would like to... but it just isn't possible."

I dwell on my painful future. The anticipation of the near future slowly drains me of all hope. Reprieve can only come in the form of a freak hail storm. I silently pray for a cloud burst to park directly above the practice field and flood it. Please God, send a high pressure cloud formation into Rossmoor. If possible, please center it over the soccer field at the corners of *Silverfox* and *Blume*. All day long I check the sky for clouds. Hoping for a storm to miraculously blow into town at the last moment and force the unfortunate cancellation of soccer practice. Divine intervention in the form of a hail storm with bolts of lightning leads to my salvation. A high pressure system colliding with a cold front is the only thing that will keep me safe.

I hate Southern California weather. Clear fucking skies for weeks. No chance of rain. So I get on my bike and ride it to practice. I have no other choice before me so I accept it and go. I pedal slowly and arrive at the field. The team is sitting in a circle waiting for the various exercises to start. Contemplating suicide is no longer a viable option. I'm going to stop complaining and run my ass off. Exercise is good for you. We run hard three times a week and there is obvious improvement among us. Those who are able to run four laps under six minutes get to kick the ball around. I'm close, but not quite over the hump. My time improves. I start at more than eight minutes to finish a mile. My legs adjust to running. I turn the corner and the soreness isn't nearly as bad as it was in the beginning. My lungs adjust. My breathing isn't as labored. The only thing holding me back is my ankles. They constantly hurt. Why don't I speak up and ask my parents to take me to the doctors? There's never enough time between practices to fully recover. I grit my teeth and bear it. I gradually get stronger. I shave my time down below seven minutes and get faster every week.

I run until I lose all hope for competitive sporting events. I run until I throw up. I run until I have to get extra padding in my shoes because my ankles are fucked up and I don't know why. Now, I know why. They are sore from running too fucking much. Thank you, Mohammad. You give me sore fucking ankles.

Eventually the team started to disintegrate. One by one we act on our disillusionment and say *"No mas."* and we walk away from club level soccer. I am not that fast, I am not that good, not that motivated, and I am under no illusion that I'm going to play varsity soccer when I get to high school. I realize that I don't have the talent or the drive to compete at a high level. I am sick of being sore and I quit the team. It is a hard thing to do. I know that if I quit, then the other boys won't be too far behind. Quitting the team creates a domino effect. One by one we all drop out.

I reclaim my afternoons. I reclaim my life. I can do what I want. I am sad because I know this will most likely be the last team I will ever play for. I am disappointed because part of me likes the competition and the physical demands placed on me. I like the idea of exercise more than the act of exercising. I am okay with knowing that I probably won't ever run a mile under six minutes. That's way too fast anyway. I am free to partake in other activities. I am free to learn a new trade.

3

Ignoring Local Building Codes

SITTING FIRMLY IN my backyard is a tree house. A sturdy wooden platform sits eight or so feet off the ground. It is centered inside the tree where the trunk ends its upward ascent and breaks off into three directions. These large branches turn out and up and form a perfect base for a platform to rest on. Three holes are cut in the wood to allow these thick trunks to both continue extending upward and out. On the left side, this platform is connected to a large slide. On the right, there is a vertical ladder and monkey bars that extend out for another ten feet. The tree house from the bottom of the slide to the edge of the monkey bars is twenty feet long. The middle section is small, no more than ten square feet, basically it is a platform surrounded by a railing, Google a picture of a treehouse, that's what it started as. When the tree is full, the branches hide the platform from view. The structure runs parallel to the back fence. My Grandfather, Uncle and Dad built it over a weekend years ago. It gets heavy use when I am young and goes mostly untouched until I get older. It is without dispute a safe and sturdy tree house.

Soccer is a distant memory and I need something to do. There are hammers and nails in the garage and the decision is made to begin a remodel of the tree house. A second floor is needed. The first floor is still just a boring platform. It is without walls and lacks privacy. We are in middle school, what else is there to do?

It is time to get the boys together. It is time to hop on our bikes and haul wood back home. Time to get our Dads' hammers out of the garage and nail some shit together. It is time to build. Afternoons and weekends are spent gathering wood. On many streets in my neighborhood there are homes with big green dumpsters in front of them. Inside is a veritable treasure chest full of discarded building supplies. All the needed materials, stashes of plywood, 2x4's, old carpet and other useful things are just around the corner and ready for the taking. These trash bins are rarely locked. All we have to do is cruise by and load up our bikes with wood.

Construction begins. We build vertical supports in the four corners of the platform. Next, we need to lift an abnormally heavy and thick piece of plywood up the tree and onto the posts. If this can be done, we have a second floor. Unfortunately, the fucker is too heavy and we can't move it. We need reinforcements and we need them now. It's getting dark. My mom is sure to call me to dinner at any moment. Leaving it until tomorrow isn't an option. We are impulsive kids with the need to be gratified instantly. We need one more person.

My dad is out of the question at this point. He doesn't exactly know the extent of our plans (neither do we) so his participation must be avoided. If we involve him in any way we are doomed. He has a parental duty to point out the various safety hazards involved. There is no chance that he will embrace the second floor. If we involve him, it's not likely that he'll just look the other way. His only move would be to shut the project down. Dad needs to stay inside and we need to get it up on the posts and nail it in. Then I need to go inside, wash my hands, eat dinner, finish my homework and watch *Family Ties* until bed, and act like nothing whatsoever is happening in the backyard.

Desperation sets in. Phone calls are made. Phone calls go unanswered. It's getting darker by the minute. We start to give up hope. We walk out front, my friends mount their bikes and are about to leave when we spot a kid riding his bike home. Not only, by chance, is he coming down my street, he is the strongest kid we know. He is just what we need. He pulls up to say hi, agrees immediately to help us and saves the day. Ten minutes later the plywood is nailed to the posts and we have ourselves a roof.

We spent the next *three years* building. The second story is soon covered by a third one. The third floor eventually gets itself a rooftop. This is all unintentional. I never signed off on the plans to build a third floor. Truth be known, I am hesitant to build higher than a second floor- where will it stop? My feeble attempts to put a stop to the madness are simply ignored. My friends come over to my house five days a week to contribute to my ever-growing monstrosity. They show up unannounced and uninvited half the time. They are always welcome. They let themselves in the backyard through the side gate and get to work. Sometimes I am totally unaware of their presence until I hear the familiar sound of hammering nails into wood. Nailing shit together is music to my ears. I have no other option but to join them.

All concerns about safety are immediately dismissed. I am convinced that this growing behemoth will fall over at any moment. Best case scenario, it defies the rules of physics and falls inward on itself- like the controlled demolition of a casino, the damage is limited, my Dad's flowers are trampled and I get yelled at. This would no doubt suck but he'd get over it. Worst case scenario? My imagination goes wild with scenes of mass destruction and carnage that continues to get more detailed and scarier the more I think about it. Aren't there city ordinances in place that prevent the ongoing construction of a tree house morphing into a rental unit? Is it crucial to build a third story den? Is it necessary to do this? Surely, it isn't in our best interest to build another wing of living space, is it? Hold on, the plan is to build it so it extends over the slide? And this is a good idea even though we lack the proper permits. Should we at least try to make this as close to "up to code" as we can? The answer to new construction is always yes. The answer to my legitimate concerns is always to stop worrying so much.

The fourth floor is never given the go ahead by me. Yet, here it is. The construction continues despite my objections. As each project ends, I forget what is troubling me. I am always happy with the finished product. I must apologize. Once again my vision is short-sighted. It is indeed necessary to build that extra room on floor three.

The tree house grows tall and wide. We reach the top of the branches and stop building up. Instead, we start to build out. There is no way to stop the natural growth of the tree house. If we finish building it what the hell are we going to do? My garage is emptied of spray paint and Christmas lights. My allowance is spent on nails. Box after box of three inch long nails disappear faster than expected. We find carpet in decent enough condition and install it on every floor. An extension cord runs from the outlet on the patio up into the tree. Lights go up. Anything we can find is used. Flood lights, someone brings over an old lamp from their garage. An old television gets carried up. It isn't long before somebody's Nintendo finds its way to the second floor. Every room gets painted with murals and pictures. Random notes and messages get scribbled on the walls with permanent markers. The tree house becomes full of memories and strange moments in time. It becomes a second home to us all. I spend most of my afternoons and evenings inside this creation. Sometimes I am with friends, other times I get to be alone.

The roof is thirty feet off the ground and level with the power lines. The threat of electrocution is a mere five feet away. A short jump away if someone wants to test it. Want to find out how electricity works? Well, there it is. An Electric Company workman leaves us a note to remind us not to touch the power lines.

Hey Guys, do not touch the WIRES. (by the way, this place is awesome.)

We all agree that this is good advice. The top of the tree grows around and above our roof. It is a natural railing that gives us a small barrier to keep us from falling over the side. The branches make the roof a tranquil spot to look out over the rooftops of Rossmoor. We can see all the way to Cal State Long Beach. We can see the basketball stadium built in the shape of a pyramid and painted bright blue ten miles away. This is no small feat. We never hesitate to mention to anyone who is unimpressed with our view that it extends all the way into Long Beach.

Building slows down and we spend our days cleaning up the leaves that never stop falling. We spend all of our free time up in the tree. We sit on branches high above the ground and are unbothered by inquisitive parents. Television becomes unnecessary. We stop spending time inside and inactive. Instead we climb the tree and take advantage of our adolescence. We are never bored again. We kick ass. And, we do this ass kicking outside. I create something with my best friends. There are spots on each floor to relax and embrace just being up in a tree. Freedom from adults is granted as soon as you climb the ladder and enter the first floor. From there, you climb up the trunk and open the trap door that leads to the second floor. Here you are free to play Nintendo, do some light reading or flip through a porno mag if you know where it is hidden.

I am in possession of a guest house in my backyard. A guest house up a tree that is rarely (if ever) visited by my parents. Mom and Dad go to bed early and aren't disturbed by the noise. I realize the awesome power the tree house has. I am thirteen years old. I am struggling through puberty. I have no place to go and even if I do, I have no way to get there. I do have something nobody else does. It turns out that it is easy to invite people to my house. All I have to say is this... *Want to come over and see my tree house....?* The answer is the same. It never changes. They all say the same thing: *YES*. It is a space that allows you to talk above a whisper. A place to hang out and make some noise. A quiet and respectful amount of noise, never loud enough to be noticed, always kept just below the level that would require some form of investigation. A place absent of curious adults. The tree house becomes the preferred destination of the cute girls I go to school with.

Young ladies come over most weekends. They bring breasts. If you are lucky, these girls might allow you to give them a feel. If you are really lucky they do not object when you get up the nerve and reach under their shirt to explore things more thoroughly. If you are really lucky you get to unhook a bra. This is critical to free up the necessary space needed to touch them with authority. Rooms are built for this specific purpose. Every floor contains a private enclave perfect for light petting and kissing with the tongue. The prime spot is the roof. Place a heavy object over the trapdoor and privacy is yours.

The youth of Rossmoor discover romance on every floor. Nervous kissing happens on the roof. This might as well be the top of the world. The full moon is stunning and the sky is bright. The success rate of rooftop kissing runs at ninety five percent. Let the ambience do the work and in an hour you will climb down the tree house with wrinkled clothing and tired lips.

If the roof isn't available, the next best place for heavy petting is the intimate space right below it. It is the size of a closet, you can barely sit up in it, but if you can get over the walls that seem to get closer and closer, not to mention the total lack of circulating air, it's a fine place to spend time with a special lady. Remember, you're in the middle of a fucking tree. Concessions need to be made.

Privacy and seclusion might be hard to come by but there is no extra charge. Without the tree house these opportunities are lost. This is the only safe place to do some heavy petting. Without it, I probably don't walk into my house with a big grin on my face. This is due to all the kissing and touching that I take part in. Which is the only reason I make it through middle school in one piece.

I never hesitate to walk outside to my front yard so I can check out how the tree house looks from the street. It is completely hidden within the branches and leaves of the tree. I see the flag that flies above the branches. It is an old rag tied to a wooden pole that's nailed up on the roof someplace. It's the only thing visible but nobody knows about it unless they know where to look. I notice it only because I know it is there and I look for it. The flag says $E= MC^2$. It is meant to be ironic. Or at least intellectually witty. We are ironic before our time, ironic twenty years before we should be. We give up trying to explain it quickly because nobody fucking gets it in 1992.

To the best of my knowledge, the structure is invisible to the outside world. It is something that doesn't hurt anyone else. Only when my dad gets the tree trimmed can you see what's hiding inside. The neighbors behind us aren't so lucky. Years before construction starts, they cut back the branches that overhang into their yard. These branches never grow back as thick and full as the other side does. They have a clear view of the tree house in its entirety. When I stand in front of my house and look back over the roof towards the tree nothing seems amiss. All I notice is a lovely tree. I assume this is the case on the opposite side as well. I am 100% wrong. When I finally see my tree from the street behind my house I am immediately sad. Instead of looking at a huge oxygen factory covered in healthy green leaves, I see it for the first time from the back. No leaves, no life giving air, nothing organic at all. All I see is a wooden shanty town hanging precariously in a tree. The view from the other side is a different story entirely. The house behind ours looks directly at the tree house. The view is not of a tree full of copious amounts of branches covered in green leaves. There are no branches. There are no leaves. Their view consists of plywood nailed unprofessionally together with 2x4's, held together with more plywood. The tree house isn't hidden from view. It is an eyesore that looks to be on the verge of collapse. The entire back side looks exactly like what it really is: built by kids and looks like it will fall down and kill someone at any moment. From my front yard, the tree house looks sturdy and well built. From their yard, on the other side, it looks like it was built with scavenged wood stolen from trash bins. I give the neighbors credit for tolerating this monstrosity for as long as they do. How is there a shanty town growing up a tree behind them and they don't complain?

The tree house survives until my sophomore year in high school. By then, we start getting too big for it (some more than others). Now there are serious concerns of a collapse. This coincides with the neighbors finally complaining about it. Something about being convinced that it's their duty to protect the community from being overrun with unsightly tree houses if they don't do something. My parents begin the demolition one morning while I am at work. I am not told of their plans. This leads to a tricky conversation with my mom. I am a big believer that it is important to communicate. If my mom gives me a heads up, nobody suffers. Instead, I return home to find my parents taking down the tree house.

Dad: We found some interesting things on the third floor.

I don't say anything. There is nothing to say.

Mom: My favorite was the *Hustler* Magazine.

I want to tell my mom many things. I want to explain why it would be beneficial to all parties involved if she had mentioned that she plans to take down the tree house while I am at work. I want to tell her that if tearing the tree house down needs to happen, then I should be the one to do it. I need at least twenty four to forty eight hours amnesty period to remove all contraband hidden throughout the treehouse, shit the amount of things on the second floor alone would get me grounded for months. I am appalled that they are up there, dismantling the entire thing without my involvement. I built it; I've earned the right to take it apart. They have no business up there. They should understand why it is important for me to tear it down. I am done with the tree house and I see why it has to go. I am on their side. It is part of me. It is something that needs to be recognized. It is worth a roll of film and the hour it takes to create a memory of what the treehouse looks like.

Every floor tells a story. Every floor has a history. Every floor is unique. Covered with artwork. Filled in with quotations. Every wall is worthy of being photographed. Every corner deserves a picture. I come home to find the tree house torn down and in the driveway. I come home to find a thousand pieces of wood lying dead on the grass. The end of my youth is at hand. I no longer have the tree house to rely on. I lost my advantage. I am on my own.

4

1984 Topps Roger Clemens Rookie Card

MITCH INVITES ME over to his house after school one day to look at his baseball cards. I'm interested in such things, and it seems like an activity I might enjoy. This is before we start high school and before I really know him. Something about Mitch intrigues me. I have never been invited to his house before, so I agree, and walk over after school. We aren't really friends but we know some of the same people. It makes sense to hang out with him and see what he's all about. I am a bit curious to see his house and have heard stories regarding his impressive baseball card collection. I'm skeptical that he actually has what he claims. He assures me that a mint condition Roger Clemens rookie card is displayed in his bedroom. I don't have any strong appreciation for Roger Clemens but I understand enough about baseball cards to know that in the world of a thirteen-year-old it is kind of a big deal and worth a lot of money.

Ten minutes into my grand introduction to the life of Mitch I find myself standing in his room, looking at baseball cards. I come over to do something benign and here I am, doing just that. We aren't really doing shit. No poor decisions are being made. We don't have our feet up on the couch. We aren't playing with fire. We aren't climbing on the roof. The option of flipping through porn hasn't even been discussed yet. This is when we hear the front door close. Mitch freezes. His dad has just come home from work.

Mitch's dad hears voices and comes swiftly down the hall towards Mitch's room. Without warning I turn around to see an angry man. Not just angry, but "I-had-a-long-day-at-the-office-and-am-still-wearing-my-work-clothes-and-haven't-gotten-to- pour -myself-a-glass-of-white-wine-or-take-off-my-shoes-and-it's-not-fair" kind of angry.

He gives me a once over and dismisses me without a word. I know that he sees me, but he looks at me without any sense of having recognized my existence. I'm unaware that he had a long day at the office, needs to take off his work clothes, put on some sweats and a t-shirt, drink something alcoholic, and that by being here I am privy to Mitch's utter disregard for his father's rules that are in place for his own benefit. I'm merely standing there in Mitch's room expecting some form of introduction. Something like this makes sense to me. This is what would happen at my house.

I would say: *Dad, this is Mitch, he is a friend from school.*

Dad would say: *Mitch, it's nice to meet you.*

But we aren't at my house. We're at Mitch's house. So instead, the man ignores me and turns his attention to his son.

Mitch's dad: *You know you aren't allowed to have people over when we aren't home. Tell your friend to leave.*

And with that, Mitch's dad turns around and walks away. Mitch has done something in the past that necessitates being cut off from all unsupervised after school visits with friends. By ignoring this rule he makes his father's long day of work that much longer. His dad is now a dangerous combination of tired, irritated and distrustful, a time bomb waiting to be set off. An explosion of frustration and anger is waiting around the corner for me. I'm not in the least bit prepared for this. My own dad just isn't this way.

Mitch recommends that I leave. I'm not about to disagree. I am stunned and confused. Unprepared to make sense of the blatant rudeness that just transpired between a kid and an adult. Did what just happen really just take place? Wow. Mitch's dad just showed up and ignored me completely.

I start to walk down the hall towards the front door in a cloud of confusion coupled with a feeling of anger. His rudeness is not okay with me. This is not an appropriate way to treat someone. I don't care that you're a grown up and you're pissed off. I don't dispute that I'm just some kid that your son wasn't allowed to invite over. But I have never met you and you've never seen me before. This means that the rational response is to find out who I am and figure out why the hell I am in your house. The easy thing to do here is to introduce yourself and allow me to do the same. Then tell me to get the fuck out of your house.

I've grown up with parents who are always interested in what is going on. If a new friend is over that they haven't met, then by all means it's time for an introduction. Are you here to work on math homework?? Well by golly, have a seat and get it finished. *IT IS A PLEASURE TO MEET YOU. DID YOU HAVE A SNACK YET?* There is no time for rudeness. No reason for uncivilized behavior. No interest in treating the local kids with disrespect. You are an adult, the example-setter; I am the child, if anyone is supposed to be the asshole in this situation, it's ME. My initial emotional state of confusion and shock turns into a more proactive approach. As I passed the hallway leading to Mitch's father's room I stopped and said goodbye.

Me: *"It was nice to meet you."*

I direct this goodbye towards his dad. I make damn sure that he hears my subtle response to his rude behavior. I am thirteen years old and have finally found my "you don't know me!" voice. My "Viva La Raza!" voice has been unleashed for the first time and I am about to unload the "I am the disgruntled youth, you are too old to understand how I feel!" voice when I realize that I am too far away from escaping through the front door. I quicken my pace and attempt to leave the house and run home as fast as I can.

Well, good try, but no. My smart mouth sets off a time bomb. Before I can react, Mitch's dad cuts me off. He's in my face, breathing fire, pointing menacingly at my chest with an extended finger. An unfamiliar level of rage is being directed towards me as I stand meekly in a stranger's hallway. My inaugural trip to Mitch's house is officially a disaster. I arrive with the intention of looking at baseball cards. I leave with the knowledge that I've started a war.

Mitch's dad: *You smart ass. Don't ever disrespect me again. I will end you.*

The lecture continues. His nostrils are aflame and his mustache is defying gravity. Mitch is nowhere to be seen, he's MIA, he's *gone* – clearly he's familiar with seeing his Dad at Def Con 4 so he leaves me to deal with the explosion. I half expect to see his dad unbuckled his belt and teach me a lesson. I'm desperately trying to convince him that

I'm a well behaved kid who respects his elders and does chores without being asked. He's not buying it. He assumes that I am the youth gone wrong and that it is his responsibility to set me straight. He is angry and tired of dealing with this bullshit. He is way past turning turning red, he is fucking purple.

And where the fuck is Mitch throughout this verbal assault? What inspired him to lead me into this hornets' nest? Why aren't there any warnings given? Mitch surely could have briefed me about the situation. He could mention that his friends are not allowed over until further notice, and that he wants me to come by but I have to do so at my own risk. He could mention that angry, possibly volatile, parents might be lurking about. Doesn't he realize that they are sure to come home sometime? All of these important details are kept under wraps and because of this, my visit is doomed from the start.

With little effort, I light the match that catches the fuse which starts the chemical reaction that produces a large explosion better known as "The Wrath of Mitch's Dad." My comment gives the green light to pillage, and plunder a small village. I am ill-prepared for any type of pillaging or plundering. I merely want to convey my feelings of hurt and displeasure that I feel towards his attitude. I have no interest in being frightened by someone who I don't know, who my parents don't know, and who doesn't have any legitimate reason for yelling at me. I am well aware that I am a smart ass. I know that in some small way, he is within his rights to react this way. I'm not stupid. Before I say anything I know that I am saying something that is out of line. I know that I am being rude, but I don't care. His reaction to my comment is disproportionately out of whack. It occurs to me that his response might include a strongly worded rebuttal that will make me think twice about being a smart ass to the parents of your friends. I am prepared to offer a contrite apology along these lines:

"Okay, I deserve this lecture. Thank you kindly for this needed reprimand. I'm overdue for a preaching on respecting one's elders and having good manners. All I wanted was an introduction. I figured that since I'm not allowed to be here, then it is my responsibility to introduce myself. I only wanted to say goodbye. My intention never involves insulting you or disrespecting your house."

But I never get the chance to apologize. Instead of civility and remorse, I get a loud voice and terror. I just want to go home and start my homework. I promise to never come here again. Please just let me go home. I'm really scared at this point and my explanations of bullshit are starting to sound legit. Ending the tirade aimed at me is my number one priority. My only hope is to convince him that I regret being and will never partake in being a smart ass *ever* again. I must assure him that I will never lose sight of living a life based on having a respectful attitude towards the home owners of Rossmoor. I must convince him that from here on forward, I am his bitch, and will never forget it.

The other option involves fighting a fifty-year-old man who no doubt would wipe the floor with me. I'm not ready to challenge Mitch's pissed off dad to a fight after school. I don't even know what time he gets off work. Can he pick me up and take me to a neutral site so we can battle? There are too many unknown variables. I haven't done my stretches and am not prepared to use my karate skills in the hallway. I don't even know any karate. Come to think of it, I don't know any form of martial arts.

He tells me that it is no longer a good idea to stop by after school, as if I hadn't already come to that obvious conclusion I tell him that he doesn't have anything to worry about. I tell him that I'm not even that interested in baseball cards. I am allowed to leave. I get the hell out of there, relieved to have escaped. My walk home is surreal. I am shaking the entire time. Still, I am somewhat proud that I stood tall and proclaimed loudly that I wasn't going to allow him, or anyone else for that matter, to marginalize me. Walking home, I reaffirm my right to stand tall in the face of irrationality and loudly proclaim that I am against it. I am ready to fight for my beliefs. In truth, I am twitching uncontrollably due to fear. I remain scared of Mitch's dad until years later when he shows his true colors as a loving and caring person who was just having a bad day. Only then do I understand this man. All he has to do is indirectly save my life in order for me to see him for who he really is.

5

The Art of a Well Toasted Bagel

ROSSMOOR IS A post-World War II master building community. It is located about five miles from Seal Beach and just across the 605 Freeway from Long Beach. It is an unincorporated community of 1.6 square miles filled completely with tract homes. Our elderly next door neighbors originally bought their house for $19,000 dollars (they get a good deal). My parents bought theirs in 1981 for $125,000. There are four or five original floor plans repeated throughout the 3,761 individual houses. The original kitchens are ugly. The bathrooms are outdated. These houses represent the bad taste of the 1970's. They can be bought, torn down, and rebuilt to fit anyone's needs.

By the time I am a teenager, the single story, three- bedroom, two bath homes that my friends and I grew up in are being torn down. They are rapidly replaced with two stories, five bedrooms, and four bath monstrosities. The original owners die off and the houses are sold, then immediately torn down. Everything is carted off except for a single wall which makes the new house technically a remodel instead of a tear down (done for tax purposes) and then built right back up again. Lots consisting of nothing more than dirt and a driveway are resold for upwards of a million dollars. Here is where new dream homes are built. Families with money move to Rossmoor for the good schools, tree-lined streets, and the comfort of being surrounded by other middle class white people who share their appreciation for manicured lawns.

High School begins. A friendly wave is given to all those I pass. I am part of a group of kids who are isolated from chaos and devastation. The outside inconveniences associated with unrest and uncertainty stay far from my dinner table. There are no real problems when living in Rossmoor. Nobody suffers injuries that a Band-Aid and a hug won't cure. I am isolated from everything considered scary or dysfunctional. Rossmoor promotes conformity. Rossmoor hides all activities that negatively affect property values. All is well. Everything is just fine. Your children are not fucked up at all. You are good parents. Nothing is wrong. Stop worrying about it. Seriously, out of sight, out of mind. Nothing will go wrong. We promise.

My family is by no means wealthy. My parents bought the house before property values skyrocket. This allows us to live in a nice area. They buy their house cheap and keep up with the mortgage payments. Any doubts regarding the financial status of my parents begins and ends when I ask for fancy athletic shoes. Their pragmatic response to my request of hundred dollar Nikes isn't taken seriously. I never seriously consider asking for the expensive shoes in the first place and am happy for the reasonably priced ones that they can afford. I don't define myself by my shoes.

We don't live large. We don't buy fancy cars. We have no use for summer homes in Holland. My dad is a well-respected principal of an elementary school in a lower income area. My mother teaches elementary school in a similar setting. We exist squarely in the middle. We're comfortable. We're fortunate that we buy our house before buying a house in Rossmoor is impossible for people like my parents. A teacher and a principal were able to combine their incomes in 1981 and buy a house in Rossmoor. Fifteen years later, this isn't a sure thing.

My parents like the area because of all the trees. They find a house on a good street and go for it. They find a house in a nice area that will bring them equity and security. We are content. We don't have money to throw around. This is fine. My parents have no interest in that anyway.

While I know that compared to the rest of America, we are solidly middle class, compared to the new arrivals in Rossmoor, my family is poor. We are only able to go to Hawaii every *other* year. Our yearly vacation is ten days at CampLand in Mission Bay. There I am content to be handed a twenty dollar bill for the week. This always seems to last long enough. My parents give my sister a used car when she turns sixteen. This is a big expenditure. By the time my friends turn sixteen, the parking lot at school is packed with BMWs and other European delights. In my world, the majority of sixteen-year-olds are usually given a car on their birthdays. Some receive shiny new red ones. Others are unfortunately frustrated with hand-me-down Honda Civics, or something comparable. On many occasions the happy teenage recipients of these clean fancy cars crash their fine birthday gifts shortly after the keys are handed over to them.

I find a job two minutes away from my house at a bagel shop that opens. I go through the entire training and opening of the store with people my age. Here, I find confidence in my abilities to be a loyal employee and a good co-worker. My sister is hired along with me. The owners are young, ambitious, and very good people to work for. The majority of the employees are only a couple of years older than me. I start just before I turn sixteen. My sister is almost eighteen. The bulk of the guys who work there are a year older than she is. The introduction of Drew, Steve, Donny and Aaron forever shapes how I feel about the influence of older friendships and their potential to unlock greatness. I look up to these guys and follow their advice for the next five years. They bring me into their older, legal and more interesting world. I am embraced completely by them. They are twenty-one-years old and are able to purchase alcohol. Thanks boys.

Bagels are the new thing to hit town. Even though they've been around forever, Southern California is suddenly obsessed with bagel shops. Saturday mornings are hectic displays of endurance. The morning starts either at 5 AM (NO...), 6 AM (acceptable), or 7 AM (tolerable) and, without fail, every Saturday involves a line at and/or out the door. From 8 AM to 11 AM there is a never-ending rush of hungry people. Before I know it, it is noon and half of my shift is over. Those with the strongest serrated knife skills are entrusted to man the cream cheese bar. This job is earned, never given without reason, this shit is serious business. This is a harder job than you would think. Some bagels are toasted, some not, some are "to go" some "for here" fuck you. Leave me the fuck alone, I am hung over (16-year-olds don't really get hung over, so I was merely sleepy) so stop ordering copious amounts of fucking everything bagels with garlic herb cream cheese. Not another sesame seed bagel lightly toasted with butter will be made this morning. That's it. *No mas.* I am done walking around the corner to add fucking tomatoes to your onion bagel (un-toasted with light cream cheese).

You do not *need* the fucking sliced tomatoes. They are not a crucial component to your fucking happiness, and are adversely affecting my ability to have *any* type of happiness on this goddamn Saturday morning (fuck it, I love this job.)

Without fail, the tickets keep coming. The printer, located next to the industrial sized toaster, is smoking by the time 10 AM comes around. But I have to say, I am fucking good at what I do and when your good at something, even when it's stressful and your'e sweating, it's fucking fun. This isn't like in little league baseball when I was kind of good. Coach may put me at second base, but I know that if I start slumping with my defense that I will be on the first train out to right field. I know I am better than right field and at the bagel shop is where I reach my potential, I am given an opportunity to showcase my skills. There aren't any balls being hit at me. I rarely have to run more than a short distance at a time. This is where I slickly field a hard hit cheese-bagel-with-cream-cheese-toasted-twice-with-a-bag-of-6-bagels-sliced-in-a-freezer-bag-to-go. I work hard and fast at getting bagels out to the community. I try harder than I ever did playing baseball, finishing homework, or whatever else has been required of me during my youth. Here I am, Chet Lemon, the starting 2nd baseman of the 1984 Detroit Tigers. To my left is Alan Fucking Trammel. Drew, the king of bagels, my immediate supervisor, fielding bagel ground balls like it was no big fucking dea, flipping them to me to complete effortless double plays. We led the bagel community in fielding that year. The customers know that my name is James and that I won't fail to get their delicious bagels out to them in a timely fashion.

Alas, Rossmoor is changing. My sister and her friends discovered a quick way to lose weight while being able to study for hours in order to keep up their insane grade point averages. I don't know what she is doing (speed? cocaine? something else?) at the time but I see a change in her behavior towards both my parents and I. She continuously made life very difficult during the last year and a half that she was in high school. I rarely get in trouble either at school or at home and it never occurs to me to talk back to my parents. Mandy has no such qualms. Nobody knows why she is so fucking angry and bitter in these days. I don't have the slightest idea how ornery and spiteful coming down can make a person. At least not yet. My parents are initially blindsided by her behavior. It doesn't take them long to fight back. It doesn't matter if my sister is 100% in the wrong and owes them an explanation and an apology for whatever bullshit she had pulled the night before, she never hesitates to turn it around on them. She never makes apologies, amends do not happen.

My sister is part of a group of friends that are *always* together. They have been close all throughout high school. I guess it isn't a surprise to find out that they all start doing speed together. Isn't that what teenage girls do? So, luckily, it doesn't take too long for one of the parents to pull their heads out of their asses, look around, and realize that all these girls are on something stronger than energy drinks (which don't exist being that this is the time before Red Bull). The parents are notified. It is a big ordeal. Tears are shed and regrets are proclaimed. They make apologies and promise to lay off the hard stuff. This act of contrition is swallowed whole by the parents. Most of whom are so confused and overwhelmed by the fact that their sweet, pretty, well taken care of daughters have gotten sucked into such a nasty habit. The parents just need a Band-Aid, a hug and to be told that everything is going to be alright. They are desperate to believe whatever bullshit the girls feed them.

The drugs continue, only now the girls hide it better and keep up their stellar grades. Out of sight and out of mind works better for my parents in matters such as these. As long as there is a change in Mandy's attitude at home, then they can sweep the whole ugly business under the rug. It quickly becomes an issue of the past. But this doesn't help ease the strain in *my* relationship with her. She is still stealing my bath towel on a regular basis (a much more complicated issue than it should be). This creates a void between us that isn't mended until we are both in college and do not live in the same house. I know that she is leaving for college soon and I am able to keep it civil knowing that there is a light at the end of the tunnel.

Mandy has a 4.0 grade point average in high school. This sends her off to college at the University of California at Santa Barbara. There she manages to last about a month. Her roommate in the dorms, a girl also from Rossmoor, calls my parents one day to inform them of Mandy's rampant drug use. An hour later they are on their way to pick her up and move her home. My junior year of high school is immediately disrupted by her return.

The shame and degradation of being brought home from the university was soon topped with a DUI arrest. Combine that with a half-assed attempt to see counselors and get credits at a junior college, and she isn't doing all too well back in the comforts of her childhood neighborhood. So, to the relief of both my parents and I, she goes back to school all the way up north at San Francisco State. She returns to higher education and reinvents her life. At the same time she simplifies our lives by leaving.

Nothing really changes upon her arrival to the big city. Her habits become more intense but she finds her niche in the city. She spends the first few years attending class sporadically while in a haze of drug addiction. Her absence from my day-to-day life opens the door to reconciliation. For me, having a dry towel hanging up in the bathroom every time I get out of the shower does wonders for our relationship. Now she is finally able to have her little brother come to visit. This allows me to forget the bitterness. This gives both of us the opportunity to have a great time together. This introduces me to the greatest city in California – San Francisco. Road trips with friends up to "the city" become a bi-yearly event. Our fake IDs work well up north and we have a place to crash after the evening turns into a drunken mush. For the first time in my life, there is a distinct aroma of a quality relationship slowly brewing between my sister and me. I have been tormented for years with her inability to hang up the wet bath towels and her causing havoc at my parent's house. Now she is four hundred miles northward and fun to visit. We go out, drink beer, smoke cigarettes and take public transportation. We rock the city of San Francisco while formulating a relationship with each other. I look over at my sister and realize that we actually are related. There is a connection reminding us about the reason that we should know each other. This connection is cut short too soon, betrayed by the bullshit of biology, genetics and chemistry, but right now it is fucking golden.

6

Mickey Fucking Mantle

MY FRIENDS AND I stick to beer. I never see hard drugs (marijuana doesn't count.) until well into my sophomore year of college. High school is defined by the discovery of alcohol. I realize that the tree house is the perfect safe house in all of Rossmoor. It is a convenient place to drink without fear of being caught. Once it is torn down we are left to our devices to find other places to party. I try to drink, trust me, I really want to be a part of it, but in the beginning I find that I can't stand the taste of beer. Every time I struggle through a can of crappy beer I feel bloated and full. It doesn't make any sense and it sure isn't fair, but that's how my body initially responds to alcohol. Instead, I smoke pot, content with that for the time being. Eventually, my body gives in to the temptation of alcohol and soon I am the poster boy for underage binge drinking. My enthusiasm for alcohol starts here and never really goes away. The influence of my friends isn't solely to blame for my dysfunction, but without them I won't be who I am. No doubt, I will be well adjusted and gainfully employed. I will be bored and happy. I will be blind and content and on the verge of a nervous breakdown. Instead of a savings account and a healthy liver I have Mitch and Bernie. Instead of John Grisham, I get Jack Kerouac. Instead of KROQ, I get KCRW. Instead of simplicity and safety, I get ideology and accountability. This is when I start to read. This is when I begin to care. This is when I start to live.

We call ourselves "The Trilogy" due to the simple fact that there are three of us (clever, I know). Bernie - The Hippie, Mitch - The Drunk, James - The Pimp. I am called the pimp because I am the only one outwardly focused on hooking up with girls. The only thing I care about is being able to convince cute girls to talk to me. I appreciate those interested in sports, academics and the arts. I can relate to such endeavors. Be that as it may, for the time being, this is the only important thing in my life.

Mitch is dealing with Catholic doubt issues that revolve around trying to stay a virgin for as long as possible. I can't relate to this, and his virginal status is never discussed. I'm sure he is having sex, but I have no definitive proof of such activities happening. His game is simple and consists of one part: Quietly hide any affection towards girls that he actually wants to date. Somehow this seems to work time and time again. There are girls our age that he is interested in. Over the years he convinces himself that they will never share the same feelings towards him. This is an easy way to be a pussy. This is how he avoids getting his heart broken. This is the first time I see him take the easy way out, only to suffer the consequences later.

The type of girls that tend to like him, also tend to irritate him. More often than not they become annoyingly infatuated with him. They are younger, not especially bright and can best be described as peppy (his worst nightmare). This is his fault. These girls are putty in his hands. Acting indifferent and aloof just makes them all the more interested. Throw in a slight hint of meanness (lingering closely to being cruel) and they are his for the taking.

Bernie drives a booger-green 70's VW bus (Camper pops out of the roof) that fits him perfectly. He is a free spirit who likes to drink beer and smoke pot. His style of dress is "stoner casual." His style of hair can be described as "a mop of unwashed brown curls" also known as "stoner casual." He is well-read, listens to good music and is the one I find myself having deeper and longer conversations with. Mitch is known as "the drunk" because back in eighth grade he signed everyone's yearbook "Mickey Mantle." He is "the drunk" because his afternoon routine includes a glass of Chablis Blanc in his living room before his parents come home from work. He is "the drunk" because he is the most talented at getting strangers to buy us beer at the local liquor store. Bernie becomes a train wreck when he drinks. Mitch becomes a lightly-powered superhero. Bernie loses his ability to stand up, has to be walked home, taken up the stairs and put to bed. Mitch finds out where the party is. Bernie pulls down his pants, whips out his dick and pees right in front of the hottest girl in our grade while riding an escalator at Angels Stadium. It's a long story. It's pretty funny actually, kinda. Mitch finds us a party *and* a ride to the party. It becomes a weekly ritual to draw straws to see who will be stuck with the inevitable task of taking care of Bernie later that night. I am always in the middle of the two. I am always aware of what my parents are going through with my sister and I don't have it in me to ignore the need to not disappoint them. I have my moments, believe me. But I don't have the ability to forget the last time I drank too much and have to have Mitch stick his finger down my throat on Bernie's side yard in order to throw up. I clearly remember not enjoying a stomach on the verge of saying "*oh shit.*" and a head without equilibrium. Having the spins pretty much sucks, so I try to avoid it.

It becomes harder and harder to keep Mitch to ourselves. Other groups of guys begin to discover that not only is he good at finding beer and house parties, but that he is a crucial component to having an unforgettable night. I am used to calling him Friday afternoon and asking him what we are doing tonight. He tells me, and that will be that. Now that he is being pulled in different directions, I am losing my loyal wingman more often than not. We still hang out every weekend. Now there are more people involved and less Mitch. Bernie also begins to be pulled in a different direction. First by a girlfriend who he spends every waking moment with, it is excessive to say the least. After they mercifully break up, he finds a group of like-minded people (hippies-in-training) who share an interest in taking acid, smoking pot and expanding their minds on a regular basis. We still speak of one another as "The Trilogy," but we see Bernie less often. Mitch and I are better suited to a scene of house parties, getting drunk, and hanging out with girls. Bernie is never overly comfortable with that scene and part of me is relieved that I won't feel responsible for his uncontrollable behavior.

In my world, everybody knows everyone else. The high school is tattered with cliques and crews with agendas and lobbyists. I am somewhere in the middle of the chaos. I claim the country of Switzerland as my sponsor. I stay neutral. I stay committed to display a good will towards the majority of the population that surrounds me. There isn't any wasted time directly related to heavy differences between myself and those around me. I rarely upset the status quo and rarely find an issue big enough to require my direct involvement. I generally enjoy and like the people around me and I have the utmost confidence that the sentiment is returned.

I benefit from the status Mitch has. We complement one another perfectly. He has the innate ability to perfect an evening with his presence and the potency of his wit. A party is not complete until he arrives. I benefit greatly from my close association with him. People want to get close to him and as a byproduct; they want to get close to me. Years later I am told this might be the other way around, but this never crosses my mind. We are seen as a package deal. We become famous based on the strength we carried when together which leads to becoming famous on the strength we give one another as individuals.

A typical Friday night involves assorted indulgent behavior at a house party. A deliberate excess of alcohol consumption is the unified goal within our small group of friends. We drink copious amounts while engaging in heated debates on history and politics. Nobody else really ever understands it. It is beyond their capabilities to translate the appeal of exhaustive discussions solely for the sake of discussions and well meaning arguments. Here we are, seventeen-years-old and we sit at the dining room table during the apex of a loud party, just to ignore it all, and argue passionately about fiscal policy, the CIA's involvement in Guatemala in the 1950's, and the benefits of Capitalism versus Socialism. The thing that sets us apart is simple. We demand a level of knowledge amongst ourselves. We read because we are young and we don't know everything yet. We read because we *choose* to, not because it's assigned. We need counter arguments to counteract the various theories and interpretations of current events that are passionately being debated at that given moment. We need documented proof that whatever bullshit we are saying is truer than whatever bullshit is being thrown back at us.

Mitch is unapologetic about his right wing fascist ideology. He is a staunch Republican. He is well-read and very committed to an argumentative personality bent on destroying the "we are the world" leftist mentality that I employ. We are the perfect fit. Complete opposites in regards to politics, religion, and values. Yet, we connect so thoroughly on all other sentiments that a simple balance is realized despite our differences.

"Oh shit. The cops are here.."

These are the last words anyone wants to hear this particular night. The party is getting large and noisy, but it is still early. The party isn't out of control and things aren't getting broken. The owner of the house is having a great time. He isn't freaking out by the large amount of strangers in his parents' house. He hasn't drunk too much Jagermeister too early in the night, only to pass out upstairs and miss out on his own party. Instead, he keeps thanking us for helping him throw a party that includes upper class females who no doubt have no idea who he is or whose house they are at. He is a few grades below us and we convince him that he should have *"a few people over."* This leads to Mitch and me working our magic and a few hours later there is a decent party about to be broken up by our city's finest. We have to act fast.

I peek out the window and see the most beautiful sight an underage drinker can see. But first, a little backstory- Cops don't want to be predictable anymore so when the bagel shop opens they start coming there instead of the donut shop located four shops down. This leads to me being on a first-name basis with the very two cops standing outside the door at this very moment. By this time, Mitch is working at the bagel shop too and knows the two cops as well as I do. Back to the present- Mitch also walks over, peeks out the window and immediately grabs onto my arm and opens the front door. Officer #1 rolls his eyes at the sight of us. Officer #2 shakes his head and laughs. We promise to keep the noise down. We assure them that neither of us is driving tonight and within a moment they are pulling out of the driveway and the party has been saved. We walk back into a standing ovation from the entire party. People give us drinks. We are the saviors of their young souls. We are the only two people there who can save a party by the sheer force of our will. On that night, we are gods.

7

Underage Plumbing

AT THE TENDER age of fifteen I find myself in love. Hope turns to disappointment and before I know it, the shattered brightness given to me is gone and I want nothing more than a quick painless death. Not quite sure how it comes to that so quickly, but it does. I have no illusions of living anything other than a normal and happy adolescence. And through no fault of her own she promptly destroys my naive familiarities and replaces them with an existence filled with uncertainty. What begins as a simple case of meeting a nice girl evolves into a melodramatic crying-for-help type situation.

I have the erroneous idea that I have some type of exclusive opportunity to get to know her. We meet on a Tuesday. Share a bit of chit-chat, small talk, see you soon, perhaps. I obtained her phone number and got up the nerve to call her later that evening.

I only meet her because she is visiting a friend before my Spanish class starts. Spanish is boring; I enter the room with low expectations. Instead, I am blindsided by the vision of an angel. (I apologize for that last sentence. It is horrible and you deserve better, but there isn't any other way to put it. Don't judge me, I am still not finished going through puberty.) I'm prepared for verb conjugations, usted, informal and formal uses of a foreign language, not for her. Out of nowhere I see someone way beyond my capabilities and surely out of my league. Yet somehow, I find myself having intelligent dialogue with a woman as exceptional as she.

The problem starts with the first phone call. It feels like kismet. We talk continuously. Instead of silence and awkward moments strung throughout the conversation, we have actual moments of connection and intrigue. She is interesting and intricate. She didn't grow up in Rossmoor and has absolutely no affiliation with a group of friends I

34

grew up with. She's the unknown. There is nothing she can tell me that I already have information about. My day at school includes meeting somebody beyond my frame of reference.

The phone conversation ends and I am unable to focus on anything else but her. The anticipation of seeing her the following day takes over every facet of my brain. All potential interests and considerations desert me. The outside world is irrelevant. I don't know where she hangs out and I have no clue what area of the quad she positions herself in. I am not concerned about when I will see her the next day. I am sure that we will find each other.

And yet, I am unable to find this girl. I expect her to be looking for me. I continuously look for her. I am frantically making myself apparent during the duration of the school day. I allow her every opportunity to run into me so we can finish the conversation we started the night before. But she isn't there. I am expecting this girl to uncover my unappreciated potential. She is capable of knowing me, but she is reluctant to fall into my intricate world. And the next thing I know... she is consciously avoiding me. She disappears during every passing period, vanishes entirely from my life, and I can't figure out why. I am clueless as to why the potential relationship falls apart so quickly. One phone call convinces me that we have a deep connection. I am left to wonder why our relationship ends before it can even begin. I continuously analyze the situation and am mystified to find the reasons for this sudden reversal.

There is no closure. There is no awkward phone call detailing her reasoning behind her reversal. There isn't any reason for this phone call. All I can do is throw smiles her way. She doesn't owe me anything. She is conveniently exempt from any and all obligations to me. I start to doubt whether there was an actual connection between us in the first place. All I accomplish is a conversation via telephone, and a few isolated moments shared during the school day. This obviously means more to me than it does to her.

The way to deal with this is to lose my mind and start writing down my feelings. The following sums up how miserable and confused I am. This is a day in my life. I am a poor sap who is in love. I have no way of turning my passion into something productive. Instead, I have this.

Breathing becomes staggered. It stops coming naturally.
The sight of her captivates me. The sight of her might just kill me.
I am always on the lookout. Just to see her face.
She is everything. My life was meaningless for so long.
I don't want suicide. I don't want to die. But I can't go on like this.
I pray to stop living. There is no hope. It is all so sad. Meaningless.
Something about her, She is the most beautiful girl.
She looks vulnerable and yet so comfortable. That just kills me.
Every moment at school is agony.
All I can think of is to see her face, her being, her aura, her presence.
Every time I see her I am tortured and frail.
She is who I can't have. She is all I want.
She kills me, eats away at my insides.
She rips away my confidence. She smashes all hope for normalcy.
She is everyone. She is everything.
And like that… she is gone.

This rejection is all it takes to destroy the foundation I am holding on to. Without being granted any sense of closure. I cannot get her out of my head. I am in a constant state of anxiety. I am miserable every minute I am at school. I walk separately from my friends and slowly melt away into a fixated state of desperation. All I can do is hope to coincidentally pass her during the day. All I want is a glimpse of her. She transforms herself into more than a pretty girl. She suddenly turns into a vision of grandeur that I can't cope without. On occasion, I walk by her. My reaction is always the same. She is someone beyond my expected capabilities. She is blond and beautiful. She is a singer and a dancer. She has talent and a certain future containing success and stardom. She becomes an idealized version of the complete woman. Bearing in mind she was fifteen at the time. Yet, somehow she portrays an inability to understand my distress. I find myself concentrating on her during lunch. I am shocked to find myself having a stalker-type personality. I try hard to keep all of this out of the scrutiny of teenager gossip circles. I really am not a crazy obsessed stalker. I'm not, right? I'm just dealing with some shit right now.

Now she is really making efforts to avoid me. She goes from slightly concerned to somewhat afraid. She is convinced that I am this weird guy that just won't go away. She only wants some peace and quiet. So now the only thing I can do is stay away from her. This is the only option I have. Somehow, I have to reverse this confused notion she has of me. I have to convince her (and her friends and family) that I am not scary. That I am indeed a pleasant young man whose only desire is to contribute to society. This strategy works most of the time. But when this plan fails, I am forced to cope with conflicting emotions far beyond my abilities as a teenager.

When we cross paths I quickly reinforce my commitment to this girl. Her beauty effortlessly disrupts every futile attempt I make to forget about her. I am miserable regardless of what I do. A few days pass without seeing her. This only compounds the problem and consumes me with a familiar emptiness. Absence does, indeed, make the heart grow fonder. This is complicated by the elated wonder and intrigue that consumes me after every chance encounter I have with her. I feel some sense of complacency during my discreet glances in her direction. As long as she doesn't notice my quick gaze I am fine. Two seconds later she disappears around a corner and my brief moment of happiness is replaced by a familiar feeling of dread. This is nothing compared to the utter horror of having to pass her head on in the hallway, occurring when either one of us turns a corner and finds the other three-quarters of the way up the hallway heading directly towards them. Awkwardness overwhelms, but there is no escape from having to pass one another. It's harder for me because every time it happens she is walking with friends. I walk alone. She is laughing and happy, while I can't remember the last time I laughed and can be described as the exact opposite of happy. What I don't do is look back after we pass. That would be too depressing. This isn't some sappy soap opera, this is real life– gazing at the one you love isn't considered cute or sexy, it's just pathetic. I am unable to survive without seeing her and I am incapable of any type of normalcy when she is in my presence. When I don't see her I am miserable. When I *do* see her I am miserable. All I think about is the anticipation of the next time I will catch a glimpse. The vicious cycle continues.

Months go by and I am *still* suffering. I quietly try to figure out how to get through the agony involved with falling in love. I turn to alcohol to help dull the unpleasantness. It's after midnight one Friday night and I am drunk at a friend's house. Having already thrown up numerous times, I now find myself situated under the kitchen sink, phone in hand. This seems like an appropriate time to give a certain young lady a call to see how everything is going. You know, a casual phone call with an old friend that I haven't caught up with in way too long. I am under a sink. I am drunk on malt liquor. I am dialing the number. Nothing good can come of this.

I return home the following morning and find both of my parents sitting at the dining room table. They have been waiting for my arrival. They have grim expressions on their faces. The night before is a complete blur. I expect to walk in the house, answer a few questions about my night and then go back to sleep. I do not expect to walk in and find my parents waiting for me with grim expressions. This is when it hits me. This is when I remember spending a good amount of time under a sink, talking on the phone.

Now, I don't remember all the details of my phone call to Kristy's house, but I remember enough of it to know why my parents look concerned. I find out that I shouldn't worry; any aspect of the conversation that is hazy to me will be retold with vivid detail by my parents. My imprudent phone call is promptly recounted step by painful step. Yes, now I remember. Last night's conversation hadn't been with Kristi at all. Instead, it had been with her mom and her older sister.

My drunken phone call contains questions such as "If I were to die, do you think she would notice?" This is followed by other melodramatic teenage cries for help. I lie under that sink and pour my heart out to her sister and her mom. I might even cry during our conversation, can't really be sure. Near the end of the phone call, Kristi's sister tricks me into giving her my home phone number. I faithfully hand out the number so Kristi will be able to call me tomorrow. I am told that Kristi isn't there, or is asleep. In actuality, Kristi is sitting right there during the whole damn fiasco. I give over the number and end the phone call with a renewed hope that tomorrow I will get a call from Kristi. We will talk, I will explain to her that I am not a psychopath; she will give me an explanation of what I did wrong. Hey, maybe my soul-exposing honesty will convince her to be interested in me. Maybe we will fall in love. Yes, that's exactly what's going to happen tomorrow. My worries are over.

Kristi does not call the next day. Instead, my parents are awoken that night by a call from Kristi's worried mother. She gives them a *detailed* account of our little chat. She gives them a thorough report of my inebriated state and my veiled threats of suicide. This is magnified when coupled with my parent's inability to locate me the night I make my ill-fated phone call to Kristi. I am at a friend's house who they don't know. I am safe. They can't call the house or drive over to pick me up. Here I dodged a bullet, because if they *did* know my whereabouts they would have come and gotten me. I can just see it now- *Where's James? He's under the sink.*

I'm grateful that specific scenarios aren't given an opportunity to develop. I'm reluctant to even speculate the damage their arrival would do to my street cred. The potential chaos associated with my parents showing up at a house party and finding me passed out under a sink is too much to bear. Even if I'm not under the kitchen sink when they arrive, the actions permeating throughout the house would be impossible to explain to them. Even if they did find me I'm sure that they would kick themselves for coming over. They would rather see none of it and stay in bed. Advantageous to all parties involved, my Mom and Dad do not find out where I am. I can only imagine the defunct interaction that would have happened if they *did* find me. It would have become my own personal after school special: A cautionary tale of what can go wrong when you drunk dial, starring yours truly.

James: A Life Spent Under A Sink

His mom and dad pull up to the house, get out of the car, and start to navigate up the driveway. They pass the empty beer cans carelessly thrown throughout the front yard. They make their way to the front door and hear the obvious commotion associated with teenage debauchery. They proceed to walk inside and are greeted by the fearful expressions cast upon the revelers. This is an unexpected appearance by James's parents. James's friends are unsure of what to do. The confused teenagers display shocked expressions as they silently stare back at these intruders.

What the fuck is going on here? There are parents infiltrating our good times. Where should I put the bong I have in between my legs? These parents don't live here. Aren't these James's parents? Why are they here? Where is James, anyway? Oh, he is so fucked. Should I run? Should I say hi? Am I hallucinating?

Mom and Dad contain the rage brewing within and are led to the kitchen where their son lays. He is not entirely under the sink. This is good. Unfortunately, he still has his torso, head and arms under the pipes. He is incoherent at this junction. His time of acceptable actions and delicate decisions ended long before his parents decided to come on over and give him a ride home. He's taking a nap on the kitchen floor at some guy's house. What's the big fucking deal? He has come to accept the fact that on occasion he might possibly overindulge on tasty beverages and find himself under the sink not entirely sure as to how he got there. He doesn't plan for his night to end this way. His intentions do not involve vomiting and blacking out. But hey, shit happens.

This doesn't excuse the pitiful situation they find him in. He makes a sadly desperate phone call which leads to his parents having to wake up and get out of bed. Their reward for being concerned, loving parents is the sight of their son passed out in a dirty kitchen on tacky linoleum. It all adds up. Soon enough their concern for his welfare descends into a more lively display of total chaos. This is all displayed through an exaggerated attempt to yell not only at him but also at all the other kids drinking forties and smoking cigarettes. Of course, he hears none of this due to the simple fact that he drank the country of Russia and has no way to operate any of his senses. His parents have long since forgotten their own reckless youth and cannot offer any sympathy for the drunk and disorderly. Thank god he is blacked out at this point. His ability to explain the situation was gone long before they got out of bed and came to take him home. He is carried out, placed in the back seat and is soon back in the safety of his house.

The End

None of this actually happens. But that is no comfort as I answer the barrage of questions hurled at me. The conversation with my parents starts with a somber tone. True to form, Mom leaves no stone unturned. Suddenly everything tucked deep inside me becomes public knowledge.

Mom: *We got a call from Kristi's mom last night.*

I've been holding in all this shit for what seems like forever and I finally get the opportunity to get it off my chest. I spend the morning talking and crying. They ask me if I want to see a therapist. My answer is an automatic no. The issue is dropped. My parents are given an explanation regarding my moodiness of late. Now somebody else is aware of my plight. Somebody finally knows the extent of my anguish.

The beauty of the situation is that on Monday I get to go to school and am faced with seeing her on campus. I go from being secretly obsessed with her, which was hard enough to handle, to being obsessed with her while she is fully aware of my dysfunction. This shit goes public pretty quickly. For her to know about my rampant fixation cripples me. I keep my head down while walking from class to class during the passing periods. I walk quickly from Algebra to English Literature. All I want is to see one quick glance of her walking across the campus. I know that I am doomed, and yet all I can think about is seeing her. This lasts until the year ends. *Every day is fucking torture.* Every day is flawed and broken. I am back in middle school, I wake up, take a shower but now soccer practice isn't three times a week, it's every single fucking day. The reality of the situation dawns on me and sure enough nothing good will happen to me at school that day. Every single day is agony. It is hell if I don't see her. It is even worse if I do happen to pass her on the way to class. She is always smiling and happy and I am barely holding on.

Mercifully, school ends for the summer. I am no longer faced with the daily torture of either seeing Kristi or not seeing her and I start to recover. I start the healing process. Every day that I don't see her, I don't think about seeing her as much as the day before. Slowly she fades away. Gradually, I rid myself of this unhealthy obsession. By the middle of July I am cured of her. I am happy again. I am back to being the person I used to be. I get invited to Disneyland. I accept the invitation. I should have stayed home.

There is no reason to go to Anaheim that day. Surely I have other options. There must be something else to do. As fate has it, I go to Disneyland with a couple of buddies and am having a nice time. Just a lovely day at the Magic Kingdom. We head towards *Frontierland* and I look over and see Kristi with a friend. If her outfit was different, maybe my reaction wouldn't be so dramatic. If her attitude was different, maybe I would be able to survive running into her.

She is happy. She is wearing a low cut shirt that accentuates her ample development. She hasn't a care in the world and she is the sexiest/ most beautiful creature I have ever run across. She says hi to the three of us, and goes on her merry way. I meekly say hi and lose all enthusiasm for a day at Disneyland. I want to die. Thirty seconds in her presence destroys everything. I spent my summer recovering from her and I think that I am cured. I think that I am fixed. I was going to be okay as long as I didn't see her. I'm betting that if I don't see her all summer then come September I'll be free from her spell. But no, instead of happiness and freedom I am back at square one. I right fucking back where I started. All hope is lost. Everything is in pieces. Everything is ruined. Go fuck yourself Mickey Mouse.

8

Getting to Second Base in a Hot Jacuzzi

I FELL IMMEDIATELY BACK into a love-clouded funk until later that August. I go on vacation to Hermosa Beach with my buddy Stan and his parents. He is dating a young girl who plans on coming up for the night with a friend she dances with at school. And wouldn't you know it, this friend happens to be Kristi. I don't know how this happens. No clue whether this is planned. Don't care about the details. All I know is that it happens.

After the night is over and the girls go home, I am no longer crazy. I guess I never really was crazy. For awhile I truly started to doubt my mental stability. Now, I am confident that my normalcy is restored. Until Kristi shows up and hangs out with me that night, I still worry about my emotional state. This all disappears when she arrives at the condo. The four of us take a walk and I am allowed to do some talking. I am encouraged to explain the misperceptions she holds concerning my character. Somehow I am allowed to walk with her and chat. When she leaves later that night she has a whole new idea of who I am. She walks away that night intrigued. Something changes after this night. We become friends. We start to hang out, we chat on the phone. I get the distinct impression that she gradually likes me more and more.

We are polar opposites. I am a bad person. She apparently is not. I am in desperate need of help. She desperately needs to help me. I became her project. She is intrigued, I am in love. I get to meet her mom soon thereafter. The same mother who listened to my drunken rambles just a few weeks before is sitting on the opposite couch, getting to know me. Kristi is on a spiritual mission to change me from a fast-living-malt-liquor-drinking-partygoer guy to a god-fearing-decaf-drinking-cardigan-wearing guy.

Her mother is, needless to say, a tad skeptical, but is willing to hear my side of the story. I win her over and am given the go-ahead to date her daughter. It is recommended that I quit drinking immediately, or at least hide it from her mom. Kristi is a special young lady and surely doesn't want to be in the company of a hooligan like myself. So I sell out and stop drinking. This is devastating to Mitch.

Kristi swoops in and brainwashes me into not going out and drinking recklessly. Mitch is distraught and disappointed at my decision. I try to explain. He doesn't understand. The first night I kiss her is a monumental moment in my short career as a lover. A moment that hangs over me for two years finally unfolds. The roles are reversed. She is cheery and buzzed on wine spritzers. I am sober and content.

The first kiss is in a hot tub. It doesn't work. We miss. We are a swing dancer and a flamenco dancer fucking up the waltz. Our initial attempt is just... horrible. Our heads aren't in the game. It is uncomfortable and awkward. We are both trying so hard to make it work that we totally kill it. In spite of this, the hot tub is still brilliant. Even though we don't know how to kiss one another, we know how to do all the other things. Actually we don't do anything. We make out and do a tame amount of touching and rubbing. I am too scared to go for the boob grab. I am not sure if it is allowed. Isn't she still a good Christian girl without interest in such devilish carnal desires?

Turns out, I am a bit mistaken that evening. After all, we are scantily clad teenagers without supervision inside a 98 degree hot tub. Contrary to first impressions, this young lady is more interested in carnal pleasures than I anticipate. By the end of the week I find myself fondling her ample bosom in the back of my dad's Honda. I am the toast of the town. All of a sudden I have a girlfriend. Check that, all of the sudden I have myself a *hot* girlfriend. I don't deserve this. Surely I'm not good looking or tall enough to be grabbing her ass on a regular basis. But here I am, not just with permission, but encouraged to grab grab it and then more.

Kristi dates me in order to save me. Her mother knows of my drinking and disapproves. Unknown to her, Kristi is herself dabbling in the same reckless behavior. But this doesn't matter. I am the established one with the issues that need sorting out. I am the project.

I don't give a shit though, I am so fucking enamored with being involved with her life that it doesn't make a hint of difference what her actual intentions are.

The relationship is doomed from the start. It's really hard to be a teenager with a girlfriend who is way too hot for you. I last for a few months before the intrigue wears off on both sides and then the relationship ends. She is my date for winter formal. We keep things PG-13, which placates me. She lets me touch her boobs and even allows me to insert a finger or two in her vagina. When we do break up I am not overly bent out of shape over it. I am content with the knowledge that I obtain the unobtainable. The great mystery of Kristi has been solved. By dating her I prove to myself that I am not crazy to have been so crazy over her. I am able to prove to all of my friends, who witnessed first-hand my pain over her, that it wasn't a lost cause. Don't get me wrong, I still want to fuck her. I am not quite done with her yet, but I am resigned to the fact that we don't work as a couple at this time. I also know there is still a chance that we can work out in the future. At some point I know that the appeal isn't strong enough for her to continue. I am all in. I want to figure out how to keep her interested, but I know that it isn't something that I can hold onto. I had a nice run and now it is over. I went from a fifteen year old kid best described as "crazy stalker guy" to something more legitimate. I am no longer crazy, I no longer am a stalker and I am no longer hopelessly infatuated with a sexy blond by the end of my teenage years. I know the relationship will end. Everything that begins in high school eventually ends. So it does.

I go away to college. She goes away to work on a cruise ship. We still talk until she ships out and remain friends. Once she leaves I start to really think about her and what she brings to the table. I made a list:

Why I Like Kristi

1. *She is hot.*
2. *She has tits to die for.*
3. *Well... Shit, that's a pretty shallow relationship. I can't come up with anything else.*

I read books, I read the newspaper front to back on a daily basis, I have opinions and passions, I listen to good music, surely I require more from a girl than nice tits and a smile? Surely there is more to her than that? Surely there is more to me than that? Is that all that I believe in now? Fuck that, surely in San Diego I will find someone worthy of whatever it is that I have to offer. I can let her go because I know that I will get another chance with her in the future. I know that only being hot and having nice tits isn't going to keep me interested in the future. This doesn't keep me from thinking about her.

I leave for College. There isn't really any reason to hold onto her. I have no interest in going away to school and have a girlfriend back at home, let alone on a cruise ship. I am going away without any strings and am confident that I will find interesting girls in San Diego without too much effort. If Kristi gives me anything it is a strong sense that I can have anything and or anyone that I want. I leave high school at the top of my game. I am well liked by everyone, and I have a newfound confidence that only a hot blond can bring. I am moving down to school with two of my best friends. What can go wrong?

9

Just Because Reagan Documentaries are on PBS Right Now, It Doesn't Mean We Have to Watch Them

AM PROUD. I am full of hope. I am excited. In my mind there is no doubt that moving to San Diego State is the right decision. I do not hesitate for a single moment. I don't go to the trouble of applying anywhere else but that's neither here nor there. Instead, I go away to college with Mitch and Justin. I share a dorm room with Mitch and live in the same dorm as Justin. Without delay we will take SDSU by storm. Show up and take it over. We'll find ourselves in a niche of smart people who happen to be attractive and well read. Higher education is waiting for our arrival. We will not fail. I can not fail. I have Mitch's wardrobe to pick from. This should be easy.

It's time to leave the hood. It's time to go get myself an education. It's time to stuff the Honda full of all my shit and get the fuck out of dodge. It's time to move out. It's time to move on. Bigger and better things lay ahead. Youthful indifference no longer holds me back. I'm finally free from the safety that boredom provides. I drive southward without concern for hastily made preparations. I have been granted my release. Off to find myself something beyond what's available around here. The anxiety of the unknown is simplified, I opt for the familiar. There will be no strange individual randomly assigned roommates to share a small dorm room with. Instead I have decided to bypass this potential nightmare and get myself a roommate with considerable fashion sense and a healthy closet full of shirts and sweater vests agreeable to my own style. I have made the decision to room with Mitch.

Mitch and I share a second floor dorm room. The third amigo is Justin, who lives downstairs. Our first educational experience together dates back to Ms. Kuther's first grade class at Rossmoor Elementary. Justin has the looks, the smarts and the athleticism to accomplish anything he wants in life (which he does, fucking asshole). We run in the same circles all throughout school, we will live together for the next four years and he proves to be one of the most loyal and important friends I will ever have. He is someone I want next to me when there are girls around because, without fail, he makes me look better and makes them more willing to consider the idea of sleeping with me.

Mitch and Justin are my forever friends. They both have my back. This keeps me from branching out on my own to face whatever uncertainty is coming my way. It also keeps me from truly experiencing anything new and scary. Nothing horrific is awaiting my arrival. No stranger awaits me who is similarly determined to make the best of things. I take the easy route and move in with my best friends. The opportunity to truly branch out from my Rossmoor roots is lost on day one, when I choose to forgo finding new brilliant friendships and instead keep my old brilliant friendships.

SDSU isn't exactly my first choice of colleges. There actually isn't any college that is of particular interest to me. I genuinely expect options to be donated upon arrival. As I pull into the dorms the environment doesn't feel right. Even though I'm not quite sure what I expected college to be, this doesn't seem to feel like what I thought it would. The hum of the adjacent roadway doesn't depart. The expected noise associated with "moving day" is a mere peep. The task of unloading cars and carrying possessions upstairs is done with polite convention. Nothing is complicated by the excitement of disorderly behavior. It's all too civilized.

My living situation immediately gives me concern. Enthusiasm gives way to worry. My group of like-minded, intellectually adept scholars never materializes. I expect to find studious young adults interested in drinking lots of beer and meeting lots of people. This surely is going to be a simple transition. I am confident that new parties are waiting for me. I naively hope that freedom lies a short distance away. Changing my location certainly will lead to amazing adventures. One hundred miles down the coast of California is as far as I need to go.

Without traffic this journey takes no more than ninety minutes, a relatively painless car ride. Remember to bring the bare essentials from home. All expectations concerning secondary schooling are shattered within the first week of higher education. I expect to find myself embroiled in the midst of conversations, something, anything. I don't know what I thought it would be, but I do know that it is supposed to be easier than this. I deserve to move into the dorms and find new friends immediately. I shouldn't have trouble finding parties. There should not be any doubt. Things appear easy for everyone else going through this journey. I have no lack of confidence in finding people with similar interests and passions. But my luck runs out. It deserts me in my time of need. I find *nobody* with the explanations I need to find success and enlightenment while knocking the prerequisites out.

My lack of faith concerning the people I go to class with is based on their apparent lack of something. I don't know what it is, but it seems to be absent from campus and dorms. I lose my confidence. I'm stuck in a rut. I'm stuck with an education filled with avoided classes and missed opportunities. I'm bitter concerning those in charge, whom I expect total intelligence and impartiality from, but do not get it. The whole college experience is a strange odyssey of failed expectations. I find the beauty of vodka and decide to sleep in and learn the minimal amount required to get by without being hassled. Regret slowly fills my mind. My body is burdened with fatigue. Wasting this opportunity turns out to be exhausting.

I spent my first year in an objective struggle to keep my identity. I spend it adjusting to the realization that things are not how I envision them and that I am completely lost without my past identity. I am unfamiliar with hesitation and ill prepared to deal with all of this doubt. I cannot understand why I can't figure things out. This leads me to drink. This leads to bad poetry.

> *The alcohol displays itself as a large jellyfish bent on revenge.*
> *Fortunately for everyone present it is peaceful.*
> *It immediately swims away into distant aloofness.*
> *Frustrated by its inability to evolve into a quiet reflection.*

What does any of this even mean? It means nothing. I am drunk in my dorm room. Dizziness is all around me, yet I confidently take another sip. My desk is cluttered with empty beer bottles. Kristi enters my mind. How can I forget her and disregard how I feel? All I can do is sit and wait patiently for my heart to break. NO. All I can do is kick ass and impress the locals. Relapse into interesting encounters with cute young females. I will lose my mind and let go of conventional wisdom. Plans will pan out when I expect them to fail.

It is obvious from the start that we have chosen a dorm that is too quiet. Too many foreign exchange students and transfers from community college. Where are the dorm babes? My expectations are simple. I am confident that I show up with better musical tastes, more complexity in the novels I have read and with more life experiences than 90% of these yahoos. I show up expecting to dazzle and inform the masses. I arrive convinced that I am good looking enough and plenty smart enough to succeed here.

I am so fucking wrong. It's weird. I try to figure it out but can never grasp how we end up surrounded by people who can't embrace us. I figure that we show up and claim similar roles that we held in high school. It never occurs to me that I might have a hard time relating to people. I have never had any trouble relating to people before.

I spend the year drinking twelve-packs of Old Milwaukee Light we purchase at a Food 4 Less. Whatever fun things that are happening around campus are not happening at our dorm. Instead, we hang out, talk about stuff, smoke cigarettes and inhale domestically canned twelve-packs. Instead of fucking dumb girls, I play video games. I *suck* at video games. I do not have sex my freshman year of college. Huh? I have been lied to by my uncle- you bastard. In his first week of college, he smoked pot for the first time AND lost his virginity. He liked it so much he *stayed* in school for close to a decade. There are occasional drunken hookups in San Diego. But, these happen so few and far between that I figure I have lost my mojo. I have more luck on the weekends when I go home. But, it isn't the same. Going home and hooking up is easy. Why doesn't it transfer to San Diego? For whatever reason, no actual cases of unprotected, ill-chosen intercourse come my way that first year down south.

Mitch spends his freshman year in the same predicament. But I never actually see him even attempt anything like flirting. He spends his time engaging in epic battles of Trivial Pursuit (1980's Edition) with a guy who lives down the hall from us named Joe. Joe is an avowed Communist (literally) and Mitch is a Catholic, Reagan Republican (yep). The Cold War is repeated *multiple* times a week in my dorm room. This version of Trivial Pursuit has an abundance of answers that are either: *a) Ronald Reagan b) Mikael Gorbachev or c) Granada*. These battles start in the early afternoon and continue until dinner time. Talking points include an equal amount of social Darwinism, Catholic dogma and threats of violence. I stay out of the game for the most part, but am secretly hoping that the commies win and Joe will get to open a self-sufficient vegan farm after he graduates.

Mitch's other pastime involves watching the *entire* series of PBS documentaries about Ronald Reagan. He literally endures (enjoys?) hours upon hours of documentary footage of Ronald before, during, and after his presidency. I have a pretty normal schedule this semester. I go to class, gain important and life changing knowledge (fall asleep), go back to the dorms, drink cheap beer until two in the morning and then fall asleep. Rinse, wash, repeat. I wake up in time to go to class the following morning in order to do the whole routine all over again. Mitch, on the other hand, watches PBS (seriously, *public broadcasting*) until 5 AM. He falls asleep with a half-full beer in his lap and is *still* asleep when I return from a day of having my mind molded in higher? education.

Here is where I find Mitch. He hasn't moved an inch and is still in a deep sleep. Part of me is impressed that someone can sleep for that long and part of me is annoyed that he clearly isn't taking this college thing seriously. He never fails to come up with an excuse for sleeping through an entire day. Thankfully his class was canceled that day so it isn't a problem.

Mitch is on a whole different path. His day usually *starts* around two or three in the afternoon. This negates the need for him to go to sleep at a decent hour. My days start with early morning or mid- morning classes depending on the day. Before I leave the dorm I make a feeble attempt to wake Mitch up and remind him that it is Wednesday, and doesn't he have class in half an hour? Instead of sleeping, shouldn't he get ready for class? In a half-awake daze he assures me that he is about to get up and head to class.

I make sure to have at least one night off from drinking each week. The alcohol is replaced with insomnia. These nights I spend sober leave me wide awake and increasingly frustrated. Am I a raging alcoholic at the tender age of eighteen? Fuck, that's a depressing and worrisome thought that I convince myself to dismiss as paranoid and excessive. How is it even possible that I can't complete the simple task of closing my eyes, calming down my brain, and falling asleep? Holy shit, am I unable to complete a single day without having a beer? On the days that I try not to drink, I am reduced to pounding a beer at midnight and then (and only then) being able to drift off to sleep. This is normal, right? Yeah, this is totally normal behavior. I am basically still awake and I have been trying to sleep since midnight. It becomes a disturbing and irritating issue that I can't sleep on the rare occasion that I don't drink. Thus, freshman year involves drinking binges lasting for weeks. I am conscious enough to realize that a night off from alcohol is in my best interest. An early class gives me an excuse not to drink. In the dorms it is an effort *not* to drink. This is my night *not* to drink. I am committed to *one* night a week without any substances. This night always ends with me lying wide awake in my bed with no hope of a good night of sleep.

Mitch is no help. He spends another night unconcerned with such silly matters, things like going to class and a normal sleeping pattern are not on his list of priorities. He deftly rotates between *Magnum PI*, instant messaging on the computer, and waiting for the final episode of his beloved Ronald Reagan documentary to start on PBS.

James: *If we watch that fucking Reagan documentary again I'm going to have to kill you.*

Mitch: *Dude, it's the last installment, we've got to watch it.*

James: *Mitch, it's 2:30 in the morning. I have a midterm at noon tomorrow and you know how I feel about Republicans.*

In the dorms you have two opportunities to use your meal card each day, before two in the afternoon and again after five. Usually, we go to the on campus market and stock up on munchies and other assorted non-perishable food items, we avoid actual food like vegetables or protein that isn't fried. I am irritated every time Mitch sleeps through the first deadline and wastes his five dollars that should add to our meager supply of potato chips. This always leads to him not having any food, which leads to him getting hungry, which leads to him eating some of my food. I am hungry enough surviving on two meals a day and this mother fucker is eating all of my Pringles. But it can't all be bad. Freshman year can't be defined by PBS and snack thievery.

Mitch notifies me that the clock says 12:01 AM. This means that it is St. Patrick's Day. I am sober and trying my hardest to fall asleep. I don't particularly care that it is St. Patrick's Day at this moment and I promise a more enthusiastic response in twelve or so hours. My lack of enthusiasm inspires Mitch to go to work. Time is of no concern to Mitch. He is either nocturnal or snorting speed on a regular basis. By 4 AM I am still miserable and awake. Mitch is on his eighth Bud Light and operating on all cylinders.

Mitch: *Wake up, Aaron is on his way down.*

ME: [sleeping] *Huh?*

He convinces our friend Aaron to drive down from Long Beach to San Diego and celebrate the holiday with us. My initial reaction to Aaron driving down to San Diego from Long Beach is that I can't *ever* see myself finding the motivation or reason to drive an hour and a half at 4 AM on a Wednesday just to have breakfast. I have a list of excuses in my head that keep me from making the hundred mile journey down south: I have no gas; I have a midterm; I'm tired; There's too much traffic; And of course, the general- I don't want to, why the fuck would I? Without a doubt, I will look beyond the potential for adventure and ignore the story brewing within. I have no problem convincing myself that being nutty and original *isn't* worth having to jump over whatever hurdles or hardships that might face me if I go for it.

The complete illogical nature of Aaron's visit aligns with Mitch's lack of a conventional schedule perfectly. This is the perfect excuse for me to step out of my own comfort zone. Their behavior is completely irrational to me. To them it is the basis on how they live. Doing things for the moment takes precedence over logistical complications. The immediate future, the one they can see and feel is without a doubt more important than any type of long term goal they may have. Things fall apart when they start worrying about trivial matters such as details and precautions that are crucial to people like me. Instead of worrying about the bullshit they just make things happen.

The three of us complement one another very well. We fit damn well together. Mitch convinces Aaron to drive down with a simple argument that we expect him to drive his ass down and that he owes it to himself to come see us. He dares him to find a valid reason why he *shouldn't* get in the car and drive down right now. He convinces Aaron that all potential obstacles are outweighed by the importance of the three of us being together. He's like Ferris Bueller in 1999 – you just *can't* say no to this guy. It is an easy sell and Aaron is on his way.

The three of us couldn't be more different, yet so alike. We all are convinced that without one another we will be reduced to something more ordinary. We would be reduced to being just another conventional white male without anything to say. Our backgrounds are varied and different, but with the same roots of growing up in Rossmoor. Mitch is the product of a Catholic, Conservative, Republican upbringing. His interests revolve around Ralph Lauren sweaters, Jazz, and supply-side economics. One theory is that Mitch was conceived in the 1950's and kept frozen until 1979. It is the only explanation we can come up with to explain his affinity for Charlie Parker, Khaki Pants and penny loafers.

Even though he grew up in Rossmoor, too, Aaron comes into our lives later. We meet him when we all work together at the bagel shop. Aaron and I meet first and then Mitch is hired. Introducing Mitch and Aaron has immediate consequences for Aaron. He is a few years older and has been secretly waiting for someone to come along and force him to start paying attention to the world around him. This starts a rapid transformation for Aaron. He changes from a somewhat shady character into a partially shady character who is also informed and well-read. His background is so far beyond what Mitch and I have experienced that it is difficult to comprehend at times. The extent of what he got away with as a youth is thoroughly impressive. The scope of irresponsibility is mind-blowing. The funniest and most animated stories are told by this guy. Getting burned to shit by the coolant in his engine - *brilliant.* Running through a field being chased by angry dogs- *please tell me that one again.*

Aaron is capable of doing what I am not ready to do. He does *insane* things with reckless abandon, just get in a car with him and find out, actually, don't do this, trust me. At the same time, his influence gives us a better perspective on how much fun we can have. He comes out of left field and lives his life for himself. He does things just to fucking do them. Fuck the consequences. The beauty of Aaron is that by the time we become friends he has mellowed down a bit and is someone who Mitch and I are able to relate to. For Mitch, Aaron is a great friend whom he can discuss politics with. For me, Aaron is the guy who I go to when I have a crazy situation that Mitch or Aleem or Tim can't relate to. Aaron's advice is legit because he has been through it all before.

When Aaron walks through the door at six in the morning I am still in bed and not convinced that starting to drink so early is the best decision I can make. Reliable as always, Aaron shows up with a case of beer and my mind quickly sees the brilliance of early morning drinking on St. Patty's day. We decide to go have breakfast at *Hennessey's* in Pacific Beach. The experience of morning drinking proves to be an entirely different experience than drinking at night or during the afternoon. By my second rum and coke (drink of choice back then- I don't get it either), I was halfway drunk and couldn't stop smiling like an idiot. The bar isn't too crowded (it is a Wednesday morning after all) and our waitress is surprisingly unconcerned that two of us are in possession of really bad fake IDs. The class that I have later that afternoon becomes less and less of a concern and I am able to see the importance of being at a bar with two close friends at seven in the morning.

Where do I fit in this puzzle? My life is similar to Mitch's, except that my parents are staunch Democrats who work in education. I harbor their basic belief system of equality for all; let the poor kids eat, gays are born that way, et cetera. Mitch comes from a religious background which influences his affinity for all things conservative. William F. Buckley, trickle-down economics and less government are how he rolls. Aaron has no religion or strong morals, but somehow is equally committed to the cause of the right. Most of the time they gang up on me on basic policy issues, but on occasion they shut up long enough for me to get my point across.

We leave the bar slightly buzzed and completely content. We all agree this is an optimal way to spend a morning. As we approach the dorms we see people beginning their day. Fuckers are jogging, heading to class, heading to go have breakfast. We represent a whole different set of priorities. Aaron is going to drop us off and head back home- I still have time for a nap before my class starts Mitch most likely has something to do today involving school but is sure to blow it off. We shake Aaron's hand, give him a hug and say our goodbyes. Just like that, he is gone. His quick appearance into our lives is over.

The morning sums up how I feel about friendship. Sometimes it is good to be forced into doing random acts of morning beverage consumption. Aaron coerces me to live a little that day. He reminds me of the importance of simple things. Food, beer and conversation are pretty much all I need. Without mornings like these our commitment to one another will slowly fade away. Our ability to connect with each other isn't easily understood and yet we all hold the unshakeable knowledge that without one another we are lost.

Does Mitch attend classes? I think the answer to that is "yes" he occasionally enjoys a class. Certain classes he attends sparingly. Other classes he enjoys the subject matter enough to be bothered to attend on a more regular basis. Does Mitch go to college? I have no fucking idea. I guess he does. I mean, physically, I know he's here– he lives in a dorm room with me. I guess he attends classes, turns in stuff and meets the professors? I am a liar if I can tell you three times I ran into him on campus. College sucks. I am convinced that he will carry me through the hard times and make the good times better. I am convinced that I need his influence to keep me hip and relevant. We end up meeting very few people, attend few parties, and find ourselves driving home most weekends. One hundred miles door-to-door from somewhere that doesn't work, doesn't make sense, to a place holding all the answers. Most weekends home offers us more to do. One hundred miles to the north of San Diego there is more to be a part of. An hour and a half drive makes all the difference in the world.

The year mercifully ends and we find a house to rent in Mission Beach for sophomore year. It is more of a shack than a house. It has four bedrooms and no more than eight hundred square feet. It is *tiny*. It is also one house away from the sand. It is perfect. It is old, my room fits a single bed and a desk and that is it, but it is exactly where I want to live. It is exactly where I *need* to live. The dorms really didn't work out. I am okay with this. I figure that a change of scenery will do us all well. The plan is to inhabit this shack with Justin, Mitch, and Larry. Larry is the wild card, the only one we didn't grow up with. He is a stressed-out transfer student who is older (a junior) who we meet in the dorms. His mom's first name is Candy. She marries a man named Mr. Smiley. Her name becomes CANDY SMILEY. Go figure. Candy fucking Smiley. He is a pain in the ass to live with. Don't butter your toast and then put the extra butter on the knife back in the butter container. Not a good idea. Don't annoy this person. He never likes to be annoyed. He is also kind and lovely, just don't irritate him.

But Mitch never makes it to this house. He drops out a couple of weeks before we are set to move in. This is the first of a long list of times he will forget to share pertinent information with the group. He fails to mention that he has failed out of San Diego State (not altogether a rare occasion). He decides not to tell us that not only will he *not* be returning to higher education but that he will not be unable to finance his room in the house that we are planning to share.

Moving to Mission Beach is, ironically, his fucking idea in the first place so this is a double-edge sword of deception and bullshit. We show up in San Diego, and Mitch says he is "right behind us, honestly" until we eventually give up, accepting the fact that he *isn't* coming and we are stuck for a significant raise in what our parents have agreed to pay for our rent for the year. At this point, I have no money, I have an insignificant job, and I can only afford to contribute the exact amount that my parents are able to support me with. But Mitch has no qualms about letting this small insignificant detail about his future (tied in to our future, no less) be unreported because he is too afraid to admit his failure. It's his dad who tells me, in no uncertain terms, that there is "no way in hell he will pay for another semester of SDSU." I am on the other line, just simply trying to see what Mitch was doing that afternoon, making small talk with his dad because it is always awkward to talk to him.

Me: *So… Mitch must be excited to live near the beach next year.…*

Mitch's Dad: [*hesitating slightly*] *James, sorry, but you have been presently misinformed. Mitch will under no circumstances be returning to San Diego State University for his sophomore year.*

No, actually there isn't a hint of hesitation. He might have even laughed a bit at my stupid assumption. The bottom drops out on me. Part of me expects Mitch's life to be too good to be true. The fucker *never* goes to class. That is indisputable. His GPA is worse than I could have predicted (and I guess pretty low, ouch). This means that his shit is *so fucking low* that he probably isn't *allowed* to participate in his next year of higher learning. I never expected him to pretend continually that summer that he is coming back. I think our friendship is deep enough that we don't need to bullshit each other in any way. Clearly, I'm mistaken. Does he not see the complications involved with him flaking out of a lease at the last minute? Does that never occur to him? Does that never occur to his father? I get no reaction from Mitch's family when he screws us out of rent. He has committed to pay a fourth of our rent next year. This never even registers in their brains for one fucking moment. It never crosses their mind that their son avoids owning up to his bullshit and there are *three* other people who are sure to be out of a place to live the next school year.

Instead, it is swept under the rug at some point. Mitch fails to tell us that he is not going to be our fourth roommate no more than one month before we are set to move out. This is a typical move from him but truly impressed by the level of unreliability he is willing to reach. I mean, come on. Really? You neglect to tell us this *insignifican*t detail about your plans for the next year? I feel betrayed and pissed. But I am also ready to hand him a pass just for old times' sake. He is out for himself and himself only. He has no fucking loyalty. He is weak. But he's still my best friend. I have loyalty. But I am fucking weak, too.

He is unfortunately a person in possession of a magnetic personality that makes all of these other character flaws insignificant. It does not matter that he shows up late, steals your favorite pair of socks and kicks your puppy. He has it. He shows up bumming cigarettes, leaving half-full beers on the counter and makes everyone's night that much better. I love the guy. It is pretty fucking annoying.

10

Playing Catch in the Pacific Ocean

SOPHOMORE YEAR IS better. We live in paradise. Our house is fifteen feet away from the sand. There is a view from our patio. We settle into our lives. We barbecue. We drink. Some of us discover ecstasy. I even find myself a girlfriend.

While all of these exciting events are happening in San Diego, Mitch establishes himself in Long Beach. He is doing just fine. This doesn't last long. Mitch's parents pull the rug out from under him when they sell their house in Rossmoor and move to Atlanta, Georgia. He has older siblings who are starting families. When his parents move, they take with them his sense of security. They take away his house to do laundry at. They uproot his place to have a warm, normal Sunday dinner with his parents. They cast him off into the world. They figure that a twenty-year-old white male from Rossmoor surely can survive without them. They assume that it isn't going to be all that difficult for him to sustain himself. At least it shouldn't be, but it is.

I wouldn't be able to handle it as well as he does. He keeps it together for a good amount of time. He moves into an apartment with two childhood friends in Los Alamitos. He gets a job, gets himself a girlfriend, drinks copious amounts of alcohol and makes trips to visit San Diego. He is fun and fun-loving during this time. He is still the life of the party and the most interesting person that I know. He intrigues me like nobody else can. He is the reason Justin and I come back to Rossmoor more weekends than not. He keeps the scene vibrant and brilliant. There is nothing better than a night out with Mitch. Sure, he "forgets" his wallet more times than I care to remember, but he is a loyal friend who makes our lives better. Wait, better? I guess, maybe *more interesting* is a better way to describe it.

He comes down to Mission Beach for weekend visits. We discover throwing horseshoes on the sand in front of our house and never look back. Justin and I spend hours throwing a baseball back and forth near the surf so we can dive in after it. We spend our afternoons running down fly balls. Worries fade every time I run down a ball; dive fully extended into a crashing wave and am submerged by the ocean water. This is when I raise my glove above the water before I come up for air. Justin sees my glove first and knows that the ball is safely inside it. Nothing needs to be said, because I know that he knows that he just witnessed a perfect catch. We do this until there is a genuine concern that our arms may fall off if we attempt another throw. This is when we call it a day and walk to each other. We congratulate each other for partaking in such an epic display of catch. We walk the short distance home dripping wet, full of sand and feeling blessed to live in such a place.

Most evenings we walk to the boardwalk to see the sunset. It seems criminal not to make the effort to walk fifteen feet and spend twenty minutes looking at something so beautiful. We look at sunset after sunset after sunset. We see so many that we start to take it for granted. We stop making an effort to see the sun disappear into the ocean each night. Before I know it, a week has gone by and I have not even thought about such activities. I feel like a fuck up no matter how productive my day is when I come home and spend hours on the couch watching television without coming close to touching the sand. Every missed opportunity to take advantage of living in such a gorgeous place makes me sick. I am filled with regret for all the time I spend indoors. I feel like I'm failing to take full advantage of where I live. I should be spending my time outside. Body-surfing, jogging, painting beautiful watercolors of the shoreline, building sand castles and meeting girls in bikinis. These are just a few things I fail to do on a regular basis. I don't even have a tan I can be proud of. What have I been doing? Why do my days tend to take place inside my shitty house instead of outside on the beach? Every single place I live in since then throws this same regret in my face. Years later, I live a mere two blocks from the beach and yet I don't see it unless I am in my car, driving by it while on my way home. The place I live in after that is actually on the water. I can see the sunsets from inside the house. A great view from the comfort of my couch. I stay inside as I watch this sunset every time. I choose comfort instead of nature. I choose noise. I choose warm slippers.

Sophomore and Junior years are spent living in a house that is located behind a larger house that is directly on the strand and on the beach. The front house is two stories, has an amazing deck and looks like an estate. Our house is tiny, has a small deck and looks like the place where the help lives. They have space to move. They all attend the local Catholic private school called USD. These are boys and girls with money. There are three girls and two boys. Up until then we've made only sporadic acquaintances, so it is a welcome change to have people our age just a house away. We slowly latch on to the girls who live up front and I enjoy the private school lifestyle so much that I start dating one of them.

It happens by accident. I fuck a girl and all of the sudden I'm dating her. It is my fault. Caught in a moment of weakness, I sleep with my neighbor. I'm not overly attracted to her. The celibate lifestyle I've been living helps her cause. Her willingness to engage in intercourse with me turns her into an attractive female. The majority of sex leading up to her takes place in uncomfortable places and in awkward situations. Sex in my twin bed while my parents are asleep in the next room isn't as much fun as it sounds. The majority of sex I experience to this point is limited, inconsistent, and stressful.

The logistics of living next door to the girl I am seeing are complicated by the fact that she originally moved in with her boyfriend who lives downstairs. They break up a few months after they move into the house. He continues living downstairs. He lifts weights on a regular basis. For some reason he doesn't mind that I am sleeping with his ex-girlfriend/ non ex-roommate. Initially, I sneak back to my house early in the morning before anyone is awake. This gets old pretty soon, so I say fuck it and just start sleeping over.

Her enthusiasm in the bedroom leads me to forget all about the scary roommate downstairs. This is the first time I get to sleep with the same girl over and over again. I figure out how to do things. These things are pretty amazing. This is how she became my girlfriend. She has redeeming qualities. She is pretty fun. She likes to party. She has money. Her grandfather invented the modern oven. The oven sitting in every house in America is the direct result of her grandfather's hard work. She attends private school. She has never worked hard. She has never had a job. Instead, she has money. She has disposable income. She uses it to buy me clothes. It's a great arrangement. We have lots of sex. Then she buys me more clothes.

Cashmere sweaters are luxuriously soft. Fitted pants from *Banana Republic* make my butt look sexy. Dress shoes bought with her parent's credit card to complete the outfit. This leads me to accept her every time she shows her crazy card. This allows me to ignore the dysfunctional childhood she grew up in. This allows me to overlook the negative influence that money has on a family. I convince myself to accept the fact that she is fucked up and that it's her family's fault. That it's all good and I shouldn't worry about such things. As long as I stay well dressed, I don't worry about the logistics.

She chips her front tooth on a trip to Cabo San Lucas during spring break. I spend the trip with a girl missing half of her front tooth. We are in Mexico. There is no way that she will agree to any type of dentistry while we are there. I suggest flying back early in order to fix the gaping hole in her tooth. This would unfortunately cut the vacation short and isn't really an option. Alternately we (she) makes the decision that the gap isn't that noticeable (it's horrifically obvious) and that there is no reason to cut the vacation short. I survive the next few days in Cabo. I go to clubs with my girlfriend who has a trust fund, but looks like she grew up in a trailer park. I realize that I hate her and I want to break up with her. I keep this information to myself until after we leave the foreign country.

My attempt to break up with her happens a few weeks later. I finally get up the nerve to break up with her. Some lame bullshit about growing apart. I tell her that I want to break up. She tells me that I am not allowed to.

James: *This isn't working.* (James thinks… I HATE YOU.) *We need a break.* (James thinks… I WANT TO BREAK UP.)

Rebecca: *I don't think that is a good idea.* (Rebecca thinks… THAT IS NOT ALLOWED.)

James: *Oh… well… okay…* (James thinks… WHAT JUST HAPPENED?)

This ends the conversation. At this point I don't know what to do. Being a guy, while still being a child, encourages me to continue dating her. I try my hardest to end the relationship, I swear it, but she convinces me to change my mind. I don't have the energy to convince her otherwise, so I drop it for now. It turns out that living with your ex- boyfriend gets old after a while, so she moves down the street. I spent the next few months sleeping with her again. She isn't officially my girlfriend anymore, but I continue to string her along every time I find myself lonely, drunk and horny. At this point, I learn nothing about dating. I learned nothing about women. I find myself in the same predicament. I find myself bored and willing to fuck with her emotions by showing up wasted so I can fuck her again (yes, I am an asshole).

It doesn't surprise me when I find her bleeding in my hallway. It should. But it doesn't. She is worthless and without any hope of recovery. Is it possible to save her? I should probably give a shit. A normal reaction would involve doing something helpful. I am big and important, right? I can give back if it involves what I can give and if it is just myself doing the giving and nothing more and nobody else is involved. I have faith in what I can do. I have faith in who I can save. I can save someone on my own. It can be done without anyone's help. I can inspire.

Before the blood, the plan is supposed to be simple. She goes to the bar, I stay home, and she meets me back at my house later that night. Her plan is to take ecstasy and go out to bars or to a club (places a twenty year old isn't allowed.). My plan is to take ecstasy and play *RBI Baseball* on Nintendo at home. Being fucked up on ecstasy focuses me on three things, chewing the inside of my mouth, enjoying the euphoria, and smoking too many cigarettes. I forget that she is planning to come back to my house so I take an extended journey to the local 7/11 to buy more smokes.

My roommate and I need a good walk late at night. Being cooped up in the bungalow all night makes us ready to tackle the outside world. A walk along the boardwalk means fresh air and exercise. I am familiar with using ecstasy and know exactly how many pills to take. By the time we leave the house we have ingested all of them and are rolling our asses off (a common term for using ecstasy– often used at raves). It takes longer than we anticipate to buy smokes. Everything takes longer when you're on ecstasy, because *everything* is SO fucking fun– no joke. Gazing at the moon, wandering aimlessly, and contemplating the meaning of life takes a blissfully long time.

We finally get back home and discover a purse lying in the alleyway in front of our front door. I don't carry a purse and live with a group of guys, so this is odd. I check the front door and realize that we locked it before we left. It immediately becomes clear to me whose purse this is. Then I realize that I left around the time that the bars were getting out and that I told Rebecca to come over.

I unlock and open the front door. The house is tiny and my room is straight ahead. The first thing I see is Rebecca laying down with the lower half of her body on my bed and her upper half on the floor. As I get closer I see that her chest and head ended up resting on a stack of books and that she is obviously out cold. Then I notice that she is covered with dried blood and has cuts all over her body. Then I see that the window to my room is shattered completely except for jagged shards of glass still encircling the edges. These are not small, soft pieces of glass. These are large enough and close enough together to fuck a girl up.

Instead of patiently waiting outside for us to return, she goes around the house and smashes *five* different windows with her hand. I personally would give up by then if I haven't found success in creating an opening big enough to jump through. There is no doubt that after one window my hand will refuse another attempt and that would be that. This apparently doesn't occur to her. She ignores the pain and keeps at it. She is eventually triumphant. The window to my room is no match to her persistence. She is able to break a hole just large enough to climb through. Her battle against the evil window panes is over, now she can pass out victorious. She is face down with the lower part of her body on the bed. Her upper half is angled downward at 45 degrees. Her pillow is a stack of books. Even in my altered state, I am able to discern that what she's done in my absence is *seriously* fucked up. My night just became significantly more complicated. This isn't how I envision my night coming to an end. The scenario presented before me isn't ideal. In fact, it kind of sucks ass. There are many things wrong with it. The fact is, I am rolling hard on no less than sixty milligrams of a potent form of Ecstasy. This eliminates my ability to do anything more complicated than lighting and smoking cigarettes. This eliminates me from all situations involving any forms of decision making on my part.

Coming home and finding a passed out (should-be) ex-girlfriend covered in cuts and glass is made more complicated by the fact that she is out cold. She isn't a small girl to begin with and now she is completely dead weight. She is breathing. She isn't cut too deeply. She has been there long enough for the blood to dry so we know that she isn't bleeding to death. She is still breathing so we assume she is alive.

We can't move her into a bed, so I sweep away any glass that is near her. The best we can do is to move her off the bed and books and into the hallway.

Normal protocol is to call an ambulance and have them take care of the situation. Dial 911 and they come to remove the crazy bitch that's asleep in the hallway. Our attempt to handle the situation by ourselves leads to my roommate Scott being bitten on the arm. His reaction to being viciously assaulted is this.

Scott: *Ouch, I think she just bit me.*
James: *Stop being a pussy and help me move her.*
Scott: *Dude, she is REALLY heavy*
James: *Be a man.*
Scott: *She is really heavy..*
James: *You're right, let's leave her here.*

And that is what we do. We lay a blanket over her, place a pillow under her head and agree that doing nothing is the best course of action. Calling the authorities is the logical response yet isn't a practical option because we are all high (including her) and doing so would without doubt create serious repercussions for her. Our fate is less certain. Maybe we can convince the authorities that we are good Samaritans. We can convince the officials that we are innocent bystanders. But I have my doubts. I have no confidence in my ability to do anything other than act totally high. The only time I can pull off acting sober is when I happen to actually be sober. This isn't one of those times. Nothing but bad things will happen if the police arrive. Nobody wins if they start asking questions.

Scott and I discuss our options thoroughly. We decide that she will sleep it off and isn't in any real danger. We take turns checking on her and eventually she mumbles something, rolls over on her side and starts to snore. I lay awake until morning in Justin's bed and eventually fell asleep. I wake when I am disturbed by the confused ramblings of a girl without any recollection of what happened the night before.

Rebecca: *What the fuck happened to me? Did I get in a fight?*

James: *Look around you Rebecca.*

Rebecca: *I did that?*

James: *Yeah, you broke five windows, jumped through the one in my room and passed out on my bed.*

Rebecca: *What time is it? Oh shit, it's after 11am. I was supposed to be at a mother daughter sorority breakfast half an hour ago. Shit. Can you give me a ride home?*

I look at her incredulously. She expects me to drive her home after what she put me through the night before? Is she fucking serious? She is. It doesn't occur to her to apologize. It doesn't occur to her to offer to pay for the windows. It doesn't occur to her that this isn't in the realm of what normal behavior entails. It occurs to me that *nothing* occurs to her. I walk out to my car and we drive in silence. I pull up to her house and she looks over at me.

Rebecca: *You can't be mad at me for this.*

James: *I'm not supposed to be mad?*

Rebecca: *I don't remember anything. It's not my fault. I'm the one bleeding here, I should be mad at you.*

James: *I don't want anything to do with you. I expect you to call a window guy and pay for all of the windows you broke. After that, we are done. I'm not mad. I'm way past mad. I'm seething with anger. How can you expect me not to be upset with what you did last night? How can you expect me to wake up and automatically forgive you? You are so fucking out of touch with how I felt about you before this and how I feel about you now. I expect the windows to be fixed by tomorrow and I expect you to pay for them. Get out of my car.*

She gets out, slams the door and walks up to her house. I drive away and realize that I finally have what I've been looking for, only I've been too much of a coward to do it on my own. I finally have a reason to break up with Rebecca for good. She can't strong arm me into being her boyfriend ever again. I won't be faced with a moment of weakness and sleep with her. I am finally free of the pull she holds over me. Cleaning up broken glass is a small price to pay for freedom. I have a reason why we shouldn't be together anymore. I have concrete proof that she doesn't deserve whatever it is that I have to offer. The window to my room is covered with a poster and there is glass everywhere but as I drive home I feel a weight being lifted. I am my own man again and I am happy. I drive home with a big smile on my face that day.

Two days later I am looking at a book of art with another roommate. I have just smoked a healthy amount of pot and am content with being high, looking at the brilliance of M.C. Escher and listening to music. I am zoned out and like really high, I look up from the book and see Rebecca standing in the doorway. Rebecca wants to talk. Rebecca doesn't want the relationship to end. Rebecca always hated it when James was stoned. James must hide this from her. Rebecca wants another chance. Rebecca suggests we take a walk and work things out. James is stoned. James has no interest in her plan. James just wants to be left alone to look at art and listen to early nineties hip-hop with his roommate. James is fucked. James walks to the strand and hears Rebecca out.

It's at this point that I realize there is an enormous full moon out and it's directly in front of us. It's at the perfect height that makes the light of the moon reflect onto the water in a perfectly straight line from the far edge of the water all the way to the shore. Rebecca is expecting a serious conversation and all I can do is marvel at how fucking incredible of a place I live in and how beautiful of a night it is. I'm having a hard time listening to what she is saying. It doesn't matter what she says because she can't convince me that our relationship isn't flawed from the start and that there is any reason for me to give it another try. I just want her to leave me alone. I apologize repeatedly for the stupid grin I have on my face. No matter how many times I tell her that I'm stoned and can't help it, she isn't convinced that I'm not laughing at her and happy to have caused her such pain. She cries more; I try and fail to be sensitive to whatever it is she is saying. I don't listen to much of it. I focus on the reflection the moon has on the water and wait patiently for the conversation to be over.

11

Learning the Import/Export business in India

THE SUMMER BEFORE senior year I moved to Boston for the summer with Justin, Bernie and Aleem. I find a job and spend the summer waiting tables and drinking too much. I meet people. Once they find out that I am from Southern California they assume that I am cool and that I surf. I never tell them that the last time I was on a surfboard was ten years ago and I have no interest in the sport. I am content to let them presume that I am cooler than they are. Sitting on our stoop one night with Bernie, I attempt to explain to him what it is like being the only kid from California working at a California Pizza Kitchen with a bunch of people from Boston. I'm not cool. I am definitely not a fan of the periodic table of elements and I have never fired a gun. Regardless, I have this conversation with a straight face.

James: *It's like everything I do is cool just because of where I am from. It's like I am this... radical... atomic.... gunslinger.... That they aren't quite sure what to make of.*

Bernie: ....

James: *yeah...*

My senior year of college isn't defined by anything I do at school or anything that happens in San Diego. Somehow I don't drop or fail a class and am on track to graduate in May. We move out of the shack and upgrade to another house in Mission Beach. Justin and I find two new roommates. We share the upstairs loft. Mark and Casey share the downstairs bedroom. It is an overpriced two story, loft-style, apartment situated over a garage and above a downstairs tenet. No matter how hard we try and no matter how quiet we are, our poor downstairs neighbor hears everything. Every time we shut a door, walk down the stairs, open the fridge, clink ice cubes in a glass, listen to music, sneeze, give someone a hug, have a pillow fight, empty the dishwasher, et cetera, our downstairs neighbor hear everything we do loud and clear. After a few months, I see the futility of the situation, and realize that she will hear every little thing we do. I give up trying to be quiet and just hope that she has accepted her fate and doesn't complain excessively to the landlord.

Christmas break this year is spent in India with my family. My second cousin Brian is eight years older than I am. He grew up in Michigan. I have fond memories of him joining the family for a summer and going camping with us when I was in elementary school. I remember him fondly from that short time spent together, but this is the extent of the time I have spent with him. Brian lives in New York and is some type of biologist/scientist/smart person. He has fallen in love with and is engaged to Sahana. She also lives in New York but was born and raised in India. All of her family still lives there. India is far away. India has over a billion Indians. India is a foreign country. This shit is far. India is India. I have no idea what India is.

Brian flies to India and asks Sahana's father for permission to marry his daughter. Her father says yes, just so long as the wedding takes place in India. Her father tells Brian that it is important for *many* of Brian's friends and family members to attend the wedding. He also says that it is of utmost importance that Brian's blood relatives come to India for the wedding. Since plane tickets are so expensive, he offers to take care of all the incidentals and accommodations after they arrive. Anyone who makes the effort to buy a plane ticket gets an all-expense-paid trip to India.

Nana calls me to ask if I have any interest in going to India for the wedding. She offers to pay for my plane ticket and for my sister's if we go to India with her. I haven't made any definite plans for Christmas break. I haven't planned on a trip to India but say what the hell and agree to it. Before long, my aunt, my uncle and my two cousins want to come too. Soon thereafter, my parents succumbed to the pressure and agreed to come to India too.

We leave early Christmas morning and fly first class to Detroit. We fly coach to Amsterdam and then fly coach-minus to India. They pack us into tiny seats with minimal leg room for an eleven hour flight to

New Delhi. Instead of sleeping with the masses, I choose to do what I do well, I drink. Halfway into the flight I find myself in the back of the plane bonding with an Iraqi dude who loves Disneyland and goes by the name Mickey. The plane is dark and most people are asleep. I head to the back of the plane in search of more alcohol. A stranger is standing at the back of the plane, he flashes a wide smile at me and says hello.

Stranger: *What the fuck mon? Glad to see you make it to where the party is.*

James: *Glad to finally see someone with similar priorities.*

A flight attendant fills up a Styrofoam cup for me with whiskey and tea. This potent mix awakens my dull senses as we continue to fly over the Atlantic. Mickey and I spend the next hour chatting in the back of the plane. A guy in the last row tells us to shut the hell up, he is trying to sleep. We ignore him, but lower our voices. Mickey tells me about the Middle East. We talk about politics and history. I impress him with my knowledge of current events; he shows off his Mickey Mouse medallion that he keeps around his neck. The conversation ends. We exchange a hug and I return to my seat. I don't see him again, but in a few hours I land in India full of confidence that I can talk to anyone, no matter where they are from, and they will like me. I walk off the plane with no fear.

We land in New Delhi later that night, go through customs, and are met at the airport by our new Indian brethren. So begins our involvement in an Indian wedding. A Sikh wedding lasts for five days.

Day One is an informal get to know your new family chat and chew.

Day Two involves the fear and anxiety that accompanies New Delhi traffic.

Day Three includes a ceremony that formally welcomes Brian as part of the Indian family. That night we dress up and go to a party held outdoors somewhere in India. The only alcoholic drink being served is scotch. My father and I struggle through a few drinks served neat. Straight scotch doesn't sit well with my father, a man who only drinks cheap Chablis Blanc bought in large jugs. It also doesn't sit well with his son. Going from a strict diet of light beer served in a can and rum and coke served in red plastic cups to strong Indian scotch isn't an easy transition. Not drinking isn't a viable option. I want to dance, but this can't happen without the presence of alcohol. I must think of something to fix this. Then I remembered my theory of lost keys.

When presented with a problem that takes longer to solve than you think it should, don't over think the solution. On occasion, my keys disappear and after looking for twenty minutes without any luck, desperation kicks in. This is when I start checking random places. Logic goes out the window. I'll check the microwave. Maybe that is where I put them last. I'll check inside cupboards I haven't opened for weeks. I'll check rooms I know I haven't been in recently just in case. My brain stops working until I remember that the simplest explanation is always the correct one. The more complicated the predicament always leads to the simplest solution. This is when I check my pants pocket and find the elusive keys.

Straight scotch is served at room temperature. I can't think of a single drink I enjoy that isn't either cold or hot. This makes me think about how much I enjoy cold beverages. Then I remembered ice. I love ice. Ice is great. Fifth grade science comes back to me immediately. I know what happens when ice melts. All say it together now- it melts. If I add ice to the scotch it will first make the drink cold - this is good. Then the ice will melt into water and dilute the beverage - this is *really* good. I've seen people order scotch and water on TV before. I never knew why until this moment. Now it all makes sense. I discover that Indian scotch mixed with water is actually quite drinkable. I share my revelation with my Dad. By drink #4 I'm convinced that it's the most delicious drink in India. We dance throughout the night.

Day Four starts with a ceremony that formally welcomes Sahana into Brian's family. Another dinner happens later that day. No dancing takes place, but I look good in my suit and tie.

Day Five starts *early*. The plan is to get ready, put on my suit and tie, place a turban on my head and meet the whole wedding party downstairs by nine. I have no idea what is in store for me this morning. The entire group representing Brian's family is in front of the hotel wearing the most formal suit or dress they brought to India. The men wear Turbans; the women wear bracelets called *bangles* that cover their arms from their wrists up to the middle of their forearms. The entire group of Westerners mill around in front of the hotel waiting to be told what to do. Fifty white people chilling on a busy street in the capital city of India. Sort of like the British invasion during the time of Imperialism, only I'm from Rossmoor.

First to arrive is a ten-piece brass band that accompanies us and plays music. Next to arrive is the white horse that Brandon and his best man ride on. The best man is his youngest male relative who happens to be my cousin, who happens to have no frickin clue what's going on. The plan is simple: The fifty of us lead the way for the white horse to get from the hotel to the temple where the wedding takes place. The band starts up; it is customary for the wedding party to dance all the way to the temple. And this is what we do. Before I start to dance, I take a step back and take a moment to run down a list of what I am about to take part in.

I'm wearing a turban.
I'm wearing sunglasses, a dark suit, and an orange turban.
I look fucking good.
I'm about to start dancing down the middle of the street in New Delhi.
I can't remember the last time I danced at nine in the morning.
I have no clue when I last danced while sober.
There is a cow across the street just standing around.
Am I the only one who is confused by stray cows hanging
out on the sidewalk for no apparent reason?

The band starts to play. It is a jazzy hook that they repeat over and over again. It is like Herb Alpert flew in for the wedding, taught these guys a few chords, and then left. It is the best live music I have ever heard. It is loud; it is full of trombones, trumpets, drums and passion. These guys don't know a lot of notes, but the ones they do know are played brilliantly. I dance my ass off this morning. I dance harder and with more enthusiasm than I realize I have. I see my sister twirling her long skirt in the middle of a street in India and I see how happy she is. I see my mom, Nana, my dad, all losing themselves in the moment.

The band plays on, we keep dancing, cars stop and people stare at this group of Americans embracing a religious wedding that no one had any affiliation to. We didn't grow up Sikh, and we don't know much about it, but we are open-minded and dancing our asses off. The locals must appreciate our efforts. We wind our way through the city. The band inspires us to keep on dancing. The band leaves us no choice but to ignore our cramping legs, sore feet and shortness of breath. Our only option is to keep going. Physical pain no longer matters, we continue to dance.

We reach the temple. It is obvious that our hard work is appreciated by the Indian side of the wedding party. It would be an insult to arrive walking and looking tired. We suck it up and arrive dancing. I save some of my best dance moves for our appearance. I unleashed vicious spin moves; furious leg kicks and unsurpassed arm gyrations just to show them how excited we are to be a part of the wedding.

The ceremony takes *forever*. Seriously, it lasts a *really* long time. It is longer than the Bar Mitzvah I went to back in 7th grade. The Sikh wedding involves Brian walking around the altar four times while Sahana follows closely behind. This is meant to demonstrate her willingness to be submissive to her husband. A holy man chants forever. My high school doesn't offer Hindi as a second language, so it all sounds like the ramblings of a holy man who speaks a language I don't understand. I sit crossed legged on the floor for at least forty-five minutes while having to use the restroom the *entire* time. The ceremony is fantastic but mercifully, it ends. I navigate myself to the nearest bathroom using two legs that are asleep. The numbness eventually wears off and the wedding moves to the reception. This is where I finally meet pretty Indian girls who want nothing to do with me, but they do consent to take a picture with me, little victories. Still, it is an amazing wedding that I feel honored to be invited to.

After the wedding ends, the plan is for all of Brian's side of the wedding party (the westerners) to get into a couple of buses and go sightseeing for the next week. The first city we visit is Agra. We drive for hours and hours through the interior of India. We bump merrily along as we make our way along crumbling roads. We repeatedly pass unfinished infrastructure projects and old men with nothing to do but squat by the road and watch our bus go by. The countryside gives off the impression that an atomic bomb detonated a few decades ago. This explains why most buildings are reduced to the shell of what they once were. All that remains is the foundation and whatever else is made out of concrete. My theory is that the cows moved back first and claimed the city as their own before the humans had the opportunity to. This explains why the roads are in a terrible state of disrepair. This explains why the men squat by the road, and the cows hang out on the sidewalk unconcerned about the crumbling infrastructure.

The bus moves onward. The trash is collected by the driver and then nonchalantly thrown out the window. We try to hide our feelings of outrage and disgust. We are Southern California pseudo-environmentalists and we feel violated and angry that trash is just thrown on the side of the road without any consideration or a moment's thought. Then I remember the smog and filth that we experience at Gandhi's tomb in New Delhi and appreciate being away from the city and out in the countryside. He doesn't throw out anything toxic or dangerous. I silence my inner-hippie. I accept their culture and go with the flow. Every time we pass an oncoming truck filled to the brim with grain, we expect to die. These trucks are three times wider than anything I've seen on a freeway in California. The grain is packed into enormous sacks that bulge outward on both sides. The width of the truck is equivalent to taking up three lanes of traffic. We travel on two-lane highways. There is no chance for us to pass these monsters. There isn't physically enough room for us to pass without dying a painful death in the middle of nowhere in India. Miraculously, we avoid the oncoming traffic. Somehow we survive the bus ride without dying. We are on Magic Toad's Wild Ride. Our bus narrowly avoids all grain trucks and the messiness of a head-on collision. We arrive in Agra. Tomorrow we see the Taj Mahal. Tomorrow night is New Year's Eve. Tomorrow we celebrate the millennium and say goodbye to 1999 and embrace the possibilities that 2000 will bring.

The Taj is beyond description. All I know is that it is composed entirely of straight lines and right angles, except for the crypt, which was installed incorrectly on purpose, because nothing should be perfect except for God, or something like that (Google it). It's pretty cool. I am excited to get to spend New Year's in a foreign country. My plan is to rally the troops, get drunk, take the elevator down to the lobby of the Holiday Inn we are staying at, find the ball room and start dancing.

My attempt to rally the troops and have fun on New Year's in India is thwarted by the fact that the majority of the people from our group are sick. Weak stomachs turn into full-blown tummy aches. I call bullshit and proclaim the entire group is weak sauce. I spit on them for having delicate immune systems. My only option is to go downstairs and party by myself.

Thankfully, I run into Sean and convince him to be my wingman for the night. Sean is Indian and also Canadian. He is the first cousin of Sandeep and is on the trip with us. He was born in India but grew up in Canada. He is a large man sent with us partially to have fun and partially to keep us out of trouble. He is another person who speaks the language. He is someone who can get anyone out of a sticky situation if the need arises. Someone who might defuse a problem before it leads to a family guest creating an international incident. Oops...

We take the elevator down to the main floor. The main hall is filled to the brim. The only drunk white guy in Agra, India at the Holiday Inn for the New Year is pretty easy to spot. Or at least I think it is, because tonight I *am* that guy. I get myself a beer and head out into a sea of bodies. My plan is to find someone to kiss at midnight. The pickings are slim. Everywhere I look, I see men. Groups of well-dressed women in their early twenties are nowhere to be found. There must be another hot spot in town because they most definitely are not at the Holiday Inn.

This doesn't discourage me. Surely there must be at least one good looking single female in the ballroom. I set out to find her. Beer in hand, Sean lurks a safe distance behind me, I start to circulate around the room. I combine dancing with walking until I spot a girl dancing up ahead. I make my way over to her and just before I get close enough to dance with her, I get cut off by a group of men. I change course and find another girl across the room. I head over in her direction, almost make it to her, and am cut off again by a different group of guys. This repeats itself over and over again. Cut off by an endless sea of overprotective males committed to thwarting their correct assumptions of my bad intentions.

I leave the ballroom and tell Sean I am going to the restroom. Upon entering the restroom, I immediately sense a different tone. Instead of merriment and laughter I am surrounded with a menacing vibe directly coming from a group of six Indian men in their mid- twenties. I enter the bathroom, make a cursory glance their way, nod, and walk to the urinal. I take care of my business and hear them laughing and talking loudly in Punjabi. It is obvious that they are talking shit about me and I immediately go from being the fun drunk white guy in India to being the nervous drunk white guy in India. I finish up quickly and get the hell out of the bathroom.

Sean is waiting for me and I tell him what happened in the bathroom. He wants to know which guys it is, but I tell him to leave it alone so we head outside to have a smoke. He is older than me, but we are in the same boat of hiding the fact that we occasionally smoke from the adults in our lives (sorry Mom). Sean is visibly upset that some guys are threatening his family's guest in India. He then tells me that if anything had happened, if any violence or aggression was started on their part, he would have only had to make a single phone call. This call would immediately (very soon) lead to...

Sean's words: *Guys with AK-47's swooping in and securing the area.*

I know that Sahana's family has money. Their house is at least three stories tall and is located in what is considered to be a very affluent area in New Delhi near the consulates. Their standard of living does not compare to India's general standards of living. Option #1- poor and destitute, Option #2- guys with automatic weapons and helicopters. Her father's official job description is portrayed to us in vague terms. He is an "Importer/Exporter" of things that require importing and exporting. His connections make him an important man. His contacts within the government allow Sean to boast, with a high degree of certainty, that we are protected. In my limited world, having the job title of "Importer/Exporter" suggests something entirely different. The only Importer/Exporters I know live in apartments in San Diego that have a bong on the coffee table and are in desperate need of vacuuming. They import my twenty dollar bill and export a small amount of weed in a *Ziploc* bag. The likelihood that they have phone numbers of people that tell men to mobilize, swoop down and secure places is very slim. Yet, it does not surprise me that my new Indian relatives just might have these phone numbers and have the go ahead to use them if necessary.

Nothing dramatic ends up happening. Nobody slides down ropes hanging off hovering helicopters to rescue me. Nobody pa onto the roof and whisks me into a safe room for my protection. and I linger downstairs to smoke another cigarette and then go t upstairs. I wake up the next day, load back on the bus and move on the next city. It is New Year's Day, 2000, and I am *not* hung over. I begin the new millennium strong in heart and with a clear head. This is a good thing? Right? We will spend the next week traveling. Eight-hour marathons were spent on the bus. Eight hours of cheating death on the Indian highways every few days. Stay two days someplace new and then move on.

HOW WE SPEND THE NEXT WEEK IN INDIA
(a partial list)

1. The family rides on the backs of elephants to get to the Amer Fort.
2. Nana haggles over the price of an Indian rug (Just buy it already. I'm sick of standing around).
3. Monkeys spotted on rooftops.
4. Dirty and hungry kids beg us for pens and candy.
5. We stay at a game reserve and see a tiger and crocodiles.
6. My sister and cousin are thrown off the back of a camel.
7. I discuss Indian Drum and Bass with Sean.
8. I attempt to grow a beard.

My parents, aunt, uncle and cousins leave after ten days in India. This is when the trip turns sour. Having the other family members around has served as a buffer between Nana and my sister and me. There isn't any bad blood or underlying issues between myself, or my sister, with Nana. The simple fact is that she is seventy years old and we are both in our early twenties. Sneaking smokes and drinking one too many becomes more difficult. The freedom we enjoy is over. She is no longer distracted. Now she has nobody else to focus on but my sister and I. This is a problem for me because I have to temper my drinking immediately. Her first order of business is to tell me how concerned she is with how much I've been drinking. From here on out I see her keeping a close watch on me Even if she isn't watching me closely, I am convinced that she is keeping a tally on how much I drink. I count on my sister to deflect some of the scrutiny off of me. She is older than me, she is better at this than me, she's been doing it far longer, she usually embraces a challenge.

My sister starts to feel sick in the middle of nowhere in the middle of India. She looks like shit. She looks pale, grey. She looks like she is in pain. Our flight home is hundreds of miles away and not for three days. The battle of wits against my grandmother now seems trivial.

My sister was diagnosed as Anemic less than a year before our trip. She is forced to move home earlier in the year, but has lived with it without serious complications. Worst case scenario is that she will take medications with minimal side effects on a daily basis for the rest of her life. Lots of people are anemic, they take their pills, nothing goes wrong, and they live a normal life.

But now, Mandy complains of stomach cramps. Sharp shooting pain that won't go away. This begins her downfall. I am stuck in India with my miserable sister and my nagging Grandmother for the final days in India. All I want to do is come home, see my friends and drink water out of the faucet without fear of imminent death.

The flight home is interminable. All I want to do is take advantage of the complimentary cocktails, drink until I pass out, and wake up in America. Nana is sitting too close, so I can't do that without being seriously scrutinized. The fourteen-hour flight going from Amsterdam to India is a whole different beast than the fourteen hours it takes to get from India back to Amsterdam. There is no alcohol, no friendly Iraqis named Mickey, no alcohol (must be mentioned a second time), and no hope. Halfway into the flight, Nana develops blood clots in her legs and is moved to the back of the plane so she can keep her legs elevated for medical purposes. Mandy is beyond miserable. She is crammed into her tiny airplane seat, sick with stomach cramps and a pounding headache. In hindsight I realize my ailments pale in comparison, but at the time I am pretty irritated and have no qualms feeling sorry for myself.

The plane lands in Amsterdam. We have a short layover and get on a direct flight to LAX. Compared to fourteen hours on India Air, the twelve hours home don't seem so bad. When our plane finally lands in

California I have no idea what day it is, and many hours I just spent on an airplane. The pain associated with the last twenty-four hours of my life is immediately forgotten after I make it through customs. My sister barely makes it to baggage check. The headache and stomach pains that started in India follow her for the entire trip back home. The last twenty-four hours she spends at 30,000 feet in the air only intensifies the pain. She hasn't slept more than ten minutes at a time. She is exhausted. She is a wreck. My parents pick us up. I go home and take a nap. Mandy goes to the hospital.

Her once treatable blood disorder which only requires monitoring and medicine, and has no serious side effects, has morphed (evolved?) into something far nastier and far more complicated. She leaves for India with a typical form of Anemia. She comes home with a rare type of Anemia that her doctors have never treated before and don't know how to treat. They assure us that she can't have gotten sicker by going to India. My theory is that the flight home is the cause. Fourteen hours straight is a long time to spend in a pressurized atmosphere at 30,000 feet. Doing this on back to back flights fucking sucks. Whatever causes it isn't really important. The truth of the matter is that when she returns home she is really sick and she never really gets any better.

I will stay home until the end of the month. The whole time my desire for the semester to start feeds my guilt for wanting to escape my parents' house. I count the hours until I return to normal. One last semester. I desert the one place I can count on and run back to finish college in an attempt to hide from the ugliness. Hiding in San Diego doesn't work. I realize that it is impossible to ignore what is happening at home. All I can do is hold on tightly. My grades start to slip. Mandy weakens. My family is falling apart. Everyone will understand if I don't graduate this semester. It is selfish to focus on higher education when my sister is sick. A degree doesn't seem important anymore.

Fuck that. My only job is to graduate and give my family something to celebrate. Just because my sister is sick and everything is falling apart, it doesn't mean that I should stop living a productive life. I suck it up and pass my final classes. My family sees me graduate and my four years of studying at San Diego State are finally over. I leave with a Bachelor's Degree in History, with a focus on South America (huh? How did that happen?) I am one of the few that graduate within four years. I'm not sure how I feel about getting out of one of the premiere party schools in the country so quickly. My four years are complete and I don't have any strong memories involving big parties. I can't count more than a handful of friends that mean anything to me. I haven't met anyone significant in four years living here. What a fucking waste of time. I imagine leaving without receiving any type of post graduate degree. Failing out, like Mitch. At least I have a degree in History. A worthless degree in *South American History* that I have no clue what to do with. I have no idea what to do with this diploma. I have no marketable skills and only a vague idea about a continent that nobody really gives a shit about. All I have is a diploma from a piece of shit state college known for Marshall Faulk and Tony Gwynn.

I don't have a job in the real world lined up after I graduate. I don't even know what kind of job I am qualified for. I am over educated, under-skilled, and not *any* closer than I was four years ago to knowing what I want to do with the rest of my life. I don't even know the first step involved with finding or actually being offered a job that I find agreeable. What do history majors do after graduation? The only obvious thing to do is to head right back to school and get a teaching credential, then a masters and maybe, eventually, a doctorate. That is the path to credibility. That is the path to benefits, a 401k and a salary that increases automatically on a yearly basis. This is also something that will take a *minimum* of two years to accomplish. I just finished four years of eighteen-unit semesters at a school that I hate. There is no chance in hell I can wrap my head around starting a credential program in the fall, spend two years completing it, get a teaching job, and then spend the rest of my Monday through Fridays going to bed at a decent hour and waking up to teach the youth of America for the next thirty years of my life. It just isn't a practical expectation for a person with my priorities.

I arrive at SDSU expecting to find a new group of friends that will last a lifetime. I arrive expecting to find people who share my hopes and dreams. If that isn't possible I will settle for being surrounded by people who share my taste in any of the following: music, literature, my sense of humor, my quest for knowledge, my anger with intolerance, my unwavering support of the poor and disenfranchised, a loud voice used in order to announce all the injustice going on in the world, mistrust of the government, my unwillingness to accept the status quo, my staunch belief that popular culture is bad for you, and that people are smart but the masses are fucking stupid. Nothing too out of the ordinary.

I leave SDSU wondering where these people are hiding. Should I join a club or try harder to meet more people? It never occurs to me how much bigger life becomes at SDSU. I don't realize that just because popularity and great friends have fallen into my lap growing up that there is nothing to ensure this will happen in adulthood. I don't know yet that my happiness is based on how much work I put into finding it. I am angry with myself for spending what can be the best years of my young adult life waiting for something to happen. I waste my potential and an opportunity to broaden my horizons. I waste my chance to find new friends. I should spend four years living in a frat house, unapologetically drunk, regretfully inebriated and without any hope of pulling a degree out of my ass. I miss the opportunity to be exposed to whatever life experiences unfamiliar people live through and want to share with me. I fail to be influenced by people who might steer my life in an alternate path.

I am content with the people I know and hang out with. I wallow in the safety of the familiar. I have friends the entire time I was there, but they are the same friends I've always had. I have fun when I am at school, but it's a watered-down version of the same fun I've always had. I know that as long as I keep up an average of fifteen units per semester and don't fail a class, or drop one, I will get out in four years with my BA. I triumph against such odds, and at the same time I feel like I am missing out on something by getting out so quickly. San Diego never consistently reaffirms my sense of belonging. My place within the community is never completely realized. Its development stalls and is unable to sustain my interest beyond graduation. This is why I leave. There is really nothing for me to do there. It is time to go home.

12

Over-educated, Under-Skilled

ARRIVING HOME IS a frightening endeavor. It is the only choice that makes any sense. Moving back into my parent's house requires a considerable alteration to my current lifestyle. I am about to leave a life whereas on a daily basis I am responsible only for myself and re-enter a world complicated by the responsibility to consider the reactions my actions will produce from my family. I spend the last four years living without the daily scrutiny involved with living at home. I am always conscious of the behavior I involve myself with. I am polite. I always (usually) pick up after myself. The last four years are spent without having to answer questions. Four years of freedom. Four years without the pressure to give explanations. Returning home means that I am about to dive back into a world filled with reminders and reiterations. These are always spoken for my benefit and always result in my frustration.

I say farewell to four years of indiscriminately consuming tasty beverages whenever and wherever I choose. I say farewell to experiencing life without having to consider what the time is. No matter the situation, I must consider how my parents will analyze the scenario. The less they know, the better it is for them, the better it is for everyone.

My triumphant return home is at hand. I officially reinstate myself into the safe confines of my parent's house in Rossmoor. My daily arrivals and departures are met with questions and inquisitions.

Parent #1: *Where have you been?*

Parent #2: *Where are you going?*

Parent #1: *What's going on?*

I walk by their intrusive interrogations concerning my whereabouts. I wish I had answers to their questions. *I've been someplace dangerous. I'm going somewhere even scarier. Nothing is going on.* Returning home is never simple. Once greeted at the door with a simple hello you are followed by questions, opinions, and more cross examination.

The phone rings. I pick it up. Words are exchanged. The conversation ends. It is always necessary for whichever parent that is present to know who it is. The questions are rarely intrusive and are mostly asked in an attempt to find out what is happening in my life. The problem is that they *never* end. After establishing what my intentions are, where I'm headed, and what my political affiliations are, more questions flood in. *What's going on? How is work? What are your plans? How is so and so? How is their job? How are their emotions?* Every time I come home I wonder to myself what is wrong with this place.

Every year of college I return home for holidays and for the majority of each summer. It makes sense. This gives me a chance to recharge my batteries in an environment that is comfortable and fun. My job at the bagel shop is always waiting for me. An added incentive to come home is that everyone else I grew up with is doing the same thing. Everyone I want to see is right back where I leave them. Every year the party comes home.

Here is where I find myself at age twenty-two. Graduated from college; ready to face the world; and not quite ready to suck it up and get a real job. Waiting tables gives the illusion of productivity. The thought of waking up and going to work everyday drives me to wait tables. Anything that allows me to avoid morning hours is appealing. Waking up in the morning is beyond my present abilities. I'm not old, yet. There is plenty of time in front of me to join the middle class. At the moment I am faced with no pressure to conform. It's time to focus my attention on finally being allowed to legally visit bars.

Various groups of friends are pouring back into the hood. Most return with a degree in hand, no money in their pockets, and are planning to move home for a while. This guarantees finding something to do on a nightly basis.

The summer after graduating isn't any different. If anything, it is better than any of the other ones. It is by far more intense than the other ones. My group of friends are considered elder citizens at the age of twenty-two. The kids who graduate the year after us have either already turned twenty-one or are just about to. This leads to a trickling down of fake ID's. The kids three and four years below us have access to alcohol and parents stupid enough to leave them in charge while they go out of town. This leads to something to do or somewhere to go every night of the week. Random house parties full of drunk and disorderly young girls who still have young girl bodies and still know how to use them. Spontaneous gatherings leave me surrounded by close friends. *"COME JOIN THE FUN.... RIDE YOUR BIKE ON OVER."*

The decision to invite a few people over at the spur of the moment means that I spend my Tuesday night close to home, drinking with friends, and loving being back in Rossmoor. Any house located in the city walls is within reach. We spend our evenings smoking cigarettes and binge drinking in someone's backyard. This is always fine by me. Sitting and talking with friends. Creating a mess that you won't be asked to clean up the next morning. Enjoyable activities attained without much hassle. Sitting comfortably and without challenges from the outside world. Under-skilled, highly-educated, and repeating the same bullshit over and over.

James: *I'm just chilling, still looking for something to do.*

Another plan involves cocktails inside a bar. We head to a bar in Seal Beach and walk in and it is always full of people we know. Leaving the house never disappoints. Leaving the house with the intention of having one drink and going home leads to nineteen shots and naked silliness. Any attempt to do otherwise leads to alcohol poisoning. There is no escape. Give up now. Accept your fate.

Either way, I get home no earlier than two in the morning, reeking of cigarette smoke, beer and sweat. Hoping that I can sneak in the front door and turn off the porch light without waking up my mom. I pray silently every night that I won't run into her before making it to the safety of my room. I sleep in till noon, wait for nightfall to come, and then repeat the whole exercise over again.

I don't plan on finding a job. Undergoing a lifestyle change is not recommended at this time. Corporate America wants to destroy your soul. They look only for those unopposed to living the lives better suited for our parents. *Be strong and resist. Don't sell out.*

Rossmoor offers this idea instead. Getting a "real job" is a poor decision. This will inevitably lead to life slowing down. This, in turn leads to the danger posed by Network Television. Sitcoms stunt your growth and invite boredom into your day. Television is bad for your health. Refuse the impulse to conform and spend the next three months with good friends. Start by hanging out at bars and drinking wine coolers at house parties. All those who are interested dare not delay. Come home to Rossmoor. Come home. Re-acquaint yourself with your youth. Try earnestly to recapture the good times. Don't move forward. Move back to Rossmoor. I need to give Rossmoor a second chance. Soon enough I am faced with the same issues that drove me away in the first place. The need for escape soon reappears. Sure, I left Rossmoor for a reason. It just so happens that for the life of me I can't remember what that reason was. Sure, I couldn't wait to get out, but I trust that getting back in will feel so much better.

I am quickly reminded why I go away to college in the first place. Living at home means that I suck at life. The lucky ones spend their early twenties in an environment that allows noise and chaos, content being poor and living in a tiny apartment. An overpriced studio legitimized by location alone. Situated within walking distance of everything one needs. Bars and food aren't too far away. Taking a walk in the city recommits oneself to a healthy lifestyle. Embracing the naked detachment of being just another worker bee living in the middle of a large metropolis leads to higher salaries and better health. My ideal plan is to get offered a job after graduating and take the mother fucker. Next step is to move someplace new, *anywhere* I don't know a single fucking person. Then jump headfirst into a situation that requires me to rely on nobody but myself. I'll find new friends slowly at first, but before long, their numbers gradually grow. Independence is available out there in the real world. All I have to do is choose a medium to large size city in the Midwest and grab a piece for myself. Chicago, Illinois; Madison, Wisconsin; Detroit, Michigan. Anything else but Rossmoor, California. But back to Rossmoor is where I go. When it comes down to it, I have no backbone. I am lacking a sense of adventure. I am unsure of myself so I keep things simple. I drive an hour and a half and then drive back home.

Living at home means that there is always a reason to give my parents updates and information. I expect and am used to such questions. I try my best to indulge them with answers that form actual sentences, not just words. My best option is to send a friend into the family room to entertain my parents while I finish getting ready to go out. This is the only way my parents get information from a source more willing than I am to sit down and chat for a while. My parent's house is our meeting place before we go out. It's the hub.

My friends appreciate the genuine interest my parents have in their lives. My house is my home base. Without fail, Mitch instigates an argument about politics or religion with my mother. We tend to linger around while we wait for Mitch to finish his monologue on conservative ideology. It is yet another failed attempt to convert my liberal mother into being a right wing conservative. Worst case scenario, an argument that combines politics with religion will break out and keep us there far longer than we anticipate.

Every friend I claim is the result of growing up in Rossmoor. My best friend lives around the corner. My sister's friends live down the street. I am lucky to get to move home and figure out my next step. I am really lucky that I have parents who are interested in my life and in the lives of my friends. Rossmoor is my home base that I know will always be there. I will be able to move to Long Beach because I know that if anything goes wrong I have my parents' house to fall back on.

Moving to Long Beach will be my only rescue from the perils of living at home. Mandy is back living with my parents by the time I graduate from college. All was well in San Francisco until she starts to get sick. It is an illness that lingers longer than it should. The common cold and basic Flu are ruled out. Nobody knows what is wrong. Weeks pass and she still doesn't get any better. My parents get nervous and convince her to move back home so she can get better. This is what she does. She leaves San Francisco, says goodbye to her independence and moves back in with my parents. Instead of getting better, she gets worse.

She comes back home midway through my last semester of my senior year. She comes to my graduation in June and I can tell that she is happy for me, yet she can't hide the hurt in her eyes. I am two years younger than her and I graduate from college first. She still has a way to go and has to transfer to Long Beach State. Taking classes is up in the air because she is sick. By the time I move back home she has been there for about a year. Living at home is difficult for her. Having her there makes my move back home impossible.

When my sister is thrown into the mix the situation becomes much more complicated. My sister is sick. She is on medication that makes her face puffy. Not only does she not feel well, she also has to take a heavy dose of testosterone on a daily basis. This fucks with her appearance. Her face becomes bloated and chubby and she stops looking like herself. She is ashamed and embarrassed and there is nothing she can do to fix it. She hates taking that medicine but it is the only thing that works. The steroids make her look horrible and she is still waiting to be diagnosed. She hasn't been given an explanation for why she feels like shit. Nobody knows anything. I move home and immediately need to leave. I have no choice but to escape. It is the only thing I can do that will keep me sane. It is impossible for me to stay here.

Her friends from her youth can be described as scattered at best. She is left to her own devices. Mitch was recently reintroduced to living in southern California after a brief stint living in Georgia. His parents leave Rossmoor soon after high school ends and move to the South. Mitch effectively is left without a home base and lives in a studio apartment near the Reno Room (a seedy dive bar that quickly becomes our home away from home) in the heart of Long Beach. Before I move home, we aren't able to see each other often, so instead he sees my sister. They develop a quirky friendship somewhat based on Mitch's commitment to marry her. This statement is made in jest, but also has more truth to it than Mitch would admit. Mandy never seriously considers it publicly, but I always wonder. Her friends from high school are nowhere to be found, so when Mandy is still feeling good, Mitch makes the effort to take her out for a drink at local drinking establishments. It has been some time since the both of us live at home. I won't characterize it as hell on earth but it becomes significantly more difficult by the week.

I lived at home for the first few months after leaving San Diego. Mitch lives across from the Reno Room, Kristi lives a few blocks away. Jennifer lives in Belmont. I have ample opportunities to escape Rossmoor and spend the majority of my nights in Long Beach. This is when I start to use cocaine. This is how I figured out how to find it.

This is when it slowly evolves from being an unreliable treat to get a hold of to being way too easy to find.

In the beginning, finding cocaine requires a third party go-between. It is an unreliable system that only works when I call Jennifer. If she isn't available, the pursuit ends here. If she is, she knows somebody who *might* be able to hook it up. This person is your typical paranoid drug dealer who only deals with her and may or may not pick up his phone when she calls. He only deals in large amounts so when she can get a hold of him there is a mad rush to find enough cash. This is when a trust fund baby comes in handy. Unfortunately, we don't have one. This usually leads to small contributions from Mitch and Jennifer, and I am expected to come up with the rest. After we come up with the necessary funds, we head over to Jennifer's house and she goes to pick it up. It is a poorly run system on many levels. It requires too much money. It takes too many phone calls. It involves too many people.

Kristi returns to my life. It starts out slowly with her occasional visits to San Diego during my senior year, intensifies during the first year home from college, and lasts until just after I move to Long Beach. Falling in love with her was a long time ago. Anything that happens when I am sixteen doesn't carry the same weight anymore. Whatever I felt for her back then, now seems childish and trivial. I am far enough removed from her to break free of her spell and move on with my life. She no longer has control over me. I am able to see her without suffering any serious side effects.

I would prefer a night of passionate lovemaking, but take solace in my ability to insulate myself from her. Her perfect body isn't worth the price I will pay if I am sucked back in. It is a fight worth fighting for as long as I keep her from having any control over my life. I already spent too much time being miserable. I have already committed too much of my youth to this girl. My undying devotion to her doesn't make much sense anymore. It is time to reassess. The time to reevaluate what is important in my life is now here. The time to be a man is at hand. It is time to stop chasing her, it is time for her to start chasing me.

When I move back home, she lives in Long Beach. The dynamic of our relationship instantly changes. I don't expect it to. When it does, I don't ask any questions and just go with it. I am the one who plays it cool. I am the patient one who waits for her to call. I am the one who plays hard to get. I'm the one who acts like I don't give a shit (Mitch would be proud). I'm the one stopping short just before she gets what she wants. I'm the one in control. She has a boyfriend. She cheats on him, with me. It's weirdly empowering. She is having an affair. It's fucking awesome. It appears that she likes me more than I like her. This is something I shouldn't embrace. There is no pride in this but still it makes me smile.

I play the game. I treat her like shit. I finally figure out how to make her like me more than I like her. I ignore my obsessive tendencies and, at the same time, figure out how to transplant these obsessive characteristics onto her. It never occured to me that she would cheat on her boyfriend with me, but she sure does. It doesn't bother her. It doesn't bother me. I am happy (thrilled) to be the "Other Guy." I accept my role without any shame. I promise myself to stop overthinking the situation, and ignore any and all feelings of guilt by association. I promise myself that I will not get sucked in by her powers, and that I will remain the person in charge of the situation. I promise myself that I won't lose sight of the fact that she isn't very interesting, she isn't that beautiful and she doesn't have anything that I don't have. I spent the next year treating her like she is just a normal girl.

13

Poems about Hair

MY ESCAPE FROM a sick sister, a pesky mother and an overwhelmed father comes in the form of a one bedroom apartment that my friend is moving out of. It is a converted garage that moonlights as a bachelor pad. Rent is five hundred dollars a month and it is available soon. I am offered a golden opportunity to get out of Rossmoor for a price that I can afford.

Within a year I'm chain smoking on the couch. I am attempting to stop my nose from bleeding. This attempt is failing. The only thing keeping the blood from flowing down my face is the wad of Kleenex currently shoved deep inside it. The trashcan is full of bloody toilet paper. Every effort I make to stop the bleeding fails. Every time I think the blood has stopped I take out the wad of toilet paper. The bleeding stops long enough to give me hope, then it starts to flow again. I run out of toilet paper. My reserves of Kleenex are running low. I am sick and tired of blood. I just want it to stop. I have no other choice. I start to lose my mind.

Within a week of moving into my new bachelor pad I found out that Mitch is *leaving* Long Beach. I hear it through a mutual friend who assumes that I know that he is leaving. True to form, and keeping with tradition, I am not aware of this "small" development concerning Mitch's life. I am the person closest to him and I am still being held at arms' length. I know that he trusts me. I know that he "loves me" and needs my support and friendship. I know that on some Kerouac-ian Sal/Dean level I am the only person that understands him. I know that a night out is not complete unless I am there to share it with him, but I also know that he is flawed and broken. I know that it is impossible for him to operate without a safety net consisting of his secrets. I understand that he has a secret clubhouse in his head that nobody else is allowed into. Unfortunately, he is not accepting applications at this time. The sign on the door reads:

Mitch's Personal Space
Back Off.
You Don't Know Me. Even if you do. Even
if you're the only one who does.
KEEP OUT.

He needs to pretend that this place doesn't exist and he doesn't even need it in the first place. But what kills me is that he hides it from me. Our friendship is based on two separate things. The first reason is that no matter how often we hang out there remains a distance between us. Since college we haven't lived in the same city. I am in Long Beach at least one weekend a month until I graduate. I am home for 90% of my breaks and we spend the majority of our free time together. My reckless youth is only reckless because of his involvement in it. The amount of fun I have is limited to whether or not he is an active participant. Don't get me wrong, great nights occur without him present, but there is always a small part of me that misses his contribution to the direction that the night might have taken.

The second reason is that I am able to look over at him and know, without any hesitation, that he is the second-most-interesting person smoking a cigarette in front of the Reno Room on a Tuesday night. Without his influence on the evening my status as the first-most-interesting person enjoying a smoke in front of the Reno Room is in jeopardy. I am excited to move out to Long Beach, I am happy to get out of my parents' house, but more importantly I am excited to do these things with him standing next to me. I know that if we live close to one another there is always a reason to meet up for a beer and shoot the shit.

Mitch: *I want to move you in, make sure everything is set up for you before I leave. I have to go. You are good. I have faith.*

Best-laid plans go to waste. His decision to leave makes some sense. What makes no sense is that we have never discussed it. The whole "I may move to Georgia" comment never pops out of his mouth mid conversation. Who knows how long he knows that he is moving to Georgia? It isn't like I am offended that he doesn't ask me how I feel about sandwiches or flightless birds. This is a *big* deal and I am shocked that he is so secretive, how he has the need to hide such an important decision from me. He figures that if I don't know anything, he can spring it on me at the last minute and before I realize what is going on, he is 2,000 miles away. He never asks for my opinion or advice on what he should do. It isn't like he is moving to Riverside. Atlanta is a *five-hour plane ride* away. It could be Alaska and it won't change a thing.

It kills me that he is moving out of state right after I *finally* move into my own crappy apartment in Long Beach. Are you fucking serious? I have plans for us. I made a list. Seriously, I wrote down a list on a piece of paper. It's in my pocket. Here it is, a fucking list. It even has a title.

List of Reasons Why Being Neighbors is in our Best Interest

1. We are both of legal drinking age.
2. We both have jobs that involve flexible working hours.
3. We have just been introduced to and can easily acquire
a stimulating stimulant that tends to make our nights out
longer, more satisfying and infinitely more interesting.
4. Combining our powers is the only thing that makes
sense at this stage of our early twenties.
5. We owe it to ourselves to see what we can accomplish together.
6. I'm not ready to face life without you.
7. You shouldn't leave because if you do then
I'll miss you and then I'll be sad.
8. Last reason, if you move away then you continue
your strange commitment to letting me down.

After #5, I run out of reasons that don't sound either overly needy or excessively romantic. He isn't my lover. But it *sounds* like a breakup. It *feels* like a breakup. It marks the start of the gradual decline of our friendship.

Here is what I don't tell him the day he leaves. It would have been cool to do but it is totally out of character. Let me set the scene...

Mitch walks down the hallway towards the front door. The taxi waiting out front honks for a second time. Before Mitch opens the door he pauses and turns around. He starts to say something, but then stops himself, regret fills his face and he turns back around and starts to leave. James starts to walk after him.

James: If you walk out that door don't even think about coming back. You fucking bastard.. Fine, go. Have fun. You'll be sorry. Mark my words. You will live a sad life filled with regrets that will all lead back to this moment. Who needs you anyway? I sure don't. I'm actually glad to see you go. Now that I think of it, you're not leaving; I'm kicking your sorry ass out.

Mitch gets in the taxicab at the same time James walks back inside and slams the door behind him. Mitch heads to the airport, James lies on the couch. Their pride allows only a single tear to trickle down their cheeks.

END SCENE

I am best friends with someone who I do not trust anymore. Best friends with someone I do not believe anymore. I'm in a codependent relationship with someone who has no qualms with keeping me completely in the dark. It is seriously like we are dating. A dysfunctional sexless love affair between two straight males based on something that no longer can be rationalized. The relationship is broken and I still can't let go. He leaves me and leaves me without giving me closure. He owes me more. He owes me an explanation. He gives me nothing. I give him paragraphs. I give him words. I give him nonsense.

I send him a coked out letter about the history of Israel, mutual friends who were involved in a boating accident on a river and a bunch of gibberish. It is at least fifteen pages long. Some of it makes sense, there are a few well articulated points about the federal government somewhere on page nine but essentially it's all bullshit. Nevertheless, I print out this nonsense and mail it to him. Weeks later I finally get a response. It is short. He writes something about dance music and gives me directions to a strip club I'll never go to.

Dear James,
What happens when your plan fails? When all along you
thought you'd be doing drugs and hop'n around to those

"RAVE 'Y- TECHNO- TUNES." I'll tell you what happens. You a) Leave Pomona immediately, b) get on interstate 10 Westbound until you come to 101 North Interchange, c) off at Sunset, about four miles (on your left will be a 7-11- buy 40's, d) drink them in a carport, e) Walk around the corner when the 40's are finished, f) Go into the building labeled "NUDE- NUDE- NUDE- 18 OK. g) Later finish packing your shit James. There's drinking to be done.

X Mitchell

Also included on a separate piece of paper is an original poem. I send him fifteen pages discussing various perspectives on Middle Eastern politics and he gives me a poem that defends a certain type of haircut. Short hair on top with long hair in the back is universally called a mullet. He worries that this name doesn't do the hairstyle justice and wants it to be changed entirely. I write fifteen pages on the Middle East. He writes a poem about hair.

THE MANNY
By Mitch

MANNY MANNY
I LOVE YOU...
MANNY MANNY
YOU FLOW LIKE THE RIVER NILE
YES YOU DO.
MANNY MANNY
IF IT WASN'T FOR YOU
I FEAR MY LIFE WOULD BE INCOMPLETE
AS MANY OTHERS WOULD BE TOO.

Years later, Mitch tells me that he has been diagnosed as Bipolar. This doesn't surprise me. His diagnosis of having attention deficit disorder is obvious. It is also apparent that this isn't the only thing wrong with him. The only thing that I can diagnose him with is being seriously fucked up in the head. Manic depression explains everything. When he is diagnosed as bipolar is it the only way to explain his behavior.

He has serious issues. Having issues is normal. I am the fucking king of having issues, but I have nothing on Mitch. He owns the patent on issue-having. He invents them. He is the enthusiastic guy you see on late night television. His million- dollar smile and fake tan tries to convince you to buy his bag of issues for three easy payments of $9.99. Instead of spending my money on a new set of knives (guaranteed to stay sharp, never rust and cut through aluminum cans) he recommends I spend my money on bags filled to the brim with his Mitch's Issues. If I don't act fast I'll miss out on this limited time offer. Call now and the second bag is free. The toll-free number flashes on the screen, operators are standing by. I pick up the phone and place an order.

It makes sense that there is, in fact, a legitimate reason for his madness. His short stint in San Diego. All the nights that he "forgets" his wallet, all the times he loses his mind (more into that later.) I am able to play it off as mere quirks of his personality instead of something that can be diagnosed as a personality disorder. His mood swings are epic in scope. His random craziness is endearing for a while, but finally becomes so tiresome that the whole friendship falls apart and dissipates into nothing.

14

Nigerian Taxi Drivers

A WELL STOCKED BAR
A Poem???? by Bernie

Those daft Fuckers.
Fuck um.
I'm going whether or not it was my idea in the first place.
I've always wanted to go to the Elephant Islands.
But well, I've never even heard of the fucking place.
I've called my lawyer and everything is arranged.
We leave on Monday and the bar will be well stocked.
It will be a long hard trip.
Fuck yeah, an island.
I imagine the place will be an iceberg.
Large obese woman will keep track of the climate.
I can't wait...

I ARRIVE AT THE Blue Door hopeful. I arrive optimistic that converting garages into one bedroom apartments is a normal thing to do and my living quarters will not totally suck. It becomes painfully clear why this house is available and why it is so inexpensive. It is a place I inherit from a friend. He had inherited it from his sister. They hand over the keys and the third generation moves in. There is no way in hell that this is a sound structure, let alone a one bedroom house.

It's located behind a small beauty salon just off Seventh Street, near the high school. It is a nondescript little building nestled closely into the lovely city of Long Beach. My neighbors don't exist. I share my only wall with a quiet salon. My front of the house neighbor is a street benefiting from the lack of streetlights and without consistent traffic. My neighbor behind me happens to be a large wall. To my left is an alley. I have a buffer zone surrounding the house in all directions.

I have the unique opportunity to be appointed to those fortunate enough to live beyond the reach of their closest neighbors. Every place I have lived in before necessitates being conscious of keeping the noise down. The walls at my parents' house are paper-thin, every sound I make reverberates throughout the house (heavy footsteps wake up my mother, as does flushing the toilet at two in the morning). The places I live in San Diego are either directly above someone living below me or are so close to the house next door that excessive noise-making is not an option.

Finally, I have neighbors who are not easily annoyed or disturbed by the noise and activities coming from my house. I am situated at least twelve feet from my nearest living entity and am under no pressure to keep the noise down. No matter how boisterous I get, I am still respectful and considerate of the people around me. There isn't anyone taking notes about my daily activities. There is nobody scrutinizing my lifestyle. My limitless options are recognized as profitable. Necessary movements unite with my late night activities. The disruption of quiet time is completely ignored by the neighborhood. They remain oblivious to the noise being created next door. They are undisturbed by the blazing saddles and blaring chainsaws.

They might as well leave me a note on the front door that says, Don't worry about these small inconveniences. We don't mind the sounds. Granted, we don't really hear them. We allow ourselves to remain indifferent to the things that have no effect upon us. Which reminds me, why are you bothering us in the first place? Who are you anyhow? Trivial matters concerning noise pollution and community relations are of no interest to us. Won't you go away?

This is where I live for the next two years. My parents cry when they first see it, I'm not joking, tears. I don't blame them for being worried. The first night I lived here I got laid. The house is a complete disaster, no bed yet, just a dingy old couch and a halogen light. For whatever reason (don't even have to get her drunk) she feels that I will benefit greatly by starting the next chapter of my life in style. She wants the first night that I live in Long Beach to be special. It is like she works for the Chamber of Commerce and is on a promotional tour spreading awareness of all the great things that Long Beach has to offer. Instead of trying to convince me to visit the aquarium or another touristy thing that one can only find in Long Beach, she gives me love in my new living room on my parent's old couch.

The former inhabitant leaves his mark before moving out. I show up to find the house a mess. I move into a house with broken furniture, littered with trash, and covered in filth. The walls were once painted white but now carry a hue closer to tan or light brown. My friend takes no time or effort to clean up and leaves his former home ragged and chaotic when he vacates. The low price of the place is of little consolation to me at this moment. I really don't care and find it amusing when he leaves without actually completely moving out. Old cordless phone here, crusty blanket there, things left without any concern. It's mostly stuff that is useful and yet not quite appealing or beneficial to my new spread - things I end up throwing away. The carpet is not very clean. In fact, it is filthy. It is defined by how many times someone says the following phrase within the last year: *Oh shit, I spilled the bong water, again.* My new home has bong water carpet. This is immediately taken out and replaced with the old carpet my parents have in their garage. I buy paint at Home Depot and repaint most of the walls. Gradually, I am able to fix the place up. Slowly but surely, it becomes cleaner and it becomes mine.

No matter how much I clean, my new home continues to be a mess. The front door leads into the kitchen. It expands to the right. Appliances are included, which means that I have a refrigerator, a sink and a stove/oven to use at my leisure. Somehow they forget to install cabinets, cupboards and drawers. This isn't an issue because I, thankfully, move in with a limited amount of plates, cups and silverware. The floor is covered with new-ish linoleum. There are no windows to speak of.

The kitchen leads to a short hallway. To the right is a wall and to the left is the small stand up shower. Located next to the shower is the toilet and after that is the sink. The shower is protected with a curtain. The toilet is not. It's right there. It sits in the middle of the house. It is exposed and smack dab in the middle of the hallway. There is no door.

There is no separation of space between the hallway and the bathroom. The bathroom and hallway share the same space. I poop in a hallway. I walk down the bathroom.

At the end of the hallway and across from the toilet is where the bedroom is located. Instead of a closet, there is a poorly installed clothes rack that bends but never collapses under the weight of my clothes. A dresser, a double bed and not much else, fit into the room. There are no windows.

Past the windowless bedroom and the bathroom that lacks privacy is a sunken living room (two steps down) that is big enough for a couch, a decent sized coffee table, a desk, a lazy boy recliner, and a couple of book shelves. This room has windows. It also has a small air conditioner.

The living room has a door that leads out to a small, claustrophobic patio. It isn't much, but it is a crucial component to the house. A private outside space simplifies everything. My everyday activities that I don't care to showcase can be hidden. It is a safe place to smoke cigarettes and hang out with friends. The patio kicks ass. The rest of the house is confusing.

The entire house lacks air circulation and natural light. The bathroom is in the hallway for Christ's sake. The former occupant never feels it necessary to do anything about the fact that the fucking toilet is smack dab in the middle of the hallway. If I am home alone this isn't a big deal. What if I happen to be entertaining guests?

The *illusion* of privacy is better than no privacy at all. I'll never figure out how the former occupant rationalizes (gotten away with) not having any type of barrier around the toilet. He is the type of person who has people over to his house on a regular basis. A toilet out in the open only makes sense if you are home alone or if you have friends over and nobody has to do anything else but pee. Nobody wants to see someone taking a shit in the middle of the hallway. Nobody should have to worry about seeing a girl wiping her ass when all they want to do is get a beer out of the fridge. How does he not sympathize with a girl's right to pee without having to worry about someone strolling by? Part of me is appalled but more of me is impressed. He carries the *I don't give a shit* gene and it leads to girls thinking nothing is amiss when they urinate in the hallway. He pulls it off for at least a year.

The dynasty of Mike and James peaks between this time. These years are filled with rapid industrial growth, major leaps forward in the field of biomedical research, and a significant reversal of the effects of global warming. The brilliant alliance of James and Mike makes all of these things happen. The masses aren't aware of our contributions to society. It is not common knowledge. It doesn't diminish our accomplishments.

Mike is a friend from high school. He spends the majority of his time dating my good friend Rebecca. They have been together since high school and have recently broken up. This frees up a significant amount of his time. Mike is now a sovereign nation. He is a free man for the first time as a legal adult. I always look for someone to share my dysfunction with. He has no clue what is in store for him.

It doesn't take long for me to introduce him to cocaine. Mike and cocaine fit together well. Coincidentally, James and cocaine are on *really* good terms. We are the best of friends. This begins the "go fast" era. I find a new partner in crime. Mike sees my bathroom predicament, takes some measurements, and goes to Home Depot. An hour later, the toilet is encircled by a linen shower curtain. Progress.

I live in a box. Walls galore, windows scarce and fresh air on occasion. A super pain in the ass because it is impossible to rationalize living in such a place but it works so well when prepared to embrace the positives on display. Activities for all. Go ahead and write something on the ceiling. A metaphorical loaf of positive energetic sourdough bread is baked on a nightly basis and is ready to be sliced and made into a sandwich. The results vary but on occasion the final product is a brilliant convoluted disaster beyond repair and remorse. A purpose is served while the deliberate sabotage continues unchecked. This is all I know and all I understand. It is all I can stick by. I promise myself to stay there until the walls start to cave in. Until there is no more room to paint and the job is complete, I will hang on.

Painting the walls starts out as a very necessary home improvement project. The simple act of going to Home Depot, choosing paint colors, and painting the walls is an uncomplicated project that gets out of hand. Painting the hallway red, the living room a soothing light brown, and an accent wall green is all the place really needs. Instead, the painting *never* stops. New colors are introduced and murals begin to take over entire walls. What begins as a simple home improvement project grows into an entity too massive to understand and too incredible to leave unfinished.

The first mural project starts with me, Bernie and Kari. Laziness has no place here. Activities are encouraged. Boredom isn't accepted. Ingenuity is appreciated. Art supplies are plentiful. Inspiration is the only thing that we are lacking (that and maybe more cocaine). The solution to our problem turns out to be the unused halogen light that is stuck in the corner. We discover that if we change the angle of the light we can create shadows on the wall.

We spend the entire night in a haze. We spend hours tracing our shadows on the wall. Depending on what positions we pose for, and how quick we are able to outline the shadows, we can fill up the wall with intersecting outlines of people. Our enthusiasm for outlining the shadows leads to an enthusiasm for filling them in. There are dozens of bodies outlined on the wall. The bodies started to overlap with one another. The overlapping body outlines start to confuse the integrity of the mural. The only solution is to treat every section as an independent entity. Every possible color is used. Any variation of color we mix together slowly fills in each section of the wall. The only thing we try to avoid is filling in sections next to one another with the same color. This is the only no-no. Other than this, anything goes.

The mural takes weeks to finish. It takes fucking *forever.* Every time people come there is an influx of outside help. Anyone with an interest in art gets an opportunity to pick out a color, choose a section to paint and go for the gold. Anyone lacking in confidence in their painting ability is encouraged to pick up a brush, choose a color and go for it. Those fearing the process are not allowed excuses. Never painted before? Well here is your chance. You think that painting is lame? Let me prove you wrong. And no, you don't have a choice in the matter. Embrace the opportunity that lies before you. Don't think, just do it.

"The Blue Door" becomes my rallying cry every night I find myself with nothing to do too early the next morning. This is when I find myself out at a bar (90% of the time it is the Red Room) flying high and announcing the commencement of a late night dance party taking place at The Blue Door. People show up, ready to dance after the bar closes. The music is blasting, nobody is dancing. Instead of dance moves, they are handed a paint brush.

First time participants are asked to pay a toll. I lead them to the kitchen, politely ask them to take off their shoes, turn around, put their backs against the wall and stand up straight. I measure their height on the kitchen wall. There is a specific place where this happens. The inches are marked from the floor to the ceiling. There is a large square marked off to look like a frame. We figure out how tall they are and then they (whoever they are, does not matter, the more random, the better for all I care) get themselves a sharpie and sign their name next to their line and date it. This happens religiously. You cannot be a first time visitor without being measured for height, signing your name and dating it. This amuses me to no end. This convinces me that I am about the cleverest person in Southern California. Any reputable news source doing an article about clever people would no doubt include me in it. Embracing random acts of nonsense keeps me busy. I fear what will happen if I stop moving. As long as I don't slow down I can continue to ignore all the things falling apart all around me.

To pay the bills, I work at a slowly failing restaurant at the South Coast Plaza Mall, a fifteen mile drive south on the 405. After working in the dining room for the first few months, I am moved over to the lounge. I essentially become a cocktail waitress. I am a useful employee because I don't complain. I show up on time and I work long hours.

My clientele includes a significant amount of wealthy (plastic surgery, pearls, fancy shoes) women. Typical Orange County housewives who order expensive glasses of Chardonnay after a rough afternoon of shopping. Top shelf is Kendall Jackson Chardonnay that goes for $7.50 a glass. This seems at the time to be an extravagant amount of money for a single glass of wine. Eight bucks for a small pour of white wine? This is just madness, I tell you. Pure madness. By the end of my table serving career five painful years later, finding a glass of Chardonnay for less than eight dollars is nearly impossible.

I work five nights a week. Tuesday's and Thursday's feature an extended happy hour. The fine people of Orange County pack the place for half-off appetizers, two-dollar drinks, and a crappy DJ. These fuckers actually stand in a line to get in. These nights are summed up with a single word: PAIN. Living in Long Beach and working in the heart of Orange County exposes me to two *vastly* different worlds. Orange County is clean and confusing. Long Beach is dirty and rad. Orange County is the world of money and privilege. Long Beach is a hard working city just trying to make ends meet. Orange County is an eight dollar weak pour. Long Beach fills it to the rim and it only costs $5.50. Long Beach is the first place I feel accepted in. It's the first place I can talk to strangers in a bar successfully. It is where my confidence grows and I start to find myself. Orange County doesn't need or want me. My pants are all wrong anyway. I am seen as the help. I am a necessary evil whose only purpose is to hurry back quickly as possible with their next round of drinks.

My shift starts at five in the afternoon and is never over before two in the morning. This is an excessive amount of time to be waiting tables. I don't know this; nobody mentions that nine hours isn't the typical length of a shift in a restaurant. In a normal restaurant, shifts last no longer than five hours. Shifts not falling on a Tuesday or Thursday show mercy. The prospect of leaving early exists. The bar closes earlier, things slow down, and every so often I am cut early and get home in time to change into civilian clothing and meet up with my friends. The chance of this happening on a Tuesday or Thursday is so remote that I don't torture myself with the hope of it actually happening. So without fail, two days a week, every single week, I bust my ass for eight or nine hours straight.

There are aspects of the job I find beneficial. I work primarily with attractive girls. It doesn't take me long to figure out how to sneak drinks. I make decent money. It is a job that I hate, but I don't hate too much. The management is borderline ridiculous. The majority of the bartenders are tolerable. I do my best to ignore the ones who aren't. The other servers don't immediately embrace me, but as time goes on I become close to many of them. I prove myself worthy of being on the team. The busboys, bar backs, and cooks are all Hispanic. They work their asses off and keep the restaurant running. I show up for each shift with one eye on the clock. I am always anxious for my shift to end so I can get back to Long Beach and get into some trouble.

Around this time, I met a Nigerian taxi driver named Tony. Our introduction happens by chance but is proven to be more than that. I am convinced that our meeting is the workings of fate. It is a typical Saturday night. A group of friends gather at The Blue Door to drink before we head out for the night. We eventually call Yellow Cab, the cab shows up and we file out of the house to get in. I have a habit of sitting up front in a cab. I insist on it. The introduction of cocaine to my life turns me into a serial conversationalist. I'm a South American History major who has read the newspaper front to back every day since I was twelve-years-old. The likelihood that the guy driving us is from a foreign country is about 100%. Who better than me to make some chit chat while on the way?

Our cab driver is named Tony. He is from Nigeria. I know things about Nigeria. There are untapped and extensive natural resources and political upheaval. That's about it. I told him this. We immediately become friends. Most of his fares get in the back, tell him where to go, and ignore him. I get in the front seat and instigate a conversation revolving around him and where he is from. I'm like the U.S. Ambassador to Nigeria and I just got in his cab. Crack kills. Cocaine gets me a ride.

Tony becomes my personal cab driver. He saves my life multiple times each week. He saves the lives of all my friends every time he picks us up. Without Tony someone has to drive to the bar. Without Tony, someone has to drive back from the bar. Without him there is no doubt that someone's luck will run out. A DUI is the last thing any of us need. A DUI is the last thing I want to tell my parents about. Driving into parked cars on the way home is also hard to excuse. Causing a fiery head on crash that kills a family of four that leaves me with months of painful skin grafts and multiple amputations sounds like a shitty way to spend my twenties.

The process is simple. Call up Yellow Cab, give them my address and ask for cab #242, and #242 *only*. Within twenty minutes Tony is outside and we are on our way to the bar. When we are ready to leave the bar, call up Yellow Cab and repeat the process. Be *adamant* that the only acceptable cab is #242. Before we know it, Tony is waiting for us out front. The meter stays off while he drives us home. He is rewarded when we hand over a generous tip. Tony has been in the country for only a few years and doesn't know too many Americans. He jumps at the opportunity to get to know us. We treat him like an old friend and appreciate what he brings to the table. This is the beginning of The Blue door and it is fun. This shit is magical.

The Blue Door allows me the opportunity to spend time with friends. My nights are consumed with endless conversations, making art, and writing. I fuck random girls in random places. I am happy. I work enough to survive. I have cash in my pocket at all times and never hesitate to spend it on whatever I need to make the night memorable. I buy cute girls shots at the bar. I develop an alter ego. I wear athletic wristbands along with headbands- fashion. I golf. I stay up late and share everything I have with people. I make art. I buy art supplies. I continue to paint on the walls inside The Blue Door. I start meeting new people. I find myself around the type of people that I have been looking for since I left home after high school. I find myself fitting in for the first time.

I smoke cigarettes, drink excessively and develop a healthy cocaine habit. Staying up all night happens occasionally. Every few months the night gets away from me. I find myself awake and up to no good when the sun comes up. This doesn't happen all the time, but a pattern starts to develop. The time between each bender gradually gets shorter and shorter. What used to happen once a month now takes place every other week. It crops up consistently. One night every other week turns into at least one night per week. It then turns into multiple times a week. Soon enough, a week is spent using it every other day.

The next week involves a bender that lasts for three consecutive days. It gradually gets worse. It sneaks up on me. Before I know it, I realize that I am fucked. I haven't slept in the past forty-eight hours. I find myself escaping the early morning light for the safety of a dark bar the moment it first opens at 6 AM.

I do drugs often. I am teetering on the edge of excess. I am the #1 candidate to cross over to the dark side where drugs take over my life. I haven't crossed over yet, but I am in the vicinity of taking it to the next step. Should I consider smoking crack? What about shooting heroin? What's it like to snort crystal meth? I may be on the verge of throwing my life away but I haven't lost my will to live. I don't have the balls to go to the next level and so the next level doesn't end up happening. I never seriously consider intravenous drug use. Cocaine works just fine in powdered form; there is no need to buy the rock version. Speed fucks with your skin. My battle with acne started in middle school and continues to this day. Victory is close. Breakouts are rare. The occasional zit breaks through. Speed, no doubt, fucks up all my hard work. If I try it once, my face breaks out. If I try it a second time I will look like a forty-year-old mother of six.

I have a degree, people! I read the newspaper daily. This shit is scary. I must respectfully decline. I'm not curious to try them out because I know that I like cocaine. This gateway drug assures me that there is a good chance any of these other options will break me. The ability to convince myself that I still have things under control ends the moment I try something new. Any chance I have that cocaine hasn't taken over my life evaporates the moment I do something stupid like try heroin. That shit is for losers.

It starts and ends with coke. Without doubt, it is something that keeps creeping into my life. It is something that I enjoy and partake in. It is something I am able to shut down when a break is needed. I stay out of trouble. I call my mother on a consistent basis and keep my habit out of view from those who don't do it. When I can get a hold of it I buy it in small amounts and then I am done with it. I finish the package. I am done with it, and then I am ready to do it again. The phone rings. Another opportunity presents itself. Coke is on its way. There is no escape from going fast. I embrace it. I love it. As long as it keeps going I'll be fine. It always keeps on going.

I want to take credit for this activity. I'm confident that originally it is my idea. It sounds like something I would force my friends to partake in. At The Blue Door we drink. We drink, but instead of drinking games, we play *writing* games. Everyone is on something, be it marijuana, cocaine, or alcohol. The majority of people are on some combination of the three. It's a fairly artsy group. It's a group of friends who would never be caught participating in drinking games. Writing is right up our alley.

There were six of us the first night. Everyone gets a pad of paper and a pen. We sit in an informal circle. Some are on the couch, some in chairs, some sitting on the floor. I explain the concept and tell everyone to begin. We all write down the first thing that comes into our minds and then pass the paper to the person to our right.

The only rule is to write the first thing that comes into your mind. A poem, a sentence, a story, a partial sentence, two words, the same word over and over, it does not matter. Once done, pass the pad of paper to the person on your right. Before long, a pad of paper is handed to you from your left. Your job is to add another bit of nonsense below the passage that was written before you. It doesn't matter what they write. Whatever is said should not and doesn't need to change you. But if it does, that works too. It doesn't have to connect whatsoever. It is actually preferable if you *don't* read what is written before you. If you *do* read it, there is no shame in that. It is all up to you. Listen to me, tell me to fuck off and ignore my advice, either way it works. I look for random prose without any concern about what is said. The pages are passed until everyone has the opportunity to add to each one. Six people sit in my living room, waiting patiently to get their hands on pads of paper. Friends and strangers sit around patiently. When the last person finishes we pass one last time. This final pass assures that everyone is holding onto their original pad of paper. One by one, each person reads their pad of paper.

This is what happens when an excessive amount of cocaine is combined with multiple packs of cigarettes, a fridge full of canned domestic beer, an ample supply of paper and enough pens for everyone.

Nothing happens. Nothing is broken. Nobody starts a fight with a rival gang, let alone an argument. It doesn't even occur to anyone to do any serious binge drinking. All I see is the uninspired sipping of people who have to do laundry later and don't want to be too smashed to separate the delicates from the bath towels. No one spills anything. Nothing is broken (yes, I already mentioned this). In an orderly fashion, each pad is read aloud. It is immediately considered to be genius. It is the first display of our soon-to-be-recognized brilliance.

> *"You can't make much progress, if you can't fix one*
> *problem, because you challenge fifty."*

> *"You can't write without a pen..."*

"Watery eyes, blurred vision, a confused thought process, nose feeling funny, a little bit disoriented, skipping songs, watch out boys, this may never end."

"He is the love inside that helps me open my eyes every morning knowing everything will be okay, he is this security that pushes me through the normal drudgery of every 24 hours. Mindless fools open your eyes and see the truth. It is in front of you. Simple, kind and soothing. YA."

"Sorry to be somber... But those 'cats' that died yesterday (US soldiers) were the direct result of Sept. 11th. Don't let that day go away. Understand their deaths with the same attention and feeling you felt that day."

"You have no game, no name, no fame, give it all to Jermaine"

"What is happening now is actually happening. Approach it with that being understood."

It is clear that we are producing some seriously *deep* thoughts.You can guess what bullshit is mine… We do this all the time. Somehow, everyone writes on each other's paper and it is read to the group. When combined with illegal social lubricants, this always seems to sound poetic. Combining random thoughts into page long essays makes everyone a writer. Everyone feels a sting of pride for contributing to something totally original. We each have a hand in doing something different and unusual with our night. Even the guy who initially is appalled by the idea becomes a believer. There is no doubt that this is an exploit worth repeating. I live in a place that is gradually becoming known as somewhere that you can go to and be involved with something out of the ordinary. I am the ringmaster of my own little artistic circus.

Soon enough the ink runs dry. The paper is all used up, and the honeymoon is over. I'm exhausted from all the bullshit. Continually entertaining has its drawbacks. I'm having serious issues each time I come down. The low that occurs the next day after binging on cocaine is killing me. The high is always followed by a low, and the low is starting to get more and more fucking difficult to get a handle on. This is before I know about various coping strategies, how to deal with its mechanisms, and feelings charts. This is before I realize that it takes a day or two for the drugs to completely leave my system, and that is the reason I'm depressed and all I have to do is remind myself of this and then ride out the storm. This is before I realize that I still haven't come to terms with my sister being sick, Mitch being gone, and me not knowing what to do with the rest of my life. I am about to explode and I don't know how to relieve the pressure.

The next thing I know, I am drunk in my living room holding a (clean?) razor blade in my right hand. The plan is to bend over and cut into my lower leg. I figure this is a safe place to do it. Below the sock line, far away from any major arteries. I drag the blade across my skin and am immediately frightened, exhilarated and comforted by the relief that comes over me. As I see the steady flow of blood running down my leg I am overcome with calmness. I am finally being released from the insane amount of worry and guilt that has been festering inside of me. I find my outlet. I figure out what will save me. Cutting open my leg transfers my mental pain into a physical one. It's not a recommended way to deal with my problems but it is the only thing I can think of. It is the only way I can give myself some type of relief. The balloon has finally popped.

I never want to say it. I never really take too much stock in it. But I still find myself thinking about it over and over. It's daylight, too much cocaine from the night before, in bed, can't sleep, been trying for hours, it looks like I'll never get some rest. No relief in sight. Mind is still racing. Which inevitably leads to self-pity and thoughts along the line of: "I want to die, I want to kill myself, I want to die I want to die I want to die...." I don't really feel this way. I do not actually want to die. But I say it over and over again. For no fucking god damn reason. I have nothing to complain about. I am fine. I am miserable. I am fucking fucked.

15

Red Blood Cells

MITCH IS IN town from Georgia for a visit. He brings his girlfriend and one of her friends for New Years. We all stay at The Blue Door. The girls give me a bottle of 18-year-old scotch. I tell them they can visit any time they want. Mitch and I meet for beers at his favorite Irish Pub on 2nd Street.

Mitch: *When Mandy catches her break, watch out man, because she is fucking due and there isn't anything that can hold her back.*

James: *I think she is going to die.*

Mitch: *Don't say that, I don't ever want to hear you say that again.*

James: *Not saying it doesn't change the fact that my gut feeling says that she is going to die. It kills me to say it but it's the only thing I can say to you that isn't bullshit. I'm sick of pretending that what's happening isn't really happening. I've been living with this gut feeling in my stomach that I can't get rid of it.*

Mitch has nothing to say. We sit quietly for a while on the patio and smoke a cigarette. He puts his arm around me and squeezes my shoulder. He knows that I haven't said this to anyone else and that I can't say it again. We sit in silence both knowing that her fate is beyond anything we can do. We sit there and he knows that I am probably right, and that breaks his heart. His heart breaks because of all the time they have spent together. It breaks because he has always loved her. His heart breaks for my parents because he always has loved them and doesn't want them to lose a child. Lastly, his heart breaks for me. His heart breaks because this is what happens when your friend's life is about to fall apart and there is nothing he can do to fix it. There is nothing he can say to make it better.

The first year that my sister lives at home, before she goes to India, before the Anemia changes into PNH, things aren't all that bad for her. She still enjoys the occasional beer. She quit smoking and hasn't touched hard drugs since she moved home. She leads a quiet life and develops a healthy relationship with my parents.

Their relationship makes sense for the first time in her life. They watch TV together on the couch. My father displays a rare tenderness towards her that I didn't even know existed. She is bored. She misses her boyfriend, who still lives in San Francisco. She deals with it and stays focused on getting better. She appears to be healing. Anemia has nothing on her. Shit… She masters the public transportation system of Northern California within a week. She can take a bus anywhere in the city. That has to count for something… Right?

Everything changes when she returns from India. For some reason Mandy switches over from being a healthy young woman in her twenties to a very sick young woman, for no obvious reason. Her blood stops functioning properly. She gets sick and then sicker.

I envision the inside of her body like a Saturday morning cartoon. The plot revolves around a magical place governed by a benevolent and kind King (her healthy red blood cells) that gets infiltrated and overthrown by an invading army of unshaven, unwashed and illiterate strangers bent on burning the crops, scaring the children, and pillaging the castle (her broken red blood cells). These invaders aren't going to stop until the castle is destroyed, the people are enslaved and the King is thrown into his dirtiest and darkest dungeon.

It is a tricky disease. She is a special case. Diagnosed with anemia at the age of twenty-three, and then re-diagnosed with some shit abbreviated as PNH a few months after that. She is the recipient of a rare blood disorder afforded to only a few dozen of her peers in the United States of America. At the age of twenty-three, just when she stops using speed and her life starts to make sense again, my sister goes and gets herself a rare blood disease. The moment she is finally at peace with herself, her body falls apart and a war erupts inside her.

Back to the Saturday morning cartoon. A growing contingent of red blood cells feel disenfranchised by the bourgeois middle class. They decide to start a revolution against the ruling class. The angry mob of pissed off red blood cells attack their contemporaries and rid her body of the ability to have any way of regulating how thin or thick her blood stays.

Our relationship falls silent one morning. There is nothing to say while we eat our breakfast together. The thing on both of our minds is too fucked up to tackle and is often thrown aside and put off for another day. It kills me every time there is silence between us. Worst-case-scenario is eating a meal together in absolute quiet. All I want to do is finish my eggs, pay the bill, and escape the awkwardness. This is when Mandy quietly begins to speak.

Mandy: *I think I'm going to die.*

James: *Don't say that, you'll get better, I know it.*

I look down at my eggs and begin to eat again. The conversation ends right where it starts. My only regret, the regret that drives me to dark places, is not continuing this conversation. All I have to do is acknowledge her fear and sympathize with her for being faced with such overwhelming uncertainty. All I have to do is legitimize her feelings and ask her what I can do to help. I could have offered to sit down with her and have her tell me her life story from her point of view. I think she would have liked being asked to do this. Instead, I finish my breakfast, pay the bill, take her home, and escape back into my own world in Long Beach where I can forget about having a sick sister for the rest of the morning.

I can't have this conversation with her because I am convinced that she *is* probably going to die. I let an opportunity to have an honest conversation with her slide through my fingers. I am afraid of what I might say, so I say nothing. Mandy is already pessimistic in regards to her recovery. Any attempt I make to convince her to think more positively is met with resistance. I'm the healthy one. Who the fuck am I to tell her how to feel?

A couple years ago we both lived through the aftereffects of a close family member gravely injured. We see our uncle survive a boating accident he has no business living through. He does this by sheer will and a positive attitude. It is obvious to me that this played a significant role in his recovery. For whatever reason, Mandy fails to make the connection. She is caught up in her own struggle. I can't understand why she isn't more like our uncle. The solution is so simple. All she has to do is emulate him, put on a happy face and get her body back to health.

Her blood is fine. It's her crappy attitude causing her steady decline. If only she smiled more often, then she won't deteriorate so fast.

It is only after her body goes into open revolt do I understand how wrong I am. Putting on a happy face isn't going to magically fix the inside of her body. Two things lead me to this conclusion. She barely survives a blot clot and a brain hemorrhage that occur only a few months apart. The first incident occurs when she is visiting Nana in Santa Barbara. She is driving to the liquor store and has to pull her car over. On the side of the road is where her body stops working. Pulled over and alone, she knows without doubt that something bad is happening. She uses her remaining strength to slightly open the driver's side door. She is barely able to reach her arm out of the rolled down window and try to summon help. This is the last thing she does. It is all that she can do. It saves her life.

Within a few minutes, something miraculous happens. In all likelihood, she is going to die right there on the side of the road. She is no more than a half-a-mile from Nana's house but on a stretch of road rarely traveled on and she needs immediate help. A minute later a cop drives by and notices her car parked on the side of the road with one door slightly ajar and an arm hanging out of the window. His initial reaction is to keep on driving but he sees her out of the corner of his eye. He almost keeps on going but notices how helpless she looks and decides to go back and see if she is all right.

A Short List of the Possible Reasons for Him to Keep on Driving.

A) He momentarily looks down.
B) A call comes over the radio.
C) Hostage situation at the public library, backup is needed.
D) An illegal U- turn happens up the street necessitating him to blare his siren and speed past her to pull over the offending car.
E) He is late to meet another policeman for lunch.
F) He is too hungry to stop, he makes a mental note of the car, and promises to investigate further (drive by again) after lunch.
G) Too hungover to notice her car on the side of the road.

There are so many excuses for him to keep driving, for him not to stop. Without this bit of luck she probably dies right now. The cop pulls over, approaches her car and immediately realizes that she is in serious trouble. Without delay, he calls an ambulance and saves her life. Her medication causes her blood to become too thin and she has a serious brain hemorrhage on the way to the store. She spends the next week in the hospital. She recovers enough and is allowed to come home. Things slowly get back to normal. My parents return to work. Mandy's doctors make subtle changes to her medication and she gradually gets better.

The medicines the doctors prescribe her are meant to balance out her blood. Too much of pill #1 and her blood gets too thick, this has the possibility of leading to a blood clot, a stroke and most likely death. Too much of pill #2 and her blood gets too thin, this leads to hemorrhaging, and an excessive amount of blood in her brain. This bleeding of the brain will most likely lead to her death. The problem is that practically nobody has this stupid disease so her doctors have limited data to help them figure out what combination of dosages will work for her.

Her version of PNH is considered to be the most serious kind. She is on the most extreme side of the PNH spectrum. Her symptoms are even more severe when compared to the few other cases of PNH that are recorded. Her doctors are smart men. Their area of expertise is dealing with blood disorders. She arrives carrying an illness that they probably haven't even heard of, let alone treated before she shows up. Now they need to figure out a way to fix her. She is a worse-case-scenario type of scenario. This forces them to make things up as they go along and hope for the best.

The second incident convinces me that there is no cure or magic combination of pills that will fix my sister. A few months after she survives the brain hemorrhage, her blood gets too thick and she has a stroke. Strokes should only happen to old people. Ninety-two-year-olds who need help wiping their butts have strokes. Lonely old people living in nursing homes who can't even remember that they have lived a full and rewarding life are perfect candidates for a stroke. Any old person whose beloved wife or husband recently died should rock a serious blood clot and reunite with their life partner. Anyone with their affairs in order and is ready to die should go before my sister. Nobody younger than the age of twenty-five deserves to have their blood do any kind of clotting. Nobody that age needs to deal with clots of blood traveling to their brain with the intention of killing them.

This is what happens to Mandy, and it almost kills her. This is by far the most serious thing she goes through. They shave her head, cut open her skull and perform emergency surgery on her brain. The surgeons are able to stabilize her. She is put in an induced coma. I am allowed to visit her a day later.

I enter the room and immediately break down. I can't hold it back anymore and the moment I see her I fall apart. I fall into my mother's arms and sob heavily until I don't have another tear left. Only then can I turn back around and look at her. Her shaved head is heavily bandaged. Her face is discolored and swollen. Her eyes are closed. Her mouth is slightly open. There are tubes everywhere. Two in her arm, two more in her nose, a breathing tube down her throat and one more going up her urinary tract. The last tube is the most painful.

She squirms, twists, turns and fights off the doctors when they insert the catheter. The doctor tells us that this is a good sign and that she still has fight left in her. A single tear rolls down her face during the procedure (I'm serious). As I watch the tears falling down her face I lose all remaining hope. My faith that everything will work out is over. It ends right there in the hospital room. By the time her tear reaches the bottom of her face I know that smiling will not save her.

Within a week she came out of the coma. Her breathing tube is removed and she slowly regains consciousness. First, she opens her eyes. Next, she slowly starts to talk. After that, she is able to move her body again. The next time I visit her, she greets me with a smile. She isn't out of the woods yet, but she is starting to recover. I smile back at her and hide the desperation that consumes me inside. I smile back and try not to think about how grave the situation is. It doesn't matter what the doctors do. It won't make any difference, no matter how hard she fights. Her blood cannot be regulated with any certainty. Even though she spends the next few months healing and getting better. In time she recovers enough to move back home. Normalcy creeps back into our lives. She has good days amongst the bad ones. We don't talk about it but we all know what is inevitable. We can't deny that the next time is only a matter of time. Without a doubt, we know that there will be a next time. We just don't know when. Nobody really tells me shit and I don't ask too many questions. I just go on with my day to day. I work, I do anything I can to avoid thinking about it, I party a lot, like all the time. The last thing I do is talk about it. I just keep on tucking it deep inside, the further down the better. I hold it all in and order another drink.

She is in constant pain. She is lucky to be alive after her blood gets out of whack and almost kills her. I lose hope right there in the waiting room of the hospital. I lost faith in her recovery. I stop believing that everything will be okay and that bad things won't happen to my family. She recovers from the stroke and comes back home, but is never really the same again. She has to relearn how to use her body. She progresses slowly. She uses a wheelchair, then a walker and eventually starts to walk again without assistance. With time, she is able to throw a ball and eventually rides a bike. Her coordination is out of whack and lives inside a broken body, but yet she makes the most of it. She works her ass off to get healthy again. She is never able to really recover from the surgery. I know that it is just a matter of time before I am awoken by the phone ringing at an odd hour only to be told that my sister is dead and that I need to come to the hospital immediately. In typical fashion, when the call comes, I am passed out, my phone is dead, and I miss it.

The evening festivities continue into a later hour than I originally planned for. Liquids and powders keep the party going until the wee hours. The rising sun complicates my return home at the fine hour of six this morning. I finally make it into my bed, close my eyes, and put a stop to the madness. I moved to Long Beach for the sole purpose of participating in such nights.

Stumbling home at seven in the morning is the reason I am finally given an affiliation to this fine city. Living in Long Beach is proudly represented.

James: *I live in Long Beach.*

This sounds *so* much better than my other available option.

James: *Yeah.... I live with my parents in Rossmoor.*

This means exactly what it sounds like, that I live with my parents. It is a loud proclamation that I am not, in any way/shape/form, mysterious.

Living in Long Beach sounds excessively better to the newly acquired friends I seem to keep making. It means that I am the unknown. I might be the dangerous type, this isn't determined just yet.

The point is, I had a long fucking night. I am not in any way prepared to start my Saturday. The plan is to commit the next six hours catching up on some sleep. I have no interest whatsoever in greeting this specific day until the latter parts of the afternoon.

Without warning I am woken up by loud knocks at my door. I live alone. I am not expecting any visitors. Best-case-scenario? The hot girl from last night followed me home and needs a bed to sleep in. Worst-case scenario is staring back at me when I open the front door.

I open the door and find Cassie standing there. She is an old family friend who lives near my parents. Her daughter was best-friends with my sister in elementary school, but they haven't stayed particularly close since then, and haven't seen each other in awhile. I instinctively know that something is very wrong. Cassie isn't the last person I expect to see standing outside my door this morning, but she is not too far off. A surprise visit from Mike makes more sense. Of course you can crash on the couch, come on in. I often hope that the members of Massive Attack are outside. They need a place to crash and are willing to put on an intimate (invite only) show for my friends and I. This is not as likely.

The only logical reason I am blessed with an unexpected visit from Cassie this Saturday morning does not bode well. My plans to sleep off my hangover and be left alone by the world crumble before me. Her surprising pop-in is made out of a desperate attempt to get a hold of me. Turning my phone to silent before passing out was an error in judgment. I soon see the plethora of missed calls I haven't heard during the last few hours.

James: *What's going on?*
Cassie: *You need to go to the hospital, something happened to Mandy.*
James: *What's going on?*

There is desperation on Cassie's face. She agrees to drive over and wake me up, but she isn't about to be the one who breaks whatever news that needs to be broken. We both know that it isn't her place to give me the crucial information that drove her here in the first place. All I know is that I need to hear it as soon as possible. It becomes more apparent what is going on. All she can do is give me the condensed version. She offers a vague explanation of the unfolding situation. Time is a factor, and I shouldn't be wasting it talking to her in my underwear. The critical nature of the circumstances is confirmed by her inability to elaborate. The fact that she is standing in my kitchen in the first place is all the preparation I need to ready myself for the inevitable.

I quickly put on clothes, ignore the impulse to brush my teeth, and start driving. The fact that I probably shouldn't even be operating a vehicle at this moment is ignored. Due to the excessive activities of the night before, I am completely exhausted. I am still both drunk and high. The simple act of successfully putting a piece of bread in the toaster is beyond my present skill set. The likelihood of buttering and eating it without burning the house down is nil. I should *not* be driving. Operating a vehicle is a bad idea. Five minutes ago I woke up a worthless mess. Now I am weaving through traffic going twenty miles over the posted speed limit. Adrenaline takes over my entire body. I am alert. I am awake. I hear my cell phone ring.

James: *What's happening?*

My father is on the line. He doesn't sound happy. Spending all morning in a vain attempt to track my ass down does that to him. He's been calling all morning. He has to send Cassie over to my house to wake me up. This is more than enough reason to irritate him. Combining these small inconveniences with how his day begins makes the tone of his voice sound reasonable. I chose the wrong night to go big. My phone chose the wrong night to die. The time he spends and the energy he uses to track me down is the last thing he needs. Sorry Dad, "my bad" doesn't cut it here.

My sister collapsed earlier that night. My parents find her on the floor of the front bathroom. She asks my mom to turn on the bathroom light. The bathroom light is already on. They immediately call 911. My dad experiences his daughter losing consciousness for the last time. She is dying in his arms. They don't know that she is brain-dead but still alive as they wait for the ambulance to arrive. My dad is having a really shitty morning. I did cocaine all night and flirted with girls. He sees his first born close her eyes for the last time. I'm such an asshole.

Dad: *It doesn't look good. You need to be prepared.*

James: *What the fuck are you saying?*

I know exactly what he is about to say. I have no doubts what his next words will be. I'm just not ready to hear them out loud. I'm just not willing to allow the gravity of the situation to saturate my life entirely and become unchangeable. I have to hold out and disregard what is inevitable. I'm not ready to deal with it. I'm not ready for it to end.

Before my dad can answer me, I tell him where I am and how long until I get to the hospital. I don't allow him to answer my question because I'm not ready to hear the answer. I still have fifteen minutes of driving to do. I need to use the few minutes I have to wrap my head around what is happening. I don't let him answer me because it is something I need to hear in person. It's something I refuse to hear over the phone.

I hang up the phone and immediately call Mitch. He's living in Atlanta. I still consider him my brother. He has the closest relationship with my parents, and to Mandy. I still consider him my strongest friend. There is no hesitation when I dial the number. My fingers automatically do it before my brain has the chance to tell them to. Before I came back home from San Diego he was living in Long Beach. My sister lives at home and isn't too sick. Mitch takes the initiative and occasionally takes her out. They get along well and are mutually intrigued with one another. Mitch is the only one who makes an effort to see her. The first time they meet for a beer my sister manages to knock over a full pint of beer ten seconds after it is placed before her. The bartender wipes up the mess and pours her another one. She promptly knocks the second one over. Their friendship runs deep.

Mitch is the friend I completely open up to in regards to Mandy's sickness. He is the one person I can articulate my fears to and express my concerns about Mandy. He cares as much for her as he does for me. Actually, I know that he secretly cares more for her than he ever will for me. This makes me thankful. He never hesitates when it comes to Mandy. He does the most for me. I am in his debt.

His phone rings five times and goes to voicemail. I start to panic when I get no answer on Mitch's cell. I'm trying to get to the hospital as fast as I can. I'm crying and I'm on the verge of hysterics. I get his voice mail. My message goes something like this.

James: *Pick up the phone you mother fucker.... It's over.... It's all fucking over. I need to talk please. Call me back right now. CALL ME BACK..........*

A minute later Mitch calls me back. He knows. We talk briefly. He asks me if he should fly out. I tell him to get his ass on a plane. Without any hesitation, Mitch's dad, the same scary dude who yelled at me all those years ago buys him a plane ticket leaving that night out to California. I fucking love this man from this moment forward. He is a kind, gentle giant who doesn't blink an eye or worry about the cost. We only got off on the wrong foot that day. When it counts he steps up and I am truly in his debt. Twelve hours and a thousand dollars later that evening, he arrives at my parent's house. Everything is forgiven. All discretions are pardoned. Everything bad I've ever said about him is taken back the moment he pulls up to my parent's house. Mitch will get me through this. He is all I need to survive.

I hang up the phone and within two minutes I pull into the hospital parking lot. I see my Dad waiting for me outside the entrance.

James: *What is going on?*

Dad: *You need to be prepared.*

James: *Prepared for what?*

This is when my dad loses his cool. He knows that I know what is happening. He knows that I need to hear him say the actual words. I know that he is pissed about not being able to get a hold of me. I don't expect him to yell at me. I'm pretty sure he doesn't expect to yell at me either. But this is precisely what happens next.

Dad: *THAT SHE IS GOING TO DIE.*

The last words are not spoken softly. The words are not eased slowly into my facilities. He says them bluntly and harshly. They are the direct result of all the frustration and anger consuming the person saying them. It is obvious to me that he is going to say it. I expect a firm voice. I don't expect him to confirm her death with such an angry outburst. The pain that is conveyed with his voice is far beyond what I think he is capable of. He articulates the gravity of the situation by the tone of his voice. He scares the shit out of me with the volume of it. It is an effective way to get the message across to me. I will not ask another stupid question again.

His words hit me like a hammer. The finality of these simple words floors me. My next move is to walk through the front door of the hospital. This is when the situation becomes real. There is no turning back. The fifteen minutes it takes me to get to the hospital is over. Fifteen minutes is more time than my parents get. I don't expect to hear him get short with me, but I know that I am in need of a firm voice. It snaps me out of my daze and lets me walk through the front door ready to face what lies ahead. The life that I had is over. As I walk through the automatic doors of the hospital I know that everything has changed. I can't count on my life anymore. Everything I have confidence in is shattered and is immediately replaced with uncertainty and disorder.

16

Hallways

I NAVIGATE DOWN THE familiar hallways of the Los Alamitos Hospital. The hallways are all empty. They are completely void of life. I move through each quiet hallway to the next. I know when to turn left, and when to go right. I know this hospital well. Nobody deserves to know a hospital intimately. My mom logs more hours here than the average part time nurse. They should offer my dad priority parking. I try my best to avoid this place as much as I can, but I still feel like I know it as well as a former patient would. The limited amount of time I spend here pales in comparison to the massive amount of time Mandy spends trapped inside these walls. I know where to go. My pace is quick and steady. I am calm. I am ready.

I understand what waits for me in the intensive care unit. My path leads straight into a situation that turns into something unfamiliar to everyone else but me. The hallways are quiet and my pace quickens as I reach the end of the hallway and walk through the double doors. This leads to the intensive care unit. I press the large square button that opens the doors to the ICU and head towards my mom. She turns around and sees me the instant the automated doors open. I walk briskly over to her and we embrace. I look over to see my sister lying on her back in the hospital bed next to me.

I approach her. Her eyes are shut. She is peaceful. She is comatose. Her eyes are closed and they won't be opening any time soon. Tubes are everywhere. The synthetic medical tubing is the only thing keeping her alive. Behind her bed is the dreaded green monitor. It keeps tabs on her heart rate and blood pressure. The line flashes across the screen. With every peak and valleys it beeps. Each peak gets a beep and is followed by a beep when it hits the valley. Every beep is followed with a pause, and every pause is followed by another beep. If the beep happens too quickly or takes too long, a nurse walks by and makes sure everything is okay. A long continuous beep will make all the nurses run over. The long uninterrupted beep is bad news. This beep hasn't happened yet. And this is where she lays. Beep, pause, beep. Her body doesn't move. She is still and silent. She is, technically, still alive.

There isn't a decision to pull the plug. It doesn't require a vote. There is no secret deliberation amongst the three of us that leads to a tense moment before we unveil our decision to either keep her alive or pull the plug and let her go. There is no grand debate over what the fuck we should do. There is no hesitation. We just collectively decide to let her go. We agree to end both our and her suffering. We agree to end our own suffering. There is never any notion that she can survive this. We suffer no such delusions. We never feel that the opportunity to freeze her and wait for science to fix her is something worth considering. Nothing like this is discussed.

Her heart continues to beat. Once it stops doing so, we will not do anything about it. On April 20, 2002, she died. That is the reality. She holds on for as long as possible and then leaves us forever. The rest of the family arrives within the hour. They are easy to track down this morning and are well on their way when I decide to face the day. My immediate family is small.

They are all close enough to get in their cars and drive to the hospital. We are located in the middle, so they are conveniently within two hours of the hospital. My sister and I grew up spending every major holiday with our immediate family. Everyone gets along. They are all on the way to the hospital. One side is driving north up the 405. The other side of the family is driving west on the 91. Nana has been picked up by my cousins and is currently driving south on the 101.

The end of the saga is here. Mom is composed. Her heart is broken and yet she is relieved that her daughter doesn't have to be sick anymore. Mandy is finally at peace and out of pain. This day has been marked on my calendar for too long. I am not sure exactly when it will come, but I've always known it is on its way. All attempts to stay positive and hopeful are thrown away the moment I see my sister lying lifeless in the ICU.

We spent two years waiting for her to recover. It was just a selfish way to avoid dealing with it. Our lingering doubts about her chances of survival come true. We all find different ways to pretend that it isn't as bad as it turns out to be. Things work out, right? Don't they? I discover that this isn't the case. My theory on life is shattered. I learn that things don't necessarily work out in the end.

So it finally happens and I don't cry. I am still unable to comprehend the fact that my sister is laying there. A loud thud in the hallway bathroom wakes my dad up earlier in the morning. The past two years train him to react swiftly to the variety of chaos that happens throughout any given night. By now he is prepared for anything. Early morning trips to the emergency room are not uncommon. On average, my sister has to go to the hospital no less than once a week. More often than not she spends three or more days in the hospital at a time. The nursing staff knows her by name. She juggles three different doctors. There is Dr. W., he is our family doctor. He has very good hair. Her second doctor is Dr. C. He is a bundle of energy and shows the most enthusiasm. He is Mandy's favorite doctor. He is a kind man who tells her that she is his favorite patient. Her final doctor is Dr. S. He, coincidentally, is the father of a girl I go to high school with. He apparently is a world-renowned doctor who has the most experience with blood disorders. He is based in Pasadena at a hospital called the City of Hope. I can't call him a charming man. I sure can't describe him as friendly or personable. But he is the expert and is good at what he does. These three doctors are responsible for figuring out what the hell is going on inside her body. They are faced with a phantom. There doesn't appear to be a clear plan. Answering this problem can't be found in a document. No matter how hard they work and how much they care, there appears to be nothing within their reach that can fix it. These are smart, capable men who are completely lacking the ability to help her.

And there she lies. I approach her. I feel obligated to touch her. I have to know for certain if she has anything alive still left in her. I have to be sure that this is for real. I run my hand over her head. There is no resistance when I move my hand across her forehead and through her hair. My question is immediately answered. She is no longer there. Her body lies before me but my sister doesn't. There is no resistance when

I move her head. This freaks me out. She is technically still alive but there is nothing left.

Her pulse fades. Her breathing becomes more labored. Her heart still beats. But she is not lying next to me. Mandy is gone. She is no longer lying there. Her body holds on. She is technically still alive but there is no doubt that her soul was left in my dad's arms on the floor of the front bathroom. She leaves the room and I can't recognize her anymore the moment I touch her. My heart breaks. Touching her body confirms it. She is gone. I can't wait to see her again. I know that I will. I have no doubt.

Mandy doesn't die just yet. Even without the aid of machines she keeps on trucking. For longer than expected she fights to stay alive. Her heart continues to beat and her lungs continue to breath. She isn't ready yet. She has one last thing to do. She holds on until the rest of our immediate family arrives at the hospital. She knows that they are coming from various places in Southern California and she understands how fickle the freeways can be. She stays patient and waits for them to arrive. Rene, Jeff, Jason, Jeremy and Teri arrive first. She is thankful they made it safely and wishes that she could thank them personally for coming on such short notice but isn't able to at the moment. This is due to the fact that her brain no longer works, her body is no longer able to move and she is close to dying. Fuck the details. She holds on.

Grandma, Ken and Aunt Weenie arrive a few minutes later. Mandy regrets not being able to stand up to greet them properly but knows that they will understand. Her heart continues to beat, her lungs continue to work, and she continues to hold on. The doctor told my parents that this might happen. He tells them that she will stay alive for as long as it takes for the family to arrive. He predicts that she will hold on until all of her family has the opportunity to get to the hospital. The last car that arrives at the hospital contains the two missing cousins, and the missing grandmother. Stacey, Josh and Nana arrive in the ICU. Everyone makes it to the hospital. Mandy can now die.

I figure out what Mandy has been waiting for these last few hours. When she first got sick and moved back home she started to visit Nana regularly. The strong bond they already shared gets stronger. The Mandy/Nana connection solidifies into something unbreakable.

The doctor tells us that after all of the family arrives, she will pass away quickly. It is clear to me who Mandy is waiting for. It makes perfect sense to wait for Nana to arrive at the hospital before she gives up. Nana arrives and within five minutes Mandy's pulse gets weaker, her heart slows down and she stops breathing. She doesn't get an opportunity to vocalize her final words. I can only guess what her last words would have been. I imagine that they are along these lines. I imagine that she smiles when she talks.

Mandy: *I would like to thank you all for coming but I've been waiting for too long for everyone to show up. I appreciate you coming but now that you are all here, I'd like you all to leave. No, wait, you should stay, I will leave. I need to stop working so hard. This heart can't keep on beating; my lungs can't keep on breathing. I am tired. I am tired of being sick. I am tired of being taken care of. I have no more fight left in me. Don't worry about me. I'll be fine. I'll see if I can call you when I get there. I don't know how the cell phone reception is but as soon as I find out I'll make sure that you are the first call I make.*

17

The Red Bowl

THE NEXT PHASE of my life begins the moment I leave the hospital. I intend to drive straight back to my parents' house. My car has other ideas. A block away from home is when navigational control of my Honda is lost. I don't have the strength to fight it. I allow it to take over. The car steers itself over to Bernie's parents' house. It pulls up in front, puts itself in park and turns off the engine. The driver's side door pops open and I get out of the car. My parents' house is just around the corner. My car is convinced that I'm not yet ready to go home. It swears to me that it knows what it is doing and I should trust its judgment. It's not wise to argue with a car made in Japan, so I get out. I close the door behind me and walked towards the house.

I open the front door and walk right in. It is that kind of house. I can't remember the last time I knocked on the front door and waited to be let in. I'm not sure if I have ever knocked. Right now is no time to start being polite. I open the front door, just like I always do and walk right in. I pass through the living room and into the kitchen. I find Bernie's dad, Hap, sitting at the dining room table reading the newspaper. Bernie is in Colorado finishing up with school. I have not seen him or his father in quite a while.

I walk towards him slowly. He hears my footsteps and looks up in my direction. He looks surprised and excited. I am the last person he expected to see in his kitchen this morning. He looks up from the newspaper, recognizes me and breaks out in a wide smile.

Hap: *Jamie...*

This is his customary greeting to me whenever we cross paths. The majority of my teenage years were spent inside this house. This place is like a second home to me. I consider him a secondary parental figure.

127

I regard myself as an honorary part of his family. His children are like siblings to me. Right now, the man reading the paper in front of me is the only person I can talk to. It takes Hap a second to see that something is wrong. The smile on his face instantly fades away. It is replaced with a look of intense worry and deep concern.

Hap: *You don't look so good, what's wrong?*

James: *Well Hap, my sister died this morning…*

The words burst out of me with shocking finality. It is the first time I have said these words aloud. It is the first time I say this to someone who I know cares for me and can comfort me. Hap stands up, walks over to me and gives me a hug. I sit down and tell him what is going on. He is like so many others who are close to me, but completely removed from what is happening with my sister.

He is one of so many people who don't know the full extent of what is going on. He, like the rest of them, never has a clue. He is aware that she might be sick, isn't totally sure what it's called, and is blindsided to hear that she actually died from it. Her death isn't something that anyone expects. It isn't even a possibility. The problem with an unknown, random sickness is that nobody can quantify it into something they can relate to. Nobody in the neighborhood has a clue. Even the people who live across the street are blind. The ambulance wakes them up. Flashing lights continuously disrupt their sleep. Paramedics arrive in the middle of the night. This happens, on average, twice a month and they still don't know the seriousness of the situation. They have no clue that the girl who grew up a few houses away is slowly dying. They soon find out that she is dead.

I don't stay long. I ramble on about how confused I feel, how unfair it is and that none of it makes any sense. Hap lets me finish, looks me straight in the eyes and then speaks.

Hap: *I know you might not be ready to hear this but it needs to be said. James, my heart aches for you and your family. I'm so sorry that your sister is dead but this is a huge part of life. People die. It's a harsh reality but there is no escape from it. People die, it's a part of life, people die, they die all the time.*

His harsh assessment initially blindsides me. I am unprepared for his brutal honesty. Then it starts to make sense. It's not what I expect to hear. It's not what I want to hear. Maybe that is what I *need* to hear.

People die, it sucks when they do, but you can't avoid it forever. *Everyone* dies. *A* few minutes later I got up to leave. The hug that Hap gives me before I go is strong and full of emotion. It only ends after a secondary extension hug that lasts a full ten seconds. This goodbye hug isn't totally unexpected. I leave the house feeling a little bit better.

I make it home before anyone else does. I unlock the front door and walk inside. I immediately realize that I can't stay inside. It just isn't a viable option. Mandy lingers everywhere I turn. Eight hours ago she was alive and inside the house. It still smells and feels like her. The place is swimming with her. Everything is still surrounded by her sickness. It is musty and full of death. All the other fucked up shit involved with death is still here. There is death in the bathroom. Death is in the hallway. Death is in the carpet. Death is hidden in the cushions of the couch. Death is still in the vacuum cleaner bag. I feel claustrophobic. It is hard to breathe.

I can't stay inside. I can't enter the house without some type of supervision. I call Cole. He lives two doors down. His car is parked out front, so I know that he is home. He is like family. I tell him to come over. Five seconds later he walks up my driveway.

I meet him outside. We walk over to a seldom used area in the front yard and sit down on a strip of grass that I have not sat on for the longest time. It is possible that in the twenty years I have lived here that I have never sat in this part of the front yard. There has never been a reason to sit here until right now. And this is where Cole and I plop down and sit. I call Lexi. I call someone I trust, and someone that I love. Someone who won't argue with me or contradict anything I say. I call someone who I am sure doesn't know what has happened and hasn't been told by or wouldn't have found out by then from someone else. I call her because I need to tell someone pure and young. I call her because I know that she will respond immediately and without anything but sympathy. I call her because I know she will drop whatever she is doing and turn her car around and immediately come in the direction of my parents' house. My mom gets back to the house while Cole, Lexi and I are still sitting on this weird patch of grass. My mom doesn't see us so she beelines it straight into the house. A moment later she reappears holding a red bowl in her hands. She sees us sitting there but doesn't stop walking to the open garage. This is where she unceremoniously tosses the bowl in the trash can. She turns around and heads back inside. Before she goes back into the house she looks at us.

Mom: *Guess we won't be needing this anymore.*

My dad gets back sometime later, followed by the family. Everyone comes inside and we sit in stunned silence. Close friends arrive next, a mixture of my parent's friends. My friends trickle in soon thereafter. Silence is replaced with talking. A joke breaks up the mood and soon everyone is telling stories. Pizza is ordered at some point, because people need to eat. Eventually my dad asks the question that is on everyone's mind.

Dad: *Is it too early to pour a glass of wine?*

No dad, I assure you, it is not too fucking early. Wine is opened. And then more. The sun eventually sets and only then do we remember that we need to call someone. Fuck. This call is going to be brutal.

Mandy's boyfriend has been living at my parent's house for the last year. This allows my parents to continue working while she is sick. This allows me to move to Long Beach. Without his presence at the house she would have to stay home alone every day. This isn't a problem in the beginning but once she starts having serious medical emergencies on a consistent basis it is no longer an option to leave her home alone. Finding him a job is no longer a priority. At first he needs to keep an eye on her. By the end, after six months or so, he takes care of her on a daily basis. Aside from the few hours he spends skateboarding each week, the majority of his time is spent caring for Mandy.

He plans to leave sometime in April so he can go back to Michigan and work for the summer. His summer job waits for him. He drives heavy machinery for three months every summer and makes enough money to get out of Michigan for the rest of the year. He does this every year. Three months of hard labor is followed by nine months of skateboarding in San Francisco and snowboarding in Colorado. The day he leaves my parents' house is April 19th. This was yesterday. Mandy died on April 20th.

When he leaves the house that morning it is hard for everyone. Mandy has the hardest time coping when he drives away but she understands that he has to go. It isn't the end of the world. She can handle being separated for a few months. Or at least she tells herself that. It is unavoidable. It is the right thing for him to do. The day after he leaves is when she dies. He leaves the goddamned *day before* and is on his way to San Francisco to see friends before he takes the long trip back to Michigan.

Joey is gone, his girlfriend is dead, and someone needs to tell him. This is a call I do *not* volunteer to make. It falls on my dad to dial his number. He makes multiple attempts, but isn't able to get a hold of him all during that Saturday. Hours later the phone rings. He finally calls back later that night. I pick up the phone. I hear Joey on the other line. I immediately give the phone to my dad. He takes it and breaks the news to him. The drive to San Francisco takes him six hours and now he is going to have to turn right back around and head back down to Southern California. The poor guy drives all day long, parks his car, returns a phone call, and finds out that not only is the love of his life dead, but he also has to get back in the car and spend another six hours driving back to the place he just left. I am glad I'm not the one who breaks the news to him.

I've known Joey for a while. I try my hardest to get close to him, but every attempt fails. We never get real close. I like him. He likes me. It just doesn't happen. He is a nice guy. He is good to Mandy. We just don't have anything in common. We never figure out how to communicate. We don't have anything to say to one another. It isn't his fault. This seems to be the problem I have with my entire family. I always pride myself on being able to talk. I usually have no trouble having actual conversations about issues and ideas and what not. I've never had a problem talking to the complete stranger sitting next to me at a bar. Alcohol and cocaine allows me the opportunity to use words. This is the setting that is conducive to the art of conversation. The minute I find myself without stimulants or with my family is when my inability to relate becomes painfully obvious. I can never figure out how to extend honest communication to my actual family. Strange people at the bar are easy. The people I want to be closest to are more elusive. They are harder to figure out. This is why I always keep them at arm's length, away from me at all times. I make them stay away for this particular reason.

The entire next week is a blur. Nana stays the entire time. My aunts come back and forth every few days. People bring casseroles. A friend stays the night. She sleeps next to me on the couch. Nothing happens, but it is good to have someone close by. My parents and I go to Forest Lawn Cemetery and pick out a plot. It is in the sun because Mandy can't stand being cold and would want to feel the heat of the sun on her face. My parents decided that butterflies will represent her memory in death. They start to collect collectable butterflies by the boatful and post them up around the house.

To this day, anytime I see a butterfly floating near me, whether it is when I'm looking over an important putt on the golf course, at a funeral, or during a backyard barbecue I think of her. Anytime one floats by, I take a second to think about her, and I know that she is keeping an eye on me.

I tell my parents that the venue is not big enough. I know that her funeral is going to be big. It will be an event that everyone needs to attend. They have no idea how Rossmoor works. This is an event that everyone that I know and everyone that my sister knows will show up to. This is the only way the masses can figure out how to show her respect and say goodbye. It has really nothing to do with saying goodbye to her. It has nothing to do with their need to let go of her. It has nothing to do with coming to terms with their loss. It only has to do with their need to be seen.

This leads to an argument with my family about how much room we need for the service. I try to convince them that more room is needed. They don't believe me and on the day of the funeral there is a packed cathedral building and another hundred other people standing outside listening to the service on loudspeakers.

Someone sees me outside before the service starts and tells me I look good. I have aviator sunglasses on. This makes me appear cooler than I am. Fuck it, why not? I am wearing a black shirt and light brown tweed pants that happen to be my favorite. As a matter of fact, I do look good. I have a kick-ass eulogy in my pocket and I am surrounded by a bunch of people that I love. They are all here to pay their respects. They are there to show support for me, my parents, my grandmothers and the countless other family members in attendance. It is a display of grief from all of her friends who have failed her since she came back home. They never call her or check in on how she is doing. They generally don't give a shit during the last few years that she is sick. They are all here now. It is sad seeing them jockey for position in the grandstands. The outpouring of grief feels false. They mourn the passing of someone who they've shown no interest in. Whatever, they get a pass, being around sick people is depressing. I'm her brother and I did the same thing. Who am I to judge?

At the cemetery I see Lynn. She is someone who understands death. She's not here to be seen, she's here for me, because she understands exactly what I'm going through. Before the service starts, we walk over to where her mom is freshly buried. The grave site is a short walk from where the funeral is located. It is the first time I have been to her mom's grave and it comforts me. I am lucky to have her there.

The service begins. I insist on choosing some of the music that is to be played during it. The fact that Barry Manilow and Celine Dion are featured prominently in the funeral does not sit well with me. It is a nightmare scenario of musical choices that my parents insist on including. I am not amused. I can only imagine what my sister's reaction would be. I lobby hard to include music at the end of the processional, and am rewarded with two Moby songs making the official funeral playlist. Mandy's first two choices of songs would, without doubt, include something from Sublime and something from Phish. These are songs that are confusing to my parents. She dies without writing a will that explicitly demands what music should be played at her funeral. This allows my parents to pick what songs are played. They agree to play my two selections at the end of the service only after they listen to them and deem them to be inoffensive. It is a small victory, but a victory nonetheless.

The service isn't especially long. My dad goes up the podium and says a few words. A song is played. My aunt has her opportunity to say a few words. Another song is played. Before I know it, it is my turn to talk. I am calm when I stand up, and I remain calm as I make my way up to the stage.

I get behind the podium and turned around to face the audience. The room is packed with people. Every seat is taken. The aisles running along each side of the cathedral are packed, standing room only. The only free space is the center aisle. Behind the last row of seats is a mass of people that continues out the door and into the outside patio. I take it all in. I told my parents that the venue isn't big enough. They don't believe me. Ha. I know what I'm talking about, bitches. Shit, there are a lot of people waiting for me to say something. I should get started.

I take another look. I scan the crowd. I take my time. I say nothing. I reach into my pocket and find my rosary. I pull out the speech, take a deep breath and begin to talk. It isn't hard to write what I am going to say at the funeral. There isn't any doubt that I would get up there and articulate what a brother goes through when he loses his only sister. I do not disappoint.

<u>My Eulogy for Mandy</u>

At the Forehan's house there is a large red bowl.
It is stored in a cupboard in the kitchen for the sole
purpose of throwing up when one of us is sick.
When Mandy first moved home and after she became ill, the
bowl made frequent visits to her room when needed.
It would then be cleaned and then returned to the kitchen.
By the end of Mandy's battle, the red bowl has its own spot in her room.
It is near her bed, under an end table.
It is in a convenient location.
It finds itself being consistently used.
The Red bowl lived in her room for the better part of almost two years.
I returned from the hospital after my sister died and
sat on a small strip of grass in the front yard.
The day was clear.
The day was hot.
The day was absolutely gorgeous.
I remember wondering if that was appropriate or not.
Then I see my mom get home.
She walks into the house.
A few minutes later she reappears carrying the red bowl.
She walks directly to the garage and tosses it in the trash.

She notices that I am watching her.
She turns to me and says
"We won't be needing this anymore."
At that moment I knew that Mandy's struggle was over.
I watch my mom throw the red bowl in the trash.
All the pain that my sister endured is thrown away at the same time.
My mother is done with facing the pain.
The uncertainty of my sister's life is now a concluded memory.
For the duration of her sickness, I had a hard time seeing past her illness.
After living with something for so long I lost the
memory of Mandy as a sister and as a friend.
All I saw was the actuality of her sickness and the pain she went through.
The day to day struggle brought a fog over the childhood I shared with
my only sibling and distorted my view of her as a young adult.
Seeing the red bowl in the trash brings back the real
Mandy and the positivity she evokes so effortlessly.
I am able to detach myself from the painful memories
so I can focus on the ones worth remembering.
In effect there are two separate Mandy's.
There is the sick one that brings a memory of helplessness that eats at
my heart because I wasn't able to do anything to ease her pain.
There is also the other side of Mandy. It is the one who still
dances in my dreams and still smiles in my heart.
Destroying the red bowl allows me to throw away all the memories of my
sick sister so I can focus solely on the time that she was able to really live.
I now look back and can only see the times when my
sister was the vibrant beauty of her youth.
I see her in San Francisco with her eccentric friends.
I see her strange sense of style.
I see her frightening driving techniques.
I see her unique perspective on life.
More importantly though, when I think of Mandy I
see a clear and vivacious vision of her face.
This vision of her enters into my mind effortlessly.
She smiles back at me.
She looks at me in that sardonic way.

It is a look that only Mandy knows how to give.
She says to me how gnarly this whole thing has been
and then she tells me that everything will be okay.

I take one last look at the crowd and then walk off the stage. Another song is played, another person speaks, and then the funeral is over. I can finally let go of the rosary in my pocket. Surviving the past few days wouldn't have been possible without them. Before Mitch flies to California his dad gives him a rosary that he wants me to have. I am not Catholic, and don't plan on converting into one, but I am touched by his gesture. God I love this man.

I keep the rosary in my pocket in the days leading up to the funeral. It doesn't leave my side. Anytime I start to lose control, I pull it out and hold onto it. I hold it in my hand throughout the ceremony. I have been holding onto it since Mitch shows up and gives it to me. He finally comes through for me the day Mandy dies. I call, he answers. I need him, and when he gets on a plane immediately, I know he's truly there for me. It is finally confirmed that he really does care. I am finally convinced that he loves me, he loves her and he loves my family. He shows up and we have one of those "oh so good to see you, it's been a tough couple of days hugs." We spend the days leading up to the funeral milling around, going for lunch, and drinking beer.

A few days after the funeral, I find myself at my favorite bar. I watch the conflicting emotions zoom past me with reckless abandon. Going to a bar with a few friends I stumble into a so-called Rossmoor event that surrounds my cocktails with pieces of my past and those who share memories with my sister. I have become a reluctant celebrity. The first to lose a sibling, the first to step into the void associated with the concept of "never again." I am the prototype for pain, loss, and confusion. I walk into the bar, a long sleeve yellow shirt on, jeans, and flip- flops. At first glance I only see the usual patrons of my life. Kids from high school, friends of friends. Then I see the concerned looks gather on their faces. They came to the funeral partly because my sister died and partly because it was the happening spot to be at. All Rossmoor kids seek is the next party and a ride to that party. I don't blame them. I do the same exact thing. I make my way to the back of the bar and see the crowd I have been looking for.

The girls of my youth rush to me in an orderly procession. I know they do this out of both want and need. I am harmless and broken and I am their friend. I am the lost drunk in a sea of alcoholics. Drink in hand, kiss, hug, kiss, hug, I weave and slide through the enthusiasm, the small talk and the bullshit.

I need to get out of dodge. I leave for Big Sur the next day. A couple of second cousins gave me a few hundred dollars the day of the funeral. They tell me to use it to take a trip. This is exactly what I do. I take off by myself and head north. I clear my head, listen to loud music and come back a few days later refreshed, and feeling better than I have in a long time. My sister is dead which means that she isn't suffering anymore. Her death frees my parents from the constant worry that has taken over their lives. Her death frees me from the guilt of not spending time with her and hating her when she is sick. Her death gives us our lives back.

A few months later I will go to a casual acquaintance's funeral. He is someone I know through the group of older guys I work with at the bagel shop. He is a well-known guy who I am definitely on a first name basis with, but there isn't a concrete reason for me to be there except that my sister was also one of his friends. He is a year older than she was, so there is a chance that her friends will be there too. I go because I want to be surrounded by people feeling that hurt again. It has been a few months since she has died and I need to be reminded of what happens when a family loses a member. I need them to see that I am still here, still fucked up, and unable to figure out what to do next. I do not know what to do next. I still do not know what to do next.

18

Tiny Scabs

Dear James,

It is nobody's fault but my own. I cannot put the blame on anybody else. I am guilty of being me. For this, I apologize. No satire has ever been directed towards your hypocritical super fascist ass. The bottom line is that I have less than I did before. The shakes that control my hands, the sweat that sometimes beads my forehead, the realization that I need to stop, doesn't heal the sores in my nose. And that's the worst part. The sores. Little tiny scabs that can't possibly heal because my nose is always wet. Little spots. I can handle the fancy for a quick little fix. I can handle these nights of Jesus knows what the fuck what where I go insane: again. But these sores hurt. And I know what will fix it. Telling people I have a cold. Telling people the weather is making my nose dry. Fucking idiots. They are all fucking new. They don't even, no can't even believe they can begin to start to fucking imagine. These sores. These little insignificant sores that no one can fucking see. I have been off for nine days. Shit constantly in my fucking nose. I know how to fix it. But shouldn't I be worried about something else? No. I can't think of anything else, and then I start to crave it just when I think I'm…Fuck. Time for a drink perhaps.

D. Tanzarian

Sportsman (day),
Reno Room (still day),
Home.

THERE ARE CERTAIN aspects of my life that don't make sense. I recognize that I am spiraling out of control but I don't know how to stop it. I understand that I am fucked up but I can't figure out a way to fix it. I know I have problems but I don't know what the solution is. I am bleeding profusely and cannot find a fucking *Band-Aid*.

I look down at my thigh and see an open wound staring back at me. My bullshit solution to stop the flow of blood involving paper towels and scotch tape is failing miserably. The problem is not fixed. It is only delayed for a brief moment. It keeps the blood from flowing down my leg for the time being. It is briefly contained and then the dam breaks. The scotch tape loses its precarious grip on the paper towels. The paper towels continue to get heavier as they get more saturated with blood. The tape isn't strong enough. It gives way and blood starts to run down my legs.

Crows,

Home.

The blood flows over my thighs and down my calves. It ruins the carpet. I can't wrap my head around explaining why there are blood stains on the carpet. It doesn't make any sense. I can't get my head around it. All I know for certain is that I am bleeding. I know that I am the one responsible. I know that I just cut myself and I'm not entirely sure why. I know that this isn't the first time, and may not be the last time. I know this hasn't happened for a while. I know that I am due. I know for sure that this isn't on the night's agenda. It is not something I plan on doing. I don't realize that I am due. It isn't something I believe in. It seems to be something I rely on.

Home.

Fuck that. It isn't something that I plan on doing. It isn't something that I want to do. I don't rationalize the act of cutting myself. I can't even respect the act of doing it. It is something that just happens. I have no control over it. It happens when I least expect it. I am minding my own business. I am content. I am peacefully folding laundry and minding my own business. Two seconds later I am bleeding, and don't know why. Without any reason and without any warning I find myself dragging a sharp razor blade across my bare skin.

Home.

One minute, I can be found focusing on folding my underwear and t-shirts. The next moment finds me cutting myself for no reason and bleeding all over the wash. I can't even think of a reason why I would do it. There is no reason to cut myself and ruin the carpet. Maybe I have one. But I don't want to go into that just yet...

Crows,

Home.

Recapping the current situation is easy. Sister dies. Mitch is gone (thanks for the visit), and I am alone in Long Beach. I am getting as fucked up as humanly possible no less than five times a week. I work at a restaurant and start to substitute teach a few days a week. The teaching turns into an everyday assignment. This is good for me because it pays well and it helps me get out of debt. It is bad for me because I have to wake up every morning at the butt-crack of dawn. This helps me to afford to buy more cocaine (yeah.). This ensures that I never get enough sleep (boo.). My only option is to burn the candle at both ends. I am so tired, like all of the time.

Sportsman (day),

Home,

Reno Room,

Red Room,

Home.

The madness never stops. The simple act of cleaning my house doesn't happen sober anymore. The moment I realize the house needs cleaning is the moment I get in my car and pick up a package. I drive to a bar called *Birds* and see the bartender. This is where I pick up a bag of the white devil. I stay at the bar for a few drinks and then go back home and clean the mother fucker.

Home.

Smoke cigarettes inside? *Sure.* Drink as much as possible? *Why not? Smoke* the tail end of the resin left in the pipe that is hidden away in my underwear drawer? *Yes, yes, yes.* Lay awake all night without being able to go to sleep? *Not the preferable way to live, but okay, why not.* Wake up at least twice a week and go to Mom's school to substitute? No problem. Do all this while operating on no more than two hours of sleep? *Absofuckinglutely.*

Red Room,
Home,
Red Room,
Home.

My routine begins. I work a lot. I sleep little. I drink too much. I eat too little. I slowly go insane. We start to paint the inside of my illegally rented shack-style house. The attempt to carry the painting outside doesn't last beyond the front door. The only thing we paint outside of the house is a tiny section of the front door. The front door is painted a shade of blue that people in the paint industry call "Deep Blue". It is considered to be two shades lighter than the darker version of blue they refer to as "Dark Blue." The rest of the house is stucco. Except for the front door, the entire house is painted white. This is something that I have spent a limited amount of time contemplating. The outside of the house is white, this is normal. The front door is blue, this is not normal, but who gives a fuck?

Home.

I invite my cousin to stay for the weekend. He is going to school in Santa Barbara. It is a two hour drive for him and it is time that we start to see each other more often. I have a few questions to ask him. I picked up a package that is larger than usual. It has been implied, yet never confirmed between us, that in fact we both enjoy the consumption of certain stimulants. As I wait for him to come over, I get more and more nervous. It's like I'm about to ask him on a date to go to Knott's Berry Farm and I'm not sure if he even likes roller coasters.

Home.

He arrives at the house and we immediately start to drink. There is never any doubt that he drinks because we do it together every Thanksgiving, Easter and Christmas. I finally get up the nerve and ask him what his official stance is on cocaine consumption and whether or not he would like to snort some up his nose at this very moment.

Still Home.

He turns towards me with one slightly raised eyebrow and the beginnings of a smile. It just so happens that his official stance on this particular issue is one of complete support. Apparently, his entire campaign loves to advocate such activities.

Home.

This is how I find out that my cousin dabbles in the same fucked up activities that I do. This is when he finds out the same exact thing about me. This is when we start to really get to know each other. After tonight, there is no looking back. With or without drugs we get closer and closer. I find the brother I never had in the form of a cousin I have always known.

Home,

Red Room,

Home.

The first night doing drugs with someone is always interesting. Most of the time it leads to good things. The conversation leads to places that would never be possible without the aid of the white powdery devil. Doing drugs for the first time with my cousin is exponentially better. I've known this fucker for almost my entire life. He is two years younger than me so he has known me his whole life. Since I have limited memories of my childhood during years 0-2, I figure that we have known each other an equal amount of time.

Home.

We grew up together. We have a shared family history. This is a history that is also very different. Our childhoods share the same grandparents and very little else. This is the perfect drug to share with him at this stage of our lives. Any lingering issues or unanswered questions from our childhoods are discussed in detail. No subject is off limits, no small detail is deemed to be too small, nobody's feelings are hurt. We end up talking until the sun comes up. Josh figures out a way to stencil **"THE BLUE DOOR"** in white paint on the outside of the front door. Taking into account that it happens to be painted blue we consider ourselves to be extremely clever people.

Home.

Now I finally have something to call the place where I live. Technically it isn't a house. It doesn't have a tin roof, so I don't feel comfortable referring to it as a shack. The presence of windows, regardless of how small they are, eliminate my ability to call it a cave. The presence of running water means that I can't call it a fire hazard. Wait, no... that is exactly what it is. Fuck, I can't call it that. My search for a name that is suitable for such a house continues. What is the name that is commonly given my place of residence? A rectangular shaped garage that recently was turned into an illegal non-house with a fucking bathroom smack dab in the middle of the hallway, limited windows, an old couch, an empty fridge and a kitchen that has the faint smell of gas that is never fixed? This place has a name. It has an identity. Starting now and continuing on until I move out. We will call this place **THE BLUE DOOR**

Red Room,

Pike,

Iguana Kelly's,

Home.

It starts out so well. A new beginning. Nothing holds back the various forms of excess. Nothing holds back my potential to discover brilliance. When it doesn't immediately come, I don't get discouraged, I just tell myself to try harder. I make proclamations to nobody in particular. I announce my intentions late at night. I imagine my audience hanging on every word I say. I have to imagine the audience because currently there isn't one. There is nobody with me. I am alone. This doesn't prevent me from standing up to boldly say the following:

James: *So this is now decreed. I shall hereby make the following resolution. Every day I will get ideas down. No more time will be wasted. No more television. Sacrifices must be made. I will get this shit done. I have the will. I have the time. I have the passion. I will do this shit.*

Home.

Nothing ends up getting done. I pass out and fifteen hours later I find myself fucked up again but this time I am surrounded by people. This starts to happen a lot. I start to see the activities happening before me in another way altogether. Nothing makes sense anymore.

Home.

At certain times I hear my front door open and I know I'll be okay for a while. Other times I quietly close my eyes and hope that someday I won't have to answer to anyone. Any form of justification is too much for my narrow focus to handle. Any and all speaking requires a level of commitment that is beyond my abilities. This house of cards no doubt collapses the moment I have to give an explanation that involves the fictional existence that is currently taking over my life. The phone rings and I can hardly look to see who is calling, let alone answer the fucking thing. I'm too afraid to answer it and allow myself to be subjected to the potential dedication that might come along once I answer it. Yes, I am coked up.

Home.

I need help beyond all understanding. I don't know how to complete myself in a way that I can respect. What change in wardrobe can I make that will turn me into a thriving adult? What new pair of shoes will stop me from being a tragic failure awash in silence and solitude? Jesus, silence and solitude? Fuck me. I try darker shades of jeans and purchase a new pair of Vans to no avail. At the end of every day I still feel the need to cut myself.

Home.

And this is what starts to happen. It mirrors my involvement in cocaine. It starts slow, every once in a while, which leads to more often than not before I know it. This leads to a habit. I have no clue how it turned into a habit but there is no way to deny that it has turned into one. And before I know it, it takes over. Once a month turns into once a week. Now it happens twice a week. This is when I promise myself a break. Two days later, I will use again. I will use again the next day. This is when I tend to stop, but on occasion I can't, and my bender goes into another day.

Home,
Pike Bar,
Home.

The cutting occurs when the blow is gone. When I am forced to deal with the after effects. I choose areas that I only consider to be within a reasonable scope of practicality. I don't cut too deep or too long. I have medicated bandages close at hand, just in case. More times than not, I end up using paper towels held in place by whatever tape I can find nearby. As long as the bandages hold together, it doesn't matter what tape I use. My first choice is masking, second is scotch, and third is electric. Worst–case–scenario involves the use of duct tape. This does the job but is never fun to take off the next day.

Belmont Brew Co.,

Reno Room,
Home.

This is not something to take pride in. This is not the healthiest way to deal with emotional pain. Most people don't feel the need to pop the balloon to let the air out, unfortunately this is the only way I know how. I would prefer to go to the batting cages when I feel overwhelmed. I imagine that if I had a younger brother I could torture him. I would much rather take my frustrations out on my fictional smaller sibling when I start to lose it. A younger brother comes in handy when these situations arise. But alas, my parents were short-sighted when they stopped producing heirs after me. As it is, this is the way I attempt to stay normal. I don't even know where the closest batting cages are, my bat is in my parent's garage, and that is the *last* place I want to drive over to at this particular moment.

Home.

I continue to cut myself. I remain conscious to avoid drawing additional attention to my bullshit. This is why I make sure to cut in places that are easy to cover up. I know that I am fucked up. I know that I need help. I know that there are at least a hundred better ways to deal with having the blues. The physical pain gets my mind off the larger issues at hand. The physical pain doesn't worry me nearly as much as the mental pain does. As long as I am aware of my own hilarity, and until something changes, I don't see any reason to stop coping in a way that confuses and freaks out the few people who know about it. As long as I recognize the flaws of choosing this particular coping mechanism, I have faith that I will be okay.

Sportsman,
Home.

Okay doesn't happen. Instead of okay I finally hit rock bottom. Okay feels like shit. It becomes clear to me that it is not okay to feel like this. Okay sucks. Okay is *not* okay. The moment I figured this out was when I bought 40 ounces of Old English Malt Liquor with the spare change in my apartment. This is when I proudly ignore all the self-respect I was once known to carry within myself on a daily basis. Self-respect no longer has anything to do with how I project my day to day activities. Self-respect disappears the moment I replace it by committing to dangerous lifestyle choices. Every single circumstance that is beyond my control becomes magnified by all the poor decisions I seem to be making.

Red Room,
V-Room,
Home.

Regret only comes when I allow it to. Regret is getting more and more difficult to fight off. I find it harder to embrace each morning I find myself still awake, wide eyed and smoking cigarettes at ten in the morning. The enthusiasm I once felt for mornings such as these is waning fast. The excitement is gone. It is replaced with dull predictability. The act of challenging the night for no reason once made perfect sense. Now it just makes me tired.

Home.

The night wins. It always does. Sleep is a necessary evil. I don't have the strength to fight against it anymore. I fear what happens if I give up the battle. I cower in the face of what replaces the madness.

El Torito (with parents),
El Torito Bar (without),
Home.

I genuinely need my life to be less complicated. I need simplicity to take over every aspect of my day to day operations. This is blocked by my need to release all of this innate bullshit. I can't handle holding back the only thing I find the most value in. Any attempt will feel wrong. I can't ignore my instinctive drive to be the most interesting person circulating the room.

Reno Room,
36/36,
Home.

Soon enough, reality sets in. No matter how late I stay up, no matter whom I spend my time with and no matter how many nights I donate to charity. I realize that I still haven't said shit. My nights continue to be void of anything real. My nights are continuously failing to benefit my peers in a constructive manner. I am left with two options. Option #1 involves sobriety, recovery and sanity. Option #2 tells me how ridiculous an option #1 is and tries to convince me to do the exact opposite. It becomes perfectly clear to me what I should do. Detoxifying, weekly appointments with a therapist and exercise are never seriously considered. I see the benefits of participating in these activities. I get it. I just don't care enough about myself to make such a healthy choice. I'm still young. My body can handle the daily assault of hazardous chemicals for a few more years. I might as well say fuck it and stay up all night. I can still dodge committing to respectable plans. Dinner, drinks and conversation with stable friends can be avoided for just a bit longer. I'll skip dinner and go straight to drinks with my unstable friends for the time being. They don't ask as many questions.

Crow's,
Home.

The decision to continue to live in this alternative secret existence isn't hard to make. The majority of my time I spend with the people I consider to be my true friends. These are people I have known since childhood. These are the friends that I have known forever and will continue to be close to for years to come. I keep the majority of these people in the dark. Aside from the few that are intimately involved with drugs, the majority of my friends don't have the slightest clue. They are kept completely in the dark and have no reason to suspect that I have a secret life.

Red Room,
Pike,
Red Room,
Home.

This is the part of my life they wouldn't understand. This is something that needs to be hidden. My brilliant journey through the sour world of drugs, death and decay no doubt would be lost on their delicate sensibilities. Attempting to explain the reasons why I chose to involve myself in such activities would no doubt fall on deaf ears. Instead of subjecting my friends to lifestyles beyond their ability to understand I pretend that no such lifestyle exists where I am concerned. What is out of sight is also out of mind. This gives me the opportunity to remove myself from conventional methods of living. No more time is wasted on silly attempts to keep my daily activities hidden from friends and family. I focus all my efforts in searching for the next high. The maximum amount of stimulation is required so I can stay busy and remain as productive as humanly fucking possible.

AM I FUCKED UP NOW? IT APPEARS THAT I AM. NOW WHAT?

Red Room,
Home (eventually).

I have no fucking clue where I am at this given moment. I have no idea why I am here, let alone what brought me here in the first place. I won't even attempt to figure out what methods were taken to get me here. Your guess is as good as mine. I won't find out where I am until I go outside and walk to the nearest street sign. Before I do that, I look around. I am in a random apartment. I am alone. No clock. Phone is dead. I walk over to the mirror and see my reflection in it. I look like shit. Oh, and half of one of my front teeth is missing. Fuck. No sunglasses. This is going to be a long walk home. Just another night that doesn't add up.

House Party,
Red Room,
Not my Home,
Home.

I arrive back home broken. I take what is left of my frazzled mind and give it a once over. Soon enough I've been sitting on the same couch in Long Beach for months and nobody has put two and two together. I am totally clear of all notoriety. I shouldn't have gone so big last night. How can I expect myself to make things proper without the benefits of sleep? I'm trying to get organized as the summer fades away. Another opportunity for a fresh start is right in front of me. It is time to take advantage of the moment and stop wasting every chance I get to lead a more respectable life.

Hennesy's,
O'Malleys,
Irisher,
Home.

My history of poor decisions is a direct result of chain-smoking-the-morning-away. It leads to a frantic search for weed to smoke after staying up all night. It leads to a desperate search to find anything that will help me close my eyes so I can fall asleep. It leads to spending the calm quiet of the early morning wide awake and totally miserable. All these poor choices leave me disillusioned. I am wary of what happens next. I stop having an interest in what will happen next.

Red Room,
V-Room,
Home.

Another night of excess is followed by another day wasted. It is almost dawn. I should be asleep. I should be waking up soon. I should wake up reinvigorated by having just slept for the last six to eight hours. I should wake up refreshed. I should open my eyes, take no longer than a minute to wake up and then immediately get to work. I can't figure out why I don't bounce out of bed full of pep within the first minute I wake up each morning. I can't figure out why I don't begin each day full of enthusiasm to tackle whatever challenges that may face me in the day ahead. Most days don't start in the morning hours. On the rare occasion that this happens I make sure to fall back asleep until it is considered to be part of the afternoon. I have no interest in how the day starts. Nothing about the middle part of the day I find curious. I don't even want to be involved with the time after that. My only interest is when the day is over. I cannot wait for the day to end.

19

The Pressures of Becoming an Only Child

THE RECKLESS ACTIVITIES and confused sleep patterns dislodge all sense of growth and prosperity. I back myself into a corner and the only way I can rebound is to attempt a complete head change. After ten months of living in constant manicured creativity I finally remember that it is nice to have food in the house. I remember the benefits of having money in my bank account. My attempt to remember what it feels like to wake up without a hangover is unsuccessful but I can imagine what this used to feel like. This doesn't lead to any immediate purchasing of amenities beyond basic survival food, but the idea is planted in my head. My reaction time is too slow and I continue to put off grocery shopping. I haven't done it for the last six months, with the exception of my trips to 7-11 to buy bags of potato chips. It is a sad and hungry way to live.

I'm under the illusion that my life is a made-for-cable mini-series. I direct, as well as star, in the story of a handsome guy who takes a break from his life of eco-terrorism. While on sabbatical from fire-bombing Hummer dealerships, he lives a secret existence as a super nice guy living in an illegal apartment in Long Beach. To keep up appearances he pretends to be a proponent for underachieving, blatant alcoholism and rampant drug addiction. This is when he finds himself on the brink of falling off a tall mountain during a risky hostage rescue mission. The meat of the story hasn't been worked out entirely yet, but in the series finale it all comes together and the handsome hero comes out on top and as a better person. Shooting starts in the very near future. I'm just waiting for the shooting locations to be finalized. I have this going for me, which is nice.

Leaving Long Beach is the only possible way to ensure my survival. I have to disappear from everything I know and everything I find comfort in. Leaving Long Beach is totally necessary only because I find myself in a repetitive cycle that leads nowhere. It only leads to my destruction. My problems start the moment I am given a valid excuse to fail. Going through the death of my sister allows me to fall into unsound behaviors. My actions finally catch up with me. The only solution I can come up with is to remove myself from Long Beach as quickly as possible.

For the duration of the time my sister was sick, I am the fortunate recipient of a life that lacks serious scrutiny from my parents. Their priorities shift once Mandy comes home. The focus turns from figuring out "who just called James" to "finding a way to keep their daughter alive." Priorities change in an instant. Who gives a shit about James's social life? They don't have the time or energy to ask about such silliness. And this is when their questions stop. The constant pestering ends right then and there. I spent the last two years flying under their radar.

The semi-mutually agreed upon exile from parental analysis ends after Mandy passes away. Every department under their control is redirected and given new priorities. All resources are directed in my direction. Every hope or dream they had for Mandy is transferred over to me. Every expectation they had for her they now have for me. If this isn't the cause of her death, then it most likely will be mine. All of the pressures and expectations of achieving greatness are handed over to me the moment I join the ranks of "only children" when she dies.

The scrutiny must be overwhelming. Being an only child must be tough. Two parents dividing their time to keep tabs on their lone child. The seven-year-old has no chance when up against two adults. Being an only child in a family leads to no good. It is the only way to grow up in a truly flawed household. A childhood spent in solitude leads to an adulthood spent in more solitude. This allows parents to continue to harass their children with impunity.

Growing up as an only child has its hardships, this is without doubt. Whatever trials they endure they do alone. That sucks, as I am finding out. Becoming an only child for the first time at the age of twenty-two is just plain weird. Nobody knows what to do. Nobody has the first clue how to act. My parents are more lost than I am. A lifetime spent relying on the fourth member of our family is no longer an option for anyone. Surviving adolescence, puberty and high school together nearly broke us. Spending our adult lives together was going to mend those old wounds. They surely won't be as challenging. We are all now considered to be grown up. We are finally all adults. We can spend the future years creating new memories. Our family dynamics will change for the better. Everything will make sense.

Nothing ends up making much sense. The scrutiny that is given to those who have recently become an only child becomes almost impossible to endure. I am new to the club and I have a hard time figuring out how to handle it. I need a break from all the focus currently directed towards me. My parents mean well. They have no ulterior motive other than keeping me close by. This creates a problem because the majority of my daily activities involve doing things that are, without a doubt, things that they wouldn't approve of. It is only a matter of time before they witness me snorting coke between the fake tits of a stripper in the bathroom of a Holiday Inn Express. Nobody benefits and everyone loses if this scenario is allowed to happen. The only chance I have to find salvation doesn't happen unless I leave everything behind and make an honest attempt to find something genuine.

I assume that the city of Long Beach desperately needs me to continue the steady monetary contributions I give to the treasury in the form of parking tickets. These tickets are usually thrown in the back seat and are of little concern to me, considering I have *weeks* to take care of them. Surely I will take care of it in a few days. This never happens, and months later they start to pile up. This is not wise. This is why I never have any money. I realize the intelligent move is to see the bill, write a check, and then immediately send the mother fucker. This involves the avoidance of late fees and extra charges. Shit. I parked on the wrong side of the street, here's thirty five dollars for the inconvenience and I'll be on my way. Three easy things that will make the ticket go away:

Step #1 - Bring it inside the house.

Step #2 - Find a checkbook, write a check, place in envelope, write return address on top left, place a stamp on the top right, lick it and seal.

Step #3 - Put it in the local mailbox.

This is easier said than done. I am able to complete steps #1 and #2 but am unable to carry out step #3. I have a plan. It is a painfully simple one. It involves a multitude of options. I give it to the postman who comes to my house on a daily basis, I pull over when I drive by a mailbox, or I take it to the actual post office. Any of these actions would ensure its delivery. All of these actions seem too difficult to handle.

Weeks later I'm driving in my car. I'm reaching behind me in the search for something hiding somewhere within the paper and trash. To my surprise and disappointment I find the stamped envelopes that contain yet-to-be-mailed parking tickets. They're still in my possession, still not mailed, still in my car. I hold them in my hand knowing I can't drive past another mailbox. These fuckers are going to be mailed today, as in, right now.

As I pull up to the mailbox the envelopes let out a sigh of relief. They look up at me with sad eyes and thank me for putting an end to their waiting. They lock the doors and don't let me mail them until I hear them out. They insist that I turn off the car and give them my undivided attention. Out of respect I do what they ask and listen attentively.

After learning about the history of the US Postal Service and the evolution of the modern envelope, they tell me how it feels to be stuck in a car for weeks on end. They tell me how it feels to be forgotten. They tell me stories of neglect and disrespect I did not know to be possible in this day and age. All an envelope wants is to be involved in the exchange of goods or information. As long as it is busy going somewhere and doing something it is content. After all, that's why they are made. An envelope thrives on its unique ability to transport papers and documents through the mail. If go to the trouble of addressing, stamping and licking close these envelopes, then what the fuck? They are ready to complete the specific job they are good at and enter the complicated process that is required of them so they can complete their journey to the City Hall of Long Beach.

But I fail. These envelopes go no further than the back seat of my Civic. Their mission is not complete. Their purpose is unfulfilled. They are destined to be delivered to City Hall. Their motivation is never in doubt, their commitment is never questioned. These envelopes are inspired and full of desire. Resolve. Unfortunately, I lack their enthusiasm for delivery and forget about their existence.

When found, they are still considered to be worthy of mailing, despite the small tears and the wrinkles. Their core is almost broken. All the time spent forgotten in the back seat leads to waning enthusiasm. Their spirit evaporates as they anticipate going somewhere day after day. Their disappointment builds as they continually go nowhere. They lose hope after the deadline passes to arrive on time and gradually flourish when the parking ticket doubles from a modest thirty-five dollar mistake into something substantially more expensive.

They stare back at me annoyed and irritated. They have been ready to go for weeks. They are supposed to be speedily delivered to their destination. They are sorely mistaken. Worst case scenario is to be placed in the mailbox after the pickup time and have to spend the night in a mailbox. They are assured to be picked up the next day and are on their way to their next destination. Within a day or two they show up at the address, are opened, and then thrown away as trash without a second thought. Their job is done, they did it well, they go to envelope heaven and are met with the respect given to those who do a job well. Ripped open and discarded upon arrival leads to the envelope brimming with pride and dying with a smile on its face.

Envelope Hell involves spending months in the back of a Civic underneath a stack of papers, a plastic cup, an old fast food wrapper and a dirty pair of pants. Envelope purgatory is when it is moved to the front seat of my car. This can last for various amounts of time. It usually ends when there is a spot in front of the mail box which doesn't require a U- turn. Whatever. Mailing things is dumb.

The Blue Door is starting to fall apart. I have lost the opportunity to make things right. I am unable to turn my gradual descent towards failure back into a fragile climb back up towards legitimacy. I have nothing to do but wonder what could have been. I am alone. I do not allow myself to second guess my choices. I will not allow myself to be consumed with doubt. I cannot allow disappointment to take over my life.

The walls are caving in. Everything is going too fast. It is way too quick and it is out of control. This is beyond my tiny ability to handle. This confuses me. This leaves me with a single option. I prefer not to yell but am left with no choice.

WHAT THE FUCK IS HAPPENING?????

The foundation is crumbling. My confused desperation is now starting to take over my able body. Rational explanations are lost. Logic has left the building. I am the only one left. The wise have made correct decisions. Sharing this debauchery of a lifestyle with old friends has ended and now I am sharing it with new friends. These are glorified strangers moonlighting as friends. The authorities who carry my best interests are nowhere to be found. They are miles away from what I still find myself neck deep in. They quit smoking months ago. Me? Not so much. They leave the excessive pace. I'm still searching for a way out.

Broken pipes lead to flooding in the hallway/ bathroom. After repeated attempts to find it, I finally succeed. I stumble into a place where my exhaustion finally catches up to me. I have no more fight left. I sit down and stop worrying. I sit there and let my mind wander without distraction. I open a new document on my computer and start to write. My fingers can't keep up with the brilliance that is flooding my brain. Every word is perfect, every sentence is better than the one before. This is my Kerouac moment. When he is hopped up on beanies, mind working in overdrive, his fingers typing so fast that he had to use a roll of paper instead of individual sheets, so he didn't have to waste precious time loading new pages of paper every few minutes. This is my moment to start the next writing generation. This is when I pen my *On the Road*.

Shattered glass everywhere. I finally begin to contemplate my invisible virtue. My life finally finds the necessary bottom. It is a grand exit. It is so much more than that. No more confusion. The explanation is no longer beyond me. I know what is left to do. My tumble down a flight of stairs is just a pathetic reflection of my prior priorities. My disproportionate response to despair ignores the logic and takes over. Sadness permeates my core belief systems.

The roof is leaking. I don't end up writing shit that night, let alone anything that makes sense. The plan is now clear. Time to focus on artwork that involves paint and go back to writing at a later date. I can't leave Long Beach with a clear conscience until the walls are done. Every inch of space gradually becomes a necessary ingredient to the monopoly the project has over me. It controls my life. I am convinced that I lack a specific reason to move and therefore won't be granted the required paperwork allowing me to.

Fucking Termites. I lack the ability to continue this art project the moment the free space is gone. I don't know how to operate anymore and don't want to return to spending my evenings with nothing to do. It is time to leave the fine city of Long Beach. There is no space left on the walls to paint. The casual brilliance once expressed on a nightly basis is over. The art produced during the era of THE BLUE DOOR has lost its relevance. It has become stale. Individuality is easy to forget and it is time to go. The run is over and the moment to flee is before me. The walls are all used up. There is no place left to paint. It is time to go. It is time to find the end of the world...

20

The Invasion of Iraq

I SEE HER CHECKING me out from across the bar. It is one of those looks that mean business. I am at the tail end of a serious bender that started yesterday. I am operating on no sleep, haven't eaten anything more substantial than chips in what feels like a month and have already spent the majority of my afternoon in the other dive bar down the street. Against all odds, I am still awake, still alive and still going strong at the Irish Pub *O'Malley's* in Seal Beach later that night. She has straight, shoulder length blonde hair. She is skinny. She is cute. She keeps catching my eye.

As the night progresses I find myself in a spirited debate about the impending U.S. invasion of Iraq. I spit out whatever bullshit I can think of to make my point. Anything that will sway the conservative (9/11= Saddam= invasion) friend who I find myself arguing with. I bring out my A game to bring down his point of view, one that obviously shows that he doesn't know what he is talking about and clearly needs to be destroyed by my words. I am in the middle of an eloquent argument that is sure to degrade every dispute he planned on throwing at me when I am distracted by the same mysterious blond that smiled at me before and is currently walking by our table.

Before I notice her passing by, she notices my side of the argument. This leads to her lingering just long enough to hear out whatever leftist principle I am trying to explain to my poor, misinformed friend. The argument ends without either of us accepting each other's point of view. Nobody concedes anything and nobody backs down from their beliefs. We leave the table without learning anything new. We leave without considering for a moment to support what the other person is saying. The most constructive thing that happens is when we walk away. We leave content and satisfied for spending the last hour of our Friday night yelling at one another. We part ways without listening to anything the other person has to say. We get up, embrace one another and go our separate ways without any regret. Neither one of us grows or develops as a person in any way whatsoever during this debate.

The difference between us is that when he leaves the table, he walks back into the bar, orders a fresh drink, rejoins his friends, gets drunk and walks home. When I leave the table and walk back into the bar I see the same hot blond. She is checking me out and is waiting for me to make a move and introduce myself. My friend's right wing ideology leads to getting another drink and going home alone. My brand of liberalism leads to something more. I talk a good game. I am focused on feeding the poor, finding a way to bring equality to the masses, and letting the kids eat breakfast before school, dammit. My brand of liberalism is long on ideas and short on actions. The fact that I do nothing to feed the less fortunate, fail miserably to bring equality to the populace, and do nothing to bring free-or-reduced breakfast to urban schools doesn't stop me from sitting down next to her. I introduce myself and start to get to know her. Who wins the debate? I do. War in the Middle East is a bad idea. Those in favor walk home, jerk off and pass out. Those opposed meet a girl and take her home.

How am I to know what not taking the pro war position will cost me later? So many *ugly* things come about because of this single night. Right-wing ideology might have saved me. One night pretending to hate the poor, loathing equality, and fearing socialism can't be that bad. It is obvious that poor kids don't really need food. One foray into compassionate conservatism would have led to a quiet night at home. Instead, leftist hardcore socialism leads me to something else entirely.

Like all relationships, this one starts out nicely. It is obvious that she wants to talk to me. It still takes me a good amount of time to walk over to where she is sitting and talk to her. We chat, make out outside in the rain and I end up taking her back to The Blue Door. She offers to drive, but I insist on taking my car. There is no reason whatsoever for me to be behind the wheel of an automobile. I should not be driving. I shouldn't be riding a bike, sledding down a hill, or on a skateboard at this moment, but I just met an interesting girl who agrees with me that going back to my place is a good idea so I should be the one who takes her there. Miraculously, I drive home without incident. Never a doubt. Sober as a goat. I am an excellent driver.

We park the car and walk inside. I give her a quick tour and within two minutes we are making out on my bed. Part of me expects to have sex with her. Part of me also hopes that we don't have sex. The majority of girls I bring back to The Blue Door are usually strangers that don't overstay their welcome. They know that the sex is casual and that I have no interest in taking them out for pancakes the next morning. The sex is expected and isn't respected.

This is when she surprises me. I breathe a sigh of relief when she doesn't give it up to me. Hell, she doesn't take off her shirt. Come to think of it, she doesn't even take off her bra. What girl sleeps with a bra on? A girl that means business. This is something. I have no clue what to do with her. This is confusing. I wasn't expecting this. I don't have a plan of attack. Sleeping over is one thing. Sleeping over and keeping her clothes on is something else. Coming back to my shitty place, sleeping next to me and keeping her bra on is something entirely different. This makes no sense to me. The angle she is playing baffles me. I somehow fall asleep and take her home the next morning wondering what the fuck just happened. I have no clue how my night ends sleeping next to the girl I just met. It makes no sense that she has all her clothes on the next morning. It doesn't make sense when I wake up fully clothed also. I don't know exactly what is going on. But I know that I am proud of myself.

More often than not, the girl I end up taking home is one that I'm not entirely attracted to. She is attractive enough to fuck. Well, most of the time she fits that description. Occasionally this isn't the case so I pretend that excessive amounts of alcohol consumption gives me a reason to rationalize taking an unattractive girl back home. I have no problem spending the rest of my night fucking her. I have no problem bringing a girl back home with the sole intention of sleeping with her just so long as nobody finds out about it.

I have no shame. My life at The Blue Door is filled with whatever girl I can trick into coming over but whom I am secretly ashamed of to bring home to sleep with. I still bring them home and fuck them but

I have no intention of ever introducing them to my parents anyway, so I avoid having to come up with bullshit reasons for finding them attractive. The only explanation confirms that I am an asshole and have no shame in using girls for casual sex. Shit, they are probably using me for the same exact thing. Without a doubt, I tell my one-night visitor that I will call her. This girl is always lacking something that prevents me from ever calling her again. Most times I can't even acknowledge to myself what happened the night before.

Once she's gone, whatever I do to her and whatever she does to me never happens. Any intimate touching stops existing the moment I close the door behind her. Within a week I can't remember her name, and I can happily deny to myself that the whole thing ever happened. This is done without remorse and with a straight face.

This Amber girl isn't stupid. She is not a slut. She is a different breed of female. It is obvious that she doesn't sleep around. She spends the night and doesn't succumb to my advances. I immediately respect her. When a month goes by and she still hasn't had sex with me, I start to believe in the power of abstinence. I have no doubt that this is love.

She is the push I need to finally leave The Blue Door. With her support I can move back home and live with my parents. With her help I can regroup, reevaluate, and reinvigorate my life. She is my reason to get off drugs and get away from destructive habits.

And just like that, I moved out of Long Beach. I find another lost soul who is more than willing to pay the $550 a month to continue the legacy of The Blue Door. He is a dealer friend of mine who sees the potential of setting up shop in a nondescript location that the housing authorities still consider to be merely a garage. It is never properly re-zoned as an apartment. The Blue Door continues to exist as nothing more than a storage unit and is kept from being the subject of any added scrutiny. It continues its existence as a place that doesn't officially exist. It is perfect for someone who lives on the fringe of society. It is perfect for someone who sells drugs and lives solely on the profits of the drugs he sells. The Blue Door doesn't make sense for me any longer.

Amber shows up in my life when I am tired and ready for a change. She is nice, she is pretty, she is an artist, and she is the only thing that can convince me to move out of The Blue Door. She is the only one who can persuade me to leave all the bullshit behind and try again. I come clean to her about my past life. I told her I used to play midfielder for the Columbian National Soccer team. I explain to her this is code for doing lots and *lots* of cocaine. I convince both her and myself that my playing days are over, that I don't need it, miss it, or want it in my life ever again. This ends the conversation. The topic of James and his affinity for illegal white powder is quickly tucked under the rug. The whole messy situation is ignored. This is a convenience for both of us.

Amber's position on the matter is firm and unwavering. Under no circumstances will she tolerate it. If I choose to do it, she promises to immediately break up with me. She reiterates this point. No matter the circumstances, I am on a zero tolerance policy from the get go.

I hold out for the first few months and keep my nose clean. It is a valiant effort that lasts longer than I ever expected it to. It turns out that going cold-turkey is *really* hard. I fully intend to stay clean. I last until she goes to her parents' house for Thanksgiving break. Intending to stay clean doesn't mean shit the moment she walks through security and leaves me to fend for myself without any adult supervision. I take her to the airport in the morning. By the time I am back on the freeway I've already made the necessary phone calls. I am assured to have something up my nose within the hour. By nightfall I'll be with people with like-minded pursuits. I am back on the team and about to have a good fucking time.

My dilemma is that Amber gives me a blanket ultimatum that isn't entirely realistic. She expects me to stay sober and committed to healthy living. She never wants to talk about my past. My habit is something she has no frame of reference of and no experience with. She never offers to help me develop strategies or safeguards that will keep me away from cocaine. Instead, she ignores the issue completely. I have no idea what her reaction will be if I tell her I slipped up. The option of working together never materializes. Instead of finding out what her response might be after my first fuck up, I keep my mouth shut and pretend it never happened. My opportunity to have an honest relationship is gone. In all likelihood, coming clean after the first time will lead to, at most, two days in the dog house. She'll forgive me and my nose will stay clean until spring.

In reality, I don't say shit. My drug use is on a need-to-know basis, and she *doesn't* need to know anything. A second time follows quickly, then a third and so on. Before I know it, coming clean entails more deception than she will forgive. The floodgates open. All I can do is to get really good at hiding it from her. So this is what I do.

Amber has never tried Cocaine. Apparently, she is absent the day they pass out the pamphlet in health class detailing certain changes of behavior and/or side effects that cocaine has on people. The pamphlet describes in detail exactly how James acts and looks after he stops off at Pedro's house after school. The entire front page is devoted to why there is an extra spring in his step. It mentions excessive amounts of energy, an inability to sit still, and the lack of appetite. Page two covers the phenomena of drinking excessive amounts of alcohol without the normal side effects. Cocaine usage can *eliminate* getting wasted to the point of passing out or falling down a flight of stairs. Cocaine usage *can lead to* WAY too many cigarettes, staying up past reasonable hours, getting into bed with a heart beating a mile a minute, and nose bleeds.

Seriously, it never dawns on her that my nose bleeding isn't a normal thing and that there probably is a logical and obvious explanation for them. The extent of her knowledge about drugs is that smoking marijuana leads to scarfing down potato chips and watching television. She can never tell if or when I am coked up. It becomes way too easy to give her the illusion that I am sober without giving up the drug entirely. I *do* cut back significantly after I move out of The Blue Door. But this is mainly due to moving back home. I obviously no longer have the freedom I once enjoyed. Blowing lines on the coffee table while my parents eat dinner and watch *Jeopardy* isn't a viable option.

And so it begins, I keep my transgressions to a minimum and I keep them out of sight. Regardless, every slip-up adds another layer of betrayal. The lies, untruths, and half- truths pile up swiftly. I am buried under the bullshit I feed her. Every moment becomes flawed. At some point I just stop keeping track because it becomes overwhelming. There is no point, and it becomes non-productive. There is only so much time I can spend feeling bad about doing something that I have control over, but can't control. No matter what I'll do, I'll still get a bad rap. Smoking pot a few times a month leads to an entirely different scenario. It isn't scary. Since Cocaine isn't socially acceptable and is considered to be dangerous she can't understand. I have no choice but to keep her in the dark no matter what.

I work as a substitute teacher on a regular basis. I start the school year as a replacement teacher at the school my mother teaches at. This lasts for three months and disrupts my freedom to sleep in and stay up all night. The late nights and later mornings I partake in since graduating from college are over. The decay and destruction seen daily is replaced with a blaring alarm clock and responsibilities. Operating on four hours of sleep ceases to be an option. A life without a good night's sleep will only work when I don't have to be up early the next morning. I discovered the benefits of eight hours of sleep in a hurry. Six AM comes pretty early. Waking up with the proper amount of rest becomes a passion pretty quickly.

I substituted at my mom's school on occasion when I first moved back from San Diego. Before long I am spending a few days a week at the school. I know all of the teachers and the principal. I spend random days as a substitute. The teachers leave plans for me, I follow them, all is good, the bell rings, I go home. I still wait tables at night. Spending a single day at school is all I can handle. I have no interest in building relationships with students. I have no experience. I should not be in charge of the youth. I am a poor choice to be in charge of anything. I am no one's role model. All it takes is passing a test (which is a test that I literally fall asleep during and still ace without any doubt) and you can be a substitute teacher in the BeachSide Unified School District. This is when I receive a call from the Principal of my mom's school a few days before the school year begins.

Luanne: *Hi James, Luanne, the Principal at Monroe Elementary.*

Luanne: *I was wondering if you have any plans this fall?*

James: *None that I can think of, what's up?*

Luanne: *Oh… Nothing… Say…. Can you take over Ms. Jackson's class for the start of the year?*

James: *You mean, like, show up on Monday and teach her class until she returns?*

Luanne: *Yeah, you would have the weekend to get ready, I'm sure your mom would be willing to help you get ready.*

James: *Um…. Sure…. Thanks.*

Luanne: *Oh. James.. You're a lifesaver. Thanks a bunch.*

What the fuck just happened here? One minute my phone rings and I go against my better judgment and answer a call from a phone number I don't recognize. The next thing I do is agree to begin the year as a fourth grade teacher in the classroom right next to where my mother teaches.

I have no formal training, no clue, no idea, no reason and no fucking chance to survive teaching fourth graders on a daily basis. I sub a few times a week, at most. I am still waiting tables full time. I am still committed to a lifestyle that isn't based on waking up early and certainly isn't based on being expected to stay awake until school is out. I am barely twenty three and have *no clue* what I am doing, I am scared shitless and have no idea what is going to happen next Monday. I realize for the first time how highly-educated and highly under-skilled I am. These fourth graders aren't going to give a shit about the depth of my knowledge about South American History. I'm about to be trusted with educating thirty or so nine-year-olds and I have no clue what to do.

What I expect to happen is different from what actually happens. There are two very different things that happen on the first day of school. I expect noise, chaos, and fire alarms. But the class is quiet, respectful, and with limited interest in flammable liquids. I find a class just as scared as I am. When I talk, they listen. When I give them directions, they follow them. When I say something funny, they laugh.

I don't realize how the other half lives. I never understand the extent of the power a teacher has when they show up for the first day of school. To establish expectations, set a tone, and refuse to take shit from anyone solves everything. I arrive weak and intimidated and go home strong and confident. I arrive knowing nothing about crowd control. I go home a badass alpha male. *I'm* an authority figure. I am in charge.

The class *loves* me. They expect an overweight, out of shape, middle aged woman promoting the status quo. They walk in expecting their individuality to be crushed. They arrive on the first day of fourth grade and don't see a burned out teacher just going through the motions. The first thing they see is a young teacher who looks equally nervous and excited as they are. The first thing they see is a young MALE teacher wearing slacks, button down shirt, a tie and a fucking sports coat. They see someone who they might be able to relate to. They see someone who just might cut them some slack if necessary. They see potential. They see me.

The class is full of oddballs, nerds, cute girls, fat girls, black kids, Mexicans, jocks, smart-asses, smarty-pants, kids with hand-me-down pants, funny kids, serious kids, poor kids, kids with involved parents, kids without dads, kids with moms that work at bikini bars (seriously), kids who try hard, kids who don't give a shit, kids without a clue, kids who know too much, kids with issues, kids without concerns, kids who make me smile, kids who make me shake my head, kids who give me hope, kids who give me headaches, kids who convince me that I am good at something, kids who convince me to show up and be my best because they deserve a teacher that gives them everything they can give and nothing less than that. The class is full of kids who motivate me to do something *more*. They inspire me to be strong. They are the reason I do something big. They motivate me. They save me from myself. I strive to make them bigger and better. My influence will solve their problems.

I struggle daily. My days are filled with an equal amount of self-doubt and self-motivation. They are a quirky and strange bunch of kids. Instead of hating each other they start to understand one another. I am the glue holding the class together. We bond more than I think is possible. I develop intimate and close connections with every student. I know what to expect of every one of them. I know how to treat them. After the second week we are a well-oiled machine.

My class knows that it is unlikely that I will stay the whole year with them. They know from the beginning that I am covering for Mrs. Jackson until she returns. When she does come back, I will be gone. Their enthusiastic young teacher will be replaced with someone who values rules, structure, grammar and all the things that represent middle aged female teachers. "Mr. F" is replaced with an overweight, overworked, burn-out who needs to retire, but instead shows up and fucks up the rest of what looks to be a pretty great year for these fourth graders.

I break the news to the class at the end of the day on Friday. I tell them that Mrs. Jackson is coming back on Monday and that I won't be their teacher anymore. Some of the class knows what is going on, the other half is blindsided by the announcement. Everyone is confused and upset. I'm pissed that she is coming back and angry that my time with them is over. It doesn't seem fair for anyone involved. Changing teachers mid-year is cruel. They deserve consistency in their lives. The majority of their home lives are fucked to begin with. School should be a safe place. Now it is less so. What begins as a positive experience turns into a harsh introduction on how unreliable things can become. I see the transformation of Yomance first hand. He arrives the first day of school as a more-mature-than-his-age–angry–raw–punk–cornrows–scary fourth grader. Now he is polite, personable and hard working. He is a model student. He has tears running down his face. He doesn't understand why his teacher is leaving him. He doesn't understand what else he could do to change into a better student. He doesn't understand what he did wrong. Why does he warrant an introduction to a life filled with disappointment and disillusionment at the tender age of nine? Disappointment and disillusionment can wait until middle school. They have no place in elementary school.

Two months later, I was offered a job teaching science at the same school. The school receives a grant and funding for a science program for the fourth and fifth graders. The principal offers me the position and I accept it eagerly. This is another case of me getting a job that I am unqualified for. Luanne doesn't seem too concerned, so I relearn elementary school science and fake my way through whatever needs to be faked. I am the new roving science instructor. My mom teaches at the school and convinces the principal to pay me more than what normal substitutes make. I am paid for eight hours each day instead of the usual six. I start to climb out of the debt I've been accumulating since college. I find a second job waiting tables a couple times a week, and for the first time in my life I am able to pay bills on time. The massive credit card debt that has been holding me down for as long as I remember begins to shrink.

My financial planner/accountant/drug dealer is all rolled up in one. She is also a bartender three days a week at a nice little dive bar. Every time I am paid I go directly to see her. I sit at the bar, she goes through my bills, tells me what card to pay off, and what card to pay the minimum on. She entered my life as a drug hookup and now is my unofficial accountant. At some point I'm pretty sure she does my taxes. She pours very strong drinks, charges me next to nothing for them, and has enormously large fake breasts. She is the best drug dealer ever.

While I am monitoring various APR rates at the bar, Amber is finishing up her senior year at the Laguna College of Art and Design. She is busy painting and finishing school, which keeps us apart enough to allow me to have independence from her. We spend more time together than apart, but it becomes apparent that she doesn't have a group of friends that she can rely on and that she increasingly becomes more reliant on me. I fight against this the entire time we are together. I need nights with my friends that don't include her. I am an established ingredient in a tasty friend pasta and I really love being mixed in with the rest of the dish. She comes across as an unnecessary side dish that I find myself having to keep an eye on and staying within an agreed upon distance to so she won't feel left out. Fuck that. I am at my best when I have the freedom to work the room, move around, partake in snippets of one-on-one conversations, and mingle, mingle, mingle. This became impossible because she isn't self- reliant enough to be left on her own and to her own devices. I became responsible for her happiness. I start to censor what I say and who I say things to because she still doesn't know about my secret life and most of these people I need to talk to are well-aware, and most likely are active participants in all the things I keep from my girlfriend from finding out about.

I choose the worst possible moment during the worst possible night to come clean to Amber and shatter her blind assumption that I am an honest person and a good boyfriend. It is amongst a group of couples that I have known forever celebrating one of the girl's birthday dinners. The dinner has been ordered but hasn't been delivered. There is small talk and light bantering, the mood is light and festive. It is at the point of the night where one glass of wine ordered by the right person can make or break the night. Unfortunately, I am the first to order one too many drinks and feel the need to come clean to Amber, right there, in front of our friends, before dinner comes and before she gets to enjoy the shrimp pasta she enthusiastically orders.

I don't have the decency to let the birthday girl drink too much flavored vodka. It is her night to go all out and I steal it from her. There is no limit to what bad behavior this birthday girl is already forgiven for because it is her damn birthday. It's only a matter of time before she starts her ascent into embarrassing behavior. She has the freedom to pillage to her heart's content, rape and murder the old and disabled, and say whatever offensive things that come to mind. Her birthday ensures that nobody will judge her, nobody will look down at her and nobody will think twice about it.

Nope, I have a better idea. I'll turn to my girlfriend and tell her that, *oops… my bad… I think I forgot to tell you that about six months ago, I started to use cocaine again and have been using it on a consistent basis ever since. And… I'm really sorry… You're not mad, are you?* The collective response from the rest of the table was to simultaneously let their jaws drop, stop whatever conversation they are having mid-sentence and look over to my side of the table. Amber's head is down, tears are welling up in her eyes, and is she is about to fucking *explode*.

She starts to yell at the table. I thankfully am able to move her quickly to the parking lot. Before I leave, I drop a bunch of cash for dinner we don't eat, and follow her out to the car. She greets me with a roundhouse right followed by a jab with her left. I'm not expecting it to escalate so quickly into violence. Part of me respects her for introducing a whole new level of dysfunction into our already flawed relationship. I expect tears and strong words, not a brawl in the parking lot.

We drive back to her house in silence. The rest of the night is spent in an unsuccessful attempt to stop her from crying. Hours go by. It gets later and later. What begins a tad after eight o'clock that night continues past midnight. The next thing I know, it's past two in the morning and I *still* can't calm her down.

This is getting ridiculous. I have to be at the golf course in a few hours. Don't fuck with my early golf time the next morning. A lack of sleep leads to bad golf. I get desperate. Hold on to that thought, let me sleep for a bit, play a decent round of golf and we can continue our conversation at a later date. Proposal denied. I lose my patience.

The guilt I should still feel is nowhere to be seen. It disappears along with whatever respect I have for her. I realize that I don't give a shit anymore. It becomes painfully clear to me that I may be an asshole, but she is pathetic. She is weak and I can't pretend to be something I'm not for someone I don't have any regard for. She looks into my eyes a split second later and asks me this.

Amber: *Did you ever even love me?*

I have no idea if I can answer this question honestly. I've always assumed that it would be beyond my capabilities. As I say the next eight words, I am shocked, confused and proud.

James: *No, I guess that I never really did.*

This isn't what she expects to hear. This isn't what I expect to say. This isn't the reply of a remorseful boyfriend who wants to do whatever he can to make it work and fix the problems. This is the reaction from a man who doesn't give a shit anymore.

These words are the last thing she expects to hear when she leaves to go to Rebecca's birthday earlier this night. Worst case scenario? Her pasta is undercooked, James drinks too much, and the night ends with a small fight easily resolved the next morning. It never even crossed her mind how bad it can get. Undercooked pasta is the least of her problems. She doesn't get to eat, she finds out that her boyfriend is quite possibly a raving drug fiend and is told that he never loved her in the first place.

The next round of violence has more to do with her having an empty stomach and less to do with her heart being broken. If she eats her pasta, maybe her reaction doesn't include fisticuffs directed at my face. I let the first few blows connect, because I deserve it. I let her hit me because she is quick and agile. That, and she catches me unprepared. Regardless, she deserves to unleash this pent up anger. I deserve another right, and then a left, and then a final right. The entire combination package meets no resistance. I am caught off guard and stand there like a punching bag.

The fury of the attack wakes me up and convinces me to take a more defensive position. I consider lying down and curling up into a ball but I decide it is tactically unnecessary. Instead, I stand my ground and don't let her punch me again. I may be an asshole. I know I am in the wrong. I also know that she has no control over her emotions. She is a loose cannon that must not be trusted ever again. I may have just gotten beaten up by a girl, but I don't care. Whatever I did wrong doesn't matter anymore because I just became the recipient of spousal abuse. *I am now the victim.*

I sleep on the couch that night. I wake up and leave the next morning without saying a word to her. I head to the golf course and play a round of golf with my dad. My drives are straight and long, my irons find the center of the greens, I chip with accuracy and I put the ball in the heart of the cup. I wake up early that morning to play a round of golf. I also wake up and leave behind a relationship built on convenience. I wake up and throw away a relationship that lacks passion. I walk away from a relationship based on deception. I walk away from a relationship that I never respect. I say goodbye to a relationship that isn't working, isn't going to work and should never have been attempted. I leave her house that morning without any regret. I leave as a free man. She wakes up later that morning angry. She holds onto everything that she hates about me. She still holds onto what she thinks I hate about myself. I leave a free man. I go play a decent round of golf. She stays home.

21

Bad Art

THE SUMMER IS a complete disaster. It is the greatest three months of my adult life. I spend all available time making art. I spend all of my free time making fucked up art. I jump head first into cocaine and am more out of control than I ever allow myself to be. My parents leave for Europe for a few weeks. I take a leave of absence from waiting tables because I can't handle showing up to work on time the two days I am scheduled each week. I make art. I make big pieces of art using expensive and powerful paint pens, colored pencils, and random pictures I find in magazines. I cut out silhouettes of human bodies that I find in fashion magazines and art books. Then I go to Kinko's and laminate them. I end up with hundreds of laminated bodies that I use over and over. Any image with clearly defined features, sharp angles, wild hair, arms or legs pointed in extreme positions is ripped out immediately. Once it is laminated and carefully cut out I have the beginning shape of my next piece of art. My next step is to organize a collage of bodies on paper and trace them out. I use straight edges to make borders. I fill in dead space with various geometrical shapes and photos of nude women. I spend too much money buying ten dollar fashion magazines with thick, high glossy paper full of images that blow my mind. I base most creations on what I find in the fashion magazines. I use anything I can get my hands on that fits my color scheme. I use anything that catches my eye. I use anything sexual in nature but not overly sexual in tone. The nudes tend to be on the tasteful side and very erotic. After I trace out all the shapes and glue on the images I find a random quote. I am a Badass. This is not the quote I use, just how I feel when I do this. Also, I put my dealer's kids through college this summer.

Each piece is fitted with some words. It transforms from a piece of random tracings and naked bodies into something more. Now I have something to say. The small snippets of prose give the art their souls and give them their identity. Cocaine. Their identity is that stuff.

I spend the vast majority of my time tracing. Trace a body then fill it in. The process requires multiple layers of ink and a lot of focus. This is where cocaine comes into play. There is nothing like being super high and having something to keep you busy. The entire summer I find myself on copious amounts of drugs. I have nothing but time on my hands. I have nobody but myself to entertain. I have an infinite amount of artwork I need to start. I have tons that still need lots of work. So many are close to being finished. I'm a fucking tweeker.

I keep this up for as long as I can. I create things, stay busy and productive. I enjoy what I am doing. I like how things look when they are done and I feel like I am doing something that nobody else is making. I convince myself that I am creating brilliant pieces of art. I'm also aware that my art is only made when I am under the influence. As good as I think it is, I recognize that it isn't a legitimate piece of creativity because it is only created with the help of cocaine. I hate that I don't have the focus to do this while sober. I can never respect my art because of this. I know my limitations. I don't have the ability to create traditional art. I can't draw, paint or sketch. I have an eye for graphic design and am good at using various mediums to bring things together. I have a steady hand. I draw straight lines. I spend my time making art because I want to spend my time doing blow. I know that once the blow goes away, making art will be next. How can I make art without the blow? Will I even want to? What will happen when the cocaine runs out and I'm left on my own?

Eventually the money runs out, my parents are due back, and I have dinner plans with an old family friend. Jim grew up with my dad, went to college with both my parents and has known them forever. The reason we have dinner is so Jim can sit me down and help figure out a plan for me. I am in desperate need of direction (obviously). He might have a solution. He wants to introduce me to a career counselor that can give me insight into what my options are. She is someone capable of finding fields of employment I may be interested in. She is someone that can help me find a job.

I've known about the dinner for days. This doesn't stop me from starting a bender the night before. I haven't slept. I use a Parliament cigarette to continue snorting coke the entire drive down to meet him. I show up to dinner with shaky hands and without an appetite. God forbid I lay off the sauce for a single day. There is nothing wrong with enjoying a free meal and spending some quality time with Jim. He is a cool guy. He is funny and generous. He has three daughters and no sons. He treats me like an equal. He makes sure that if I need money or help in any way that he has my back. He is my father's age but he isn't my father. I sit down to dinner knowing that I need to talk to someone soon. I'm still not convinced that he will be able to relate to me but I am pretty sure that he is the only one who can help me.

Jim: *James man. What's going on? How are you?*

The dinner starts with the basic catching up, *how are you? Fine. How are you?* chit chat. I go through the motions of the conversation until I convince myself to come clean. I finally say fuck it. Here you go Jim. Do you really want to know how I am? Because if you don't, then I'm making a big mistake in confiding in you. I'm out of options. I'm desperate and I'm going to tell you the truth. I hope you can handle it.

James: *Well... to be honest with you, I'm really depressed. I've gotten involved with something that I need some help with and I don't know how to fix it on my own anymore.*

Jim: *What's going on?*

He says this with genuine concern. I'm pretty scared at this point, but there is no turning back. I lay it all out for him.

James: *I have a drug problem. I don't feel that I can approach my parents with it and I need some advice on what to do. I need help. I need you to help me.*

Jim: *What drugs are we talking about?*

James: *Cocaine.*

Jim: *Oh, James, oh no....*

Oops. His reaction conveys to me that he has no experience with this drug. Maybe pot is something he can relate to. Cocaine? Not so much. His initial reaction makes sense but isn't expected. I assume that at one point he has tried it. He spent his twenties in the 70's. He was a well-paid lawyer all throughout the 80's for Christ's sake. His reaction conveys none of this. He looks back at me like I just told him I am hooked on crack, HIV positive, running from the law and am going to die sometime later in the week.

I misread the situation entirely. I've now made this a much bigger and scarier issue than it actually is. It takes serious back pedaling on my part to convince him not to contact my parents right then and there. He is well-aware that my sister struggled with substance abuse growing up. Here I am, following in her fucked up footsteps. Jim also recognizes that I go to him in confidence. He sees that I am mature enough to realize that I need help. He understands that he is the person who has the means and the ability to save me. He also recognizes that my parents don't stand to benefit from this knowledge.

Discovering that their only son is hooked on drugs and struggling to stay afloat might break them. He knows my parents just as well as I do. They have been through more than they can handle. Everyone wins if this is fixed in-house. He knows that the less they know, the less they have to worry about and the better off they will be. He sees all of the variables. He agrees to help me out. He consents to keep it between us. He is the right person to reach out to because there is nothing he won't do to protect my parents. He helps me and I still keep him in the dark when I need to. It is for his own protection.

I arrive to dinner high on cocaine. I leave dinner still high. He has no idea. I promise to stop doing blow. I agree to see a counselor on a weekly basis that Jim offers to pay for. He promises to keep it between us as long as I stay clean. I intend to do just this. I expect to keep my nose clean. I look forward to spending an hour each week talking about my feelings with my new therapist. I can't wait to figure out what ails me. I embrace the opportunity to kick the habit. I have faith that I'll be able to show Jim that his investment in me is money well spent.

I haven't seen Amber for a couple of months. My summer of excess is almost over. I'm still fucked up, but there is some hope. I don't know why I call her, but I do. There is no reason to call her, but I can't stop dialing. I feel like I owe her something. I have a moment of weakness. Ten seconds of loneliness leads to meeting her for dinner. I know it is a bad idea. I try to reschedule. It's in my best interest to put it off until later. It is of no surprise that I'm on the tail end of another bender. I have no business meeting my ex-girlfriend for dinner in the state I'm in. I've been up for the last thirty six hours. I shouldn't even leave the house. There is no reason, whatsoever, to get in my car and drive over to her house and see her. What if I have to parallel park? Fuck, I don't think this is a good idea. I don't want to go. I am too fucked up to brush my teeth. I'm operating on no sleep and shouldn't be asked to do anything more complicated than putting on some pajamas and going to bed. Contrary actions, right? I rally the troops and get in the car. I have no clue what to expect when I walk through her door.

I'm not ready when she opens the door. I don't expect her to look so good. I don't plan to rush over to her. I don't intend to immediately hug and kiss her. It just happens. Her hair is cut short and she looks fucking amazing. We immediately start kissing like we haven't seen one another for years. It feels right. It is full of passion and intimacy. We walk to a restaurant and have dinner. She cries. I struggle to eat. Every bite is torture. Eating on cocaine is not exactly a pleasurable experience. She doesn't notice. We go back to her house and fuck. Before I know it, we are back together.

I have no choice in the matter. I never plan to get back together with her. I have serious doubts about our compatibility as a couple. I can ignore these doubts as long as we are happy. I want her to mold me into the man that I want to be. I want her to fix me. I figure that if I give her another chance I will, in effect, give myself another chance to put cocaine behind me once and for all.

I know it is a mistake the moment we kiss. I'm looking for a way to stop using cocaine. She is still my best bet. We have a connection and I still have feelings for her. I use her as a way to stop being such a delinquent.

Every Tuesday I spend an hour with the therapist/life coach that Jim introduces me to. He knows I can't afford to pay for it, but agrees to foot the bill so long as I stay away from the white devil. I want to stay clean but I keep slipping up. I spend an hour with Lydia, my therapist, every Tuesday afternoon. She expects me to attend meetings daily and stop doing drugs. It takes me awhile to commit to the system. I start to dread Tuesdays. I fail to attend meetings. The few that I do attend are very uncomfortable. I can't get through the weekend without doing blow. Linda assures me that she isn't mad, just disappointed.

Six weeks pass before I'm able to show up to my weekly Tuesday meeting with good news. My nose stays clean for the entire weekend. I spend two days at my parents' cabin and break the cycle. I could have easily gotten some before I left, but I didn't. I survive the weekend without drugs and it isn't even that hard. I finally made it through a weekend without cocaine. I continue to drink, but I stay away from drugs. The drug-free days add up. I attend meetings a few times a week. I get my first Narcotics Anonymous (NA) chip, then another, and another.

Going to NA meetings is a trip. I agree to go to one per day. Linda makes this the number one priority. She agrees to see me only if I go to thirty meetings in thirty days. This is beyond the scope of what I am willing to do, but I agree to it nonetheless. I diligently search online (before the internet was the internet) and find local NA meetings that fit into my schedule. The meetings start at 11 AM. The first day I showed up was pretty nerve racking. I've never been to an AA meeting, let alone an NA meeting. I have no clue what to expect. I drive to a park in a part of Long Beach that I'm normally not allowed in. If my mother knew where I was she would kill me. I park my car and walk over to a group of people gathered around a couple of concrete picnic tables. I immediately regret getting out of the car. I am the only white person in attendance. I am the only white person in a ten block radius. Embrace the moment. I'll be okay. Staying sober another day is all that matters. The important thing to focus on is making it through another day without doing drugs. Fuck that. All I need to do is survive for the next hour, get my sheet signed and get the fuck out of dodge.

The meeting starts. People share their stories. I sit and listen. I don't say a word. I do get in a circle and hold hands with two crusty crack heads to recite the serenity prayer at the end of the meeting. I have a lady sign my check off sheet that Linda gave me and I get in my car and drive away.

I go to meetings in the park a few more times. I make coffee at the sober living house across the street one day. Entering a sober living facility scares me straight pretty quickly. I lose all interest in drug-use two steps into the sober living house. A single minute encircled with the remnants of communal meals and dirty furniture is all I need. If I'm still not sure that drugs are bad, then standing in the park with broken people convinces me it sure as hell is. I finally open my eyes. I hold hands and say the serenity prayer with people who have infinitely more fucked up lives than me. This is more than enough reason to get clean and stay clean. I have no business at this park. Never having to see it again is all the motivation I need to get my shit together.

I never go to enough meetings. I see Linda every week and every week I show her my NA check off card. Every week she is disappointed. I find a meeting in Los Alamitos. I go to another one in Huntington Beach. I get up the nerve to talk a few times. It is uncomfortable because I am claiming to be sober, but I'm not completely sober. I'm unwilling to stop drinking but am focused on my attempt to stay away from drugs. Linda agrees to this reluctantly. I show up to meetings and stand up and announce how many days it has been since I have done drugs. I stand tall and introduce myself knowing full well that I can't own up to the entire story. I should use this opportunity to actually get sober and give my liver a break but instead I keep on drinking.

I hate meetings because they bore me to tears. I hate them because I am claiming to be something I'm not. I show up hungover. I smell like Wild Turkey one day and strawberry daiquiris the next. I stand up and announce how many days I've been sober. Sober means *staying off cocaine*. I fail to mention that I continue to drink. I bite my lip and keep going. I get my "Thirty-Day" chip. I am proud. I am still drinking, but I make it an entire month without doing cocaine.

Things are going well with Amber. I am on my way to legitimacy and I want her with me. I am the one who asks her if she wants to move in together. I am living with my parents. She lives in a tiny studio. It makes sense. We find a one-bedroom apartment that is the lower half of two units. We have outdoor space and we start accumulating stuff. I become domesticated. I start to garden. It takes at least an hour to water all of the plants. We built ourselves a picnic table. We buy a fish tank. We invite people over for dinner. We convince everyone that we are a well-put-together couple. We try really hard to convince each other that the relationship makes sense. No matter how hard I try to tell myself that I am happy and I have everything I need, there is something missing between us.

We *never* discuss cocaine. We never allow ourselves to be completely honest with one another. She will never accept me for who I am. She will never be enough for me. Boredom leads me back to cocaine. My girlfriend is boring. She doesn't have it in her to hold my attention long enough so I don't feel the tug of the drug. She keeps my attention while I'm at home but it is impossible for me to stay home all the time. She doesn't like going out. She finds faults with just about everyone I am friends with. She doesn't understand how I work. She doesn't care much for who I am but sees my potential. She never understands me. She likes the concept of me, but is committed to mold me into someone more compatible with her. I am flawed no doubt but I don't see the need to completely overhaul my wiring. I understand why she feels the need to do so. I get it, coke is bad. Eating more vegetables is a good thing and quitting smoking makes sense. It's hard to argue against such logical advice. It makes sense to do these things. I understand her point, but I start to resent her for it.

Nobody likes to be told what to do. Nobody likes to argue with their girlfriends. These simple statements are magnified exponentially when it comes to Amber and me. She has a couple of friends. I have lots. I have friends all over the place. I'm at my best when I am around them. I operate on a higher level when I am surrounded by people I like. I keep in contact with everyone I've ever met. I literally keep in contact with every person I have ever met. Amber keeps in contact with her mom. She has one close friend in Washington but other than that she is alone in the world. She is all alone and it doesn't seem to faze her. Wait, she isn't all alone, she has me.

We never figure out how to disagree with each other. Opposing opinions cause an excessive amount of drama between us. This is a normal part of any relationship so I assume, but in reality this is just another flashing red flag that I fail to understand. This is a big red flag that I don't see. Amber isn't an easy person to disagree with. She doesn't understand the concept of constructive criticism. Any fight, no matter how small, becomes a battle. Logic and rationality disappear and are replaced with raw emotions and spite. I start to bite my tongue.

I let things go. I look the other way. I "choose" my battles. I stop any form of opposition and let her have her way. We never figure out how to disagree with one another in an appropriate way. I become quiet. Any small disagreement has the potential to mutate into a large argument. I stopped caring. I nod my head, smile and approve.

This is what destroys us. I keep my mouth shut and go with whatever bullshit she is focused on. Feuding isn't allowed. Strife leads to tension. I lose the motivation to oppose. I don't have the energy to object. I spent the majority of my youth arguing with my friends about politics and social causes. I enjoyed every minute of it. I embrace the opportunity to tell someone that they are wrong. I have the utmost confidence in my words. I fear nothing. Nobody can silence me. Nobody, except Amber. She is able to do it. She figures out how to shut me up.

Next step is obvious. Buy a ring and ask her to marry me. That's exactly what I do. I am a stupid person. I go against my gut instincts, ignore my doubts and go for it. I convince myself that I can live with her flaws. I assume that I'll be able to overcome them by sheer will alone. I am willing to live the rest of my life without blow jobs. I ask a girl to marry me and at the same time I know that it will end in divorce. I can't explain the madness that takes over me, but I embrace this foolishness and go ahead with it anyway. I marry her because I'm too lazy to break up with her. I don't want to go through the awkward situation of breaking up and moving to separate apartments. I envision a couple of tense days while we move out of the house. Let me repeat this. I marry her because I am afraid to break up with her. I am weak. I have no excuse for what happens next. I bring all of this upon myself. I am an idiot. I am a fool. I am… I am so many things. I guess I always have been.

22

Conversations with Squirrels/ Assault Charges at the Dallas Fort Worth Texas International Airport

THE FIRST THING I do is drink a bottle of wine (this is in of itself, not really a surprise.) I wash it out and hide it in my sock drawer. The next step involves putting a certain amount of money aside after each shift at the restaurant. I count my tips and diligently put between ten and twenty percent in the bottle. I never touch the money in the bottle, and soon enough it is full of cash. A friend of a friend knows a guy who can make me a ring on the cheap. For $1,200, I get a diamond a shade under a carat.

I hand over a dozen hundred dollar bills to a guy named Berg who assures me that the ring will be finished "soon." He is impossible to get a hold of. He never calls me back. I have to pay him up front. He has all my money. Each time I call him he tells me that I'll get the ring in a few days. Week after week he tells me the same thing. Just a few more days. Delays, more delays. I wonder if handing a bunch of money to a stranger is such a good idea after all. The deadline is mid-December. Time is running out. I'm getting nervous.

My faith in Berg is finally rewarded. Berg comes through. The ring is finally ready. My father and I go to pick it up and all my worries fade away. The ring is perfect. The diamond is perfect. It is set on a simple ring that I know she will love. I am the bargain shopper of the year. For $1,200, I get a ring that will appraise for almost four times what I pay for it.

We are going to her parents' house in Washington for Christmas. I plan on proposing during Christmas dinner. My parents are flying to Washington to spend the holidays with her family. It is the first time that I won't wake up on Christmas morning with Nana, my aunt and uncle, and my two cousins. My streak of twenty six years alternating between houses is broken because I decide to ask my girlfriend to marry me. Nana makes sure to mention that it is the first Christmas in fifty years that she will spend without her entire family. I ignore her none-too-subtle passive aggressive discontent.

The dinner at her parents' house is loud and festive. It consists of the two of us, my parents, her mom, her step dad Frank (he's the shit), her step-brothers, her step- sister and her husband. Midway through dinner, I stand up to give a toast. This is expected, as I tend to do this at holiday gatherings. I ramble on for a bit and then turn towards her. I tell her some nonsense about my feelings and how much I love her. Then I get on my knees, pull out the ring, and ask her to marry me.

Looking back on the proposal, wedding and the actual marriage, I must admit I nailed two of the three. Unfortunately, I peaked entirely too early. The proposal is perfect, the wedding is amazing and the marriage is a train wreck. She has no idea that I am going to ask her to marry me. My system of stuffing cash in an empty wine bottle hidden in my sock drawer works beautifully. She has no idea I've been saving money for a ring, let alone actually buying one.

I propose to her on her home turf and in front of our families. The ring is exactly what she wants. The rest of the night turns into a roaring party. Frank (her stepdad) tells me it is the best Christmas he has ever had. Everyone is excited for us. It is the first day of the rest of my life and I am content. Doubts be damned. There is no reason why this won't work out. There is nothing holding us back. My reservations are put aside and I am confident that I can make this work. I ignore my lingering doubts for a day and enjoy the celebration.

Our first decision is to set a date. I favor a longer engagement, but Amber is set on a wedding next August. This gives us a mere eight months to pull it all together. My gut instinct tells me that the smart move is to wait until the next summer to get married. This gives us time to make sure we actually want to marry one another. Amber wants none of this and is dead set on legally binding me to her as soon as possible. I capitulate and we set the date for the first Saturday in August next summer.

The months fly by and before I know it, I'm at the Men's Warehouse in Tacoma, Washington picking up my suit the day before the wedding. The ceremony and reception take place at her mom's house. This isn't negotiable. Her dream wedding takes place overlooking the Puget Sound, where the majority of her childhood was spent. The house sits on ten acres of land with two hundred feet of waterfront property. Their house is an hour south of Seattle. You cross a spit (look it up) and drive the final eight miles up a two lane highway. On the right is a wall of dense trees. On the left, you guessed it, more trees. Everywhere you look you see trees. Civilization fades away in the rear view mirror. By the time you get to the house, you find yourself in the middle of nowhere, on the edge of the fucking world.

The first time I go to her parents' house I am in awe. The driveway is made of dirt. It is only wide enough for a single car. Both sides are overgrown with trees and shrubbery. Her stepfather guns it down the path without concern for speed limits or safety considerations. The never ending driveway eventually flattens out into a driveway that leads to a garage. To the left of the garage is a path that leads to a carport. This is where Frank keeps his Russian made tractor (it's a red one). To the right is a manicured path that leads to the house.

The house was originally a one-room cabin with a fireplace, a small kitchen, a tiny bedroom, and a tiny bathroom. Amber's stepdad, Frank, bought it cheap and has spent the last couple of decades remodeling, expanding, improving, and perfecting the property. Along the way, he meets Amber's mom, Hannah, and marries her. They move into Frank's house and live with his three kids from a previous marriage. The melding of the families isn't easy. Amber treats her new dad like shit. Frank's kids treat their new mom in a similar way. For years the house has been in chaos. Luckily, by the time I came around, everyone had grown up a bit and doesn't act like assholes anymore. They realize the benefits of a close family and commit to be well adjusted and happy.

The house is truly amazing. The first thing you do is walk up to a large deck that appears to be hanging over the water below. A large tree grows through the deck and holds a swinging bench. The deck continues around the corner to the far side of the house. The deck makes you wonder how you've survived so long without having something so majestic in your life. The house appears smaller than it is. The main floor contains a large living room, a modern kitchen, an updated bathroom, and a guest bedroom. Upstairs is a master suite. The downstairs basement has another bedroom, a bathroom, and an office.

My first time in Washington helps me understand the appeal of a life spent surrounded by nature. I escape the perils of strip malls, fast food, and freeways. Everything is green. The air is fresh. This is not a bad place to live. I spend my time chopping wood and throwing rocks at things. I pick up starfish the size of large Frisbees along the shore. I wake up each morning, look at the water for a bit and feel rejuvenated. I wonder why anyone would ever leave. Seeing where Amber grew up helps me understand her more completely. I see her clearly for the first time.

As I'm reading a book on the deck one morning I hear a loud thump a few feet in front of me. I look down from my book and see a squirrel crouching nervously in front of me. He just fell about twenty feet from the tree and doesn't know what to do.

James: *Hey, you okay?*

Squirrel: *I think so…*

The squirrel lands on his feet but bounces a few inches off the ground upon impact. He looks around sheepishly. He feels embarrassed. He wonders if anybody else saw him fall.

James: *Do you need anything?*

He appears fine.

Squirrel: *Nothing seems to be broken… thanks anyway… I'm going to go… Can we keep this between us?*

James: *I won't tell a soul.*

Like it never happened, the fucker turns around and climbs back up the tree. I share a brief moment with the wildlife of Washington State. Three hundred days of rain a year doesn't seem so bad. I understand the appeal of breathing in fresh air. I support the idea of eventually moving to the Pacific NorthWest. It comes sooner than expected and I'm not ready for it.

The majority of my close friends are able to make the journey to Washington for the wedding. The only important person missing is Mitch. After my engagement, I have to pick the best man for my wedding. The smart choice is my cousin. We are the type of cousins who make the most out of the time we spend together. I am given a "get out of jail free card" from Amber every time he is around. I get to do whatever and stay out till whenever. He is the only one that is granted a "limited edition just don't break anything and/or die" pass for the night. Amber is the youngest and the only step sister with four older siblings who party, drink and stay up late any time they get together. She tolerates my participation in such reckless late night activities because he is family. In her mind, this is completely appropriate. This is what *family* does.

This gives us a free pass to do whatever we want, without fear of repercussions. We take advantage. He isn't a typical cousin. Our connection intensifies at the Blue Door and just keeps growing after my sister's death. Our bond escalates and increases into something much bigger. He is someone I respect and admire. He is the obvious choice to be my best man. He is honest. He is loyal. He has a good heart. He is reliable. But, he is not Mitch.

Mitch moves back to California and lives in Big Sur for a while. He may or may not dabble in heroin, something I can't independently confirm or deny. But now, he is back living in Georgia. He claims to be on the straight and narrow path. He allegedly has a job and a girlfriend. Unless independently verified I can't be sure about anything he tells me. Old habits die hard. The trust and faith I felt throughout the ordeal with my sister have been dissipating slowly only to be replaced with a healthy amount of skepticism. By now I take everything he says with a grain of salt.

James: *Oh, you're working later tonight? That sounds great.*

Does he have a job? Does he own a car? Did he brush his teeth this morning? Your guess is as good as mine. I still love the guy. I know that I will probably always love the guy. I just don't believe anything he says anymore. I stopped listening to his answers. I stopped asking about the details.

Mitch's phone number changes bi-monthly. As long as he makes occasional contact, I remain content. He is hard to get a hold of. He is bipolar, whatever that means. He abuses his ADD meds and drinks too much. Details about his daily activity lose all relevance. As long as he is alive and eats every other day, I can rest easy. We talk more regularly after I get engaged. He is naturally my first choice to be my best man. He knows the most about me. He is the only person I have ever met that has the ability to somehow transform me into something… better. He has been the closest friend I've ever had. He is still my best friend. Any time I look around at all of our friends, I can't see a single duo who can claim to have what Mitch and I have or at least what we once had.

Mitch is mine during a time when everyone wants a piece of him. He means more to me than I can explain. I'm in his debt for what he did when my sister died. I owe it to him to choose him. If I choose him it will validate the close bond that we have. I choose him and I authenticate all the good times, as well as the bad ones that we have spent by each other's side. His words are something like this…

Mitch: *I've waited for this since I was sixteen. I need this. You know this is what should happen. I won't let you down. I swear.*

He is hard to argue with. Mitch never has a problem convincing me to do something that my gut tells me not to. His logic is sound. I agree with him. I tell him that if he makes it out to California for the engagement party then, yes, he is my best man. He has a lot more convincing to do. He isn't the most trusted person that I know. On the contrary, he is pretty much the only person who nobody takes seriously anymore. He deserves a chance to be my best man. He deserves a chance to show everyone that he is capable of getting on a plane and showing up on time. This is his final opportunity to prove myself, my friends and my family wrong. I hang up the phone with my doubts. I hope to God that he can keep his word. I have my fears that he will drop the ball. The smart bet is that he will. I am cautiously optimistic that he won't let me down. Just this one time, don't fuck up. Prove them all wrong this one time. Do it for me. Do it for yourself.

I know that my mother doesn't approve of my decision. My dad keeps quiet but is obviously skeptical. Nana isn't at all too pleased. None of my friends meet the news with enthusiasm. The general consensus is that it isn't a good idea. The dialogue revolves around the simple fact that Mitch is not reliable, and I should not rely on him.

Mike: *Who is your best man going to be?*

James: *I'm going with Mitch.*

Justin: *Mitch?*

James: *He's the only Mitch either of us know, so yes. That's my plan for now. That is,*

until he gives me a reason to reevaluate my choice.

Mike: *I'm not going to say that is the worst idea I've ever heard. Wait… No… on second thought, that is a horrible idea. Best case scenario? He shows up on time, drinks moderately and writes down a speech beforehand. Worst case scenario? He ad–libs the best man speech, hasn't slept in the last two days, knocks over the cake, spills red wine on Amber's dress, ruins the wedding and needs to borrow money. You are a brave and stupid man. I will pray for you.*

James: *Have a little bit of faith. He will surprise all you cynical bastards. He won't let me down.*

I have the identical conversation with *everyone* involved in the wedding. Amber is unconvinced, but trusts my judgment. My entire family lost faith long ago. My future in-laws haven't met him, but have heard stories and are somewhat concerned. My friends all think I have lost my mind. I gradually become more and more worried. On the day of the engagement party I am scared shitless that he won't show up. Small concerns escalate. Nothing he tells me makes much sense. The hours pass by and at the end of the night I promise to listen to the people close to me more.

<u>Ten Causes for Apprehension</u>

#1 I still don't know when or where his flight is landing.
#2 He smoothly changes the subject each time
I try to find out his flight itinerary.
#3 There is no contact whatsoever the entire day of the party.
#4 At 4:55pm he calls to tell me that his connecting flight is delayed.
#5 The party starts at 5pm.
#6 He is still at the Dallas/Fort Worth Airport.
#7 He isn't flying into Long Beach- a ten minute cab ride away.
#8 His plane lands in Ontario- at least an hour away.
#9 Texas to Ontario is three hours. Ontario
to Rossmoor is another hour.
#10 There's no way in hell he's showing up
before the party ends at Midnight.

The party rocks without him. The turnout is huge. I drink in excess. I am pulled in every direction. I am surrounded by all my close friends all wanting a piece of me. It's my party and this is when I'm at my best. I work the room for hours. I circulate. I never stop moving. I don't have the time to dwell on the fact that Mitch isn't here. The night goes on. Only when the party ends do I realize that he never showed up. Only now do I recognize his failure to call. It doesn't even bother me. That is, it doesn't bother me too much.

I'm mad that he failed me. It makes things easier in the long run. I feel stupid for telling everyone close to me to trust him. I feel like an idiot for convincing them of his reliability. They must wonder what pills I have been taking. It doesn't surprise me that he is still such a fucking train wreck. Trust and dependability have never been his strongest suits and they still aren't.

Two days later he calls me. The conversation should begin like this.

Mitch: *James, I'm so sorry. I feel so bad about missing the party. Please forgive me.*

If the conversation kicks off in this manner, then I won't care as much about the convoluted story that is sure to follow. It isn't in his nature to say he is sorry. An apology is all I need. He is still out as my best man, but he might get to come to the wedding. Sadly, this does not happen.

I pick up the phone. Without even saying hi, he starts attacking me with words. He tells me what happened, attack style. It involves a lost credit card, the Dallas Airport and a misunderstanding. Mitch is just an every man trying his best to get to his best friend's engagement party on time. I don't buy any of it. Before he can tell me the whole story I tune him out. I don't give a shit. Just say you feel bad for not showing up. Then go ahead and tell me what happened.

This is what allegedly happens in the Dallas Airport. This is his story and he is sticking to it. He and his girlfriend kill time in the airport bar waiting to board. After boarding the plane they realize that they left their credit card at the bar. Mitch clears it with a flight attendant to get off the plane so he can run and get the credit card. He leaves the plane, grabs the card and runs back to the gate. The gate is closed. The guy in charge won't let Mitch back on the plane. Mitch pleads his case and gets nowhere. The guy won't listen so Mitch punches him in the face. He assaults an airline employee (a federal crime?) and is arrested. He spends the next few days in jail.

This is his story. This is the reason why he never showed up. *He* is the victim here. He has gone through so much the last few days. Anything I've had to deal with can't be as bad as what he just went through. He tries to convince me that he is arrested on my behalf. He implies that it is somehow my fault. He can't figure out why I haven't apologized to *him* yet. This is when the conversation ends. I hang up on him and he disappears. I don't hear from him again. None of my friends speak to him. He doesn't make a single attempt to contact anyone. He doesn't come to the wedding. He isn't my best man. He falls off the planet and nobody hears a thing.

23

Swimming in the Puget Sound

MY COUSIN JOSH is my best man. He was my first choice anyway but I foolishly cast him aside when Mitch says "pretty please." He knows all about Mitch. He knows the situation. Before I ask Mitch to be my best man, I take my cousin aside and explain the situation. It feels weird to ask him to be my backup, but he understands. The marriage ceremony has dual officiates. Mike and Aleem take the honor of marrying us. They perform flawlessly. We say our "I do's" and ten minutes later we are officially married.

I put together a playlist on my IPOD that plays in between the ceremony and the following dinner. The ceremony is finished, pictures have been taken, the keg is full and dinner isn't ready just yet. I am standing on the beach with my groomsmen, my cousins and my uncle. Someone picks up a stone and throws it out into the water. Someone else picks up a stone and throws it. A buoy floats about a hundred yards from shore. This becomes the group's mutual target. Nobody has to say this, it just happens. A collective understanding/Jedi Mind Trick. Whoever can hit it will live forever in infamy. My cousins start to throw. Next, my groomsmen start *heaving* rocks. Within seconds, everyone one the beach is picking up rock after rock and throwing them out into the water. This is when I take off my jacket and throw a stone. I look back towards the deck to see if Amber is watching. I can't see her and wonder, for a split second, if I'm allowed to throw rocks with the boys. Throwing rocks on your wedding day is an acceptable activity, right? Most weddings include rock throwing contests, don't they (maybe in the Nordic lands)? Oh yeah, I remember, only the cool ones do. That's right bitches. I miss the target over and over. Everyone misses it. Apart from a few close calls, the rocks splash harmlessly into the water. Most efforts aren't even close. We spend the next forty five minutes trying to hit the damn buoy. The majority of the guests are drinking wine and mingling up on the deck. Even if they have an interest in rock throwing, they most likely will throw out their shoulder in the process. They are much more comfortable watching the youth throw rocks.

This is my moment. The music I chose is playing. I'm sharing a moment with my closest friends. The pure randomness and spontaneous nature of this moment ensure that it will be a memory none will forget. It's my wedding day, and right now the high point is listening to music with my friends and throwing rocks, minus my bride.

The next song on my playlist overpowers me. It is the perfect background music for such a scene. My concerns wash away and I start to dance. The wedding is finally something that I can call my own. Up until this second, all the time and energy planning this fiasco is a waste. I have no interest in spending so much money on a wedding. Shit, the wedding is comparatively small and cheap, by most wedding standards, and it is still pricey. But here, listening to a dance song that I'm sure that not another person here has even heard before, I see that it all was worth it. I'm surrounded by the people I love the most. I'm dancing on the beach. It's my wedding day. I am smiling. The wedding is finally mine. I had limited influence on the direction of the wedding. My hands-off approach worked for everyone involved. But for the next two minutes, I'm going to enjoy this song. I chose this jam. I am content. Nobody can stop me from dancing.

Bernie is the first to go swimming. His parents, brother and sister fly for the wedding for two reasons. The first is to support me. I am an honorary son. The second is for additional security to help keep Bernie from doing something stupid. They forget to bring full body restraints and fail to stop him. Bernie does not disappoint. He is brilliant.

The buoy remains elusive. A mere two rocks manage to hit it. It is a pitiful yet gallant effort. We throw hundreds of rocks at it and only made contact two times. At this point we are all disillusioned with our throwing abilities, our arms hurt and we are getting hungry. We give up just before dinner is served. Nobody can find Bernie.

It takes a few minutes before somebody sees his floating head about fifty feet from shore moving slowly out to sea. Unable to wait for dinner,

Bernie jumps in the Sound for a leisurely swim. It's his first time here and he treats it like he owns the place. He acts like it's a typical Saturday afternoon, nothing big is going on, time for a swim. My reaction is mixed. Part of me wants to kiss him and jump in after him so I can catch up. The other part of me is annoyed that it is such a spectacle. Come on man. Don't confuse all of the old people in attendance.

The crowd is forced to watch him because it isn't safe to swim alone. Allison soon wades in and swims to him in her silk dress. They stay out in the water for a while. The majority of people eventually lose interest and focus on the actual wedding. Bernie and Allison come ashore, soaking wet soon thereafter. Bernie comes out of the water wearing his suit. He is dripping wet and soggy. Allison thrills every man lucky enough to see her get out of the water. Even the newly married can't resist looking when she reappears. Her silk dress sticks to her body- the lack of underwear, the cold air... put two and two together. Everyone glances at Allison's body. The body is curvy, I already mentioned the silk dress, cold air and water, do the math. Obviously the men take a double take. Some just blatantly stare. Even the older women take a look and reminisce about days long gone. There is no choice in the matter.

This is a delightful wedding. We dance, we drink, we have a great time. The reception is great. Cutting the cake is memorable. Our first dance is fabulous. We run out of beer too soon. Next to go is the wine. My cousin Jason approaches me and asks me if I have my wallet, keys or phone on me. I check my pockets and find nothing. He walks over to Amber and asks her if he can throw me in the water. She gives him the okay and the next thing I know I am swimming in my tux. It doesn't take long for my groomsmen to follow me in. Amber's brothers jump in next. Floating on my back in the Puget Sound with my tuxedo on is not how I envisioned my wedding. Best wedding ever.

The water is surprisingly warm. I am not alone in the sound. Cole is the next to jump in. He does so naked. Well done, man. Amber's step brothers are floating around me somewhere. Much to the dismay of my aunt, my best man is working on his backstroke nearby. It occurs to me how random this moment is. I take a deep breath and take in what is happening. I need a minute to appreciate what's happening. I take another minute to situate myself. I float on my back and embrace my surroundings. I float calmly. I am given amnesty by the water. All mistakes are forgiven. It is my wedding day. I am given a clean slate. The rest of my life is waiting for me. I can and will make this work. It's time to grow up, be a man, and do right for my wife. It is my wedding day, I am swimming in a rented suit, and this moment is mine. I am alone. I own it. I will not fail. I stay floating on my back for a while longer. I recognize that this isn't the way I intended the night to end. But then I figured out why it makes so much sense. This is a good and pure way to start fresh. All of my sins are washed clean. I have control over the bullshit. I swim to shore. Someone hands me a towel. I dry off and leave my history behind. My past isn't important anymore. I have a wife to look after now. I must remain focused. Need to keep my head on straight. I can embrace this opportunity. I have a clean slate. Fuck cocaine. Fuck the lies. Fuck the bloody noses. Fuck all the bullshit. The salt water washes me and I am reborn. I can do this. I can stay clean. I don't need outside help to do it. I don't need therapy. I don't need to find out the root causes of anything. I don't need to think about what it means to self medicate. I don't need to process anything. I can make this marriage work. I can do it. All I have to do is believe in it. Forget out the past, enjoy the present, and embrace the future. All that, and find some dry underwear.

24

Things Fall Apart Quickly, Like Ninja Quick

THERE IS NO reason why my marriage should fall apart as fast as it does. It should work. I want it to work. I want to believe that I can change and she can make me happy. We are married in August and by December I discover that my wife is clinically depressed. She keeps this detail from me until after the ring is on her finger and we are bound together for richer or poorer. This only comes to light because my dad has to take a shit in the woods.

My father has zero interest in pooping in the forest. It just isn't his style. He prefers to take care of business in the front bathroom at home. The first thing he does after buying a house in Rossmoor is claim the front bathroom, declaring it to be off limits between the hours of 5-6 AM. What begins in 1981 continues to this day. He wakes up, eats a light breakfast and then takes a shit every morning before he goes to work. He requires toilet paper, privacy, and nothing more. Pretty sure not even a magazine. On the day he poops in the woods, he receives none of these things. Instead, he has to get dirty. Primal. Leaves. Fertilizer. I gain a whole new level of respect for him that morning. I have no clue that by the end of the day I will lose all respect for Amber.

We spend our first Christmas as a married couple in Washington. My parents, Nana, Amber, and I spend the holidays at her parent's house. We take a walk the day before my parents fly back to California. On the way back I notice that my dad is walking more quickly than usual. I keep pace with him. We separate ourselves from the rest of the group. Unfortunately, my dad can't make it back to the house in time. He darts into the woods, pulls down his pants, and reluctantly takes care of business in the forest. I don't know for sure, but I suspect that his business includes shooting liquid #2 out of his butt. This is what it smells like.

I assume he'll go native for a while, sharpen a branch into a spear for protection and reappear sometime later in the afternoon. This is how I would handle liquid #2 in the woods. I would immediately cover my naked body with mud, make a crude lean-to for shelter where I use some local flint to make a fire. My obvious next step is to learn the ways of the forest, kill a small animal, eat it's still beating heart (as a show of respect) and cook it on a spit while I gather dry moss for a bed. I'd kill fish with a spear, make friends with some local woodland creatures and then reappear months later. I return to society a wise and more quiet man blessed with tracking skills and with a new found respect for mother gaia.

My dad busts back on the trail and ignores whatever may be running down his leg. He looks at me briefly, but doesn't say a word. There is really nothing to say. Maybe quiet reflection is the way to go. Witnessing what just happens is more than enough. There is no reason to discuss it. All he can do is head to the house and take a shower. All I can do is forget it ever happened.

Oddly enough, I am so proud of my dad. I don't know if I have ever been as impressed with him as I am at this moment. I'm not sure if he knows that I am proud of him. This is a delicate situation. Our relationship has never been one that involves heart to heart conversations about bowel movements. All I know is that his secret is safe with me. I'm not going to tell anyone about it. I'm certainly not going to bring it up with him. The following words are never spoken.

James: *Dad, I'm really proud of you for shitting in the woods and not being a bitch about it.*

Dad: *Thanks son, don't tell your mother.*

I lower my head and follow him at a distance back to the house. We never speak of it again. My plan is to keep what happened to myself and forget about it as soon as possible. I never envisioned that eight hours later I would use this story to defend my family's honor.

It's one of those nights. Too much wine, too much food, too much whatever. We have the option of passing out without having sex. Consensual drunken sex between newlyweds is also an option. I'm content to just fall asleep. Amber has other plans. There is a third option I'm not aware of. This option involves being blindsided by my belligerent wife. She has things on her mind. She has stuff to say.

Amber: *I am mad.*

James: *What are you mad about?*

From my perspective, this is when all logic disappears. Rational thinking ceases to exist. Amber loses her mind. She starts to attack. Trench warfare, mustard gas, bows and arrows. My plans of sex and or sleep are thrown out the window. She isn't happy about how my family *behaved* while they were at her parent's house. She feels that Nana and my parents haven't tried hard enough. She is upset about something. I can't figure out what exactly it is. She doesn't think that my parents have made a strong enough effort to embrace and appreciate the Washingtonian lifestyle. She thinks they have been bitching the entire time they have been here. My parents are well-behaved house guests, they don't complain about anything. I tell her about my dad and his adventure in the woods. Her response is along the lines of...

Amber: *Who gives a shit? Big deal.*

James: *Actually, for my dad, it was a big deal. Did you hear him complain?*

I tell her that my mom has been going with the flow of the whole trip. No complaints, a perfect attitude, give her some credit. Amber comes back with this.

Amber: *What are you? A Mama's Boy?*

There isn't anything I can say. My wife of four months calls me a "Mama's Boy." I don't even know what that means. All I can do is shake my head and walk away. Attack me if you need to, I can handle it. But what gives you the right to pass judgment on my parents? It makes no sense. It is beyond my ability to understand. Where is all this coming from? I was under the impression that I married a nice girl. I never signed up for this. Then I remember a conversation I had with a girl I worked with right after I got engaged.

Kendra: *What would you do if right after you get married Amber stops having sex with you, gains weight, completely changes as a person and you can't stand her?*

James: *That would suck.*

Kendra: *Yes it would.*

James: *Please don't speak to me for the rest of the day.*

The next morning is quiet. My parents are unaware of the chaotic end to last night. I spend the next morning killing time until they leave for the airport. Amber's mom knows that something is wrong. She keeps quiet until later. Amber spends the entire day downstairs. She lies in her bed with the lights off and stares up at the ceiling. I tell her she should make a brief appearance before my parents leave so she can say goodbye. She walks upstairs, says goodbye and then immediately turns right back around to go downstairs. Her day of laying and staring continues.

Mercifully, my parents leave. I waste the whole morning counting the minutes until they have to leave. The unspoken tension is unbearable. They are in the dark, but I am fully aware of the underlying anxiety. The air doesn't seem right and I'm sure that they sense that something is wrong. After they leave, Amber's mom, Hannah, heads downstairs and checks on her daughter. She returns a few minutes later to tell me that Amber wants to talk. I am skeptical. I am angry. I go downstairs regardless. My fucked up wife needs a word with me. My only option is to walk down the stairs and hear her out. I enter the room and see that her eyes are red from crying. She stares back at me with a look that pleads for forgiveness. She looks at me hoping to garner some type of pity. I am not ready to make up. I am not ready to forgive. The pity I can give her is not the type of pity that she is looking for.

Amber: *I need to tell you something…*

James: *Go ahead…*

Amber: *I am so sorry about last night. I have been replaying it in my head all day long. I had no right to say those things.*

Her genuine remorse is evident, but she isn't going to get off that easy. I'm *glad* she has been crying all day long. I'm glad that she spent all day lying in bed with the lights off, staring at the ceiling. I'm glad she feels like shit because she *should* feel like shit.

James: *Listen, I understand that you're sorry. But you need to understand that you can't talk about my family like that. You have no fucking right to talk badly about my parents. Talking shit about me is one thing, but attacking my parents is inexcusable. What the fuck happened last night?*

Amber: *I'm depressed; I don't know what is wrong with me. Please forgive me.*

I make no promises and go back upstairs. I sit on the couch. Hannah comes over and sits down next to me. She apologizes to me for Amber's behavior. She feels horrible for what happened. She can't explain it and promises to do whatever she can to make sure it won't happen again. She opens an expensive bottle of wine and pours us each a glass. After my second refill, I begin to feel better. Amber comes upstairs. She desperately needs a hug. Holding a grudge doesn't make sense to me. It's just not who I am. I've never seen the point of holding onto anger longer than necessary. I tell her everything will be okay and put my arms around her.

We leave a few days later and head back to our lives in Long Beach. I return home with my new bride - my bride that just so happens to be clinically depressed. This diagnosis is news to me. She's gone from cranky to clinical in a few days (as far as I know). No more than five months after we are married, I find out that Amber needs a therapist. Before we even get to start the rest of our lives together, I am faced with a *manically depressed* spouse. She needs Prozac. She needs to get better.

My return home leaves me doubtful. There are too many things to be skeptical about. It really is too soon into the marriage to be skeptical about anything. It doesn't make sense. Paranoia creeps into my head. It seems quite convenient that she waits until after the wedding to let me in on this small detail. The fragility of her mental state was never mentioned before. Is this the reason why she is so gung ho about getting married so soon? Was this her plan all along? Trapping James is easy. Hold off on disclosing your mental illness until after he marries you.

But I love this woman. I want nothing more than for her to be healthy and happy. Depression doesn't scare me off. Shit, this is a fixable problem. I want her to get some help. Therapy is a good thing. Medicine that comes in pill form can help. Pills that come in pastel colors are even better. Doesn't that shit make you cheerful and sweet. These pills are made with rainbows and are full of hope. Take them daily and you'll be riding magical unicorns in no time. It is a fantastic idea. Stop with the questions already. Close your eyes and swallow the pill. Wash it down with this glass of water, and we both live happily ever after... right?

She needs to make an effort. *She* needs to call her doctor. *She* needs to talk about her feelings. *She* needs to pick up a prescription at the pharmacy. *She* needs to go home, fill up a glass of water and swallow the pill. She does *none* of these things.

Amber has reservations about going on meds. She isn't ready to commit to taking a pill every day. Her mother takes anti-depressants daily. Hannah has been doing it for as long as Amber can remember. Shit, Hannah is fucking lovely. Amber doesn't want to be reliant on medicine like her mother is. She convinces herself that she doesn't need to do it. I know she is wrong, but I accept her argument, like I always do. I nod my head and smile. I go against my gut and don't try changing her mind. I choose to do nothing. No proactive measures are taken. Instead of dealing with the problem we agree to pretend that there isn't one. We don't even get around to discussing our "plan" to ignore the entire situation. We just ignore it and pretend that everything is okay.

I am so good at ignoring my marital concerns that I forget about them completely. Our plan is to stay in Long Beach for the next few years and then eventually move to Washington, where we can afford to buy a house and start a family. Amber has a successful landscaping business that she started with another woman. I finish school and have a teaching credential. I don't have a contracted position yet, but I have a long-term substitute job that will last for the rest of the year. By next summer, I will finish school completely with a Master's in Education. By the following school year, there will be nothing holding me back from getting hired as an elementary school teacher on a permanent basis. Once I sign a contract, I'll make fifty grand a year and have full benefits for both myself and my wife. Amber's business is booming. Her client base continues to expand. Referrals pour in and she has more work than she knows what to do with. We live in an awesome place, on a good street in the best part of Long Beach. Everything is falling into place. Everything should be perfect. I am excited for the future. She is less so. I don't see the grounds for dysfunction. I miss the explanation for her discontent.

There is no sensible justification to uproot ourselves and move to Washington before our first anniversary. But this is exactly what we do.

She promises to stay in California for two years. This gives me time to digest the move to the Pacific NorthWest. I'm okay with this plan. I actually want to live in the forest. I want to buy an affordable house on the water. I want to start a family. I want fresh air. I want my tap water to come from a well in my yard. I want to own and use an umbrella daily. All of this sounds like a good plan for the future. This sounds doable in about three years. This *doesn't* sound doable in nine months. But she talks me into it. My inability to disagree with her bites me hard on the ass. We break the news to my family the following Easter at the dinner table. This news comes as a blindside to my parents. They do not attempt to hide their lack of enthusiasm about this turn of events. My mother is literally horrified at the prospect of our imminent departure.

Mom: *Well… that is the most depressing thing I've ever heard.*

James: *Happy Easter?*

She refuses to look at Amber for the remainder of the holiday weekend. I don't blame her. In three months her only child is going to move twelve hundred miles away. I would be pissed off too. I blame myself for being talked into leaving so soon. It's my responsibility to be a man. It's on me to stand up for myself. I fail miserably on both accounts.

I am well aware that my parents will have a hard time dealing with my move to Washington, especially so soon after the wedding. It's entirely too soon to make such big decisions. It's way too soon to go anywhere. When I leave, they have nothing left. Their daughter is dead and now their son is moving two states away. Amber should understand that by leaving California I am abandoning my parents. She knows my parents well. She recognizes how they operate. She gets that my sister is dead and that I am all they have left. These reasons should be more than enough for her to wait. They should be sufficient but they are not. She can only try to be sympathetic without having any sort of empathy (or is it the other way around?) with how my parents feel. But that won't change the fact that she is miserable in Long Beach. She convinces herself that the only way she can find contentment is to move to Washington. The elusive golden chalice of happiness is located up north. My parents' needs are secondary to her need to find it. Amber teaches me that marriage is about sacrifice– me sacrificing my own happiness to placate hers.

25

Wild Seals Will Rip Your FACE Off

AMBER AND I start to save all the money we can. We discover that moving far distances is more expensive than expected. We slowly start to box up our stuff. We then book a moving van. The school year ends for me in the middle of June. We plan to leave in five days. We need to drive a moving van and two cars to Washington at the same time. We need reinforcements. My mother would jump at the opportunity to help move us, but she is never under serious consideration. The official reason for her disqualification is that she drives way too slow. There are other reasons but I keep them to myself. I love her with all my heart but a three-day road trip with her might cause me to reconsider such positive feelings towards her.

Amber gets two of her friends to fly down from Washington in order to help us pack, and drive our cars up the coast. My parents give us a going away party the night before we leave. Unbeknownst to Amber, my friend's girlfriend shows up with a baggie full of coke. This is her going away gift to me. It is the last bag of cocaine I will see for a long time. The blow keeps me up for the majority of the night. My mind races as I get into bed. Sleeping isn't in my near future, so I lay in bed thinking. Counting sheep doesn't work. After five minutes of visualizing and counting them I give up. I toss and turn for hours until the sun is almost up and then finally fall asleep. I wake up an hour or so later the next morning. I'm running on fumes and I feel like shit. These are two reasons why I shouldn't get behind the wheel of a large moving van. The other is that I shouldn't be moving to Washington in the first place, but that ship has sailed. It is not in my best interest to drive for the next seven hours. My options are limited at the moment, being that I don't have a choice in the matter. I put on my sunglasses and drive away.

Our first stop is in the Bay Area. We spend the night and pick up Tim, his girlfriend and my cousin. Next stop is somewhere in Oregon. Then full steam ahead to my new life in Washington. Driving the moving van is not easy. It is the opposite of easy. It is fucking hard to do. It scares the shit out of me. The bright yellow beast is twenty five feet long. It is a *Penske* moving van that is filled to the brim.

I share the front cab with three goldfish that are barely staying alive inside an old Tupperware container and my confused cousin. He has no illusion that the goldfish are going to survive but he keeps all reservations about it to himself. He doesn't ask if I did a quick google check on methods to keep four dollar goldfish alive while traveling long distances. Shit, he probably would have checked the internet for us if we had bothered to mention our plan. But we kept him in the dark so now he gets to watch them slowly die and keep his damn mouth shut about it (boy isn't family the best?). The van is full from top to bottom with almost everything we own. It's packed too full, making it top heavy. It sways dangerously from side to side if it is driven too fast. Sometimes it sways if we drive too slowly. It sways whenever it isn't traveling on a direct straight line. It sways occasionally when there aren't any curves in sight. It sways when the wind picks up. It sways when the wind is calm. It sways randomly and for no damn apparent reason. It is my first time driving a moving truck so I don't know if it is swaying a normal amount or if the swaying is excessive. All I know is that I'm driving a fucking death trap on wheels and I still have a thousand miles to go.

Following the *Penske* death mobile is Amber and her two childhood friends from home driving my Honda Civic. Tim and his girlfriend bring up the rear driving Amber's truck. After twelve hundred miles of driving we finally all pull into our new driveway in Lakebay, Washington. Hannah and Frank are already waiting for us at the house. There are balloons on the mailbox. After the cars are parked and before any unloading begins, everyone starts to look around. My friends from California are awestruck. I can see clearly that whatever expectations they had don't do justice to the reality. Seeing the property for the first time erases all unpleasant memories that twenty hours in a car can bring.

The house sits at the end of a cul-de-sac, located at the end of the Key Peninsula. The house is only reachable after an eight-mile drive along a two-lane highway. Each mile leads deeper and deeper into the trees. The nearest city of any substance is a few miles away. The term city is generous, it's not a city, it's barely a town, but it's all we have.

The house has two bedrooms and one bathroom. It is about a thousand square feet. It is old, creaky, and slanted. It sits on a full acre of land, at the end of a three hundred foot long driveway. There is a carport located on the left side of the driveway, about halfway down. To the left of the driveway is a large open area of grass surrounded by trees. To the right of the driveway is the property line. Its border is marked by an assortment of bushes, shrubs, and more trees. Straight ahead is a garage that we don't get to use. To the left of the garage is the house.

We enter the house by going through a covered, yet not fully enclosed, mudroom that leads to the kitchen. This is a kitchen meant for a cabin. It is a kitchen that should only be used a few times a year. It is meant for holidays and long weekends. It isn't meant for daily use. The kitchen has deplorable off-yellow laminate countertops that are impossible to keep clean. The floor is cheap linoleum. It fails to pull off the look of rustic brick. It looks like a cheap brick version of brick. It looks tacky and shoddy. It looks like a floor made of linoleum that tries not to look like a floor made from whatever it is that linoleum is made from. Instead of looking like an authentic brick floor, it looks like a fake plastic floor struggling mightily to be a real floor.

The cabinets are made of cheap wood that doesn't fit together. They look poorly made and unfinished. The decent refrigerator that was there when we toured the house a few months back is gone. What stands in its place is no doubt the oldest refrigerator in the entire state of Washington, if not in the entire United States of America. Any attempt to find an uglier refrigerator in the entire Pacific NorthWest would no doubt end in failure.

But, thankfully, the refrigerator is in working order. I don't need it to be pretty. I need it to keep things cold. It does just that, I get over it and walk into the living room. When we first tour the house, there is an enormous shag carpet that covers the entire living room. The landlord asks us if we prefer to live on outdated shag carpet, or if we would rather live on the hardware floors that lay underneath. It is an easy decision. We ask her to remove the carpet and expose the hardwood floors that lie underneath.

The floors are beautiful. They are made of actual wood, original to the house, and still in pristine condition. We discover that this is all true except for the enormous space in the middle of the living room that was never finished. Smack dab in the middle of the main living space is a huge area of unfinished flooring. The floors are refinished at some point. The entire house is done, except for a six by nine space in the living room. What appears to be the size of a rug in the middle of the main living area is raw wood. The entire house has wood floors. Every other inch has been sanded down, polished and lacquered, except for this one spot in the living room. The landlord has the balls to pull up the tacky carpet, see that a significant portion of the floor is fucked up, and leave it how it is for us to discover when we move in. It's a ballsy move on her part, that and the old refrigerator switch-a-roo. Now I know why the rent is so cheap. For eight hundred and fifty dollars a month, she can get away with it. We never even mention it to her.

The rest of the house contains two small bedrooms and a bathroom, if you can believe it, the bathroom is more outdated than the kitchen. The house is a piece of shit. It is also on the water. I don't agree to move away from my family and my friends to live in a shit hole in the middle of nowhere for nothing, unless there is a view. As long as there is an outdoor space, I will be happy. I quickly forget about the bare spot on the floor and the ugly refrigerator.

The living room is the core of the house. It has enormous picture windows and leads out to an enormous deck. We're talking about a *huge* wooden deck that doubles the living space of the house when the weather is decent. The deck overlooks the Puget Sound. This crappy little house lies directly on the water. I can look past the brick colored linoleum that fails to look like brick. The unfinished patch of hardwood floor doesn't bother me as much. Once I walk out onto the enormous deck and look at the water, I forget all about California. I can't even remember the names of my friends I leave behind. It takes me a few moments to remember what my mother's name is. This isn't a *partial* view of water located miles away. The water isn't off in the distance. The water is pretty and blue and in three minutes, max, I can reach my hand in to touch it. The water sits right there in front of me. This water is all mine. All I have to do is walk out the back door, cross my deck, and then my small lawn. Tucked away is a path hidden by overgrown bushes that leads to a rickety old staircase. It is without doubt, structurally unsound. It is sure to collapse at some point in the near future. It is perfect.

We discover that there is beer in the fridge- courtesy of Frank. We love this man. Everyone cracks one open, finishes it, grabs another one, and then starts to unload. We make steady progress all day long, only to pause later that afternoon when the welcoming committee starts to show up. Hannah, Frank, and Amber pretty much know everyone in town. The Key Peninsula is full of two types of people. The majority of inhabitants are white trash. Dead cars collect rust on unkempt lawns in the front yard. Menthol cigarettes, poor dental care, and old sweat pants litter the community. Every year or so, a meth lab catches fire. I am told to stay away from the riff raff. I follow their advice.

The rest of Lakebay is well-educated. They are firmly entrenched in an Upper Middle Class lifestyle. They live either directly on the water, or they have a view of the water. They are artists. They are far to the left. They are politically engaged liberals. They are well-read, opinionated, and articulate. These fine people are our welcoming committee.

They arrive with bottles of wine and platters of appetizers. They have all known Amber since she was a child. They are best friends with Hannah and Frank. They can't contain their excitement that Amber is returning home. They all can't wait to get to know her new husband more intimately. I've met most of them before and I like every single one of them. They discuss politics. They are talented artists. They are my kind of people.

The night ends on a rowboat out on the sound. Josh and I are drunk and determined to use the dinghy that we find overturned on the bulkhead. We find oars in the shed and carry the boat to the water's edge. We ignore all attempts made by the more sober people to turn back from the water.

Frank: *Bad idea guys, if you're fifty feet from shore and in fifty degrees water your chances of survival are slim. If something goes wrong, you're in trouble.*

James: *Where did you get this information?*

Frank: *The Coast Guard website.*

James: *Good to know.*

We walk back to the shed, find life jackets and toss them in the boat. Frank accepts that he won't be able to talk us out of going out on the boat. He follows us down the stairs and hangs out on the shore while we row away from the beach. He, of all people, can understand our reasons for doing this. As long as he can keep an eye on us, he won't stop us.

We are quickly reminded that rowing a boat requires effort and skill. It takes us a minute to synchronize our paddles but soon we figure it out and start to make progress. We stop far enough offshore so the water surrounds us completely. We are in complete agreement that our actions are totally necessary. Failure to spend quality time on the water within the first twenty four hours of moving into a house sitting directly on the water sets a bad precedent. I don't plan on drowning tonight anyway. We last twenty minutes and row back to shore. We stare death in the face and survive. We stare down the glassy calm water and don't even get wet.

We spend the next two days hard at work. The unpacking never ends. Interior walls are painted. Between sips of bourbon, shelves are made in the kitchen and a bookshelf is built for the living room. Amber organizes the bedrooms. Tim does whatever is asked of him. I don't stop moving the entire time. We listen to music, sip on beers, buy more beer, and enjoy every minute of it. In a few days, our unpaid help will leave us. The rest of the summer belongs to Amber and I. Our bedroom has a window that looks out onto the water. Every morning I open my eyes and see clear skies and blue water. The days are warm. Three months of summer weather makes up for the nine months of non-summer weather. We arrive at the start of the nice season.

Our first few months in Washington are pretty fucking awesome. I have no complaints. I am happy. My life starts to change. I start to do things that I haven't done for a long time. I start to do things that I've never done. Sex for no reason? Sounds lovely. Eating meals outside? Sure. Mow the fucking lawns? Fuck me.

I have experience mowing lawns. There's no reason I can't do this. I mowed a family friend's front lawn for a few months one summer when I was a kid. This was fifteen years ago. I haven't looked at a lawn mower since then. Part of the new lease agreement I recently signed before moving to Washington stipulates that I'm responsible for all lawn care at the house. I don't think twice about it. How hard can it be? I'm an experienced lawn mower. I mowed the shit out of a lawn every other week for an entire summer. I practically invented the modern lawn mower. I have no fear of grass.

I quickly discover how wrong I am. Mowing the lawn is more intense than I initially expected. The average amount of grass in a front yard in Rossmoor is tiny. At most, it is ninety feet long and twenty feet deep. Even if the mower runs out of gas and you accidentally kill the next door neighbor's cat, the job is done within twenty minutes.

The grass here is long overdue for a cut. I looked over the excessive amount of lawn for the first time. I can only pray that a twenty-year-old mower and a backup supply of a half tank of gasoline will get the job done. I spend the next ten minutes using all my strength pulling the cord in a futile attempt to start the engine. Only after I am out of breath do I look at the directions printed on the top of the mower. I turn the ignition switch to the on position, flood the engine with a bit of gas and pull on the cord one last time.The fucker starts right up. I got started.

Mowing the lawn takes *forever.* It requires a commitment that lasts no less than two hours. It only takes longer than four if I am super hung over. It usually takes me three hours to cut both the front and back yards. Week after week I completely ignore the lawn. The grass keeps growing. I keep ignoring the situation. I continue to put it off until my neighbors start giving me dirty looks. I see my next door neighbor atop his riding lawn mower taking care of his grass every Saturday. Every Saturday I consider mowing my lawn. Every Saturday I ignore the impulse and promise myself that I will do it the following weekend.

The vicious cycle continues. Only when my neighbor offers to cut my grass for free do I take any action. Under no circumstances will I allow anyone to cut my grass but me. It may be up to my knees. I'll no doubt have to set the mower at its highest setting. What should take two hours, will no doubt take six. I slowly battle my way through a full acre of grass that is eight inches high. I have to constantly angle the mower upwards in order to keep the blade moving and the engine running. I waste the majority of my time restarting the motor. Every time it sputters to a stop I have to flip it over so I can clear out the grass.

I then put it back upright and then pull the damn chain so the fucker will start up again.

The bulk of the grass is located behind the house. It looks challenging. It doesn't seem impossible at first. After ten minutes busting my ass I look around and see that I haven't even made a dent. Finishing this lawn is going to be harder than originally thought. This is a true test. Do I have the stamina? Do I have the commitment? Do I have a choice? No, on all counts– so it's back to cutting.

I start cutting the grass near the house. I head up the left edge of the lawn, turn around at the carport and head back towards the house. I repeat this display of back and forth lawn mowing for hours. Each time the bag fills up with clippings I have to stop the mower, remove the bag, walk to the far end of the yard and dump the clippings on the compost pile. I take the empty bag back to the mower, restart it, and continue the process until the bag fills up again. Rinse and repeat. This gradually leads to long grass becoming short grass. I stay focused on going back and forth. I continue to keep the vision. I am persistent and keep the lines straight. I keep on going. It never ends. I keep going strong. The uncut portion of the lawn keeps getting smaller and smaller. Before I know it I am done with the largest part of the yard. The back is done. I am tired and sweaty. Then I remember that the grass continues on either side of the house and into the front yard. My job is not yet complete. There is still more grass that needs to be cut.

My first moment as a real man happens later in the summer. The local Chamber Of Commerce gets wind of my arrival. It is their civic duty to make sure I can withstand the various pressures and hardships of being a Washington State resident. They require a feat of strength. They send Mark and Seth. They are deep undercover operatives in Kitsap County. They are teenagers. My options are limited. I can survive the test, drown in my front yard, or go back to California.

I met Mark, his younger brother Seth, and their parents a few days before. Amber and I go with Hannah and Frank to an event out on the Peninsula. It is a fundraiser of some kind that has a silent auction, live music and more importantly, a beer garden. I check my calendar and discover that I don't have any plans that day. Actually, I don't own a calendar and I don't have any plans scheduled for any day soon. My shit is wide open for the foreseeable future.

Sitting across from me in the beer garden is John, his wife and their two sons. Mark recently graduated from high school and is going to Gonzaga in the fall. He is a super polite, good looking, well-adjusted young adult that I like the second I meet him. Seth is fifteen; he is ornery as hell and hates authority. I say something mildly sarcastic to him. He tells me to fuck off.

Seth: *Fuck off.*

These are the first words he says to me. I immediately like this kid. He reminds me of an angrier version of myself ten years ago. He tells me to *fuck off* exactly how I would tell me to fuck off. It isn't an angry *fuck off.* He doesn't say it with a big stupid grin on his face. He looks me straight in the eyes and tells me to *fuck off.* This is not a threat. This is not a joke. This is so much more.

James: *Are you a Kid A or OK Computer fan?*

Seth: *Both, what do you mean?*

James: *I mean, if you had to choose one album, which one would you pick? Which album more accurately describes you as a person? Which one do you listen to more often? We all have one that speaks to us on a deeper level. Which album gives you more hope? Respect? And appreciation of Radiohead music?*

Seth doesn't expect me to say this. He assumes that when I say something sarcastic to him that I am blowing him off, discounting him as a kid. The moment I ask him a serious question he is able to let his guard down. We spend the next few hours talking about music.

I find out that Seth and Mark's parents own a cabin further down the Peninsula. They live in Seattle and come out here on the weekends during the summer. The two boys get their parents' permission to come to our house later that afternoon. Amber and I feed the underage drinkers beer. We play a game of Bocce ball and they eventually go back to their family cabin.

My phone rings late the next day. It is Mark on the other line. He wants to know if Amber and I have any plans that day. One of the two friends I have in Washington is on the phone right now; my other friend is his fifteen year old brother that's probably sitting next to him on the couch. Fuck no. We have absolutely no plans to speak of. Come on over. After I hang up the phone it occurs to me that we might have plans that I just don't know about. Then I remember that we live in the middle of nowhere and if we had plans I would be the first to know about them. Mark and Seth arrive no more than five minutes later. Mark doesn't mention that he is a government agent. His ulterior motives are unknown to me when he nonchalantly suggests that we swim to the other side of the bay and back. A leisurely swim sounds nice.

A skinny eighteen-year-old who may or may not be working for the local government talks me into swimming across the bay and back. I'm on the wrong side of twenty-six. I have skinny arms, skinnier legs and an impressively large belly. He is over six feet tall, skinnier than a bulimic middle school girl, and has no more than 4% body fat. In the fall of 2007 he will start his freshman year in college. My freshman year started in 1997. I am so out of shape that my survival is in question. This never even enters his mind. Fat people drown, skinny people keep on swimming.

I am given no choice in the matter. I have to say yes. My honor is at stake. The honor of the Californian swimming community is in my hands. I have no other option but to embrace what is sure to be a leisurely midday swim. What could go wrong?

The initial shock of the cold water only lasts for the first few minutes. I dive in and sooner than expected, the water temperature becomes pleasant. I remember the swimming lessons I took when I was five. My swimming strokes come effortlessly. My body adjusts to the water quickly. I transform into a part trout, part blue whale swimming machine. My arms start moving faster. My legs start kicking harder. I swim faster and harder than I ever imagined possible. Not only can I do this, I can do this in record time.

I stop swimming to see how far I've made it. I pop my head out of the water and look around. Mark is swimming close by. He comes from a good family, so leaving me behind has never been an option. This is when I discover how much more swimming we have left. We're still really fucking far from the other side. We haven't even made it past the half-way point. We can see the other shore, but we know it is farther than it looks.

I am treading water in the middle of the ocean and I have no other choice but to continue swimming. This is when I start to get nervous. I abandoned the freestyle immediately. My survival depends on making it to the other side. Consideration of swimming strokes becomes a distant memory. From here on out I will rely solely on the backstroke.

As I tread water and catch my breath in the middle of the ocean I see something break through the surface of the water. Twenty yards off to the right I make eye contact with two eyes connected to a smooth head made of blubber. Our gaze is only broken when the seal winks at me. A second seal surfaces soon thereafter and smiles at Mark.

Without saying a word, and with nothing more than a look, we start really swimming. We don't have to say shit. Two wild seals bird dogging us is all we need to know. It is time to start moving. I forget that I am fucking exhausted. I am done for if the seals decide to attack. On my best day I can't out swim a seal. This isn't my best day by far. My only hope is that they have already eaten lunch that day. What if they haven't eaten in a while and are hungry? Am I about to fall victim to a vicious seal attack?

Turning back now isn't really an option. Even if there is ravenous sea life nearby, we *must* keep on swimming. This is what we do. We keep swimming across the bay. I try not to think about the seals that continue to follow us. I ignore the blood thirsty seals that shadow us. I can only hope they are friendly seals. I pray that they don't have murder on their minds.

I agree to this swimming adventure unaware that oceanic wildlife could play a part. I needed the exercise and looked forward to burning some calories. Half an hour later, I am nowhere near the safety of land and I am about to be eaten by a ravenous seal. *Let's go for a swim? Good idea. Let's go across the fucking bay, touch the sand, and then swim back. That's a great plan. No seals will eat you on the way over. You won't die of exhaustion on the way back. Nothing will go wrong. Be a man. Where's a piece of driftwood when you need it?*

Thankfully, the seals don't attack. We make it to the far side of the bay. We arrive on the sand and collapse in exhaustion. We lay on the safety of land for a few minutes to catch our breath. Then we prop ourselves on our elbows and look back over what we have just swam across. That shit was far. It was way farther than what it looked like.

Two seconds later it occurs to me. The only way I can get back is to swim back across the bay for a second time. Will I offend the seals by attempting to swim back to the other side? Did they not attack us in an act of pity? Will their kindness abate if we attempt to swim across again? Will their fury be ignited? Will they keep us alive until we are almost to the other side only to then eat us bite by bite? Do they like our resolve? Will they let us hold onto their ears and swim us across? Do they even give a shit? Did they even notice us swimming in the first place?

Neither of us thought to bring an inner tube. We have no inflatable arm floats. We have nothing to hold onto as we start our swim back across. We are swimming farther than we should be and we have no form of safety measures to help us. There are also a couple of menacing seals circulating around the bay. Hungry seals more than ready to fuck somebody up.

We swim back slowly. We expect that at any moment a seal will surprise us and rip off an arm or a leg. We continue to swim. Every leg kick and arm stroke gets us closer to shore. The seals seem to have moved on. Our lives don't seem to be hanging in the balance as much as before. Blood thirsty seals with murder on their minds don't seem to be an actual thing. The swim back doesn't take as long. My body isn't so tired after all. I will swim freestyle again. I made it back to shore. I return triumphant. I am, afterall, a strong capable human. All concerns that the local government has regarding my ability to handle the rough and tumble world of Washington State living are answered. The local seals don't want to fuck with me, and that is more than enough reason to let me live here. I pass the test.

I spend the summer playing bocce ball, mowing the grass, working on the house, and applying for jobs. Amber cooks dinner, we drink wine, we play dominoes, watch television together and take showers together. Life is pretty good, my marriage is fine. I am content. My skill at backyard games improves steadily, the grass looks amazing, and the house looks better each day. Finding a job proves to be more difficult. Every attempt I make to find one ends in disappointment. The local school district just won't hire me. Getting an interview is impossible.

The few interviews I go to lead to nothing. The school year begins and we start to get nervous. Our rent is half of what it was in Long Beach. Our expenses are much smaller. Amber saved a bunch of money before we moved here. We are fine for now, but we can't survive for much longer without an income.

Amber and I return to California for a week in August. I can't wait to go home to visit. She can't wait to come back to Washington. Our plane tickets are paid for so I can officiate a wedding in Santa Barbara. The wedding falls the weekend before my ten year high school reunion. This is the perfect excuse to spend the next week visiting my friends and family and then attend my high school reunion the following Saturday night.

The rapid decay of my marriage begins on a Saturday night in Costa Mesa. The reunion starts off well. The reunion continues to go well until it falls apart. It turns to shit faster than I think is possible. I work the room. I bounce around from friend to friend. I look over and see that Amber is occupied at the moment with Mike. I figure that she is happy and I'll get the next fifteen minutes to walk around without her so I can be me for a bit.

As I circulate the room, Amber and Mike start to talk about me. Mike complains to Amber about the people I hung out with before I moved to Washington. These people have less than perfect reputations in regards to the use of a certain drug. Amber asks Mike if I have done Cocaine since we got married. Mike doesn't say yes, but he doesn't need to. His body language and attitude say it loud and clear. With that, he sells me out and I am *fucked*. Amber quickly corners me. She asks me point blank if I have done drugs since our wedding.

Amber: *Have you done cocaine since we were married?*

Any amount of stalling won't change the fact that she already knows the answer. My only hope is that English is my second language and that I don't understand the question. If only I grew up in China. I know that she knows the answer. My Mandarin is poor at best. The only option is to come clean. I have no choice but to admit my transgressions to her.

James: *Yes.*

Before I can even finish the word, she throws a coffee mug full of red wine at my head. As she storms off down the hallway, I realize that

I have to follow her. I'd rather not. I'd prefer to go back into the reunion and drink some more. Sadly, this marks the end of a fun night. My time at the reunion is over. My night is just beginning.

I spent the rest of the night in the hotel room. Countless hours are spent fighting, arguing, pleading, promising, begging, yelling, and trying to reason with Amber. She takes a couple of swings at my face. I let her connect because I deserve to get hit. She calms down a bit when the blood drips down my face where her engagement ring cuts into me. The physical violence calms her down. Once she sees blood she can fall asleep.

We wake up early the next morning. She won't look at me but we are supposed to go to a baseball game with my parents in a few hours. We have no choice but to fake it and watch Angel's baseball. Mike just so happens to have tickets directly behind us. Amber and I show up and do a decent job of pretending that there is nothing wrong. Mike sits directly behind us. I do not look at him for the entire game. He makes no attempt to talk to me. The game ends and we mercifully get on a plane and leave California later that day. Even after the plane touches down a few hours later in Washington, I still don't fully understand how fucked I am. Even after I grab our luggage and wait for the ride back to Gig Harbor do I figure out what awaits me? No. Only after we get home do I *truly* understand how angry my wife is. It takes me awhile to figure out how much she really hates me. And how painful my life is about to get.

26

Build Fire, Stay Warm, Fold Laundry, Ignore Wife

LIFE SLOWLY GETS back to normal. Dysfunctional, but normal, which come to think of it, *is* pretty normal, whatever, it's tolerable. I find a job teaching first grade about forty-five minutes away that fall. It's fine. It's whatever. I survive most days. Some days it's all I can hope for. Other days are better. I don't really know what's happening a lot of the time. Makes me question my decision to go into this particular field of work. Oh well, it's a job. Someone needs to have one.

The warm weather ends in October. November is when I start making fires. The weather starts to suck and we discover that the main heating vent blows directly into the back of the TV. Fearing a premature death by electrocution is what leads me into a life of fire building. On a daily basis I arrive home from work to a cold house. I have no other choice but to make a fire. Even with roaring flames in the fireplace, I still must wear a beanie and flannel pajama bottoms. Without a fire, Amber would have to make dinner wearing a heavy coat and multiple pairs of socks.

I build a Lincoln Log-style tower of wood every single night after I get home. I originally went through numerous layouts before I settled on an acceptable design. I start by laying two medium sized logs parallel to each other on the bottom of the cast iron stove/fireplace. I then lay smaller pieces of wood across the first two logs. After that, I place a piece of wood that's a bit larger on top. Lastly, I add kindling in various strategically important places and then stuff the space underneath with newspapers. I take a brief moment to inspect my work and then light themotherfucker.

The flame starts slowly. I keep an eye on its progress and, if necessary, continue to feed it small pieces until all of the wood has caught fire. Only after the fire starts to roar and creates heat do I add the final log. This single log is significantly larger than the rest. It is the key to keeping the fire strong. This log keeps the house warm until it is time to go to bed.

I spend no less than three hours a week collecting and chopping wood. What begins as a chore turns into an activity that breaks up the tedious nature of living in isolation. I build something beautiful every day after school. I destroy this creation soon after it is built. I use fire on a daily basis. I burn wood every day after school. My inner pyromaniac is let loose. I am allowed, nay, encouraged to play with matches. Each fire is my masterpiece. I watch the wood burn like I did when I was seven years old on a camping trip. Yes, I am a man. I can prove this statement with the roaring fire I just made. I created this heat. I'm responsible for the comfort it provides. I do this for anyone that needs it. I bestow this warmth for all to enjoy. If anyone is hungry, I will hunt and kill animals. I will track down a large moose and strangle it with my bare hands. Then we will smoke the beast over damp leaves laid over a fire. On second thought, I will gather assorted berries and fruits for a nice salad. The likelihood of either of these activities happening while living in a city is very slim. I have little interest in gathering berries or killing large game but I appreciate that building a fire makes each activity possible.

I am still the only one working when Christmas break comes around. Amber hasn't gotten around to starting up her new landscaping business. What was originally supposed to happen last summer is pushed back to the fall. This will now be pushed back to spring because she can't do any work during winter, it is too cold. After six months in Washington she has done *nothing* to rebuild her successful landscaping company. I am the sole breadwinner of the household. She is the "Stay At Home Mom."

The problem with this is that we don't have any kids. She spends her days doing a healthy amount of nothing. The only reason she gets out of bed is so she can watch her soaps for two full hours each day. I can't figure out what the rest of her day is spent doing. It's obvious that cleaning isn't high on her list of priorities.

This is when I start to get resentful. I come home from a long day at school to a house that is never clean. If I take over the role of man who brings home the bacon, then she needs to embrace the role of wife who makes sure the house is clean and dinner is ready. That's how it works right? It is a small house. I'm not there for at least eight hours every day. All she needs to do is rally for a half hour before I get home so the house is picked up. This never seems to happen.

It is still dark out most mornings when I leave for school. If Amber cooked the night before, then I'll do the dishes after dinner. I fill the dishwasher and leave the heavier pans and pots to dry on the counter. This is where they still sit when I get home later that day. Amber has *all day* to do a *single* load of laundry. This never seems to happen. I come home from work and put in a load. I never complain about this. I simply put it in the washer and then transfer it into the dryer. Once the clothes are dry, I take them out and fold them.

My day starts before six AM and I find myself folding laundry after ten PM. I don't mind folding clothes. The problem is that I only have a few hours after I get home from a hard day at work and I have to go to bed. My wife has *all day* to do these things. Why am *I* folding undershirts at 9:30 at night? Why am *I* folding anything? Why the fuck don't I say anything?

I finish folding, but don't put it away. I leave the folded laundry on top of the couch. I am tired. First graders are exhausting. I'm going to bed. My hope is that Amber will put them away tomorrow. And there it waits for me the next day when I return home. I'm too big a softie to call her out on it. She won't even pretend to keep the house clean. She either doesn't realize how much this bothers me, or she is well aware of it and just doesn't care anymore. Every time I come home to a dirty house I have to tuck more resentment inside me. This doesn't make sense to me. I can't figure out why this is happening. Oh yeah, I know exactly why this is happening.

I reach my breaking point when I walk through the door when her mom is over at the house. She is there to paint with Amber. The sink is full of dishes. Clean ones are still on the counter. The folded laundry is on the back of the couch. I took care of all of this last night. All she had to do before Hannah comes over was clear away the clutter. She has all fucking day to do this. All fucking day to do some light tidying before her mom comes over. This is not a lot to ask. Doesn't she have any *pride*? Doesn't she want her mother to feel pride for where we live? I do not understand this bullshit. These days frustrate me the most.

January comes and I organize a surprise birthday party for her. It is like a second homecoming party for Amber and an attempt to get off her shit list. A well-executed surprise party just might be the first step on my way back into her good graces. I am pretty desperate at this point.

The party is a great success. I get my hands on some strong ADD medicine and spend the night running around at a hundred miles an hour. We bring a small group of friends back to our house. Then the night starts to get weird. Amber's first order of business is to lose her engagement ring. A caravan of three cars drive down our driveway and park, Amber gets out of one of the cars and somehow manages to fling her diamond ring off her finger and into the dark, vast void of the backyard. At least this is what she alleges to have happened. She explains to me that she is in the middle of an animated conversation when she gets out of the car. This causes an excessive amount of arm flailing. Without such arm motion she can't articulate the important point she is about to make. This in turn causes her engagement ring to fly off her finger and directly into a pile of leaves, lawn debris and dirt. She doesn't immediately notice that her ring is no longer on her finger. She doesn't see it land. She has a general idea regarding its whereabouts but isn't certain. The ring could be anywhere.

The entire group goes into the house, finds flashlights and turns right back around and starts looking for the ring. It is really fucking dark and cold outside. The ring is pretty fucking small. If we can't find it in the next five minutes, then we won't find it no matter how long we search. Our only hope is that it lands on a large leaf near the top of the mound with the diamond facing up. Even if this does happen, there are a half dozen people trampling around the area. The search perimeter is being compromised. This ensures that it is getting more and more buried by the minute. The ring evades us. The search is a total failure. We stay out there for twenty minutes looking. Then, I call off the search. I figure that the ring will be easier to find the next morning. I'll wait until it is light out to dig through the shit and find it. After all, we do have guests at the house. This rarely happens so I must take advantage of the situation. Everyone is in complete agreement. We all would rather be drinking inside. Nobody wants to continue digging through the dirt. The ring isn't lying in an obvious place as it should be. It should be easy to find but it isn't so our only move is to give up for the time being and tackle the bottle of vodka I have waiting for us in the freezer.

The night continues on with a spirited game of Trivial Pursuit. People start to leave. The party dies down gradually. By three in the morning, there remain only three of us. Amber is still going strong. This is way past her usual bedtime. I still have a few pills left. I won't be going to bed any time soon. The third person at the house is Jerry. The playlist I made for Amber is full of music she loves. Classic rock is loudly coming out of the speakers. We play cards in the dining room and keep on drinking.

I am happy that Jerry is here with us. I like Jerry. I know that Amber likes him too. Amber has known his family since she was a little kid. Her parents have known his parents forever. She grew up with Jerry and his brother. Their childhood homes are no more than a mile apart. I like Jerry. He is polite. He looks like he might be waiting for the bus. He looks like a guy who just might eat an ice cream cone (vanilla) either at a community event or in the sunshine outside an ice cream shop. I never consider him to be a threat on any level. His attempts at hiding the fact that he is a dork are not successful. His nerdy side shines bright, but it doesn't matter because I know that Amber enjoys his company. For the most part I am excluded from their conversation. I feel like the third wheel on a date they are having. They continue to reminisce about shit I have nothing to do with. Stories are followed by more stories about things that happened back in elementary school. Inside jokes are brought up. Secret handshakes are reintroduced. I know, he is that guy you can rely on that always brings ice to a barbeque.

They forget that I am still sitting at the table with them. My presence isn't necessary. They would prefer if I would leave them alone and go to bed already. Sleep isn't an option for me, so I found an art project to work on. Anything to focus my attention on that doesn't involve their boring stories will save me. My desperate attempt to find something else to do leads me to the shed. My need to get away from their stories is strong. I actually turn on my table saw and cut wood. It is four in the morning when I measure out and make the cuts for a new wooden box. The saw is pretty quiet. Cutting plywood with it is not. It's the middle of the night. I have no business making loud noises right now. I have neighbors that would freak out if they find me in the shed doing some woodworking at this time. My only hope is that the sound won't carry too far and wake anyone up. If Jim has to walk over and ask me to stop using power tools at four in the morning, I'll feel pretty fucking stupid. If Jim's wife has to come over and tell me to keep the noise down then I am truly fucked. I abandon my ill-conceived project and find another one that doesn't involve so much noise. Oh yeah, Jerry probably prefers mild salsa.

I find a box that was ready for staining. I set up shop in the mud room and get to work. Amber and Jerry stay in the dining room and talk. The front door is wide open which allows me an unobstructed view of the two of them. I can see them, they can see me. The minutes fly by. We've made it deeper and deeper into the night. At some point I realized that the night is almost over and that the morning is closer than we think. This is when I turn my head to glance into the house. As I look towards them I notice how engaged they still are in the conversation. Next, I notice how close they are sitting to one another. I lastly notice how close their faces are to one another. Jerry probably knows where the breaker box is and has labeled all the switches.

As I see my wife gaze intently into the eyes of another man I imagine seeing her lean in to kiss him. I imagine watching both of them slowly lean closer and closer. I can visualize them kissing each other right there in the middle of the dining room. I allow my mind to wander for another second so I can consider what an appropriate reaction should be. How do I respond? How do I react? Standardized social conventions require a strong response. The community looks forward to an elaborate act of crazy to come from me. I will be forgiven for any and all acts of violence. Any blood I am directly responsible for spilling won't be held against me. I am issued a pass the moment I see them kiss. My reaction would look something like this. This is my plan if they start making out. This doesn't happen. But you can never be too prepared. Also, Jerry is an excellent parallel parker.

I burst through the screen door and enter the house yelling obscenities while waving my arms in a threatening manner. I tell them both in a stern voice how shocked and appalled I am. I shamelessly hurl cliché after cliché at them.

James: How could you do this to me? I let you in my house. I trusted you. This is how you repay my generosity? I thought we were friends. Get out of my house you dirty whore. Your betrayal will not go unnoticed. I am very disappointed in you at the moment. I'm not mad, just disappointed- which should make you feel worse.

My anger and rage can't be contained within words. I pick up an expensive vase and throw it through a window. I punch Jerry and knock him out on the spot. I fully intend on punching him until I remember that the last time I was in a fight was when I was in middle school.

The mature thing to do is ask him to leave. If I am anything at all, then I am totally a mature adult. I'll escort him out of the house with a firm grip. I turn my attention towards Amber after he leaves. I launch a second volley of clichés in her direction. My performance deserves an Oscar.

James: How could you do this to me? Why? Blah, blah, blah, et cetera, et cetera.

I can barely suppress a smile as I say this to her. I struggle to stay serious and somber when all I want to do is cheer for joy. She fucked up and I get to divorce her. It's all on her now. I had nothing to do with it. It's all her fault and there's nothing she can do or say to fix it. There is nothing she can do to sway the public's opinion on the matter. No matter how hard she tries to repair her image, there is no disputing that she is a bad person. All of my bullshit stays hidden while she sews on a big letter A on her petticoat. Crappy weather, wood chopping and loneliness will soon be just a bad memory. My near future will be filled with traffic, strip malls and warm temperatures all year long. I will return to California embraced with the open arms of a sympathetic audience. Years of lies and dishonest behavior are swept under the rug because she kissed another guy. Her infidelity wipes my slate clean and gives me a fresh start. I get to pick and choose what I want to leave with. I'll claim as much stuff as I want to. She won't say a single word while she watches me do it. The entire peninsula community throws me a going away party before I move back home. Amber is the only one who isn't invited.

James: Get out of my house, you cheating whore!

This is what I want to scream in her face. Instead, I snap out of my delusional fantasy. They sit closely together. They stare into each other's eyes with serious intensity, but they don't kiss. The clarity of what I am doing consumes me -The fact that I spend the last ten minutes thinking about it, happily, is pretty sad. The reality of hoping that I witness my wife cheating on me speaks volumes. My plan to catch my wife cheating on me falls apart right there. My marriage is falling apart as the sun starts to break through the darkness; and I have no incentive to fix it.

The sun eventually rises and I take Jerry home. Not only did I just give her an unforgettable birthday surprise, but it's looking like she gave me one, too. The clarity of my failure as a husband is all-consuming, I cannot forget the way Amber looks at Jerry, the way she used to look at me. Everything is different, and yet nothing has changed. Amber goes to bed and I spend the rest of the morning digging through an enormous pile of leaves. I thank my lucky stars for the little blue pills that are keeping me awake. Lying in bed next to someone who I used to know, pretending to be asleep, would be torture. I shift my focus - create a game of *Where's Waldo: The Engagement Ring Edition*. The search for the engagement ring keeps me occupied. As Amber sleeps, I dig. And dig. And dig. I think of the urban legend that warns if you dig too much, you'll reach China - at this point, an escape route to China feels more welcoming that my marital bed. Hours later I am still searching for it and about to give up. My hands are filthy, dirt is embedded into every fiber of my body, and I'm pretty sure I look like a crazy person out here. Has there ever been an incident of a man digging holes at dawn that ended well? The ring turns into my obsession - if I can just get it back, then everything will reset, right? I've been either sitting on the ground or on my knees for the past three hours. My back hurts and I'm tired. I bring my arms above my head and close my eyes while I crack my back and stretch like a senior citizen - slowly and with painful acceptance. I open my eyes ten seconds later to find myself staring directly at the ring. Mother fucker. If I didn't know better I would say that it has been sitting there the entire time. The search is finally over. The ring has been found. I hurry back inside and show it to her. She thanks me groggily and falls right back asleep. Her lack of enthusiasm concerns me. The absence of appreciation annoys me - I was expecting a demonstration of love for my HOURS of hard labor, and was given the equivalent of a one-armed (friend-zone) hug - leaving me awake to ask myself, *Is this what love is supposed to feel like?* I would love to hop in bed and fall asleep, I don't want to allow myself to answer the question, plus I still have way too many milligrams of legalized blue pills full of amphetamines in my system that I don't have a prescription for. The devil comes in the form of small blue pills. They appear to be harmless but keep me from falling asleep. Churning in my weary thoughts about my dying relationship. Resting isn't an option as of yet. Instead of sleeping, I spend the next hour cleaning the kitchen. Ironic.

I eventually fall asleep. I wake up later that day to discover that the birthday party hasn't magically fixed the marriage. For me, it's the beginning of the end. Weeks go by and it becomes clearer and clearer that things are getting worse. We stop talking. We stop having sex. The marriage is disintegrating right before my eyes, and I'm done.

We spend the majority of our relationship trying to steer clear of arguments. Constructive criticism doesn't exist. Throwing the most vile insults at each other, neither of us is trying to "help" the other with our passive-aggressive/aggressive-aggressive put downs. We never learn how to argue productively. This leads to secrets. We're at the point where we would rather lie to each other than deal with the reaction of the other - we just don't care. The fear of being honest with one another finally catches up to us. All tactics that can help to keep an argument from escalating into a war are lost on me.

But regardless of the obvious divide, I am not ready to quit this union - only I have no strategy or plan of action. My only choice is to continue to avoid dealing with all the things that bother me. I am no longer "James: Witty Wordsmith", instead I'm "Silent James" - leaving everyone who has known me pre-Amber worried about me, my silence scares me. I keep my mouth shut. I come home to a dirty house and a wife still wearing her pajamas a few days a week. I force myself to smile and I tuck more bitterness inside me. Every day I get home from work I add some more pent up anger to the enormous tumor of frustration that is building inside me. The tumor gets so large that I can't even talk to her. Making the effort to verbalize words becomes too hard for me. I simply stop talking to her. She follows my lead and ends all spoken communication with me. We spend the next *ten days* in a vow of silence. We barely even look at one another. We don't say a single word to one another for a week and a half. I am not exaggerating. I'm not even aware it is possible to completely ignore someone you live with for ten days straight. It turns out to be quite easy. I don't really even have to try.

A How-To Guide For Ten Days of TOTAL SILENCE Between Spouses

1. *Wake up early and leave the house before she gets up.*
2. *Leave without poking your head through the bedroom door to say "bye," "have a great day," or "I love you."*
3. *Work until five PM and then drive forty five minutes to get home.*
4. *Park the car, enter through the kitchen door and see that the dishes you left in the sink last night didn't get washed and will need to be washed by you.*
5. *Find your significant other lying on the couch; she does not turn to look at you.*
6. *Return to the kitchen, do the dishes.*
7. *Change out of work clothes, she leaves the couch and cooks dinner.*
8. *Do not offer to help her cook, instead, pour yourself a drink.*
9. *Sit on the couch and watch television.*
10. *Spend all of dinner eating food while watching pre-recorded TV shows.*
11. *Go to the kitchen alone and clean up the mess.*
12. *Return to the couch and continue to watch TV until it is time for bed.*
13. **Another option is to watch TV in different rooms.*
14. *Fall asleep without saying goodnight.*
15. *Repeat this sad charade for nine more days.*

This is how I will spend the next few months of my life. The silence is broken and we inevitably start to communicate again. We communicate, but our sex life is nonexistent - we no longer even try. I never give up hope, and keep on attempting to turn her on, so I don't feel like the only one trying. But, our sex life (or lack thereof) is *trying*. It sure as hell is trying me. Her defense is strong. She assures me that she totally wants to have sex. She unfortunately had to change her birth control dosage a few days ago and it'll take at least a month for the new pills to kick in. I try to convince her that pulling out before I orgasm never failed me in high school and only failed me once in college. She never considers this option thoroughly– even though we're married and have always planned on having children at some point, she acts repulsed by the idea of it. She never even takes this simple solution seriously. This alternative method of birth control may not be scientifically proven, but is no doubt equally effective in the prevention of pregnancies. It never even occurs to me to buy a box of condoms. I completely forget about their existence. It is a simple solution to my problem. It can solve everything. It is the answer to everything and it is sadly overlooked.

I am totally blind to the possibility that the only reason she changed her birth control is to have an excuse not to sleep with me. I never doubt her when she tells me that we can't have sex until her birth control kicks in and blocks her uterus from producing babies. It never crosses my mind that she may have alternative motives. I go with the flow and take her word for it.

It doesn't take me long to realize that this relationship cannot survive without some form of intimacy. Taking away sex is one thing, taking away hugs and kisses as well as sex is something entirely different. No relationship can survive without the minimal amount of physical touching. No bond is strong enough to withstand being completely separated. This appears to be her plan. She doesn't care enough anymore to fight for it. I am in complete agreement with her.

A few weeks later, I stop caring altogether. I abandoned my wife on Valentine's Day weekend. The fact that she has strep throat and the flu doesn't stop me from leaving. She is super sick and I am super out of there. To my defense, I only found out how sick she is after getting off the airplane. Not until I arrive in San Francisco do I find out that she is actually sick, like really sick. Flying back to Washington isn't an option. I have no intention to turn back around. She might be contagious. Instead, I spend the weekend with my cousin and try to drink away my problems. Also to my defense, if I don't leave this weekend, there is a good chance that I will lose my mind and kill my wife. She gets off easy. The original plan is for Amber and me to fly to San Francisco for the weekend. We are given two free tickets courtesy of Tim. The whole trip is based on getting to fly for free. Amber gets sick the day before we are supposed to leave. Amber is *always* sick. Amber *never* feels good. This is what happens. I am more enthusiastic about this particular trip. I can tell that Amber doesn't really want to go away for the weekend. Getting away for the weekend is important to me. She would rather stay home. I am skeptical when she tells me that she is too sick to go. I've been dealing with this shit all throughout our relationship. I get a nasty cold every other year. It lasts no longer than a week. I drink lots of fluids. I get lots of rest. The cold goes away. I am miserable for a few days and then I fully recover. This won't happen again for at least two years. I don't have the time or the interest in being sick. I have no desire to have a cold. Amber is always sick. There is something wrong with her multiple times each month. It is rare when she avoids catching some type of bug.

Living with a girl who constantly announces that she doesn't feel well gets old pretty quickly. It is a bit too convenient for her to be sick the day before we are set to leave on a trip that she isn't really excited about. At this point, I am hesitant to believe her. I'm sure that her mind has convinced her body to pretend to be sick. The brain makes a convincing case. The body and the mind need to stick together. Solidarity is essential. Her brain is sick of being the only part of the body that feels like crap. Wouldn't it be better to share the burden so that nothing feels good at all? Her body agrees to go along with it. This is when I stop believing that she is actually sick. She never wanted to go to San Francisco in the first place. It is way too useful to get sick right before we leave. She never wants to go anywhere. This is the last time she gets to use evasive action to keep me from doing something I want to do. Then again, when I do get a cold all I want to do is curl up in a ball and be left alone. Who fucking knows.

I leave my sick wife on Valentine's Day weekend without any regrets and with her permission. She recognizes that I am about to lose my mind and sets me free for a weekend in the city. I spend the weekend at my cousin's house. It doesn't take him long to figure out that things aren't going so well with me. It is pretty obvious that things are fucked up when he picks me up at the airport. He is expecting both Amber and I to walk out of the terminal. I see him at the curb and walk towards him. He sees that I am alone and knows instantly that we will spend the next few days drinking heavily.

He lives with a bunch of roommates. He has a good group of friends that also live close by. They all know me from past visits. When I show up to the house, I am not sure that my marriage is over. I am almost convinced that it is, but I still retain the slightest bit of hope. After I arrive at the house I start to talk.

And this is what we do. I wake up and open a beer. I self-medicate the entire time I'm in San Francisco. I hold it together until the last night I'm there. At some point I can't hold it in any longer. I've kept all of these emotions tucked inside for so long. I have an early flight the next morning. I have every intention to drink heavily tonight. This is my last night in the city. I can handle it. There's just no reason to embarrass myself, so don't do it. There is no reason whatsoever.

The last thing I want to do is cause a scene at the karaoke bar, so I don't. I do not fall over. I do not knock over a tray of beers. I do not say anything offensive to the locals. I do none of these things. I almost left the bar without causing any damage. I am so close.

This is when I start to cry. The tears flow down my cheeks. I'm at a Karaoke bar in front of a group of ten friends and I can't stop crying. I am a total wreck. I fall apart. I am broken. I am shit faced for the entire weekend. My cousin does all that he can.

The flight back to Seattle takes forever. I fly standby. I get dropped off at the airport at five in the morning. I am entirely too hungover to do anything. I haven't showered. My teeth haven't been brushed. I reek of cheap bourbon, thrift store furniture and bar food. Part/all of me wants to die.

I am at the mercy of the airlines. I'm flying home on stand-by. The first flight to Seattle leaves super early that morning. This is my best chance to find a seat. Every flight after this one is full. There are a few seats open for this early flight. I can get home if I can get on the airplane.

I sit in the terminal hoping that my name gets called. I wait. I continue to wait. I watch patiently as the plane fills up with passengers. My name gets called. I make my way towards the counter. In the corner of my eye I see a man walking briskly in the same direction. He arrives at the gate a second after I do. I am about to check in. I am about to get the last seat on the plane. I am so close.

This asshole has a ticket. He shows up at the last possible minute and walks on the plane. I get bumped from the flight and walk away. I spend hours after hours waiting for another flight to Seattle. I finally find a plane with an extra seat. I dry heave the entire way to Seattle. I am without a doubt the biggest train wreck in the history of the commercial airline industry. It doesn't matter how many times I apologize to the person sitting next to me. She has the aisle seat and I am stuck near the window. The last three days have caught up to me. The lack of food and the excessive amount of Jack Daniels don't sit too well with my insides. Enough is enough. My body draws a line in the sand and makes it very clear that this behavior will not be tolerated. The plane finally lands. Asking Amber to pick me up at the airport isn't a viable option so I take a shuttle to the nearest city to my house. It is late in the afternoon when I finally get home. Amber has made a miraculous recovery and is able to pick me up at the bus stop. It doesn't take long for her to see through my attempt to hide my vicious hangover. She may not be sick anymore, but there is no doubt that she is sick of me. She spends the weekend drinking lots of fluids and getting lots of rest. She also finds time to discover more reasons to distrust me. It appears that the vitamin C pills she has been taking are laced with angry dust. Her subtle hatred for me seems to have grown since I left. I've read about vitamins that are laced with a chemical that makes you hate your husband. Once the drugs wear off things will go back to normal. There is no way that she can hate me so completely.

The drugs don't appear to be wearing off during the first half of the week. I start to consider that the anger may not be chemically induced. She stays pissed off until Thursday. Easter is three days away. We are sitting on the couch watching television like usual. It appears to me that I should try some intimacy so I lean over towards her and go in for a kiss. She immediately recoils from me. She blocks my attempt to touch her with Kung Fu moves. Her use of defense is totally unnecessary and a bit frightening. I back off instantaneously and ask her what is wrong.

James: *What is wrong?*

Amber: *It just doesn't seem right.*

James: *What doesn't seem right.*

Amber: *Doing that.*

Once she says this, I immediately get off the couch and stand up. My plan is to avoid another confrontation and sulk in the bedroom. I immediately feel sorry for myself and intend on ignoring the situation so I won't have to deal with it. This is how I usually handle things like this. I make it all the way to the bedroom. I am about to close the door behind me. Then I pause.. I take a single deep breath while I stand in the doorway and decide to turn back around. It is time to act like an adult. An adult doesn't get under the covers and fall asleep. He turns around and walks back into the living room. This is exactly what I do. I sit down on the couch and start to talk.

James: *I don't know what just happened between us, but I know that we can't live like this any longer.*

Amber doesn't say anything. She looks at me and then she looks down at her shoes.

James: *We have two choices. We either need to see a marriage counselor so we can work through our issues or we need a divorce.*

I expose the elephant in the room. I lay it all out for her. I say the one word that both of us are too afraid to articulate. I verbalize the one thing that is on both of our minds. It is without doubt that she will need the next twenty four hours to give me an answer. It is only fair to offer her some form of quiet contemplation. I imagine that she needs some time to think about her options. Sleep on it. No rash decisions.

I discover then that she has already made up her mind. She doesn't need time to think about it. She already has. She has been thinking about it for weeks. Her mind is all made up, it happened a long time ago. She's just waiting for the right moment to come along.

Amber: *I don't think counseling will do any good. I think we should get a divorce.*

It takes all of my effort to listen to her say this while fighting the urge to smile. It is almost impossible to display the joy that envelops me.

The happiness is overwhelming. I've spent the last six months without a reason to be happy, and now that I am and I have to keep it off my face. I manage to hold it back. My relief I am feeling at this moment pops the balloon. I can pretend to be sad. So I do just that. Holy shit.

I should be devastated. My wife tells me that she wants a divorce. This should be a big moment. My life is totally upended. My marriage is over. Why doesn't this bother me? My marriage ends prematurely. It is over after a year and a half and I can't figure out a single reason to mourn its conclusion.

All I need to do at the moment is to get out of the house. She wants me to stay and talk, but I can't figure out what we need to talk about. She wants a divorce and I have no interest in talking her out of it. I have more pressing issues to deal with. I need to get in my car, stop holding back my need to smile and find a bar.

I need to suck down a beer and then call my parents. I leave the house and drive down the peninsula so I can get cell phone reception. My cell phone doesn't work in the forest, so I can only break the news after I get off the peninsula. My first call is to my cousin. He isn't totally blindsided and knows better than to interrupt me. He pledges his allegiance and lets me vent for the next ten minutes.

I promptly dial the number to my parents' house after and I hang up. I pull into the parking lot of a McDonalds and wait for them to pick up the phone. It takes my mom a few rings to pick up the phone because it is later than they expect to get phone calls. She groggily says hello and I have no choice but to tell her the entire story.

She wakes my dad up and I have to repeat every last sordid detail. I tell them the truth about everything. I hold nothing back when I tell them why it is over. Their reaction is what is expected of them. They are initially shocked and appalled. This soon turns into a mixture of concern and confusion. I wake them up and tell them that my marriage is over and that the main cause for the end of my marriage is my secret cocaine habit that I've been keeping from them.

They shouldn't be happy to hear this right now. I shouldn't be happy right now either. They should be sad. I should be sad. I should be embarrassed and full of regret. They also should be embarrassed. Twenty minutes ago I had to walk to the other room so I could hide the enormous grin that took over my face. My mother doesn't have to walk to the next room so she can hide her smile. All she has to do is pretend that she isn't happy to hear this news. It is pretty easy for her to hide the fact that she is happy right now. It is obvious that I am coming home soon. She can't pretend that this doesn't make her happy.

I let go of all of my pent up sadness in a McDonald's parking lot. I am defeated as I sit in my car and cry my heart out. I eventually return home only to find Amber gone. She returns back at four in the morning. She tells me that she went over to Bobbi's house to talk. Bobbi is Jerry's mother. At the time I think nothing of it. It takes me a long time to figure out the connection. I don't connect the dots until months go by and I am back in California.

27

Frank

I AM ALONE ON Easter Sunday. It is the first time in twenty-seven years that I spend a holiday by myself and without my family. I spend the day sipping bourbon on the couch, at peace with the world. Amber shows up to her parents by herself and breaks the news to her family. My family is two states away, so I spend the day by myself. Monday morning I go to school and tell my principal that I won't be back next year. I contain myself for five seconds before I break down crying in her office.

Amber is at the house when I get home from work. She plans to continue living there with me until the school year ends and I move back home. Her parents live ten minutes away. My parents live twelve hundred miles away. I have nowhere to go. I have no friends. I have no options. She wants to continue *living together*. This isn't going to fly with me. I tell her there's no way in hell. For once, she actually listens to me. She moves into her parents' house within the hour. I can't imagine coming home from work every day to find her car in the driveway and her inside the house. Even though she leaves, I still get anxious every time I drive down the long driveway until I see that her car is not parked out front.

We start the negotiations to see who gets what. I expect the dialogue to be civil. Everything should be split more or less down the middle. The only exception to this rule involves the big ticket items that were given to us by our parents. Any large gift given to us by my parents should go to me. Anything that her parents gave us should go to her. This is a simple way to ensure that I leave Washington with a few expensive items. This plan works in my favor considering that my parents have been significantly more generous gift givers over the years.

231

Amber doesn't agree with me on this matter. In fact, Amber *hates* this idea. She doesn't take into account that I was the only one who worked during the past year. She never considers that the move to Washington was really expensive. She fails to see that a two-income household makes a good deal more money than one that only has a single revenue stream. *She* is the reason that we are over our heads in debt. It is her time to make a few sacrifices. This unfortunately isn't how she sees it. She expects our sizable debt to be split down the middle. I suggest that she sell her engagement ring in order to pay off a good amount of this debt. She flatly refuses to sell it. This is the beginning of her unwillingness to meet me halfway on anything. She fights tooth and nail for the majority of the things that I have a legitimate claim to be mine.

We reach a stalemate and nothing changes hands. The final battle is still a few months away. A few weeks go by before I hear from anybody on her side of the peninsula. My soon-to- be-former-in-laws and soon-to-be-former-neighbors make no attempt to contact me. Every relationship I made here dissolves into nothing. I expect this from the wives, but don't understand how all of the husbands can sleep at night knowing that I am alone and could use their help. I can only guess what horrible things they've heard about me in the last couple of weeks. I expect too much when I expect them to hear my side of the story.

Not a single effort is made by any of them. The only one to reach out to me is Amber's stepdad, Frank. He has always liked me. He is the first person from the Washington contingent to call me after the break up. It takes him a few days to make contact. I expect him to wait for the dust to settle before he reaches out to me. I'm not entirely sure what protocol he has to follow in this situation. He has an obvious allegiance to his wife and stepdaughter. He risks feeling the wrath of his wife if he calls me. Most men would simply wait for me to move away. This is the safest course of action in these circumstances. Fortunately for me, Frank is not like most men. He does what he thinks is right and picks up the phone and dials my number. He called me late one afternoon during the middle of next week. I look at the number on the phone and pick it up.

Frank: *James, It's Frank. Good, you're home. I'm coming over. I'm bringing cigars and beer.*

He hangs up before I have a chance to say a single word. Ten minutes later he enters through the front door with a six-pack of beer and four cheap cigars. I walk directly over to him and we embrace. It's a long good hug. I tell him how much it means to me that he came over to talk. The thing about it is that he is the closest male friend I have in the entire state of Washington. He is seventy-two, I am twenty-seven. But we are two peas in a pod. We spend the next five hours talking out on the deck. We open the next beer right after we finish the one before. We smoke cigars and we start to throw bean bags. The first game to twenty-one begins. We toss our bags and then walk to the other side. Then we toss them again. We walk back and forth across the deck continuously until someone is victorious. We are locked in a one on one battle that gets closer and more heated after each game. What starts as a friendly match keeps on getting extended. The best out of three matches are quickly amended to best out of five. Neither one of us is satisfied after five games. Best out of seven should do it but turns out to be a trivial number of games that won't please either of us. We finish nine games and decide that only the weak would stop there. We reach eleven games. This should be enough, but it isn't. Only after we play thirteen games back to back do we finally stop. I've surely torn a rotator cuff and Frank is seconds away from a massive heart attack, but neither of us say a word. We both don't want the game to end. When the game is over, we both recognize that our friendship will be the next thing to fall apart.

We shake hands. I'm not sure who ends up winning the match. All I know is that it is brilliantly played on both sides. An epic battle. The game lasts longer than expected. Frank is way past tipsy and shouldn't be out this late on a school night. I'm way drunker than he is and I have to get up early the next day to teach. Frank is retired. He doesn't have to do shit tomorrow morning.

The only true friend I have in Washington leaves my house. He drives back home to the only other house in Washington that I've ever felt at home at. My soon-to-be ex-wife and my soon-to-be ex-mother-in-law are waiting for him. As he walks out of the house, we realize that both of us are about to lose something important. I lose someone I respect and admire. I lose a person who cares about me and understands me. I lose a person I consider to be a father figure. Frank walks away from someone he has expected to know for years to come. He loses a friend who surprises him and makes him laugh. No longer will he be able to consider me to be like a son to him. Soon there will be nothing left to connect the two of us. It is a friendship that is cut short prematurely. It will end soon and then we will be strangers.

We figure out who gets what. I'm not happy about any of it and it turns out to be a lot worse than it seems. I am robbed. I get hosed. She takes whatever she wants and lets me have all the leftover shit that she can live without. I am such a fucking pushover. My lack of a backbone is complicated by my complete lack of arguing skills. I fall apart when it counts. Every opportunity to use my words in a constructive manner is missed. Every valid point I intend to make escapes my mind right before I plan to use it. My mind goes blank every time. It is nowhere to be found when it can still help me. Once that time is over is when it enters my mind. My brain starts to work again fifteen minutes after the argument is over. I really need to keep a pad of paper and a pen in my back pocket at all times. This is my only chance for success. This idea is quickly forgotten. I am such an idiot. What it comes down to is simple. I am fucked on a karmic level and there is nothing I can do about it. I might as well give up.

The truth of the matter is that I feel like I don't really deserve anything. I am dishonest and sneaky. I was never a good husband. I mean, I did shit for her and tried to make her life easier and more pleasant but there was always that other side of me that refused to give her every part of me. I never hesitated to keep things from her. There are things I continue to do that she can't support. I know that if she finds out about my behavior, it will break her heart. I never make a serious effort to stop my involvement with the bullshit. She has the right to be married to someone who doesn't lie, cheat, or steal. Just because I don't cheat on her and I don't steal things won't justify all of the lies. Everything I hide from her and every half-truth I tell her makes me wish I was stealing cars and cheating on my taxes.

The only way I can make amends is to give her the Magic Bullet. This is the only way I can have peace of mind. Maybe if I give her the household items, I won't feel so bad. If she is so bent on keeping all of this shit and if I can walk away from it, then I should just do it and get it over with. This is the only way I'll get back to even on a karmic level. Give her what she wants, and hopefully my karmic balance will be restored.

Frank continues to make occasional visits to my house while I'm still living in Washington. He shows up with a six pack of beer and cheap cigars every other week. We throw bags and shoot the shit. He doesn't hide how he feels about the situation. He quietly suggests one afternoon that I should stop taking shit from Amber. He thinks I should fight like a rabid dog for the dining room table.

Frank: *Don't roll over on that stuff. Your parents were the ones who bought it. There is no reason why you shouldn't get it.*

All I can do is smile. If only I had a leg to stand on. The moment that Amber mentions the word "alimony" is the moment I get scared. Everything I know about the word freaks me out. All I know about it is what I've learned from the movies. Alimony is bad. Best case scenario? I'm Matt Dillon and I try really hard to set up my ex-wife with a new love interest so that they will get married and I won't have to pay alimony any more only to find out that I still love my ex-wife and she may still love me and it may be too late to re-fall back in love before it's too late. Thankfully I figure it out just in time and convince my ex-wife to date me again so I don't have to pay her alimony.

But, I'm not Matt Dillon and I'm sure I butchered the plot of multiple horrible movies in my best-case-scenario fantasy, but it doesn't change the fact that Amber tricks me into thinking that if I don't give her everything she wants then I will spend the rest of the next decade sending her monthly alimony checks. Our divorce happens quickly. Our marriage doesn't last two years. It is over before we can buy any property. It dissolves way before we acquire any money. The marriage ends before the discussion of kids even begins. The conversation involving court ordered provisions should not yet exist. Even if she is interested in a monthly handout, there is no way that she is delusional enough to expect anything significant. She knows as well as I do that I don't have any money to give to her on a monthly basis. This is how she gains her upper hand. I don't know shit. She figures this out and takes advantage of my stupidity. She expects that I don't know my legal rights. Once she discovers that I actually don't know any of them, she doesn't hold back. This is when she discovers that she has the right to make the rest of my life really, really difficult. This is what she plans on doing. Pure evil.

I am angry and frustrated. The fear of paying alimony angers me. The phobia of monthly payments breaks my spirit. I have no interest in seeing what will actually happen. The fear of supporting her in the future turns me into an angry and frustrated individual. The conception of alimony payments destroys the expectations of a good life. The monthly costs would without doubt mean that I won't have any money and that I'll most likely starve or go to debtors prison. The divorce is her idea. I'm sure to stick around and fight harder to save the marriage. But without a doubt, I know that she is right. I can't forget that I betrayed her every time I hid my drug use from her. I can't forget how many times this happened during our relationship. Actually I can't remember most of it but I know it was a lot. At this point I need to be prudent. This is when being responsible for alimony payments are not in my best interest. I have no doubt whatsoever that my life might involve more pain and difficult scenarios than I will ever be able to understand. My ability to eat on a daily basis is at risk. I need to fight hard right now. If I fail to do so, then I just might go hungry.

I want to battle for the dining room table. It wasn't so long ago that we picked it out at a fancy furniture shop in Gig Harbor (fine, it was at Pier 1 Imports, but still.) It is a generous housewarming gift that *my parents* pay for. After the shit I pull over the years, it makes sense that she gets it. But she *shouldn't* get it. I'd never have the balls to insist on something like that if the situation was reversed. But she does not hesitate. My parents didn't buy it for *her*, they bought it for *us*. But if it is going to only cost me this dining room table then I am willing to pay that. I guess I owe her at least this much.

I can throw her a bone (the bone being a dark wooded beauty of a dining room table) her way. I am getting off cheap. No kids, no property, no money, no future as a couple all thrown into the communal pot. She gets to be rid of me. I, more importantly, am finally rid of her. I am finally done with the questions and the glances my way when I make a drink after work, open a beer or pour a glass of wine. I am finally free of my second version of a mother. The first reaction I have is to start up the healthy and productive habit of smoking cigarettes. I quit these foul sticks more than two years ago at her suggestion. My lungs get a much needed break, now is the time to reclaim them, no matter the cost.

Once she moves out, I am again responsible for feeding myself on a daily basis. I immediately start to lose the weight that I steadily gained in the past year. The reintroduction of Jack Daniels and cigarettes goes a surprisingly long way to a slimmer waist- line. I replace the elaborately planned gourmet meals that Amber cooks nightly with a simpler approach. Having chips for dinner works perfectly for me. I cut out vegetables, homemade meals, and domestic dysfunction. I replace them with heavy drinking every day after school. This is how I stay happy and healthy.

The house starts to empty. First the little things start to disappear. One day the stainless steel measuring cups are gone so I am forced to use the plastic red ones instead. The good salad bowls (did I agree to this?) are next. The various cooking utensils fade away. All the pretty baking pans, the good cookie sheets, the silverware, candle sticks, every single vase, all the cute little cups for holding sauce, and the newer half of the dish towels are suddenly no more.

She takes all her clothes and her shoes, as expected. She packs up everything, except for the robe that my mother gave her for Christmas. I probably read more into this than I should, but for some reason this pisses me off. She doesn't hesitate to take the big ticket items that my parents bought us, but when it comes to a robe she can't be bothered with it. She leaves it there to tell me that she doesn't need *shit* from my family anymore. She has what she really wanted in the first place and has another robe she can wear. This confirms my long held suspicion that she never really gave a shit about my parent's feelings. By leaving the robe she officially wipes her hands of me and my family.

I have to convince her to leave the furniture at the house until I move out. She actually expects me to live without a couch for the next few months. But I won that argument and lived in a house with a normal amount of furniture for my final few months in Washington. She leaves for good. From this point on, she never comes back to the house while I am there. After I sign the divorce paperwork, I do not see her again. I am an alone loner alone in this lonely place. After a few too many glasses of whiskey I sit down at the kitchen counter and actually write down this phrase.

"I am an alone loner alone in this lonely place."

Writing such horrible prose is rationalized as poetic at this moment. This inspires an immediate gut check. This is some seriously crappy writing. It will not be allowed again. I am not proud of this sentence. I usually *spit* on such drivel. I normally respect myself enough not to say such things. Ninety eight percent of the time I immediately delete this entire sentence and try again. Not now. Now I embrace it. Fuck, I need to find something to do.

The forest is starting to close in on me. The emptiness that I come home to every day is beginning to take its toll. One more weekend spent in the middle of nowhere might be my last. One more weekend might lead to more desperate attempts at even crappier alliteration. Where will it stop? A paragraph leads to another, soon enough all I can do is write bullshit about my feelings. I refuse to subject people to this drivel. There must be someone I can call.

28

Handstands

I'M NOT GOING *to say I love you, because I don't. But I do.*

I say this in my kitchen a few weeks later. The ink isn't yet dry on my divorce papers and I tell a woman I've been seeing (for less than a month) that I love her. The funny thing about it is that I mean every word of it. This was made possible a few weeks ago when I made a successful attempt to get out of the forest for a night.

One of my roommates from college has a younger brother who lives in Seattle. His brother Rick and his ex-girlfriend Lisa both live in the city. Lisa is the younger sister of Diana. Diana is a friend of mine that I've known since middle school. Diana used to spend "quality time" in the tree house making out with my neighbor Cole. In short, we all went to high school together. Rossmoor's reach does, in fact, reach up to the Pacific NorthWest.

I don't know Rick very well. I haven't seen Lisa since I saw her at a wedding five years ago. My friendship with Diana peaks in eighth grade. We head in different directions at the start of high school, but I still consider her a friend. The reason I don't hesitate to track down Lisa's number is because we both grew up in the same area. I have faith that we can easily pick up where we left off. I always have confidence in people whose childhood home I've been to. I am loyal to the younger siblings of the friends I grew up with. I'm on a first name basis with her parents for Christ's sake. The fact that I haven't seen them since the early nineties doesn't dissuade me. Desperate times call for desperate actions and right now there is no doubt that I am desperate.

I contact Lisa via email, and then on the phone. I tell her my situation and ask if she wants to meet for drinks in Seattle next weekend.

Without any hint of hesitation, she agrees to meet up. Next weekend I escape the boondocks. I head to the civilized part of Washington State.

It doesn't cross my mind that something will happen between us. My intentions are honorable and platonic when I show up to her apartment. She is three years younger than I am. When I was close to her sister we were in middle school which means that the majority of time I saw Lisa was before she hit puberty. She was a kid. She was still subjected to weekly spelling tests. I knock on her door. A few seconds later she opens it and I see a woman before me. It takes me a second to get my bearings. Holy shit. Little Lisa has grown up, and did so very successfully. It is obvious that she hasn't had to take a spelling test in quite some time.

Lisa is half-Chinese and half-Caucasian. She wears her hair parted down the middle. It is jet black, straight, and ends high above her shoulders. Her haircut looks expensive. It is kind of what I expected. I can't help but smile. It is very hip. It looks amazing. Her hair is cut shorter in the back and gradually gets longer as it comes towards her face. She wears designer reading glasses that are black and of medium thickness. Her clothes initially give off the illusion of being from a thrift store. After a second glance I immediately recognize them to be vintage chic. There is no doubt in my mind that they are designed by someone I've never heard of. I can only imagine how soft they must feel and how much they cost. She opens her door and I instantly see a woman who is the total opposite of Amber. She is well dressed. She is wearing expensive boots. She is hip. She is cool. She smiles at me when she opens the door. That must mean that she doesn't totally despise me.

We plan to meet her ex-boyfriend and a girl he is dating for dinner (this makes more sense than it sounds). They dated for years during high school and college and then eventually broke up. They remain close friends. We meet for dinner and drinks with dinner leads to more drinks. We end up at a packed bar in the industrial part of Seattle. Lisa and I spend the night next to each other. The loud music ensures that we both lean in towards one another. The conversation is held at close range and flows easily.

At some point in the night she agrees to have a shot of Jack Daniels with me. Without hesitation she says, "Yes." I am greatly impressed. She tells me that she dates both men and women, also impressive. We walk outside and share cigarettes. We are facing each other and standing very close. I surprise myself as I lean closer towards her and ask if I can kiss her. Liquid courage takes over and does its job sensationally.

The exact words I use are lost to me. I can't say for sure that I smoothly executed the question. The degree of nervousness I cannot judge. It's not the ideal way to go about it but give me a break, I've been out of the game for a long time. All I do know is that it works. And thank god it does because If I fail I just might lead a lifetime of celibacy. Thank God I choose this moment to ask her because my timing is good. So I go for it. I lean closer and ask her. She leans in and answers my question wordlessly.

The instant connection I feel towards her is reciprocal. I am not the only one who feels a strange and powerful energy when she opens her door. The electricity in the air that infatuates me the moment I see her is shared. I thank God that she feels it also and doesn't turn her head. It just so happens that she likes me too. We finish our kiss and smoke the rest of our cigarettes. Neither of us wants to spend another minute in a public place. The sooner we get back to her place and lock the door the better. We should already be there, god dammit. We should have been there an hour ago. Why the hell did I wait so long to kiss her? Argh...

We convince Rick that he is sober enough to drive us back to her place (he is not). He drives like a really super drunk person. He should not be in charge of a moving vehicle. The girl he came with is long gone. Neither Lisa nor I offer to get in the front passenger seat of the car. We both get in the back seat and start to make out. Poor Rick. He is wasted; driving a car that isn't his, and his ex-girlfriend is making out with his brother's ex-roommate from college in the backseat. He is our unpaid chauffeur that may kill us all. He has to watch the former love of his life get felt up in the back seat. None of these factors elicit a single complaint from him. He rides a bike to work and is happy to drive a Volvo way too fast through the back streets of Seattle.

We survive the drive and say good night to Rick. My original plan was to sleep on Lisa's couch. The new plan is much better. I spend the rest of the night naked and sweaty. Lisa reintroduces me to all the benefits that sex has to offer. She shows me how great an enthusiastic lover can be. She moves around. I forgot how important it is for the girl to do this. Amber usually just lied there. Lisa is like an alternate on the Russian Olympic gymnastics squad. She does handstands against the wall. This is how it should feel to fuck a woman. I can't believe I married someone who didn't do this. Everything Lisa does is magic. Everything I do is met with a fervor that I forgot was possible.

I explore the entirety of her body for hours. We fuck, rest for a bit, and then go at it again until the sun rises. My penis comes through big time. It recognizes how important the situation is and stays hard the entire time. We finally fell asleep early the next morning. We wake up a few hours later and fuck again.

A night like this hasn't happened in a long time. The last few months lack any reason to even get aroused. Come to think about it, the last year was full of uninspired sex. Marriage sex doesn't have to be but turned into being dull and boring. Newly divorced sex is the complete opposite. I realize that I totally owe my penis an apology. It didn't do anything wrong. It doesn't deserve such predictable sex. I ought to have offered it a higher level of love making. It merits amazing sex. It should be a happy and well- adjusted penis. After last night it better be. There should be no complaints at all. The entire time Lisa and I have sex she yells "FUCK." as loud as she can. I am the greatest lover that ever lived. From out of nowhere I morph into a pleasure giver. I orgasm and within five minutes I am hard again. I can't explain any of it. The only explanation is that great sex is back in my life and that my penis has been waiting for a really long time. It is committed to make up for all the lost time.

Lisa and I started dating at once. She starts out as my rebound. In no time, she is my girlfriend. Our sexual chemistry is off the charts. Our conversations last for weeks on end. She understands me. She accepts me. She likes who I am and doesn't want to change anything about me. Also, she listens to really good music.

I tell her everything. I hold nothing back. There is no time to ease into it. I jump in with both feet as does she. We have only a limited time to spend together. She has a good job and has no intention to leave Seattle. My job ends in late June and I have no intention of staying in Washington. My plan is to spend as much time as possible with her until

I leave after the school year ends. We both accept this reality without reservations. We both know that there is limited time to spend together but neither of us expect things to progress so quickly. Neither of us anticipate the relationship to build with such intensity or so rapidly. We both know that we are setting ourselves up for heartbreak but there is no way around it. There is nothing we can do to avoid the end that will eventually come. She will be fine, I'm sure of that. I just don't think about it. I can't focus on the inevitable. Each day brings me closer to it and each day I fall harder for her.

Our relationship is doomed from the start. *A torrid love affair.* I'm serious. *An undying love without a future.* These are words that run over and over in my head. We both know the exact day that it will end. It is like a summer camp romance. I feel like I'm thirteen again. It's like my parents have sent me to a summer camp that I don't want to go to. I fight tooth and nail not to go, only to meet the girl of my dreams half way through the summer. Aside from canoe trips and flag football I spend the rest of my summer touching boobs and participating in heavy petting. My parents never sent me to a summer camp when I was younger. It was never even discussed. But here I am at the age of twenty-seven discovering what a summer romance is like.

We both know that extending this romance into a long distance relationship isn't an option. This doesn't stop me from making a couple of futile attempts to persuade her to date me after I move back to California. This is how hard I fall for her. It only takes a second. She shows me what a relationship should be like. She is the kind of woman I deserve in my life. She gives me hope that there is life after a break up. The ugliness that occurs between Amber and I won't go away until I leave Washington. This ugliness doesn't sting so much because of Lisa.

Lisa reintroduces me to optimism. I have the love of a good woman and this changes everything. I start listening to new music again. I create a Facebook account (it's a new thing). I reconnect with old friends. New ideas are happening. New stuff is afoot. New things present themselves. Newness has undeniably arrived. New is the new new, who knew?.

I take a quick trip to California the weekend before I am set to leave Washington. My Uncle passed away and his funeral is on Saturday. I have to attend his funeral. The timing couldn't be worse but there is no way I can rationalize missing it. Other than bringing home empty cardboard boxes from the cafeteria at school I've completely failed to start packing. The situation is now serious and I need the weekend to pack. I need to make up for lost time. This forces me to plan on missing the funeral. I seriously consider it. It doesn't take long for me to get my head out of my ass. This is my Uncle. Fuck packing, it can wait. I book a flight to California and go to the funeral. My cousins' *dad* just died. I am closer to them than anyone else in the world. Once Mandy died they became my de facto sister and brother. I consider them my siblings. They need me to show up. I need me to show up. I fly in late on Friday. I emcee the funeral and drink an excessive amount of Makers Mark. I play ping pong in the garage and sneak cigarettes in the side yard.

Luck has it that I cut myself the week before I go to California. They aren't deep but they are long. I am anxious, drunk and bored. Two minutes later, a razor blade is found, ten seconds after that, I am tending to fresh wounds. The outsides of both of my calves have two to three cuts on them. Luck also has it, that it's freaking hot outside at the funeral so I change into shorts. Two minutes after I put them on, someone loudly asks me what happened to my legs. He does this in front of a significant portion of my immediate family. This leads to all of them looking down at my legs. I have no choice but to explain the reason why there are various cuts covering my calves. My explanation is pretty lame. All I can think of is that I fell into a viscous bush covered in thorns. Nobody believes me. They immediately take a closer look and know that I'm full of shit. These cuts are straight and clean, surgical even. They look nothing like what would happen if I fell in a bush. These cuts should be hidden behind pants.

I evade more questions and get a beer. My cousin is obviously concerned. I pull him aside and tell him to shut the fuck up. Then I tell him the truth. He looks at me like I've lost my mind. Cutting his legs with a razor blade isn't something he has ever considered doing. It's beyond his ability to understand but he promises to not bring it up again. Everyone else moves on and focuses on less fucked up topics. My night ends late. I finally fell asleep after a good cry and a trip to the Jacuzzi.

I get on a flight the next morning. My mother is able to book a flight at the last minute and flies with me. I have three more days of work and then two days to pack. Afterwards, I leave Washington forever. Getting back to California is the only thing that matters. My total lack of preparing to pack makes the next week a total cluster fuck. Packing up the house would be impossible without the arrival of my mother. I initially didn't want her to come. I have a first class ticket (free booze) back to Washington that I give to her. A short plane ride in coach (no free booze) is the price I pay. Four days alone with my mom has never been attempted before. I have no clue how it will turn out. These concerns prove to be without merit. The benefits of a four day long mother/son bonding session are endless. My mom is the shit. I can't believe I considered not having her come just so I would get free drinks on the plane ride home.

Lisa picks us up at the airport and we all watch playoff basketball in Seattle together. After the game, my mom and I drive the hour back to my house. We stop at the store so I can buy my mom a bottle of her favorite wine. It is a jug of cheap Chablis Blanc that she drinks nightly. Without the Chablis, she probably wouldn't make the trip. While I finish out the school year, mom starts to pack. She packs *way* better than I would have. Each glass and every dish is individually wrapped and put in a box. Once she is done she moves on to cleaning the entire house. She does the oven, fridge and everything in between.

She makes it possible to finish the job before the movers arrive. She is the only way I'm able to get my ass home. This qualifies her for *Mother of the Year.* It doesn't matter how little the things are that need packing, they start to add up. The amount or large stuff I'm leaving with, combined with all the small things, didn't look like much on paper. But, in actuality, I own a lot more stuff than I thought. It all adds up quickly and the pile of shit continues to grow. It is expanding faster than I am comfortable with. Part of me is now a bit thankful that Amber takes so many things, without her help I'd be overwhelmed with furniture and completely out of boxes.

29

Loose Change

A MBER TAKES THE rest of her stuff from the house when I am out of town. My mom and I walk in to discover this small detail I was vaguely aware of. All of the furniture is gone, except for the things I am taking and the couch. She isn't happy that she has to come back to get the couch, but I don't give a shit. My Mom and I need somewhere to sit. She can pick it up later. I am under the impression that she is clear on what she can take. I know who gets what and I figured that she does also. Up until this point there isn't that much animosity. She originally proposes that lingering resentments won't overtake the end of our relationship. She proposes a civil and mature divorce. Shit, at one point she talks me through a cooking question. I am naive. She promises fraternity and brotherhood for all. I ignorantly take her word for it.

When we discuss who gets what, we fail to write anything down. A lot of things are left unsettled. We talk about most things, but forget to be thorough. We don't discuss every last item. It is easier for both of us if she takes her things while I'm out of town. I have no interest in standing around while she packs up her shit. I have even less interest in helping load things into her moving van. My nightmare scenario involves carrying out the dining room table (that she has no claim to) and putting it in the back of a truck. I'd rather avoid the entire awkward scene. I plan to safeguard myself completely from the whole mess by being in another state. It never occurs to me that being so far away will make it that much easier for her to just take whatever she wants.

I leave the iced tea pitcher on the counter. I happen to like this pitcher. She knows this. This is my first mistake. It is empty and clean. She takes it. This is the first low blow. All I had to do was leave it half full of old tea and in the refrigerator. She wouldn't want the pitcher if it still has iced tea in it, right? Would she have the balls to empty it out and then take it? Would she pour the tea into the old crusty iced tea pitcher and leave that in the fridge? I wonder about these things when I realize it is gone. I fail to protect my pitcher from her evil grasp. My dumb ass cleans it and leaves it out for her to take. For some reason it seems appropriate to drain the pitcher, scrub it clean and leave it on the kitchen counter the day before I leave.

This more or less sets the tone for the last five days I live in Washington. Each day I find something missing that I assume I am getting, but we don't talk about it. I'm supposed to get the bed, but she takes the duvet cover that was on the comforter. All the *Le Creuset* baking dishes? She takes the majority of the expensive wine glasses. Another low blow. I love wine. Well, then again, so does she. But that's not the point. She comes in and takes all the best shit. She leaves me with things that are chipped or missing a part. She walks away with everything new and leaves the secondhand bullshit behind.

She is already getting all of the fancy cool cookware. She is getting all of the silverware, the majority of which was bought by my parents and was not cheap. I get a Zip-lock bag of assorted silverware that is found in the back of the cupboard. This is a bag of old, cheap hand me downs that don't match. We only kept them just in case we go camping. We never go camping. She cleans me out of salad bowls. There are at least five of them. Nobody needs *five* salad bowls. She takes every last one. She doesn't even leave behind her least favorite, the one that we never use. It's like she wants to ensure that my future doesn't include the option of making a salad. Spending the last five years trying to get me to eat lettuce has left her bitter. It is just another way she reminds me that the days worrying about my eating habits are over. A not so subtle way to tell me that eating balanced meals is no longer any of her concern.

I am trying not to be bitter and petty about the material bullshit, but once I discover that she takes the blender, I am done being nice. I clearly remember the discussion we had about the blender. It came up specifically in our initial negotiations. The conversation goes something like this.

Me: *I want the blender, it is important to me.*

Her: *Fine*

The blender? Really? This is a low fucking blow. The blender marks the end of civility between us. It was a wedding gift from Bernie's family. End of story. The fact that I don't know how to use it other than to make margaritas is beside the point. We agreed that I should get it. I make delicious frozen cocktails. She gets everything else, the least she can do is give up the blender.

I don't even notice that the blender is gone until a few days after I get back. I'm not even looking for it when I realize it is gone, yet sure enough, she takes that too. There is no reason for it to be missing. She claims that she doesn't remember having the blender conversation. She argues that since she doesn't remember agreeing to give me the blender that I have no claim to it. She refuses to return it and tells me that I am being *petty*. The word petty wakes me up and makes me mad. This is when things get nasty and I actively hate someone for the first time in my life.

When I discover the blender's disappearance, I take a closer look around the house to see what else is missing. Then Amber hits a new low. She has the balls to take the *change dish* that I have been depositing money in for the last few months. She grabs the dish AND the change inside it. What fucking message is she trying to send me? When I walk in my bedroom I see that the small clay bowl that sits next to my bed is gone. The moment she calls me *petty*, my original plan of letting the change dish go without mentioning it ends right then and there. She probably made that ugly bowl in a ceramics class in high school. It's not really that impressive. But all I know is that this is the bowl I put my change into when I get home each night. Amber might have had a claim to the change that I put in there before she moves out. I would have had no problem splitting up the six dollars in change when she leaves. But, all the change I've added to the bowl since she left should be *mine*.

The clay bowl sees significantly more action after she leaves. Every night I come home from work my pockets are heavy with change. The bowl is overflowing with dimes and quarters. I have hopes and dreams for these coins. I understand how important a crappy clay bowl can be. All she has to do is take the bowl, walk into the kitchen, open the drawer with the *Ziploc* bags in it, grab one, walk back, put the change inside the bag, close it tightly, leave it on the nightstand. All she has to do is follow these simple steps and she will avoid my rage. Failing to do these simple things confuses me.

When she takes the six dollars in change, she assures herself that she will live forever in infamy. The word will slowly spread every time I tell this story to a stranger when I am drunk at a bar. And spread it, I most certainly will. Any chance she had of being a sympathetic character goes out the window when she *steals my change.* I am forced to make a list. I'm tired of making lists. Usually I love making lists but making lists like this is a waste of my time. Whatever, this list is going to be made anyway. This list is for you Amber. Thanks for wasting my time.

Things You Can Do When You Have A Lot Of Change.

Park a car anywhere with a meter for the next six months.
Wash clothes at a Laundromat.
Buy gum.
Play a game of darts at a bar.
Buy a bag of chips at a vending machine.
Make a phone call.
Find another homemade bowl that is way
cooler than the old one to keep it in.

This is the first time I yelled at her. It takes two months for it all to fall apart. I believe her when she says that she still wants to remain friends down the line. I never doubt her when she tells me that she wants to do things fairly. We even have a civil conversation when I call one night and ask her how to cook pot stickers. I only attempt to reconcile with her once. Just one time. I make a single call to her and ask her to come home. I will not make that call again.

I never envision that things will take a nasty turn. Up until now, I never really hated her. I am thankful to get out of a marriage that has no future. I can't hate her because I am so lucky. We are both really lucky. We have no children. No custody battles. No every other weekend. Shit, if there was an infant involved everything would be a shit ton more complicated. Would I stay in Washington in order to be a father? I want to say that I would, but I honestly don't know if I am man enough to pull it off. Either way, I'm paying child support for the next couple of decades.

We have no property. Two days after we decide to break up, our landlord comes by to tell us she wants to sell us the house. A week ago we'd have been super excited. This is our future plan. Buy a house, fix it up and live happily ever after. A mortgage payment now would fuck us both over. Who knows how long it would take us to sell it. We dodge another bullet.

We have no money. No 401K to split. No stocks or bonds to cash out. All we have is a meager amount of money that we split and a huge amount of debt. With that, we get to walk away. We walk away clean. There is no reason to talk to each other again. We will never again see one another. It's like the marriage never happened. It doesn't really count. Our marriage is like we spilled a glass of red wine on a beige rug. We spill something on the rug that can be cleaned up without too much trouble but only if we act fast. Of course, we feel bad about the stain, but it never occurs to us to do anything about it. All we have to do is walk into the kitchen and grab a clean dish towel. Instead, we just stare at it. A proactive amount of blotting and some carpet cleaner will fix the stain. Neither of us moves a muscle. We both make no attempt to do anything. We say… "Oops, my bad" and ignore the situation.

The entire marriage is fraudulent. Every gift we receive is tainted and undeserved. Every item on the registry that was generously bought for us should be sent back. I really like all the new stuff during our brief marriage. But all of it should be broken. Every single thing that our family and friends gave us should be given back. We should give it all to charity. All of these gifts should be earned. Everything new has to stay in storage for two years. Only after we prove that we are a happy and a well- adjusted married couple do we get the new shit. Two years without the new sheets and twenty dollar wine glasses will ensure how much we actually like one another. All marriages that last less than two years are an embarrassment. It shouldn't count. We shouldn't get all these nice things.

As I think about being more accountable and consider doing the right thing, I am reminded that I am currently on the phone yelling at my soon-to-be ex-wife. The notion of returning all the gifts is just plain silly. I resume screaming at Amber for stealing my blender and all of my change. Fuck giving things back, I'm focused on getting my stuff back.

Amber: *What do you want me to do?*

James: *I want my change back.*

Amber: *Are you serious? You're really being so immature about a handful of coins?*

James: *Absolutely. You have no right to that change and I want it back.*

Amber: *This is ridiculous.*

James: *It may be, but that doesn't change the fact that you stole from me.*

Amber: *Fine, what do you want me to do about it?*

James: *I want you to bring over the change you owe me or drop off a check for the amount that was in the bowl.*

The line goes dead. The conversation is over. Asking for a check is brilliant. It's the funniest thing I've done in weeks. It is the last thing I say to Amber. She doesn't want to hear another word from me after this. This is the last time we speak.

30

Sweat Lodges on the Oregon Coast

TWO DAY LATER I leave the forest for the last time. I make it up the driveway without incident. As I'm driving, I start to cry as I realize that this will be the last time I get to drive on this two lane road, enveloped with so much green. I am not expecting to get emotional, but it happens on my way out of Lakebay, Washington on a road bordered heavily with trees. I cry and drive. I seriously consider listening to sad, depressing music.

The movers showed up earlier than I expected them to. Right off the bat they have issues with getting the truck down the driveway. This will cost extra. I called my dad. He tells me not to worry about it. He tells me to focus on getting home. At this point his only concern is that I get out of Washington and it doesn't really matter how much it costs to get me home. They charge extra for driving down the driveway. No problem, just make sure the truck makes it back up the driveway and is heading in the direction of California as soon as possible.

It takes them more than four hours to load everything into the van. The estimated cost to move me doubles pretty quickly after they arrive. This is partially due to my lack of understanding how much things weigh and paying an extra $3.50 for every roll of tape they have to use. If it isn't in a box or a suitcase then they are required to wrap it up, or put it in a box. I have a lot of things not wrapped properly. A laundry basket full of stuff doesn't count. They have to repack it. Every time this happens my moving costs grow. The process repeats itself. A good chunk of my mom's hard work goes to waste. Every large box costs an extra forty dollars. We have no clue how this works. If we did, then we would have invested a hundred dollars in cardboard boxes at the local post office. Poor planning on my part and blatant price gouging on the moving company's part turns out to be pretty expensive. Every time I see the movers grab another piece of cardboard and make a box out of it I want to cry. After ten boxes I stop worrying about it and accept whatever enormous amount of weight I'll be charged for. All I can do is hope that it arrives at my parents' house in one piece and that they will pay for it.

The landlord arrives for the official checking out ceremony. She shows up intending to be a hard-ass landlord. Her plan is to walk the entire property and make sure everything is perfect. After no more than two minutes her demeanor changes and she turns back into a nice older lady. She smiles and gives me a big hug. Her effort to hold me responsible for anything wrong with the house ends quickly. She approaches me and sees how stressed I am. She takes one look at me and understands how long my day has been. She sees how exhausted and scared I am. She looks at me and gives me a pass. I gaze back at her and thank her for her kindness. We both know that I'm leaving regardless of what she wants me to do.

All the improvements I made to the house over the last year cancel out anything she could possibly complain about. The only thing she mentions is the shed. She fails to notice how great it looks. I spent a good amount of time in the shed over the past year. Living in the middle of nowhere forced me to find new ways to spend my time. I develop a healthy interest in woodworking. I started to make boxes. I spend hours in the shed perfecting my technique. I make small boxes. I make large boxes. I cut, sand, and stain wood for hours. I turn her ratty old shed into an actual workshop. The floor of rotten plywood laid down decades ago has been replaced. I use whatever wood I can find. It is an uneven mess of recycled shelves and particle board. It is a hodgepodge of wood that was never intended to be used for flooring, but works pretty damn well. I expect that she will look into the shed and be thrilled to see a brand new floor. She no doubt will appreciate the hard work that I put into it. This can't be ignored. This brilliant feat of engineering will hopefully make up for the fact that there is a broken AC window unit hidden behind the garden tools.

She looks into the shed and doesn't notice any of the improvements I've made to it. In the fifty years that she has owned the place, she has probably gone into the shed only a handful of times. She doesn't care about the shed. This doesn't occur to me until later. For some strange reason I expect the new floor to negate anything else that may be wrong with the house. In my ideal scenario, I reckon that even if she shows up and walks into a house full of broken windows, dead bodies and bags of heroin that she will forgive me for once she checks out how good the shed looks. She'll walk around the dead bodies, notice the pool of blood just in time and step over it, and won't give in to the temptations of hard core drug use. But, of course, none of this faux debauchery will matter after she sees the new floor in the shed. She'll tell me how much she always wanted a new floor in her shed. She'll hug me and then offer to pay for my gas on my way home.

But this ideal scenario doesn't happen. Thank God there are no dead hookers or bags of heroin in the house when she comes by, because she doesn't notice shit. The only thing she *does* notice are some shelves I put up on the far wall. She sees them and complains about them. She wants me to make another trip to the dump to get rid of them. I point out to her the new floor and how clean the shed is. I can only hope that she doesn't inspect it from top to bottom. I'm not sure that a crappy new floor made out of scrap shelving will make up for the fact that I've filled it up with a good amount of crap. There is a bunch of stuff I have tucked away in the far corners that isn't there a year ago. If she notices the broken ceiling fan in the far left corner of the shed I might be in trouble.

There are only two people that come over on the day I leave. They both probably shouldn't be there but don't stay away. They risk pissing off Amber but don't care too much about that. Kate arrives first. She was Amber's maid of honor at our wedding. She is Amber's oldest and closest friend. Amber would be super offended if she knew that she was at my house, but Kate is a strong independent woman (like Beyoncé) and comes over. She helps me clean up and she drinks a beer with me. This isn't surprising for is the main reason that I am obviously way more fun than Amber. There is no disputing the fact that she totally likes me more than she likes Amber. Mark one in the "Win" column for James.

She made this clear a few months back when she invited me to go camping with her and a group of our mutual friends. She calls me and asks if I want to go camping a few weeks after Amber and I break up. The invitation surprised me and I immediately accepted the offer. I've known these people for a few months. Amber has known them for her whole life. She doesn't get to go. How do you like that? Kate has to pick one or the other and she picks me. I'm confident that she never considers inviting Amber. She didn't ask her to go before me and only takes me along because Amber can't go. She never asks Amber. She only asks me. Even if she did ask Amber first, it wouldn't matter. I spent the next few days on the Oregon coast with six of Amber's friends. The weekend confirms what I've always thought to be true. I am extremely entertaining and people generally enjoy my company. In other words, I am 100% fantastic and wonderful and that's why I get invited places.

I am sure that camping in Oregon in late summer is lovely. I discover that camping in Oregon in the middle of April isn't as nice. It makes sense why the campsite is so cheap. Gray skies, fog and the occasional downpours of rain makes camping pretty miserable. Combine the bad weather with unavoidable heart-to-heart talks about going through a divorce and you get a horrible way to spend a weekend. Or so it would seem.

I am proven wrong. Talking about it is inevitable. Talking about it is a necessity. Talking about it clears my head and a huge weight is lifted off of me. I lay everything out on the table for everyone to see. The group briefly sifts through it and moves on. Thankfully, nobody brings it up again. Thank god nobody wants it to take over the weekend. It makes more sense to build a large fire and try to stay warm. It's really fucking cold.

There are two options facing me after I wake up the next morning. A decision must be made. Option #1 involves spending the day feeling sorry for myself. Option #2 requires some form of physical activity. Option #2 means that I'll do something productive and I will feel a lot better afterwards.

The group has a plan. I don't know about it until after we start implementing it. I need to do something amazing. I need to do something new. I need to create and or build something that benefits us all. I need to find a way to start my life over. I don't know what I need exactly, but everyone else knows what it is. They all have the solution to my problem.

The six of us spend all day building a sweat lodge. An entire day is filled with tasks. A lot of thinking goes into this. A lot of physical labor is required. We walk miles on the beach in order to gather driftwood. We have to find large stones. Then we start digging a hole in the sand. A big hole in the sand is essential. A big hole will lead to a shelter. We start a bonfire with the wood we collect. We place five large stones in the middle of the fire. Large and heavy stones are the key to the whole thing. We continue to add wood to the fire. We keep finding wood and adding it to the fire all day long. The stones stay put and start to get really hot. I have no idea what we are doing. I do what I am told and don't ask questions.

This is my first sweat lodge. I'm only an amateur, the rest of the group seems to do this professionally. Apparently, this is something that people do north of California. It makes sense to me. The shitty weather forces them to adapt. This leads to a life that involves sweat lodges. Making a sweat lodge while camping never occurs to me. It has never even crossed my mind. The basic essentials needed for a successful camping trip are pretty simple. I know that I need a sleeping bag, a pillow, a tent, an ice chest, a bottle of Wild Turkey, some wood, and my toothbrush. This group is hardcore. They show up with green tarps, metal poles and a plan. They set up camp and build a sauna. None of this makes sense to my Southern California mentality. Camping usually involves warm weather and cans of beer. I realize that I haven't been camping since college. This is the first time I am camping without fear of getting in trouble for underage drinking. Shit, I am getting old.

The first step is to find a good spot on the beach. This is crucial. We need a flat space that is backed up with a wall of sand. We need the sand to form a wall so we won't have to dig so deep. We find a good location and spend the next few hours digging. We don't stop until there is enough room for everyone to sit down comfortably. We use the tarps to create a crude lean to. We secure the tarps at the highest point of the sand wall and drape them over the hole. Then we use sand to weigh down the tarp and keep it secure. The tarps are pulled over tightly over and across the hole and so that the space is air tight. More sand is used to weigh down the lower side. We use more sand to plug any remaining holes. This creates a space big enough to fit all six of us comfortably. The sweat lodge looks like an obtuse triangle. After we secure the tarps, the lodge is air tight. We then nominate someone to dig out a stone from the fire and bring it into the lodge safely.

The sun has already set and it is dark out. Visibility is severely limited at this point and it is colder than shit. We are all sitting on damp sand in a hole in fifty degrees weather. We are all wearing nothing but our underwear. We nominate Kate's boyfriend to grab the first stone. He begrudgingly agrees and disappears out into the wild dark abyss beyond.

We make small talk for the first few minutes he is gone and then shiver in silence for what seemed like forever. He is our only hope. It is cold. We aren't wearing much. He should be back by now. It shouldn't take this long to run fifty yards down the beach and pick up a stone buried in the embers of a bonfire. It shouldn't be too complicated to balance the stone between two sticks and walk all the way back without dropping it. Oh, yeah, it's pitch dark out there.

The stone finally arrives and is put in the middle of the lodge. We pour water on it and feel the benefits immediately. The steam fills up the space and warms us all. We continue the process until all the rocks are used. Why didn't we heat more stones? Are you sure there is only one left? Every rock added and every cup of water poured on it convinces me how brilliant of an idea this is. Nobody minds having sand in their hair. Everyone is in their undies and nobody feels weird about it. No one cares that the walk back to the campsite is far away and it will be fucking cold. Nobody cares about divorce. Nobody is going to judge. Nobody is going to choose sides. The steam fixes everything. The steam purifies my life. The steam makes everything okay. I don't want this moment to end. No one does. This is perfect.

It occurs to me then that I will remember this moment for the rest of my life. The hut is making me sweat. I'm sitting in my underwear with a group of people I probably shouldn't be with and I have no interest in seeing them in their undergarments. The only thing that matters at this moment is that I am a part of it. I used to think that I am too smart to get divorced. I never envision being involved in the construction and actual use of a sweat lodge on a beach in Oregon. If I have to go through a nasty divorce before I can be involved in activities that don't make sense and confuse me then I say bring the pain.

I am more passionate about creating a sweat lodge than I am about my divorce. I am more passionate about building a fire than I was about my marriage. I return home from camping feeling refreshed. My feet are filthy, my hair smells like smoke and my priorities are flawed. I love camping but I usually hate getting home from camping. This time, when I get home, I feel pretty darn good.

Before I drive off the peninsula my next door neighbors come over and say goodbye. I don't think they will miss me too much. The past year wasn't easy for them. We arrived in the neighborhood and brought chaos with us. They have limited interest in music, drinking and divorce before we move in. Ten months of living right next door to it is about all they can take. They see me off for the sole reason to make sure that I don't come back. All is forgiven as long as I leave. I give their eight-year-old daughter three enormous goldfish that have lived in my kitchen for the past year. Traveling with fish in Tupperware isn't an option. It didn't end well the first time I tried it and I have no interest in doing it again. My options with the fish are limited. The unlimited amount of water in my front yard is no help to a freshwater fish. I have serious doubts that Francois, Bonnie and Steve will adapt quickly enough to survive. I am about to flush them down the toilet when I remember that small children love taking care of living things. Gifts that require daily maintenance usually don't make parents happy, but in this case it seems to work. Introducing the community to noise, alcohol, and dysfunctional relationships is forgiven the moment I hand over the fish. I have no idea my next door neighbors are fervent gold fish enthusiasts. I kick myself for not bringing over a twenty-five cent goldfish earlier. I could have won over the whole family months ago. I see them all wave as I drive away.

The other person seeing me off is Frank. His contribution is significant. He offers to haul all of my trash to the dump as a final act of kindness. He spends the day helping out and hugs me before I leave. I take a last glance at the property before I get in my car. At this point, the water view bores me, the trees surrounding the property should be cut down and made into paper towels, the entire state of Washington should be clear cut, the acre of grass behind the house should be turned into a really big parking lot.

I drive eight miles down a two lane highway for the last time. I pass a couple of gas stations. I drive past three bars and three restaurants. I passed a grocery store, a lumber yard, and a liquor store. My music of choice is sad and for about six miles I cry. I can't help it and I call my mom when I am almost off the peninsula. I tell her how disappointing it is to be leaving, but it makes sense at the same time. Our conversation is brief but it makes me feel better. I hang up and immediately change the music. I make it off the peninsula. I berate myself for my music choice. It is ridiculous to listen to sad music. I need to find a song that will save my life. I need something upbeat.

This is the second time that pop music saves my life. The first time it happens is the week after my sister dies. I am a few hours into a solo drive up the coast of California when I pull over and buy a couple of CD's at random. The first song on the first CD reintroduces hope and joy to my life. It has fast beats, a catchy hook and is just the right blend of techno and electronic. I drive faster. I hit the steering wheel with my hands. I start to appreciate the scenery as it passes by. For the duration of the song I am fixed. All of my pain is tucked back inside and replaced with five minutes without worry.

This time my savior comes via my iPod. Technology. I scroll down to Lily Allen and push play. Witty lyrics, great hooks and short songs make it a pop music masterpiece. My smile returns, my fists bang on the steering wheel, life isn't so bad. I'm picking up a good friend, my rebound love and her sister in Seattle. It's the start of what will turn out to be an amazing road trip. It's the first leg of my journey back home and the final moments of a very tumultuous year living in the Pacific Northwest.

The only way I can get back home involves two things. A moving company and a road trip. The moving company ends up costing almost three times their initial estimate. The road trip isn't free either, but it is totally worth it. My original plan is to drive the entire twelve hundred miles by myself. This is negatively responded to by just about everyone. It's just a bad idea. It doesn't pass inspection. I look forward to the long drive. I have books on tape. Driving home is totally something that I can pull off. It is something that makes sense to me. It is only twelve hundred miles. I won't have a problem driving down. It is something I should do. It is something I owe myself. With the help of tobacco and caffeine I might just make it back home. If I can get a hold of a stronger substance the skepticism won't be as strong. But I don't have that phone number in my cell, so it isn't an option. Come to think of it, if I had that number and drove down all coked up I would totally die. I would no doubt get pulled over and taken to jail, hit a deer at ninety miles an hour and kill the both of us, or fall asleep at the wheel and drive off the highway and into a ditch. Driving across three states alone is madness. Doing it while sniffing cocaine out of the back end of a Parliament Cigarette is a good way to die. There is no way I can rationalize doing the drive by myself. The act of contemplating driving alone is scary enough. My only chance to make it home to southern California in one piece is to find some friends to do it with me.

I am in need of some help. It doesn't take long to find some. I find some and then I find some more. My journey home starts with one. It quickly finds one more, and then another. By the time I am crying while driving the trip involves four of us. I spend the next three days on the road. The next three days are perfect.

31

Manly Beards

CHAUNCEY IS THE first to commit. He has a manly beard, like, it's fucking amazing. He hears that I plan to drive home alone and won't allow it. He understands that driving a thousand miles after a break up is a bad idea. He goes on the internet and books a flight later that day. He lands in Seattle that next Friday. The next person to commit is Lisa's older sister. Diana just so happens to be visiting Seattle the same week I am due to leave. Chauncey and Diana are long-time good friends. They both book one way flights to Seattle and plan on getting back home with me. The last one to commit is Lisa. It is a brilliant move. Convincing her to take a road trip with us changes everything. The whole dynamic shifts the second she books a flight home from Oakland.

I pick up Lisa and Diana in Seattle and then we pick up Chauncey at the airport. I drive until we hit Portland and then Chauncey takes over. Lisa and I cuddle in the back seat for hours. We hold hands, give each other kisses and then some. The blanket covering us hides the fact that my zipper is down and her skirt is up. The last time I did this was in high school when I was dating Kristi. Her mom happened to be driving the car so it was pretty stressful. This time is way more relaxed. Both Chauncey and Diana have some idea what is going on in the back seat and make sure to keep their eyes focused straight ahead.

We leave Seattle and only stop for fast food and gas. We drive for eight hours straight the first night. We pull into the Holiday Inn Express in Medford, Oregon around three in the morning. Our only hiccup occurs when Chauncey almost hits a deer at eighty MPH. Thankfully he misses and we get to the hotel in one piece. Lisa and I get permission to go swimming in the indoor pool after hours by the night clerk and Chauncey and Diana hop into bed. We swim around for a bit and discover that sex in a pool isn't as good as it sounds. We go back upstairs to the room. The four of us are sharing a room with two queen beds so our only option is to hop in the shower. As long as we are quiet, nobody will be the wiser.

We wake up early the next morning and start to get ready to leave. I notice that Chauncey and Diana keep exchanging glances and smiling. Finally, I ask what is so funny.

James: *What's so fuckin' funny?*

It turns out that Lisa and I were anything but quiet the night before. We were blissfully unaware how loud we were the entire time we had sex in the shower. Diana has to listen to her little sister getting fucked in the shower. It is so obvious that she is able to discern what position we are currently in. Anytime we change, she can easily figure out what position we are in next. This is what she and Chauncey discussed for the half hour we were in the shower the night before.

Thankfully Diana is a cool chick. Sex is a topic that the sisters have discussed freely forever. Neither girl is embarrassed and by the time we check out it is like it never happened. After breakfast we get back on the road. I drive for the first few hours and then Diana takes over. We cross into California and get through the mountain pass. We briefly stop in Weed, California for some gas, once we pass this tiny town we are out of the cool mountain air. For the next six hours we drive south in oppressive heat. A heat wave never seen in the history of weather surrounds us as we drive. Our only hope is to get the air conditioning at full blast and keep the windows shut tight. The two chain smokers up front derail this plan. Every time someone wants a cigarette, the windows are rolled down and a blast of hot air enters the car. After they finish and roll up the windows it takes a few minutes to cool the inside of the car back down. Just when the back seats are almost cool again is it time for another smoke. This process continues over and over again until we arrive at Uncle Leo's house.

We will stay the next two nights just outside San Francisco in a city called Lafayette. This is where people move when they get a bunch of money. Uncle Leo and Aunt Kris have an amazing house surrounded by woods and nature. They welcome us into their home and treat us brilliantly. We play the *Rock Band* video game with Lisa's cousin for hours. We head into the city for dinner one night and meet up with more of their cousins in a park in the middle of the city. Our last night was spent at the house. We have an amazing dinner and end up playing poker until early the next morning. Uncle Leo breaks out some expensive bourbon and pours me glass after glass. Nobody bats an eye when I put my entire leg through their screen door. They assure me that they need a new one anyway and it isn't a problem (not my finest moment).

The problem is that I just walked into a screen door. I no longer can hide the fact that I am drunk. My objective was to not drink excessively. I have obviously failed to meet my goal. I have no one to blame but myself, and Uncle Leo's brown liquor. This is my last night with Lisa and I am entirely too intoxicated. I don't black out or pass out and am able to lead Lisa upstairs to bed. We spend our final night together in a loft totally lacking any form of air conditioning. We ignore the heat and sweat and make love one last time.

We take Lisa to the airport the next morning. We hug and kiss and then she walks into the terminal. The final leg of the drive is over before I know it. Diana drives like a woman possessed and we make it back to Long Beach in the latter part of the afternoon. I spend the final hour of the drive making contact with everyone I have ever met. Text after text contains the following message.

I'm back in the hood. Meet me for tasty beverages ASAP????

Chauncy and I drop Diana off at her parents' house and plan our next move. The first thing I do is call my mother and tell her we made it back safely. Neither Chauncey nor I are ready to call it a day just yet. We drive to a restaurant I used to work at and set up shop on the patio. Friends come by. We spend the rest of the day drinking and smoking on the patio. Once the sun sets we move the party to the Sportsman. It is located on the outskirts of Rossmoor and offers all of the same safety features that Rossmoor does.

Chauncey and I make a quick stop on the way to the Sportsman. I haven't been home for more than a few hours and I'm already on my way to meet my Peruvian drug hook up. It doesn't take me long to walk into the same dive bar I wasted away in during my twenties. I am back home and nothing seems to have changed. My triumphant return is before me and I am not sure how I feel about it. I am happy to be back. I am thrilled to be drinking in the bar closest to my parents' house. I am surrounded by close friends and I am back where I belong. I am back. I am doing the same fucking thing I have been doing all my life. Nothing has changed. Everything is different. It feels delightful.

32

Jerry's Revenge

I ARRIVE HOME WITH nothing. It takes a couple of months for the moving van to show up. Until then, I literally have no possessions. Aside from the two suitcases filled with clothes and my iPod, I have nothing else of value. All I have are answers to the questions that don't end. *Why? How? What?* I actually forgot my answers back in Medford and quickly tire of trying to explain. I run out of ways to tell people what went wrong and how it all fell apart. All I know is that it did and I can't take the questions much longer. Ugly thoughts begin to creep into my mind. I am starting to get desperate. I am close to falling apart. I wrote this on a scrap of paper late one night.

I want to cut myself.
I want to hurt myself.
I want to make my life a waste.
I am sick of comfort and predictability.
I want to be skinny and smoke cigarettes in front of my parents.
I want to drag a razor blade across my skin.
I want to blow shit up my fucking nose.

What I need and what I want is some fucking exercise. I don't want to cut myself. I don't want to give up. All I want to do is lift something heavy and then move it somewhere else. I want to spend my days lifting and moving things. I want to come home sore and dirty. I don't want to think. I want to act. I want to move shit around and then move more shit afterwards. I want to dig a hole and immediately fill it right back up again.

265

I return home depressed and bored. My arrival coincides with my mom's summer break. This means that she is home every day of the week. I don't last more than two weeks. Every time I make it home at four AM smelling like strippers and cocaine I know that my mom wonders where I've been and how I got home. Every time I sleep past noon I wonder what time my mom got out of bed. I wonder how many hours she spends waiting for me to wake up and start looking for a job. This shit can't continue. I need something to do with my days. I find it in the warehouse that Chauncey runs.

He hires me and I start that next Monday. He pays me ten dollars an hour and tells me that if I work hard he might bump me up to twelve. I never see the pay raise, but I go to work for him. I spend my days embracing physical labor. I sweat out all of my anger. Every muscle on my body is sore except for my broken heart (jesus…). I lose more weight each week. Another eight pounds disappears from my body. My beer belly starts to disappear. Next to go is my lingering resentment. After that, my bitterness fades away. I spend the rest of the summer in the warehouse.

The return of a content and well-adjusted version of me becomes official later that summer. A few weeks before the start of the school year I got hired to teach a third grade classroom. The offer of a contracted position with benefits immediately replaces the bitter taste of clean Washington water and fresh Washington oxygen. The moment I find a real job is the moment I can forget about the past year. The past twelve months never happened. I wake up from a bad dream and recognize the comforts of home. I don't mind the traffic. The concrete feels right. Being around factories, industry and filth makes sense. Anything man made must be good. Anything that replaces the tedious greenery of Washington is okay with me. Poverty, strip malls, and fast food return with a vengeance. Every day is filled with the opportunity to buy something worthless. The days spent climbing trees, hunting game and building log cabins are long gone. I now spend my days climbing ladders, hunting for the nearest Carl's Jr., and playing with Legos. I can't even remember what fresh air smells like, let alone appreciate its benefits.

Months go by and I am almost past all of my issues regarding the breakup. I am working and saving money by living at home. I am in a good place. I am at peace. This happy place doesn't last long. I glance at my phone and see that Kate is calling me. Thanksgiving holiday is over and I am about to get in the car and head home with my parents. I press talk on the phone and say hi.

Kate: *I need to tell you something.*

James: *Okay, let's hear it.*

Kate runs it all down for me. It is both highly unexpected, yet highly predictable. Amber starts dating Jerry immediately after she moves out of our house. This is planned way before she moves out. I'm not sure if she has an affair while we are still married. I can't say for certain that it was physical, but I have no doubt that an emotional affair is in the works. Her birthday party is the beginning. Nobody mistakenly loses their engagement ring without a good reason. I witness close talking between herself and Jerry, but don't see them kiss. I forget about it until Kate calls me. Now that I look back at it, everything makes perfect sense. She was ready for the divorce because she already had a plan for afterward.

I am not surprised. I predict that this might happen. I remember having this conversation, months ago. As I am driving home from work I am talking to my future ex- brother-in-law Terry. The conversation goes something like this. I do most of the talking.

James: *What are her options?*

Terry: …

James: *Who the fuck is she going to date?*

Terry: …

James: *I seriously can't see her dating people. I can't picture her going out on a date. I don't see how she gets a boyfriend. How does that work while she lives at her parents' house? The only people she hangs out with are old people. Will she find love at her parents' friends' house?*

Terry: *I see your point.*

James: *It's not like she is going to go out to the local bar and meet someone. The option of making out with a handsome guy at the local bar isn't necessarily available to her. The likelihood that she will find a man who has all of his teeth is slim. Fuck, she hates leaving the house. Finding a single guy with knowledge of environmental policy who firmly believes that he doesn't have the right to bear arms doesn't exist in these parts. So what are her options?*

Terry: *I have no idea.*

James: *I'll tell you what she will do. She will probably become utterly predictable. She will take the easy way out and hook up with Jerry.*

This scenario makes logical sense when I think about it now. It isn't out of the realm of possibility that she would cheat on me. I expect her to do it back in January and she doesn't do it, so I don't give it another thought. I will hear about it again next November. I don't treat it lightly this time. The accusation isn't discounted so easily this time. Everything that seems strange at the time starts to make sense. The blinders are removed from my eyes. I start to see what really happened. I am a day late and a dollar short, but I finally know the truth.

Every aspect of the divorce is based on lies. When Amber tells me that she wants a divorce I assume that *I* am to blame. Because *I* betray her trust when I do cocaine after we are married, *I* am to blame for the break up. She tells me that she won't ever be able to trust me again and that it is *my* fault. She tells me my failure as a husband is the sole reason we can't be together. She fails to tell me that she has a plan. She makes sure to convince me that it is entirely my fault yet she has an exit strategy the whole time. She goes as far to convince the entire community to keep her relationship with Jerry secret from me. It's for my own good.

Amber: *It's important to spare James's feelings. He is fragile and I think it is best not to tell him that Jerry and I are dating. I'll tell him when the time is right.*

This is why nobody came by to check on me. Frank isn't allowed to tell me what is going on and it kills him. Every time he comes over he has to keep his mouth shut and just toss bean bags. He knows that if I find out about Amber's new relationship that all hell will break loose. He knows that I have the right to find out about it but he can't tell me. His future sex life is at stake and he knows it. Hannah is in Def Con 4 mother hen mode and has to protect her chick. Frank has no choice but to toe the line no matter how he feels. He brings me beer and cigars in an attempt to make up for all of their lying. He stops by, smiles and conceals the truth from me.

While I am still in Washington, Amber and Jerry actually invite everyone to a barbecue so they can officially announce that they are a couple. I sign divorce papers pretty quickly after she moves out. She seems to be in a hurry for me to sign them. I think nothing of it and do what I am told. The ink isn't even dry yet, the divorce is still a few months away from being official, and they are organizing community cookouts. This is when we are haggling over who is getting what and fighting over the dining room table. She doesn't want me to know about her relationship with Jerry because she knows I'll be able to connect the dots and figure out when it began.

Hannah knows full well that if I find out about the relationship I'll start to fight harder for the stupid dining room table. She sells out her soul when she sends me an email that I read at school one afternoon. I open it up and am chastised for "pitting her husband against her daughter" and attacked for disrupting the harmony of her household. She types the following email.

"Joy called and she wants the bedroom and living room painted back to off white. Thanks for totally pitting my husband against my daughter. I personally couldn't be more depressed between last night and the call from Joy this morning."

She knows full well that her daughter is dating Jerry and is hiding this from me and she still has the gall to blame me after Frank goes home one night and speaks his mind in defense of me. She knows that her daughter's actions are shady, at best, and still finds it prudent to attack me via email – not even in person. I manage to hold things together at work until I check my email right before lunch is over. I read the message and had my time-allotted break down. I have trouble breathing normally. I feel overwhelmed to the point that holding it together until school lets out isn't a possibility. I pick up my class from recess and start them on an activity. I then call the office and ask for help.

The literacy coach walks into my room within two minutes, takes one look at me and sees that something is wrong. She immediately sees that I am holding on by a thread and that I needed to leave five minutes ago. She sees that I won't be able to hold back the tears much longer. She points to the door and sends me out of the room. I walk down the hallway and into the main office and don't have to explain anything. The secretaries know my situation and don't ask me any questions. I peek my head in, they see how fucked up I am, and reassure me that it's okay that I am leaving early - using only their facial expressions and without the need for actual conversation.

I drive home slowly that day. I don't worry about work because I know that everyone there has my back. It's normal to have a break down during a breakup. If I make it to the end of the year without having one at school, I will surely have a much larger one at the next school I will teach in. I don't even know about what is really going on and it still fucks me up. Hannah knows about everything and still sends this email. On top of being convinced that the divorce is my entire fault I now am told that I am breaking up another marriage.

I have no clue that Amber is deceiving me at this very moment, but it doesn't surprise me that she hooks up with Jerry. She proves to be sadly predictable. My theory ends up being right. She has no sense of adventure. Her sense of intrigue is limited. She sells out for the sure thing and takes the easy fix. She quickly settles for the safe move. She instantaneously forgets that she never was and never will be attracted to him. Every time she mentioned Jerry in front of her friends and me she always made it clear that he was a total nerd and she would never be caught dead with him. Amber and Jerry grew up together and he was referred to as his brother's nerdy older sibling. I know that she knows that I will see through their relationship instantly. She can't let me know about it because she is embarrassed about it. She knows that the moment I find out the gloves will come off and she won't have any legitimacy anymore. I find out and she loses her leverage over me.

She instructs her family to keep quiet. They do not tell me anything about anything until it is way too late. She needs to send thank you cards to Frank and the rest of her family for keeping their mouths shut. The cards I should send them carry a different message. Hallmark doesn't make a card that conveys my exact feelings, I checked, it isn't there. If there had been one I would have written words in all capitals. These capitals would imply my outrage.

I didn't find this card and am left to wonder. None of it makes sense, yet all of it fits perfectly. The entire situation is dirty and false. The fact that she is shacking up with someone else so quickly shouldn't be an issue. I waste no time myself in finding a warm body to console me and don't expect her to keep her legs closed forever. I make no effort to hide my exploits from her. Her intentions are shady only after she hooks up Jerry. She has no reason to hide it unless she has a reason to hide it. What exactly is she protecting herself from?

Kate tells me that she is living in Alaska with him. He promises to take care of her so she can focus on painting. She spent all of her energy fighting for the wedding gifts and then promptly put them into storage. She hides the fact that she takes the majority of our stuff and now has absolutely no inclination to use any of it. As long as I'm not enjoying the blender, she doesn't mind that it is collecting dust. I am left to wonder what she wanted with any of it anyway. She has no need for it presently, but makes sure it will be there waiting for her in the future. Just in case.

I am sipping bourbon in my childhood bedroom with the door closed two days after finding out about Amber's alleged infidelities. I am living at home with my parents and have just written an email that I am hesitant to send. It is not a long letter by any means. It is straightforward and to the point. I think I should send it.

> *Dear Amber,*
> *"Did you have an affair?"*

I don't send it. I stop feeling sorry for myself in time and remind myself that sending it will not make me feel any better. I know that it won't help me. I know that if I send it to her the stress alone will kill me while I wait for a reply. It will give me no closure. It won't help me. It will solve nothing.

I erase the email, but I keep on typing. I bang away at the keyboard with strength. Every letter I touch uses the perfect amount of force and is backed with pure intention. I kill it. I stop fixing spelling errors because I don't have time to stop typing. The keyboard becomes an extension of my fingers. I know what the prudent thing to do is. But I do not want to do the prudent thing. I want to keep on typing. I want to destroy something. I want to bleed and see the sun rise. I want to break everything that I used to think was pure. All of the bullshit that used to matter when I still believed in my flawed marriage needs to disappear.

I want to send the email so she knows that I know. I know that she will never reply but I don't care. Jesus fucking Christ. Are you kidding me? Come on James, you know better than to contact her. This can only end badly. Or even worse, nothing will be said and I will be left wondering. Once things end it is only a matter of time until things further apart. I imagine she hates me. I don't know why she hates me, but sure enough, she does. It doesn't surprise me that she hates me, but yet I can't figure out why she does so thoroughly.

The best part about her moving to Alaska is that I have an extremely low chance of running into her in the lower forty eight states. Jerry promises to support her financially so she can paint full time. "Full Time" consists of no more than three times a week. She will cook on a daily basis. She will drink wine. She will be engaging. She might be somewhat fun. Hell, she may even do light dusting and a random load of laundry. She can put on the façade of someone who is not spoiled and lazy.

I don't want to cut myself anymore. I don't need to do it again. I figure out how to take that away and right now it is no longer important. I no longer need to feel like I am evil. I no longer feel fucked up. I don't feel any remorse. I'll accept my own decisions from now on. I discover that I am not to blame. I wasn't the most fucked up person in the relationship. She can carry that distinction now. She is way more fucked up than I am. She is the broken part of the relationship. I can live with this. I can accept things now. It doesn't bother me that she lives in Alaska. I don't feel bad that she moves there and lives with Jerry. Let them cut wood to stay warm.

It is appropriate that she is hiding things from me after the divorce. I hid a second complete life during the entirety of our marriage so it's only fair that she gets to return the favor. What evil have I done to change her? She used to be a sweet girl. Now she is just bitter. What drives women into the arms of a goateed bush pilot living in Alaska? James does, that's who. I'd want to get as far away as possible too. That is, if I were in her position. But I am not, so there.

33

Wearing Suits for Absolutely No Reason

James: *Have you talked to Mitch recently?*

Justin: *Not in a long time.*

Mike: *Where the fuck is Mitch?*

James: *Last I knew, he is somewhere in Georgia.*

Justin: *Is he alive?*

James: *Is his real name even Mitch?*

Mike: *Good point.*

James: *Exactly, I don't remember anyone ever taking the time to independently verify his identity.*

Mike: *Let's call him. Do you have his number?*

JUSTIN AND I check our phones. The number he has is different than the one I have. Neither number works. Both are out of service. This happens all the time. I've kept the same cell phone number for the last six years. My parents' phone number has been the same since 1982. If anyone really needs to get a hold of me, they have the option of leaving a message. Mitch lives a different reality. He is on the fringe. He prefers to make sporadic guest appearances into our lives. Mitch has a cell phone for no longer than a month before the number is disconnected. What follows these brief reintroductions into our lives are months without contact.

None of this makes sense to me. I'm pretty sure he isn't a deep cover operative in the CIA or in the witness protection program. I'm somewhat confident that he isn't a deadbeat dad doing his best to avoid child support payments to his various baby mamas. Running from the law makes more sense to me, but I'm not entirely convinced that he warrants the attention of the local police. Sadly, the answer is probably that he is fucked up and unable to call any of us. He most likely wants to talk but knows that will involve answering questions. Wrapping his head around partaking in that conversation must overwhelm him. This is my theory. This is also something I can relate to. This is why I always pick up the phone when he calls me. This is why I don't ask him too many questions. In my head, I question whether or not Mitch is his real name. Asking him questions doesn't mean that I believe any of the answers he gives me. I stopped asking questions a long time ago, what's the point? I don't really believe anything he tells me anyway, so I would rather not allow him to feed me his bullshit.

My summer ends and I am gainfully employed again, back to the comfort and stability of teaching the youth. I have full benefits and decide to continue to live with my parents for the next year. I convince myself to act prudently for the time being. A year without paying rent will allow me the opportunity to climb back out of debt. I can avoid utility bills and start paying back my parents. I come home with three maxed out credit cards that are beyond my ability to pay off. My parents rescue me and write three large checks to erase the monthly suffocation. Now, all I have to do is pay them back each month. This won't happen if I am living in a one-bedroom apartment in Long Beach. This won't happen if I am living in a studio. The only thing that makes sense is to be a twenty-eight year-old divorcee that lives at home. The difficulty of writing this sentence is beyond computation. Shit, I even enjoy spending time with my parents but still...

Nobody pulls off the act of 'suit wearing for no reason' as well as Mitch and I did. He doesn't hesitate for a moment to put on a tie. He is no doubt willing to pull this off with me. We should be, without a doubt, doing this together. Traveling to someplace together still is appealing. It could be a bocce ball tournament in Puerto Rico or a glue sniffing competition in Ohio, whatever, we should go, just us. There is no reason why we shouldn't be sitting on a plane together, wearing suits for no good reason. I wouldn't be questioning my ability to drink scotch successfully without cocaine if he was here. Even without his magic pills, I know that it won't be a problem to stay up past midnight without blacking out. His presence is like an amphetamine. The years dealing with his bullshit fail to convince me that I am better off without him. There is still a part of me that wants him sitting in the seat next to me. All of his lies and all of the times he takes advantage of me teach me nothing. My brain tells me to let him go but my heart wishes that he is here. Anytime I wait for a red light, order a burrito or wait for a plane to take off it occurs to me that some part of me would be more content if he was doing it with me. It bothers me to no end that I still think this way. It kills me to hate someone that I love. The one person in the world I want to go places with is someone I can't stand. My life becomes a complete mess when he is around. It becomes complicated and disorderly and it smells like cigarette smoke. Without his presence, my life has clean socks and exercise. Without him, my life is missing something. I spend way too much fucking time wondering if my life is better with or without him in it.

Mitch isn't here. He is far away. Blah, blah, blah... Life gets in the way. I understand this. Lives change and priorities switch. I can live with this realization. The compatibility of our lives ended a long time ago. Our lives are no longer closely related and the things that connect us don't exist anymore. The occasional phone call is the extent of our friendship. There is nothing left between us to inspire taking a trip together. We missed our chance. The opportunity to wear suits, for no good reason but to look good and fly somewhere for a house party, is over.

Neither of us have the ability to fix this. We both lose the motivation to make the effort. From here on out, I am unavailable. I've been unavailable for a long time now. It isn't that important anymore and that should make me feel ill, but it doesn't. I wait for the plane to depart and it becomes clear to me that I am failing in my attempt to keep the important people in my life close by. Mitch and I no longer see the benefits of knowing each other and it makes me sick. I wonder where Mitch is. I wonder what he is doing. I wonder whether or not I even care.

Something that should be simple never is. A simple question such as what specific city he is currently residing in requires an explanation.

James: *Where are you living right now?*

Mitch: *Well...*

Five minutes of uninterrupted talking on Mitch's part mercifully ends without answering my simple question that should have taken a single word to answer. If he chooses to include the state, this still leaves the maximum amount of words to answer the question at a whopping two. Mitch takes an uncomplicated question and turns it into something way more convoluted than it needs to be. This is his hobby. Every attempt to master the art of knitting scarves, playing indoor soccer, or collecting stamps, fails. Normal avocations don't intrigue him. Instead of kayaking, he takes up the art of deception.

I gave up trying to figure him out a long time ago. I stopped asking questions. It becomes too tiresome to keep up with him, so I just stop trusting any and everything he says. It is boring being lied to. I'm weary of the lies. I'll see him eating a ham sandwich for lunch and if I ask him what he is eating there is a fifty/fifty chance that he tells me that it is a turkey on rye, hold the cheese because he is lactose intolerant.

He burns every bridge with everyone he grows up with. One by one, bridge by bridge, friend by friend, they all stop caring. He loses his California privileges. He was once considered to be a crucial component. He once was a substantial asset. Now all he is a headache. It stops making sense when he comes to visit. He is no longer a welcome addition to a night out. Now he is just a drain on everyone around him. At one time or another everyone defends him. At some point we all enable Mitch. We all say that he is good for it. We all wait for him to change. When it never happens, we all lose our faith in him. Our ability to defend him is finished and we all quietly swear to never do it again. I promise myself that I will never be fooled again. I pledge to never defend him about anything again. I made an oath never to do that for the rest of my days.

I always know that sooner or later I will simply stop listening to his bullshit. I'll grow a backbone and stop being a victim of his charm. I have faith that eventually a situation will present itself that leads me to lose all respect for him. I am confident that the firm grasp he holds over me will soon loosen. The end is near and I can feel it. The tragic off-Broadway play detailing the friendship of James and Mitch is about to end its run. Sales have been slow. The actors do nothing more each night than go through the motions. The investors made back their money months ago and have no reason to extend it. It is finished. Then the phone rings. It is Mitch. He is engaged. He asked me to be in his wedding. I consider my options.

#1 The Enthusiastic Payback Option: AKA The Sassy Mic Drop?

This involves hard lobbying on my part to be the best man. I make elaborate promises to be the greatest best man ever. I then fail to show up at the last minute, concoct an elaborate story about being wrongfully prosecuted in Texas while en route, and then fall off the face of the world for the next year and a half.

#2 The My Feelings Are Still Hurt Option AKA Get Over It Already

I respectfully decline to participate in his wedding.

#3 The This Is Seriously Your Last Chance, I'm The Bigger Person, No Hard Feelings Option.

I spend an ass load of money to fly to Atlanta, Georgia. I am a willing participant in his wedding and then I don't speak to him again for almost an entire year.

The first option is too complicated and is never seriously considered. The second one is never really an option either. No part of me could refuse a friend's request to be in his wedding. That's just mean. Also, I like being in weddings way too much. My only real option is to say this to him.

James: *Of course I can be in your wedding, Yay.*

What I should say to him involves raising my voice and using emphatic hand gestures.

James: *There is no way in hell I would even consider participating in your lame ass wedding. I hope it rains, you slip, twist your ankle and can't dance.*

I should remind him what happened not so long ago when I got married. Do I need to remind him that he flaked on me, disappeared, and never even acknowledged, let alone apologize for what happened? The fucker makes me look bad. I convince everyone to have faith in him. I reconditioned everyone's automated skepticism and convinced them to trust my instincts and ignore their own. He proves once again that when there is a healthy amount of skepticism that it exists for a reason.

I should break his heart. I should destroy him. I should make him feel small. The only reason I should agree to be in his wedding is so I can kick him in the shin with those shiny plastic tuxedo shoes. Fly out there, kick him, turn around and fly back home. This is what he deserves. There is no disputing that I owe him a good hard kick. This is why I have to go. I have to show up and ignore any and all impulses to physically harm him. It is impractical to fly all that way to kick someone. Instead, I'll fly all that way so he can see that I don't give a shit anymore and that he just isn't worth it. Declining to attend the wedding means that I am still bitter. Showing up makes me the bigger person. There isn't anything I can do. I should reject him and say no. I should leave him at the altar, but I can't do that. It's an excuse to wear a tuxedo. It's also a reason to fly to Atlanta. Fuck it, I get a haircut and make sure to shave. I'll look damn good, and that is all the excuse I need. It is all that I require.

At one point I think that Mitch is going to ask me to be his best man. I imagine the awkward silence and nervous laughter when the crowd realizes that the best man can't come up with a single positive thing to say during his best man speech. The best I could come up with?

James: *Mitch really liked golf.*"

I am not a good liar (I'm totally serious) and I can't imagine talking about how great someone is when all I really want to say is that they kind of suck. Thankfully he finds someone else to be in charge of that duty. He asks Bernie, Justin and I to be a groomsman at his wedding. We all accept. Three other couples travel from California to Atlanta for the wedding. It looks like a fun weekend in the south.

I try to act like an adult by going to his wedding. I expect him to appreciate the level- headedness/rad-ness/maturity-ness that I possess. At least he will acknowledge my involvement, buy me a drink, and give me a hug. I have no illusions that I will actually receive any of these things. The moment I show up it is obvious that I am a visitor in his new world. Here in Georgia he is no longer called Mitch. He is now called Mitchell.

He has carved out a new identity that involves the elongation of his name. He is no longer known as Mitch. His new name is more refined. It has more letters. It has two syllables instead of just one. He is now called Mitchell. His last few visits to California began his subtle requests to be called Mitchell. We forget to do this and within minutes his petition is forgotten and he is, once again, Mitch. Here in Atlanta he is known as Mitchell and known as Mitchell *only*. Here in Atlanta, I quickly discover that calling him Mitch does nothing but piss him off. It isn't simple anymore. Exercising my given right to use a familiar name in order to call upon a familiar person is no longer allowed. The name "Mitch" is banished. It is the last thing associated with him and the final thing that connects him with a past that he can no longer afford to be acquainted with.

He becomes vulnerable the second we touch down in Atlanta. His new identity becomes fragile the moment we arrive. We are his biggest liability. He left "Mitch" in California years ago. He spends the next few years working hard establishing a fresh, cleaner identity. His driver's license identifies him as Mitchell. He is a new man. As any new man will tell you, missing the opportunity to extend your name leads to regret. A new identity comes along rarely. Changing a five letter name into an eight letter one became his number one priority. A name with only a single syllable won't cut it anymore. Five letters isn't enough. Eight letters and two syllables will do just fine.

At this point he needs a clean break from his youth. A new beginning is required. Burning bridges is exhausting. Losing his California privileges isn't fun. Signing three extra letters every time he writes his name is a necessary evil. Remaining Mitch only reminds him of a past that is best forgotten. Becoming Mitchell relieves him of all past transgressions.

When his California friends arrive in Atlanta he is faced with his past. His secret life as Mitch is in danger of being exposed. Every time we call him Mitch he is reminded of being infiltrated by a group of friends that know all about his past and may or may not have reasons to expose such transgressions. We are the exception. We show up with all his hidden baggage. We are the only ones with the ability to fuck everything up. Best case scenario? Justin, Mike, James, Aleem, and Bernie stick to beer. Worst case scenario? Fuck, who knows, light arson?

I'm in the heart of Atlanta on the day of the wedding. I'm wearing a tux with a bow tie and a fucking cummerbund. I can't get over the fact that I'm wearing a cummerbund. I am not even aware that the cummerbund option still exists. It turns out that cummerbunds are the shit. I am just not hip enough to realize this. My numerous attempts to give Mitch shit for the cummerbunds are met with a glare that is meant to shut me up. I miss the obvious implications and continue to press the issue. The longer and harder he frowns at me has a reverse effect on my mood. My smile gets bigger and bigger as his mood gets more sour. His disposition is slowly going in the toilet and I can't stop myself from fucking with him. I can't figure out why he is so tense. The only solution I come up with is to annoy him as best I can. He should be happy. If he is too nervous to embrace the moment then I have no choice but to grab it for him.

I'm the one about to participate in a full mass Catholic wedding ceremony thing. I'm not entirely sure that I'm even allowed inside the church. It's all about me, dammit. What is he so nervous about? He is the most Catholic person I know. He knows where to stand and what to do. My only chance to figure out what is expected of me is missed yesterday. I arrive at the rehearsal just when it is ending. I am directly involved in a church wedding and have no clue what is going on. When the ceremony finally ends I am still in the dark about what just happened. The last hour of my life found me utterly confused about what the fuck was going on. I spent the last sixty minutes standing up and sitting down. I repeat this over and over until the service finally ends.

The reception takes place at the locally world-famous Botanical Gardens in Atlanta. There is a quesadilla bar - usually right up my alley but I've been popping Ritalin for the last three days and I have no appetite.

By the time Mitch's best man takes the microphone to give his speech, I am on my ninth glass of ice mixed with Makers Mark. I realize that I have something to say and that I am drunk enough to go up and say it. I make a beeline towards his cousin. My plan is to grab the microphone, raise my glass, and tell a group of two hundred right wing Republicans to give it up for the newly elected president Barack Obama. I don't know if I'm going to hand the microphone back to someone or just drop it and run. I make it up to the front of the room; begin to reach for the microphone only to be met with a straight arm from the best man. He keeps me back and turns me around in one motion. I start my retreat. He smiles big and tells the crowd.

Best Man: *James just wants to say congratulations..*

Thank God I don't get a hold of the microphone. No good would have come of it. After the best man speech ends, Mitch takes the microphone. Some part of me expects him to acknowledge his childhood friends that traveled so far to be a part of his wedding. Surely, he will recognize his amazing friends that traveled all the way to Atlanta in order to come to his damn wedding. He mentions *nobody*. It is like we aren't even here. Why the fuck are we here? Why did I decide to come in the first place anyway?

The open bar saves the wedding. It is full of high-end liquor and it is brilliant. It is the one thing that makes up for everything else. I walk outside to the bar, order a drink, and head over to a group of people. This is when I trip. Somehow I save the glass from breaking. If I drop the glass and it breaks it is a small addition to the bar tab for whoever is paying for it. That isn't how I roll. There will be no broken glass on my conscience. I save the glass. The Makers Mark and ice don't fare so well. It flies in all directions. The bar is close by, I know there is a refill waiting for me once I pick myself off the ceramic tile and walk back across the patio. What I don't notice is the blood dripping down my hand as I stand back up.

Leave it to me to trip, save the glass, get up, head back to the bar, glance at my hand, and discover that I am injured. On the back of my left hand, near my pinky finger, is a cut a half an inch long. This isn't a problem until I realize it is a pretty wide cut that might need a couple of stitches. This is when I realize that someone who works at the gardens may feel obligated contractually to convince me to go to the hospital to get stitches.

I don't want to leave. I have no interest in being the guy who goes to Atlanta Mercy Hospital to get a couple of stitches in the middle of a wedding with an open bar. I saved the glass people. I need a *Band-Aid* and a hug. One of the workers hears of my predicament and kindly brings me the medical assistance I call for and, without delay, the bleeding has stopped. I'm ready to refill my beverage. Unfortunately, they also bring a waiver form and a pen. At this juncture of the evening I doubt my ability to read a form and sign it. I have no doubt that I am in need of another cocktail. I am on the fence about whether or not I should sign anything implying that I am of sound mind and should just sign it. I respectfully decline.

My gut instinct says *don't sign it.* The crowd slowly surrounding me says otherwise. Reluctantly, I sign away my life, give the guy a hug, and move on with my night. The reception ends. The party moves on back to the hotel and my night gets fuzzy from there. I fly to New York the next day thankful to make it out of Atlanta.

Two days later I receive the first text message from Mitch. Very seldom do I receive text messages with so much unspoken anger. The subtle edge attached to the words carries an undeniable tone of voice. The tone of the text messages scream accusations. I am about to be blamed for something.

Mitch: *How many times did they tell you not to smoke in the garden? They are charging me $750 for all the cigarette butts.*

James: *I smoked where they told me to.*

Mitch: *Tell me exactly what happened when you fell and cut your hand.*

James: *I fell, the staff gave me a Band-Aid, I thanked them, end of story.*

Mitch: *Call me.*

James: *Obviously you have something to say to me. If you want to talk to me then take the initiative and dial my number.*

I admit that I smoked in the rear outside patio which is the "Non-Smoking" section of the reception. I admit to being reminded on multiple occasions by the staff that I am not allowed to smoke there. This is where the bar is located and this is where all the smokers are taking care of business. After a while I ignore the staff like everyone does and keep on lighting up in the forbidden zone. I tell myself that as long as I pick up my butts and throw them away then on a moral level my smoking isn't hurting anyone and can be justified. I am somewhat confident that I pick up every one of my cigarette butts and throw them away. I am not one who litters without remorse. I was raised better than that. In all likelihood my cigarette disposal rate is not perfect. Without doubt I picked up the majority of them but at some point I probably flick one in a bush and leave another one on the ground.

Mitch expects me to call him. I am not overly interested in getting yelled at the moment. If he has something to say to me, then say it. He finally realizes that I have no intention of calling him, so he calls my number. When I see his number on the caller ID I am drinking with Aleem's fiancé at a speakeasy somewhere in New York City. This has the markings of a phone call that has little chance of remaining a pleasant one. The cool New York hipsters surrounding me at the bar don't need to witness, what they can only assume to be, a lovers quarrel. I don't have time to thoroughly explain the situation to the entire bar, so I step outside.

The phone call leads off in typical Mitch fashion. A relentless diatribe of words- he talks, I listen, there is no back and forth. I stop listening after the second minute, but from what I can gather, he is being unfairly prosecuted for the actions of others. He is an innocent bystander caught up in a web of blame. The Botanical Garden is charging him some ungodly amount of money because of all of the cigarette butts found in the "Non-Smoking" Section. He needs someone to blame. *Somebody* needs to take the fall and it sure as hell isn't going to him. *Someone* should be held accountable. Apparently that *somebody* is me.

I listen to his well-rehearsed tirade on the importance of personal accountability when one visits botanical gardens. It is obvious where this is leading. Mitch knows that he has the ability to confuse me with big words and numbers. Starting at the age of sixteen and continuing to this day, anytime he finds himself in a dead end argument about politics, when I am right, he knows it, I know he knows it, he is backed in a corner and should concede the point and move on, but he can't so he resorts to throwing out random data that proves his point. He quotes percentages and hard data from articles he recently read. According to the *National Review*, you have no idea what you are talking about and my words are the truth. This always trips me up. Using fictional data to prove a point never occurs to me. This baffles me and fucks up my abilities to defend whatever it is that I am arguing for.

Without subtlety, Mitch implies that *I* am solely to blame for all of the cigarette butts. Since I am the *only* one who smoked that night, I am morally *obligated* to wire him seven hundred dollars to cover the damage. He tries to convince me the twenty people also smoking in the forbidden zone have *nothing* to do with the fine. *I* am the evil ringleader. It is my *entire* fault. He has to blame someone and he figures I am the easiest target.

But this "social" call isn't over yet. He also needs to inform me that he is also being charged for the amount of time the staff had to spend trying to convince me to sign the waiver after I cut my hand. I am accused of taking over an hour to consent to sign the paperwork. There isn't a chance in hell that I spend an hour fighting off the staff. Mitch's oldest brother (the lawyer) walks over to me.

Paul: *Dude, just sign the thing.*

James: *Okay.*

Once he tells me to sign it, I sign it. The entire episode takes no more than ten minutes. Eight minutes is a more realistic estimate. Mitch's estimation of how much time it takes is just over an hour. He suggests that spending such an excessive amount of time refusing to sign a waiver has led to additional penalties, and more fines. He accuses me of being rude to the staff. He tells me that I told them to *fuck off.* When Mitch tells me this I immediately lose the last remaining amount of respect that I have for him.

I have counted on him for so long. It is apparent that he no longer knows anything about me. I rarely tell people to fuck off. I never say it in a menacing way. I reserve that phrase for friends who won't take offense from it. In my heart I am a blue collar worker. These are my people. I spend a significant chunk of my life in the service industry. I have *never* disrespected a fellow slave to the middle class. I have no reason to tell them to fuck off. They have gauze and a plan to stop the bleeding.

Thinking about it, my hand is bandaged up by the largest black man in Atlanta. I rarely tell black men to fuck off, let alone the biggest one I've ever seen. I have a healthy level of respect and admiration for this man. The staff loves me. The next day I look through the pictures on my camera. Near the end of the roll I see a picture of my new friend and myself smiling at the camera. I'm hugging my new amigo just minutes after telling him to fuck off? This makes no sense. Mitch has either been grossly misinformed or he is making this shit up as he goes along. He expects an apology. He isn't going to get it from me. Not now anyway.

Mitch: [to his wife] *He refuses to apologize.*

His wife takes the phone from him and starts to speak.

Julie: *Listen, he is just under a lot of pressure from the families right now.*

James: *I understand that Julie, but I don't really appreciate being blamed for everything that went wrong during the wedding.*

Julie: *I know.*

James: *Let me just say this, you were a beautiful bride, it was an honor to get to participate in your wedding, tell Mitch he can go fuck himself.*

Julie: *You don't mean that.*

James: *For the first time in my life, I do, tell Mitch to erase my number from his phone and never fucking call me again. Have a nice honeymoon.*

I say bye to Julie and hang up the phone. I go directly into my phone and erase Mitch's information. I don't feel tempted to call him. I know that I need a break from him. We don't talk again until Aleem's wedding. When I see Mitch again, things are calm between us. We got drunk together, just like old times. I stop trying to figure him out. I stop trying to change the things that bother me about him. I stopped needing him. I finally can let him go. I am able to take him for who he is. I accept his good points and his faults. I want him to be happy, I realize that I can't expect him to make me complete. We had a good ride, but it is over. I can handle that, it makes sense to me.

34

Deep Cuts

"**J**AMES, YOU'RE SO *flawed. But, like, I get it. I seriously get it. We're both so frustrated and anxious for something more. I don't know, I just get it I guess… I don't have anything more really.*"

The last time I cut myself is an utter failure. I cut too deep. I have no reason to do it and before I know it, blood is everywhere. I am bored. On some level I am disenfranchised. Some part of me is abused by the world. There is no doubt that I have been wronged in some way. The irony sets in just about now. I have no reason to cut myself. I have no interest in causing a scene. The moment the blade goes in my thigh I regret it. I have no intention to cut myself deeply. Once I finish and look down is when I realize what I have done.

Shit. I am gushing blood. I use paper towels and scotch tape to stop the bleeding. I bleed through my sad attempt to contain the gushing blood. My plan of relying on super thick paper towels fails the moment I fall asleep. The blood seeps through the sheets, past the towel I laid under me and into the deep recesses of the comfortable bed ready to give nightly pleasure to all who sleep atop it.

I wake up the next morning and see the extent of the damage. My leg is a bloody mess. My bed is soaked in blood. I can't believe what I did to myself. For the first time, I am genuinely afraid. I get in the shower and then I really start to regret the cut. The warm water rinses off my leg. The water turns red as the dried blood goes down the drain. The gaping wound in my leg is massive. Without doubt, I am in need of stitches. The pain brings me to tears when the water first hits. It is unbearable as I gingerly rub soap into the cut. I promise myself that this will be the last time I cut myself. I've made this promise many times before. I've never been able to keep it. I say to myself *Never again* and a few months later I find myself with a razor blade in my hand. Something different happens this time. I find a reason to stop the self-destructive habits. The need to cut myself goes away. I have no interest in it anymore.

I meet a girl. She changes everything. Cutting myself is no longer an option. It doesn't even occur to me to do it anymore. I never cut myself again.

My marriage fails. Mitch and I break up. My leg is bleeding. I live at home. I have no money. I drive a lame car. Things are bleak. Things are all fucked up. And then, all of a sudden life turns around.

I am one of three new teachers at my school. There is me, I teach third grade. There is another male teacher who teaches fifth grade. He is prematurely balding, overly enthusiastic and ridiculously excited to be there. He is the anti me, he stands for everything I hate about teachers and the teaching profession. Without fail (and every fucking morning) he walks down the hallway and says *hello, hello, hello...*

Every single morning I wait for him to just say *hi*. Each day I wait for just a simple *hello*. I patiently wait for this unnecessary enthusiasm to end. Day after day, it continues. I can't wrap my head around his positive attitude. His enthusiasm confuses me. I want to like him, but I just can't do it. I am the one with problems. It is my character flaw. He annoys me. His open-faced honesty is the antithesis of *anyone* I could even consider to be a friend - he is nice. Nice is gross. I am cynical. I cannot take this person seriously, he either has no skeletons in *his* closet or he's a fucking liar. We get it, you are rad, you have a good attitude, you are what we should strive to be like, you are the worst. Whatever...

The third new teacher at my school is another story altogether. She is tall and beautiful. Her hair flows in the wind. She wears makeup effectively. She looks amazing in turtlenecks. I usually hate turtlenecks but not on her.

Our first conversation...

James: *This traffic sucks...*
Future Wife: *Totally...*
James: *I'm serious. All these drivers suck bags of dicks...*

Future wife: *Don't say that…*

James: *Why not?*

Future wife: *An entire bag? That seems mean spirited…*

As I finish reading her last text I know without a doubt that I am fucked. All my plans go out the window. Live with my parents, pay off debt, move out to hip bachelor pad, fuck fuck fuck fuck fuck everything in sight. Drink bourbon while I take a shower. Color-coordinate my closet. Have a stocked bar in my living room. Make cute girls drinks with vodka and soda water. Store cocaine in my sock drawer. All of that doesn't make sense any more. All I want to do is be with her.

I find my first true love. I discover the sexiest, most beautiful woman in the world. I luck out and find someone funnier than I am. I hold nothing back. I tell her every last ugly detail. I show her the cut on my leg. It doesn't scare her off. A week later she shows up to my parents' house on Christmas night. She brings a bottle of scotch and meets the entire family. An impromptu dance party starts the moment I put Madonna on the stereo at the party. The night comes alive and becomes something more. She dances on the coffee table with my aunt, my cousins and my dad. I watch from the kitchen and know without a doubt that my life is about to become good again. "Lucky Star" fills the house and I see that there is hope for the future. I see my future singing along to vintage Madonna and I know that everything happens for a reason. Things just might work out in the end. There is hope and she is dancing right in front of me. There is a reason to get my shit together. A reason to be a better man, an excuse to do things right. I am given a second chance and there is no way that I'm going to fuck it up.

35

One Way to Spend a Sunday Morning

10 Years Later…

THE HEIGHT OF the sun suggests that it's just past 11am on a Sunday morning. This is in itself a ridiculous statement. My phone says it's 11:14 and the sun is already too bright and it isn't suggesting shit. I am currently walking down Cerritos Avenue in the direction of my house. Being that I did not plan on any strenuous exercise today I am poorly dressed for it. But there's no turning back now, and God knows I need the exercise.

The plan was simple. Don't fuck things up. That was all I had to do. Contrary actions. Learn from past mistakes. Be better. For the most part I did all these things. I honestly thought I *was* doing better. Married the girl of my dreams, had a couple of children, checked all the boxes on the "Adulting" Checklist. My body tells the world I'm middle-aged, but why do I still feel like that volatile teenager. Now my day has a wholesome itinerary of Church coupled with the plasticity of suburban family life: Church, lunch, then Dollar Tree. This should be enough, it is enough for many, I want it to be enough for me, but no matter how hard I try and all the things I do, I still feel on the verge of a breakdown. The fucking Dollar Tree cannot be the highlight of my day, but that's where I'm at. Without the rigid structure of teaching, the infinite possibilities become finite with the realization that having no income sucks. But I can't be anyone's role model today, at least not until I pick up my boys from school later - then I will force myself to be an adult, but it never feels 100% authentic. I am not someone an old friend would look at with admiration and think, *damn. James has his life together. I want to be like him.* But I'm also sick of looking at everyone else that way - why are morons capable of paying mortgages and taxes, securing that 401K, and are able to happily settle into an existence that often makes me want to crawl out of my skin at the idea of the boredom it inspires? Who the fuck *wants* to live *that* way? I guess part of me does. And that's the part that is kicking me forward; I have to believe that I can change.

11:18 AM *I wait for the light and then cross the street when it told me I was safe. I am getting old. Such a rule follower. Follow the rules of the law, holy shit. That car was driving fast.*

I make it to church, park the car, drop off the boys at the free childcare center and go inside. There, I proceed to stand up like everyone else for the next twenty minutes of new wave Christian Rock. What I did not do, and refuse to do on principal, is sway from side-to-side or reach an outstretched arm or arms in an upward fashion. There are some lines I refuse to cross - and grandiose religious gesticulating is a hard "no" for me.

The music ends and everyone sits down. Before the service starts, quick church-related videos play on the big screens. Join this, do that, be of service et cetera. Usually this is when I check my phone, but something catches my ear, I look up, and before I know it I have to leave. I usually power through this part and make it to the service. But not today.

The fact that I am at church in the first place still blows my mind. I must admit, some parts of it I find interesting. Don't get me wrong, I still think it's all ceremonial bullshit, but without the righteous anger and solid conviction as before. I'm long past the age where it's considered "cute" to be engaging in anti-religious sentiments - so I work hard to hide it well. The work pays off. I don't love it all, but the services that remind me of the History Lectures I used to enjoy in college can actually be quite interesting. When there's actually history being taught, when the places are familiar and I know they existed, when the names are based in fact, and I saw them on the *History Channel*, then I'll sit up in my chair and pay more attention. That's all good. Church and I can be friends.

Then comes the other part of it. You know, the *Jesus* stuff. I just can't wrap my head around the main reason everyone else is there. Whenever it isn't secular, keep in mind, this is the one place where it's supposed to be unsecular, I am just not there yet. Jesus is in the building and there's a bunch being said about that specifically and the people around me are eating it up. They believe without question and that pisses me off because part of me is jealous that I don't have what they have but another part of me can't ignore my inner skeptic. But that's not why I left a few minutes ago and started walking.

I really didn't have a good reason to leave church but I did anyway. It was a combination of everything really, church finance reform is really the least of my worries but that's what got me up and out of my seat. Basically there are all of these extracurricular church events and they promote them before the service starts and today there was an event coming up about grief counseling for people who lost their long time spouses. There was information about how to sign up and how much it cost. My issue was that eight dollars seemed a tad high, especially for grieving widows. What if they couldn't afford the eight dollars? What happens to those poor souls who are on a fixed income? Why does the "Junior" Pastor (who is younger than I am) drive an Audi and is building a million dollar home when the older and newly bereaved have to dip into their social security to get help with the grieving process? Why am I such a fuck up that I'm not teaching this year? Why is everyone so nice here? Why aren't they surrounded by the same doubt and sadness that I am? Are they though? Did they replace it with Jesus and that's why they seem to be doing just fine when I am spiraling?

11:20 AM *I am running in flip flops. Running. The flip flops I am running in are grey and cost me two dollars. I have another pair of the same flip flops at home that are black. These also are not made for running. They are barely made for walking. Yet here I am, running past a donut shop...*

Turns out I do have a bad memory from childhood. It's a long story that needs proper telling. That's the thing about this one in particular, I wasn't exactly aware of it. Ahh... the old repressed childhood trauma thing. It makes perfect sense when I think about it. Something did happen so many years ago. No, I did not fall down a well. That would have been cool though. It happens in fifth grade. The shitty parts of puberty are beginning to happen but none of the cool things are yet. My face is breaking out. I still don't have any new hair in exciting new places. My mom is dealing with some major shit which stresses my dad out even more than he usually is. I'm not getting along with my sister for a bunch of reasons that seem important then but in hindsight aren't really such a big deal. But at the moment it all seems huge and I don't know what to do with it. What do you do with all of this? Where does it go? How do you deal? How the fuck do you deal?

11:24 AM *I am no longer running. Running is serious business. I make it a few blocks until I have to slow things down. Keep in mind, these are large city blocks. So the eight dollars is the catalyst that gets me out of church, I am currently waiting for the light to change... And now I continue onward...*

A repressed childhood trauma that led to situational depression. Nobody freaks out the way I did over having soccer practice. The fucking cloud was thick those days. My reaction to being rejected by Kristi wasn't an uncommon one, kids freak out all the time over that shit, what made it uncommon was how far past extreme I took it. That cloud enveloped me and took me way past *normal reaction boulevard,* up the street, around the corner and all the way into *what the fuck?* city. All I know is I felt this overwhelming sadness that I couldn't get rid of. Maybe this wasn't normal. Fuck, what did I know? I just figured it was.

First, before taking this ill- advised walk, Nana dies. Months ago this happened and I was too busy to mourn her. Too many things. Not enough time to process it properly. Too busy to think about it like I needed to. She had such a unique and special connection to my sister and just like Mandy was close to Nana, so was I. She was the only person I had this weird bond with. Mandy had the same bond with her. Now Nana is gone and I can't call her to check in while I walk which is hard to accept so the best I can do is think about her which I never properly did after she died. I've put it off until now, months later, I never made the call to Nana before she died, I wasted an important opportunity just like I did before.

11:27 AM *How is there another donut shop this close together? Seriously, how many donuts does one community eat? This cannot be right. Quick fact, I have only eaten one type of donut my entire life. Rainbow Fucking Sprinkles. Go figure...*

She had been living with an aneurysm for the past few years that could burst at any moment. Life goes on, she was still active and awesome, part of me even forgot it was there. Years went by and nothing happened so part of me knew it could be any minute but I had other things to do so I went about doing them. Gotta fold laundry, feed the children, go around a be a consumer, you know life. Well, the fucker bursts one morning and she miraculously calls 911 and gets to the hospital but there's no saving her, it is going to kill her, who knows how much time she has left, the clock is ticking.

I get a call from my parents so I leave work early that day and rush up the 101 to see her before she goes. Of course, the shakes are fucking bad that day. So bad that even though Nana is clinging to life and time is of the essence, she is literally waiting for me to get there so she can go (her words) I still have to pull off the freeway to find a liquor store so I can buy a pint of booze and drink it while driving just to steady my nerves. I don't even try to get the smell of bourbon off my breath after I park the car. I just showed up.

She wakes up briefly, sees me and tells me to get into bed with her, a few minutes later she loses consciousness for the last time. My parents are there along with my aunt and uncle and my cousins. We sit and talk while we wait for something to happen. Nothing does so we slowly leave to go back to Nana's house to sleep. I stop at another liquor store in route because at that point who gives a fuck. The next day she dies and I am already back home because I woke up hungover and spending another day in the hospital isn't in my best interest.

11:30 AM *Walking past a Korean Church. Services today at both 11 and 5. It's right next to a nail salon. Maybe someone left some shoes in my size that I could buy. Shit, maybe they'd give me water if I get a pedicure. Oh wait, I don't have my wallet…*

A childhood trauma leads to situation depression which turns into outright depression. I saw a therapist after my sister died. I went once. The issue was dropped after that one visit. I was twenty two. I saw a therapist (or was she a life coach? Someone's neighbor? Not sure who she was really) in my mid twenties no more than ten times. Amber wanted me to stop doing cocaine, I guess I did too, but what I wasn't ready to do was to stop drinking. I stopped the cocaine for awhile and the issue was dropped. It was conveniently brushed aside until it wasn't convenient to be ignored anymore. I needed therapy when I was ten but that was before kids went to therapy. I had therapy after my sister died but I didn't know what I needed. Christ! How can anyone wrap their head around any of that shit when they're so young?

11:38 AM *Ahh, I pass the first liquor store of the day. Fuck, no wallet. Even if I had money there's too much of a walk ahead to be carrying a paper bag. Fuck I may not even make it past Aleem's parent's house if I stop and buy something...*

Nana isn't the real reason why I left church this morning. Nana called me out on it years ago, because that's what Nana's do. I, of course, ignored her, because that's what grandsons do. The real reason involves the river of alcohol I've been floating down for all these years. What was once a lovely stream is now a medium sized creek. The pond is now a lake. The chair is now a couch. Whatever it is, it is harder and harder to fly under the radar. I know it's a problem. I've always known it was a problem and now I am considering actually recognizing the severity of the problem and potentially doing something about it.

Red flags. So many of them. So many helpful tests one can take online if you're brave. The tests are free when you are desperate to learn the truth. But I already know the answer. I don't really need the internet to tell me that normal and healthy behaviors include routines. Routines are good, structure is important. What's concerning is where these routines are taking me every morning.

After I drop the kids off at school, my car makes a stop on the right hand side of the street because I know I can park easily there. There's usually not a line and I'll be in and out within five minutes. The liquor store lady knows me, not by name, of course but she knows that lately if I don't stop by before 8:30 it's only because of a local disaster or my car is broken down. Sometimes I try to outsmart her by going to the other liquor store, but that one is more expensive so I usually don't make the effort, also, there's a U-turn involved.

I only switch up locations at all so I don't appear like a total degenerate, even though I kinda am one. Only the truly fucked up go to the same liquor store everyday before nine in the morning. The non-degenerates are on a rotating schedule. You have to mix things up so they don't see you everyday of the week. They know all about my rotating liquor schedule but they don't say anything. But it doesn't matter anyway because this isn't when I normally stop by so the other guy is working now. Which means that today I show up at a more socially acceptable hour and therefore appear to be just a run of the mill fuck up. This guy knows me too but he doesn't say anything either, just like normal.

11:50 AM *I am seriously regretting this walk. I am passing my old middle school. I could call an Uber but at this point it would make this grand scheme of walking home so much less dramatic. Right foot, left foot, right foot... This walking business is a serious business. And now there's a hill. Fuck me, this better be the fucking freeway near my house...*

The stash is getting deeper in the garage. The original stash was not too close to the door but close enough to locate, twist open, pour and then replace. The shelf that the glass sat on became progressively worn and dirty and wet over time. Over time, this hiding place was discovered. Over time, it was discovered again. One time, a bottle was let to slowly drain onto the floor of the garage. It was time to get rid of the garage stash. This happens off and on for awhile. Thirty days straight without a drink. I play an entire round of golf with all my drinking buddies, absolutely sober. I play another round sober and in the midst of a green smoothie cleanse. There is no garage stash. Until there is a stash in the fucking garage. Now it's deeper in the garage, hidden in a drawer underneath some towels that I have saved for painting.

When there is a stash in the garage it only lasts two days these days. I don't even make it to the grocery store to buy my alcohol. I can't wait long enough to drive the extra eight minutes, so I spend an extra six dollars and buy a handle at the liquor store that's on the way home. I assume that the checkers at Ralph's know that I was just there, buying the same thing two days ago, I know that the Middle Eastern guy at the liquor store loves me- he doesn't give a shit, no judgement, he loves it when I pull up three times a week and point to where the over priced bottle of dark Bacardi rum is located on the shelf- he does not judge me, or at least I don't care if he does. Anyway. The garage stash is fucking destroying me. It kills me that there is one in the first place. It kills me that it's there. Fuck dark rum. Seriously. But then again, fuck everything else.

12:20 PM *That was not the fucking freeway, nope, just a false alarm. Now here it is, holy shit, where did the sidewalk go? Now I am getting nervous...*

Secret lives... Mitch lied about nonsense and real things. What he had for lunch, whether or not he ever had a plane ticket to California and if he was actually arrested in Texas. My lies are continuous. I play the long con. I live entire second lives. Mitch lied to other people. I lied to myself.

I've been depressed for a long fucking time and I didn't know what to do about it, it just seemed normal. I never knew that feeling this way wasn't normal so I dealt with it the only way that made sense. I self-medicate because it's the only way I know how to feel something different. Fucking stupid how long I lived this way. Seriously, who fucking cuts themselves? Who does that shit over and over again. It's all such a waste of time. That's the thing about it, I do not currently have a plan. There is no way that any of this will figure itself out right now. I don't know what the future will bring. Will l figure it out? Am I actually depressed? Do I have a mental illness? Raging drug problem? Or do I just need a fucking hug? Regardless, things aren't working. Things haven't been working for awhile now and I may just be time for a change, But fuck if I know. Fuck if I know anything about anything, I don't have the solution. I don't know what the fuck is going to happen. I don't know if I can pull this off, be sober, go to therapy, fix what's wrong with me. Fuck, what is wrong with me? As I walk I contemplate these things and I can't figure it out. All I know is that I don't know shit. I can't sum all this up neatly. I do not know what will happen to me. Fuck, I may relapse the moment I get home (If that ever ends of happening.) I may get hit by a bus, smoke crack, run away, start a clothing line, Fuck, who knows, what I am going to do. The only thing I know for certain is to put one foot in front of another, and then another, all the way until I get my ass home.

12:40 PM *By the grace of god, an hour later, I finally limp up to my house. A few things become painfully obvious. 1) I am very out of shape. 2) That was a long fucking walk. 3) I left my keys in the car and nobody is home. 4) I am locked out of my house.*

My immediate future includes drinking out of the hose on the side yard. And I am certain that next time I will take a fucking Uber. Regardless, of all these uncertainties, and there is no doubt whatsoever that for the first time in a long time, my head is clear and I know what I need to do next. My path forward is unknown. I don't know what is going to happen next. But I know what needs to be done. My only option is to accept that this moment has passed and another one is on its way.

The End

Made in the USA
Las Vegas, NV
14 October 2023

79110832R00184